# THE UNWANTEDS

## Island of Graves

# Also by Lisa McMann

» » « «

*The Unwanteds*

*Island of Silence*

*Island of Fire*

*Island of Legends*

*Island of Shipwrecks*

*Island of Dragons*

» » « «

Coming Soon . . .

The Unwanteds Quests Book One: *Dragon Captives*

» » « «

FOR OLDER READERS:

*Don't Close Your Eyes*

*Visions*

*Cryer's Cross*

*Dead to You*

# LISA McMANN

# THE UNWANTEDS

## Island of Graves

Aladdin

NEW YORK   LONDON   TORONTO   SYDNEY   NEW DELHI

**ALADDIN**

An imprint of Simon & Schuster Children's Publishing Division

1230 Avenue of the Americas, New York, New York 10020

First Aladdin paperback edition August 2016

Text copyright © 2015 by Lisa McMann

Cover illustration copyright © 2015 by Owen Richardson

Also available in an Aladdin hardcover edition.

All rights reserved, including the right of reproduction in whole or in part in any form.

ALADDIN is a trademark of Simon & Schuster, Inc., and related logo is a registered trademark of Simon & Schuster, Inc.

For information about special discounts for bulk purchases, please contact Simon & Schuster Special Sales at 1-866-506-1949 or business@simonandschuster.com.

The Simon & Schuster Speakers Bureau can bring authors to your live event. For more information or to book an event contact the Simon & Schuster Speakers Bureau at 1-866-248-3049 or visit our website at www.simonspeakers.com.

Book designed by Karin Paprocki

The text of this book was set in Truesdell.

Manufactured in the United States of America 0321 OFF

10 9

The Library of Congress has cataloged the hardcover edition as follows:

McMann, Lisa.

Island of Graves / by Lisa McMann.

p. cm. — (The Unwanteds ; book 6)

Summary: The battles continue for young mage Alex and his friends as they search for Alex's abducted evil brother, Aaron.

[1. Brothers—Fiction. 2. Twins—Fiction. 3. Magic—Fiction. 4. Fantasy.] I. Title.

PZ7.M478757Iqk 2015

[Fic]—dc23

2014050311

ISBN 978-1-4424-9334-6 (hc)

ISBN 978-1-4424-9335-3 (pbk)

ISBN 978-1-4424-9336-0 (eBook)

For Unwanteds fans everywhere

# Contents

# THE UNWANTEDS

## Island of Graves

# A Momentary Lapse of Judgment

Alex Stowe, head mage of Artimé, stood alone at the helm of the magical white boat called *Claire*, speeding eastward over the waves. The island, his friends, and all the people who were gathered on the glorious green lawn grew smaller and smaller behind him. He didn't know where he was going. He only knew that his identical twin brother, Aaron, was out there somewhere. In trouble, definitely, but *alive*—Alex could feel the life in his own broken soul.

He also knew that there was no one else in the world who would rescue Aaron.

LISA McMANN

Not that Quill's high priest deserved rescuing, especially by the head mage of Artimé, after everything Aaron had done to hurt him and his people. And even though Aaron wasn't technically responsible for either of Quill's organized attacks on Artimé, he had killed Mr. Today. An unforgiveable offense. Yet the invisible bond between the brothers was ridiculously stubborn, and it wouldn't let go of Alex, no matter what Aaron did. It was wrong and maddening, but it seemed they were irrevocably tied together. And thus, here he was.

With nothing but open sea before him, Alex closed his tired eyes as he traversed the waves, letting the cool breeze wash over his face and flutter at his shirt collar. He hadn't been alone like this in ages. Neither Spike, the intuitive whale of Alex's own creation, nor Simber, the winged-cheetah statue who protected Artimé, had noticed his impulsive departure, so he remained gloriously alone and vulnerable. It was exhilarating. Feeling rejuvenated from the weariness of battle and grief of the past weeks, Alex filled his lungs with fresh air.

He opened his eyes. The gentle swells of deepest blue seemed to stretch out forever before him. So serene and peaceful—he loved the sea.

LISA McMANN

Now and then a spear of doubt over his sudden departure pierced his conscience, though he tried to ignore it. His intense premonition that his brother had been so near death and was now most certainly alive had clouded his judgment. It felt like a second chance . . . but a second chance at what?

He rubbed his side where the pain had been. His premonition was more than magical—it was physical. Something much deeper than magic could ever be. What was Alex supposed to do, ignore it? It seemed irreverent to do so.

Granted, he knew this was an impulsive move. It was the kind of move Alex rarely made these days. And it might cause problems in the near future, with the looming presence of Gondoleery Rattrapp growing larger and remaining completely unpredictable.

Alex's actions might even be considered reckless by some. After all, he and Lani had just managed to rid the entire island—Quill included—of the ice spell Gondoleery had cast upon the land. And even though Liam Healy had reported that Gondoleery's palace takeover was spur of the moment, no one really knew what she had up her singed little sleeve, or when she'd attack next.

Alex's mad dash to rescue Aaron had more immediate problems as well, which he realized as he looked around the boat. He'd brought no food. No water. If this was to be a rescue trip, Alex was sorely unprepared. It might take days or weeks to find Aaron. What was Alex supposed to do? He couldn't stop for provisions at the nearest island to the east, since it was a jutting cylinder of sheer rock that looked completely unconquerable and inaccessible. And paying a visit to the carnivorous-gorilla island beyond it was not something Alex would ever do if he had even an ounce of life left in him—that place meant certain death to anyone who landed on its shores. He couldn't get the image of the saber-toothed silverback attacking the pig out of his mind.

Alex paled. What if Aaron was on that island? If so, he must have found a place to hide, at least temporarily. He'd know in his soul soon enough if Aaron got killed. He was quite sure of that.

Alex searched his robe pockets, disappointment growing at his inadequate provisions. There was nothing there that could help him take down a monstrous fanged gorilla, other than a smattering of nonlethal spell component options. He had no idea if the spells would work on such a creature. These same spells had done nothing to stop the horrible eel that had plagued them on their previous journey.

Now that Alex had spent a few minutes really thinking about the consequences of his actions, he realized that he was more like someone in need of rescue than someone who was setting out to help another.

"What am I doing?" he muttered.

He slowed the boat and glanced over his shoulder. He could no longer tell who stood at the shore watching him go, only that there was a large group of people gathered there—scores of Unwanteds, but also abandoned Warbler children and mistreated Necessaries from Quill who had all found acceptance and protection in Artimé. They were people and creatures who had come to trust in Alex and rely on him to protect them. They were loyal, and they'd fought valiantly and tirelessly as thirty of their friends and loved ones, including Alex's best friend, Meghan, had fallen in the ferocious battle with General Blair and his Quillitary. They were resilient, and they'd withstood Gondoleery Rattrapp's ice spell. But they were most certainly in for more trouble from the new high priest and dictator of Quill.

Alex looked within himself. What kind of leader and protector would willingly and selfishly leave his faithful followers at a time like this? The head mage of Artimé should have one goal—to protect his people. And Alex was doing the exact opposite, leaving them horrendously in danger while he went out on a lark to save somebody whom nobody else wanted to save.

As the truth set in, Alex released a heavy sigh. He'd lost his mind, or at the very least he'd had a severe lapse in judgment. Aaron Stowe, former high priest of Quill, enemy of Artimé, wasn't worth it.

Aaron wasn't truly worth anything.

And it was high time Alex let go of him. Forever.

With new resolve, Alex took one more look at the sparkling sea, then swung the boat around and headed home.

# Clinging to Life

Inside the rock shelter on the Island of Shipwrecks, the afternoon air was heavy with moisture, which was almost too thick to breathe for someone who'd lived all but the past several days of his life in a desert. Outside the thunder crashed and the wind howled. Ishibashi, Ito, and Sato kept watch over their unconscious visitor. There was little else they could do now but wait.

Aaron's eyes remained closed, his breath labored, his body feverish and broken, and his mind trying to make sense of the strange environment. Over and over he dreamed about a rare day when he was ten. Water poured from the sky as he and Alex did chores in the backyard. It was the day Aaron drew with a chicken bone in the mud, and Alex took the blame for it.

Because of Aaron's altered state, the dream turned in a dozen odd directions, repeating incessantly. His brother's face was replaced by the High Priest Justine's. His father became Gondoleery Rattrapp. And the bone turned into Panther's tail. He could even hear Panther's scream alongside the thundering of the giant rock's voice.

As the dream raced through Aaron's head, he tried again and again to rouse himself, but he was paralyzed, unable to move at all. When the panther appeared and raced toward the boys, fangs dripping, Alex jumped in front of Aaron. Aaron watched in horror as the panther tore Alex apart. And then their father came outside and mistook Aaron for Alex.

"Oh good!" said Mr. Stowe. "Aaron's dead. I guess you were the good son all along, Alex," he said to Aaron. "Aaron got what he deserved. I'm glad he's gone. Now you can be the Wanted son."

In the dream, Aaron was tired of pretending and tried to explain. "I'm not Alex! I'm Aaron!" he cried again and again.

But his father only laughed. "Your lies won't work on me anymore, Alex. Stop covering for your awful brother, and accept that you are the only son we want."

No matter how many times the dream played out, it always ended in confusion, with Aaron desperate to explain the truth. But no one would listen.

On the cool damp floor of the shelter, Aaron's body lay still, but inside his mind he was struggling and fighting, kicking and shoving, trying to pull himself out of the fog and nightmares that enveloped him.

He was not successful.

# An Unsettling Feeling

Alex was a little embarrassed driving the boat back to the lagoon. His friends saw him coming and gathered to wait under the tree where the platyprots often perched. Lani held the robe he'd shoved at her, folded neatly and draped over one arm. Samheed, at her side, had a smirk on his face so exaggerated that Alex could see it from the boat. Simber lounged in the shade on the beach, casually nibbling at a claw and pointedly not looking at Alex, while Spike swam nearby and trumpeted water from her blowhole as he waded back to shore.

Sky stood with arms crossed, a teasing sort of smile on her

LISA McMANN

face, which made Alex blush all the more. It was clear they all had heard by now what he'd set out to do. And he knew he wasn't going to hear the end of it.

Automatically he looked for Meghan—she'd stand up for him. But then he remembered, and her death ripped Alex's heart in two again. Would it get easier? Would he ever get used to her absence? Or would he have to live with this ache every single day for the rest of his life?

He swallowed hard, hesitating in the shallow water, and then forged ahead toward his friends.

When he reached land, Sky met him on the beach and fell into step with him, linking her arm in his. "Is everything running as it should?"

Alex shot her a puzzled look. "Huh?"

"The boat's working all right?" she asked, a little too innocently. "No damage from the ice?"

A hint of a smile twitched at the corner of Alex's lips. "Oh. Right. No damage," he said. "Glad we got that checked out. What's next on the list?" He cleared his throat and dared not look at Samheed.

Lani pushed her long black hair over one shoulder and held

the robe out to him, her piercing orange eyes dancing with glee. She didn't say anything.

Alex slipped his arms through the holes. "Thanks for keeping it dry while I, ah, checked on the boat," he said, fastening it at his neck. Maybe they were going to let him off easy.

But then Samheed let out a snort.

Alex looked at him. "Shut it, Sam," he muttered in an attempt to remain perfectly straight-faced. "Don't start with me."

"Seriously, Al," Samheed said. "What exactly did you think you were going to accomplish? Stupid move. When will you finally realize that Aaron isn't worth it? You are such a—"

Alex lunged at Samheed, plowing into him and throwing him off balance. As Samheed stumbled, he grabbed Alex by his shoulders and shoved him to the lawn, where they rolled around, arguing and gasping and laughing at the same time. Platyprots and rabbitkeys scattered, giving the boys a wide berth. They took up a lot more space now than they had a few years ago, when they'd had their first tussle in Artimé.

Lani looked at them with disdain, and then she and Sky turned to Simber, who was lumbering to his feet and shaking

LISA McMANN

his head ever so slightly. Together the three of them left the boys on the lawn and strolled to the mansion for dinner.

"Of course you're right," Alex admitted to Samheed about ten minutes later. The two lay on their backs on the lawn, chests heaving from the fight. "I'm ready to give up on Aaron now." It felt okay to say, which gave Alex a bit of comfort. He pushed himself up on one elbow. "And thanks to Gondoleery, we have plenty of other things to think about."

"I think she's a little nuts the way she was talking and cackling after the battle," Samheed said, staring at the sky. "Which is even more scary than dealing with a somewhat sane dictator like Aaron. Gondoleery's unpredictable. Any idea what she's going to do next?"

"No." Something about the question bothered Alex, but he couldn't quite put his finger on it. "I'm planning to see what we can find out about her from Liam. Maybe tomorrow. Did Lani melt the ice in Quill, too, or just in Artimé?"

"It's gone everywhere."

"So Gondoleery knows we did it," Alex said.

"I would assume so, you dolt. She's not stupid."

LISA McMANN

Alex laughed and elbowed Samheed hard in the ribs. "Shut it."

"Ow! All right," Samheed said. "This time. Only because I'm exhausted. I'm still sore from the battle, you know."

"Yet you still managed to pin me. Like always."

"I have my pride."

"Yes, you do." Alex yawned. "You know what would be nice?"

"What?"

"If we didn't have to constantly worry about being attacked."

"Yes, that would be nice," Samheed agreed. "Maybe someday."

Alex frowned. It seemed endless. And it was unsettling and exhausting not knowing what was going to happen next. It felt like all they did these days was fend off attackers.

After a while Alex and Samheed got to their feet and limped into the mansion. It had been a long few weeks with little sleep. And after being away for so long, it was nice to be home and have a chance to explore more of the many secrets left behind by Mr. Today. Alex was glad he'd come to his senses and turned back home.

After dinner Alex stopped in the hospital ward to check on the injured. Henry Haluki was there, administering medicine as usual. He seemed busy, so Alex didn't want to disturb him too much. But he knew how tirelessly Henry worked, and he was worried about him.

"You don't have to do it all, you know," Alex said gently. "Get some sleep."

Henry kept his head down. "I will when I'm done here."

Alex watched him work for a moment, but the boy didn't look up. "Are you okay, Henry?"

Henry paused, then nodded. "I'll be okay." He looked up, finally. "Thanks."

"Sure," Alex said. "Let me know if you need anything. Or if you just want to talk. I know this is hard." Alex waved his hand, indicating the injured among them.

"It's not hard seeing the ones who are improving," Henry said. "It's the other ones . . ." He dropped his eyes once more and continued his work.

Alex smiled grimly. He understood. Or at least he thought he did. But Henry gave nothing else away, and Alex respected the younger boy's need for privacy. Still, Henry's mood seemed off. "The offer stands," Alex said. "I'm always here for you."

Henry nodded, then began counting aloud the number of drops he was putting into a small vial. "Six, seven, eight . . ."

Alex pursed his lips, then turned and quietly walked away. He remained thoughtful the rest of the evening. But with his mind turning back to Gondoleery and the issue at hand, he soon forgot about Henry.

# Taking Care of Business

**W**hen Alex woke up the next morning, he was desperately trying to hang on to a thought that had burrowed around in his mind for a good part of the night. It concerned Gondoleery and the conversation he'd had with Samheed the previous afternoon, about wondering what she would do to them next.

*Hasn't Gondoleery already done enough?* He stared at the wall, cocooned inside his luxurious bedding, which he'd missed so much on the ship. "Maybe we're doing this wrong," he said, his voice rough with sleep. He thought some more, and after a time, sat up rather quickly.

Taking a notepad and pen from his bedside table, he began scribbling. A minute later he paused and looked up at his blackboard. "Clive?" he called.

Clive's face pushed out. "Yes, m'mage?"

Alex closed his eyes and expelled a breath. He tolerated Clive's attitude, which had gotten better ever since Alex had given Clive more responsibility. Threatening to assign the important jobs to Samheed's blackboard, Stuart, seemed to work well too. But Clive still liked to give a smug greeting now and then, especially when Alex had been away for any length of time.

"Really?" Alex asked. "Must you? It's getting tedious."

"I assumed you missed my charming personality," Clive said.

"Oh, but of course."

Clive nodded serenely. "Continue, your excellence."

"Clive," Alex said, "I want you to assemble a meeting in my office for tomorrow evening after dinner. These advisors, please: Simber, Florence, Ms. Octavia, Claire, and Samheed and Lani and Carina and Sean—"

"Whoa, hang on," Clive said. "Not all of them can access the secret hallway."

"They can now—they just need to go through the 3-D door I made. Lani has it. Have the ones who need to use it connect with her." He thought for a moment. "Invite Sky, too. She has great ideas."

"You got it, your imperial majesty."

"Knock it off," Alex said. "Also, can you arrange for Liam Healy to meet me on the lawn in an hour?"

Clive blinked. "I'm sorry. Who?"

Alex crinkled up his nose. "Drat. Don't you have him in your . . . system, or whatever you call it?"

"No." Clive frowned. "Is he new? One moment. My assistant is going to be in big trouble for this. . . ."

"You have an assistant?" Alex asked.

But Clive had disappeared. Alex watched the black screen with curiosity. Soon Clive pushed his face out of the blackboard once more. "All set. Mr. Healy has been located and a blackboard personality assigned to him. I imagine he'll be quite shocked to hear from it. I almost wish it were me. . . . It's *such*

LISA McMANN

fun the first time. But then, well, you never know what sort of chump you'll end up with. . . ."

Alex ignored him. "So he'll meet me on the lawn in an hour? Near the fountain, please."

"We'll relay the message," Clive said. "Anything else?"

"The babies . . ." Alex tapped his chin. "I suppose I should visit them like Florence wants me to. Where might they be?"

"I don't know. They don't have a blackboard. I'm not sure where they keep things like that."

"What, extra blackboards? I hardly think they need one yet."

"No, I meant babies."

"Oh. Don't worry," Alex said. "I'll ask Florence. I didn't see them in the hospital ward."

"If I hear anything about their location, I'll let you know, of course."

"Thanks, Clive. That's it for now."

Clive melted into the screen.

Alex got dressed, ordered breakfast up to his room through the tube, and started back to work on a plan.

After three quarters of an hour, he made his way downstairs and outside. It was a beautiful morning, and many Artiméans

LISA McMANN

were taking advantage of the lawn actually being pleasant to sit upon once more, now that the ice was gone. The fountain bubbled merrily, perhaps even more enthusiastically than usual, for the water in it had been frozen under Gondoleery's ice spell too.

Liam wasn't there yet, so Alex swung by the border between Artimé and Quill, where the three girrinos stood quite a distance apart, trying to do their job of protecting the entrance to Artimé. Now that the wall was down everywhere, they had quite an expanse to cover.

There were others stationed along the border as well. The ostrich statue and the tiki statue were among them, as well as Jim the winged tortoise, who rose and fell with the flap of his wings between five and ten feet off the ground. The ostrich stood on one foot, looking quite bothered by anything and everything.

"Summon Simber, Florence, and me immediately if you suspect any sort of invasion," Alex said to each of the creatures and statues as he walked the border. "Gondoleery is not finished with us yet." He asked them if they needed anything and, finally, praised them and thanked them for their work.

LISA McMANN

When he was finished, he circled back and headed to the center of the lawn, where he saw an anxious-looking Liam Healy, clad in sporty new Artiméan clothing. His sleeves were quite a bit too long and needed hemming, and he used one of them like a handkerchief to mop the sweat off his forehead.

"Liam," Alex called out. He moved forward and held out his hand in greeting, and Liam sort of bowed over it while shaking it at the same time.

"Hello, High Prie—I mean, your honor. Ah, sir? I'm sorry. What am I to call you?"

"How about Alex?"

"Oh. Well," Liam said with a nervous laugh. "Alex. How easy."

"That's the way we like it here," Alex said. He could see the man's hands trembling and wished he knew how to put him at ease. And then he thought of common ground that might help. "By the way, do you happen to know where the babies are? I'm not sure where we keep them."

Liam looked startled. "Keep them? They're not supplies, you know. Loaves of bread or extra linens or whatnot." He tittered nervously, forgetting himself for a moment. "They're not likely to be in a box somewhere, I hope."

"Of course not," Alex said warmly.

Liam clamped his mouth shut. "I mean, ah . . ." He paled. "I spent several days with them, sir, so I feel quite defensive of them. I apologize for speaking out of turn."

"Not at all," Alex said. "You're absolutely right. It's a bit demeaning the way I've been talking about them, isn't it—I've only just realized it, thanks to you. Let me rephrase: Do you happen to know where my sisters are at the moment?" That he had sisters at all still felt very strange.

"I—I believe the theater instructor is watching them today, along with an orange-eyed fellow. In the, ah, the theater, that is."

"Shall we go visit them together and have a chat along the way?"

Liam let out a breath. "Yes, I think so. That would be nice."

Alex gave Liam a friendly slap on his shoulder.

"Oh!" Liam exclaimed, startled by it.

"Sorry," said Alex.

"My fault," said Liam.

Both of them knew it wasn't Liam's fault, but Alex decided to let it go or risk the conversation heading into an even more awkward direction.

LISA McMANN

"Well, then," Alex said. "Let's go."

They set off. Liam seemed to calm down after a bit. Alex wondered if he had always been such a nervous person, or if it was just the vast change in environment that had him feeling edgy. Time would tell.

"So," Alex began, "tell me everything you know about Gondoleery. Whatever you can think of. Even if you've mentioned it before."

In fits and starts, Liam described what little he knew of her, beginning with the time they served together as Restorers for Aaron. He told of her lengthy disappearances and her strangely glowing house, her more recently singed eyebrows and fingertips, and her sudden takeover of the palace once she learned that Aaron had been abducted.

"I see," said Alex as they approached the mansion. He paused before entering. "Do you think Gondoleery has the people of Quill behind her?"

Liam pondered the question. "I don't know," he said. "And like I told you when I first arrived, I don't think she is prepared to take over Artimé. Not yet, anyway. High Priest Aaron's disappearance was unexpected, and it caught her off guard. But I

LISA McMANN

believe she is scheming, and she won't waste time."

"What about the other governor? Strang, is it?"

Liam scowled. "Strang is completely inept. He has no passion for anything, one way or another. I don't think he cares for Gondoleery. He only spent time with her rallying the people because he had to."

"Rallying them for what, exactly?"

"Oh, getting them ready to fight Artimé. Same old thing."

"But they're not ready? The people?"

"Heavens no. They are dead inside, as I once was. It'll take a miracle to rouse them. Only Aaron had a special touch with them when he wanted something, what with offering them extra fruits and vegetables and such. Incentives, I think he called them. He was very clever that way."

Alex set his jaw and nodded. "Well, I see their lack of enthusiasm as good news. Thanks." He opened the mansion door and ushered Liam inside. "To the tubes," he said. "Let's go visit those adorable babies." He tried not to cringe. But spending time with a couple of smelly one-year-olds was pretty much the last thing he wanted to do.

LISA McMANN

# Tiny Personalities

The theater was awash in sound and light. Onstage was an entire ensemble of actors and singers, warming up their voices to rehearse the new musical. In the orchestra pit in front of the stage sat the musicians, tuning their instruments to accompany them.

Observing from the seats were various student directors and crew. Alex spotted Samheed, who was trying his hand at directing. He was furiously scribbling notes, and Alex knew better than to distract him.

There were a few curious onlookers in the seats as well, including Fox and Kitten—musicians of a different kind, though they kept to the lounge for that. They bounced with anticipation for the dress rehearsal to begin.

Several adults and statues moved about the aisles and backstage, multitasking like crazy. Some used magic to adjust the lighting; others tried spells to coax a stuck curtain into opening and closing properly. Captain Ahab stumped across the stage once, grumbling under his breath, just like old times.

Watching it all from the back of the theater, Alex couldn't help but smile, remembering the shows he'd been a part of. He'd have to see about reprising his role in *Perseus! Perseus!* one day. Maybe the next time Lani wouldn't break him into tiny bits.

Beside Alex, Liam was a bit jumpy because of the noise, but he was handling it. He was eager to see the twin girls, and it was he who spotted them first. He nudged Alex and pointed them out, toddling near the front row. Sky's younger brother, Crow, sat on the floor watching them as the theater instructor, Sigfried Appleblossom, spoke to some actors. Mr. Today's daughter, Claire Morning, instructed the musicians and singers.

Alex glanced at Liam, whose eyes landed on Ms. Morning.

Liam was clearly in love with her, and apparently had been since they were children. Everybody knew it but nobody talked about it, because Liam had blown his chance at reuniting with her. His terrible decisions as a Restorer would likely haunt him for life. And while Claire had been kind enough to allow Liam the safety of remaining in Artimé, at least for the time being, she had made it painfully obvious that there would be no love reciprocated.

When Liam noticed Alex looking at him, he dropped his gaze. Alex shrugged. He didn't feel sorry for the man. Not much, anyway. He was an adult, and he'd made his own decisions. But Alex was glad Liam was making such great strides in reforming his ways.

The two made their way down the aisle toward the stage. Crow saw them coming, chased after the twins, and scooped them up. They giggled and kicked their feet as Crow held them and began moving up the aisle toward Alex.

Their features were just as identical as Alex and Aaron's. The boys resembled their fair-skinned, dark-haired father, but the girls had the sharper features and deeper complexion of their mother. Alex hadn't noticed it before, but now he couldn't help but see his mother's face in the angle of their jaws, the tight spring curls in their dark brown hair, and the most unusual trait—their eyes. Alex had known only one person in all his life with true, jet-black irises, and that was his mother. The girls had inherited those. But while Mrs. Stowe's eyes had looked tired and dead, the girls' looked alive and full of mischief.

It took Alex aback for a moment—a disturbing reminder of the death of his parents from the crashing wall in Quill. He was so far removed from them since the Purge, yet their deaths had brought them screaming to the forefront of his mind. He didn't feel sad about them, and that bothered him somewhat. Maybe he was still numb from Meghan. How much grief could a person hold at one time? He took a deep breath to clear the thought from his mind and studied his sisters, gathered up in Crow's arms.

The one in purple held a smashed jam sandwich in one fist, and she wore most of the jam on her cheeks. In her other hand she held a tiny wind instrument that Alex recognized as a quarter-size fife. In between bites she blew into it.

The one in red pounded on Crow's chest, trying desperately

to get down and back to the business of toppling piles of books, which Crow had been stacking up for her. Her determination now got the better of Crow, and after one especially well-placed jab to the throat, he let her down. She shrieked with joy at her freedom and quite adorably tottered to the pile of books and knocked them over.

From the stage, Mr. Appleblossom noticed the visitors. He called for a break and headed down the steps toward them as Alex greeted Crow.

"Hi, Alex," Crow said. He hoisted the girl in purple higher on his hip. "How've you been?"

"Not as busy as you appear to be." He leaned forward to align his face with his sister's as she sat contentedly in Crow's arms. She looked back at Alex, her face innocent and sticky as could be. It wasn't quite as awkward talking to her now as it was last time. "What have you got there?" Alex said. "Huckleberry jam?"

"It's fig," Crow said. "She can't get enough of it. She knows her way to the kitchen from almost anywhere in the mansion."

"Oh my. Already?" Alex said with a grin. "Just wait until she learns how to travel the tubes."

LISA McMANN

Island of Graves » 30

Mr. Appleblossom reached the group. "Greetings one and all," he said pleasantly, and crouched to pile up the books for the twin in red. When he was finished, he turned to Alex. "It's good to see you. These nameless girls must learn that you're their kin." He straightened up and smiled as the one in red tugged at his trouser leg. "I'm not sure Red and Purple suit them well. Perhaps you've come to dub them Sage and Flynn? Or Amelie, or Eleanore, or Quinn?"

Alex grinned and shook his head in admiration. "I should have come here before—of course you'd have lots of names to offer. What do you think? The one in red seems . . . bookish. And dramatic. And this one, with the fig jam all over her face," he said, looking at her almost fondly, "she needs a musical name, don't you think? What with that grip on the fife?" Hesitantly he tickled her tummy. She didn't seem to notice, and Alex gave a sheepish laugh and pulled his hand away.

"Do you want the names to start with the same letter?" Crow asked. "Like you and Aaron?"

"Hm," said Alex. "I think maybe not. Let's see what suits them. Mr. Appleblossom, what other literary names do you like from your plays and stories? Any tragic heroines or secret queens or spectacular fighters we can name this one after?"

Mr. Appleblossom looked at the girl in red and tapped his chin thoughtfully.

"No hurry," Alex said. "I imagine it takes time to find just the right name." He glanced at the orchestra pit, where Ms. Morning was straightening her papers.

Crow followed Alex's gaze. "Hey," he said, "maybe Ms. Morning can help with a musical name for the purple twin."

"Great idea," said Alex. The thought of having to name them had been weighing on him, and he just wanted to be done with it. Did it really matter what somebody's name was? Why not just call them Red and Purple? He didn't care all that much.

Alex waved to get Claire's attention and motioned for her to join them.

Ms. Morning, who had given her students a break at the same time as Mr. Appleblossom, came over to see what the discussion was about. "Good morning," she said. She didn't look at Liam, who had shrunk back slightly and pretended to be fascinated by the workings of the aisle seat next to him.

Alex explained his idea for naming the twins.

"I've never named a person before," Claire said. "I'm not sure I have a gift for it, but I'll try." She studied the one in purple. "Hm. This might be too easy. Clearly she's a fifer. I mean, it's simple, but what do you think of that?"

"Think of what?" asked Alex, confused.

"Fifer," said Claire. "It makes a beautiful name, and I don't know anyone with it. She'd be unique."

"Fifer?" Alex asked. He thought about it. "I like it. What do you think?" he said to the girl in Crow's arms. "Fifer. Shall we call you that?"

The girl held the figgy crust of her sandwich out to Alex. "Da!" she said, and blew into the fife. A shrill note came out.

Alex looked at Claire. "Either you've got beginner's luck, or you're secretly talented at naming children and just discovering it now. I think it's decided." He reached out hesitantly for his sister, and the girl leaned forward into his arms like she'd been waiting for him to take her. He held her, a little cautiously at first, and bounced her gently on his hip. "There, little Fifer Stowe. Do you like your name?"

She bonked him on the head with the fife, then slapped her sticky little hand to his mouth.

Alex licked his lips. "Mm, tasty," he said. "A bit warmer than how I normally take my jam, but I like it." He looked at Crow. "What do you think? Does Fifer suit her?"

Crow's face was more animated than Alex had ever seen it before. "I think it does!" he exclaimed. "And . . . maybe we can call her Fig for short?"

"I love it," said Alex. It was nice to see Crow feeling so comfortable without Henry at his side. Perhaps he had found his niche with caring for the little ones. "Fifer Stowe, and Fig for short." Alex looked at Mr. Appleblossom. "And what about the other Miss Stowe? Nothing's coming to me at all for her, I'm afraid. Have I given you enough time to think?"

Fifer's twin rubbed her eye with her fist. She looked tired and sweet and full of goodness. Then she reached her pudgy hand in the air whimsically, grabbed Mr. Appleblossom's hair, and wrenched his head to the side.

The theater instructor cried out in surprise and pain. When he'd managed to release his hair from the girl's grasp, he spoke. "So sweet, yet thorny as a rose, you see? Determined, full of life, this one will be."

"She seems to be," said Alex. "Not sure Sweet or Thorny are

LISA McMANN

good names, though—she might hate me for either, one day."
He looked at Crow. "Do you agree with Mr. Appleblossom's
description?"

"Oh, she's definitely sweet and thorny," Crow said. "And
determined. Fifer is mostly content, but the one in red doesn't
stop until she gets what she wants."

Alex nodded and turned back to the theater instructor. "Do
you have a Shakespearean name to fit her, Mr. Appleblossom?
Or something else, maybe?"

Mr. Appleblossom craned his neck to look at the girl and
eyed her pinching fingers warily. He studied her while the others looked on, waiting.

Finally Mr. Appleblossom's face lit up. "Forget the
Shakespeare names. I know of thee!" he cried. "From Ovid,
you are *clearly*"—he bowed with a flourish—"our Thisbe."

"Oh yes!" said Claire. "From Pyramus and Thisbe. I remember it. Forbidden love, tragedy, death . . . It's absolutely perfect
for the dramatic one. And the character of Thisbe is so strong-
willed, so passionate . . . so brave." She sighed, remembering.

"Thisbe?" Alex asked, sounding out the two syllables.
"Like T-h-i-z-b-e-e?"

"Spell it how you like," Mr. Appleblossom said as the twin in red lunged toward Alex, "and read the story." He tilted his head and said conspiratorially, "Inspired Juliet, our brave Thisbe."

"Really?" said Alex. "So some guy named Ovid wrote about Pyramus and Thisbe, and Shakespeare got inspired to write *Romeo and Juliet* because of it? That's pretty cool. And I don't even want to know how you know all this."

Mr. Appleblossom looked ready to rant, but Alex stopped him with a grin. "I know, Mr. Appleblossom," Alex said. "Books. Thank goodness for the ones that wash up on our shores or we'd have no stories at all."

"We'd have our own," Claire said quietly. She nodded at the twins. "I wonder what their stories will be."

Alex smiled. "I wonder too." He reached out and took Fifer's twin in his free arm. Almost immediately she laid her head on his shoulder and popped her thumb into her mouth. Her lids grew heavy and she relaxed, like she'd found a perfect resting place there in the crook of her brother's neck. Alex was surprised to feel a wave of emotion come over him.

Mr. Appleblossom wrote the name on a piece of paper and showed Alex.

"Thisbe," Alex said, noting the spelling. It sounded smart and important, and the more he said it, the more he liked it. "I think it fits her well," Alex said. He looked at Crow. "What do you think?"

"I like it," Crow said. "Thisbe and Fifer. Fifer and Thisbe. They sound good together."

"Better than Red and Purple?" Alex asked.

Crow laughed. "A lot better."

"It's a perfect name for her," Claire said. "Oh, look, Thisbe's asleep. Just like that."

"And Fig is next," Crow said. "Look—her sticky cheek is locked in and she's down for the count." He laughed. "They like you, Alex."

"Yeah? Do you really think so?" asked Alex. He craned his neck to look narrowly at one, then the other. "This feels very weird," Alex said. He'd never held two sleeping toddlers before. He turned slowly toward Liam, who had been standing back respectfully, saying nothing, as he was used to doing when he'd gone anywhere with Aaron. Or maybe he was just hiding from Claire.

"And what do you think, Liam?" Alex asked. "Do the names

LISA McMANN

fit them? You've had more time with them than anyone."

"Yes, indeed," he said in earnest. "If what Mr. Appleblossom says is true about the story, the name Thisbe is perfect for the one in red, for she's nothing if not filled with intensity and passion. She cries hard, plays hard, and sleeps hard. And gentle little Fifer, why, the name suits her well. Delicate and sweet. And even her laugh is musical—you'll know her when you hear it. That's a promise of her musical future right there." He faltered, and his eyes filled. He turned away, embarrassed.

"What's wrong?" Alex asked.

"Nothing. It's just . . . I've never felt so strange," he said. "So full of hope." He swiped at a tear and regarded the group, trying desperately not to look at Claire. "Thank you for letting me stay in Artimé. Getting out of Quill—it changes people."

# Unfamiliar Territory

**W**hen Aaron Stowe finally opened his eyes in the dark shelter, it took him several minutes to figure out that the howling noise he heard wasn't coming from any of the jungle creatures. It wasn't Panther screaming her affection, or the rock growling his melancholy loneliness, which Aaron didn't really care about. He stared at the ceiling without thinking at all for quite some time before any thoughts began to form.

A few hazy memories floated above his head, and he wasn't sure if they were real or if they were dreams: The pirates attacking him in his office and dragging him to the fishing boat, throwing him in and leaving him there, broken. Then pulling his boat behind their ship for days and the awful rocking on the waves. The extreme pain in his shoulder and face was real—he was sure of that, for it was still present. And the horrible thirst was real too. He swallowed reflexively, finding his throat still sore and parched. And his body ached all over. But why? Why had this happened to him? What had he done to deserve it? The questions ran through his mind endlessly, exhausting him.

Eventually he became aware of a few things, like the fact that he wasn't in a boat anymore. There was a blanket covering him, and he seemed to be lying on something soft. With great effort, he slid one hand to the edge of the soft bedding and, to his disappointment, felt the cool, rock floor below it. He had hoped, however silly it seemed, that he had somehow made it to the jungle, where he had come to feel the most comfortable he'd ever been with the other misfit, dangerous ones. But this floor was not the jungle floor, and this noise was not jungle noise, and these smells weren't jungle smells.

Too exhausted to pull his arm back under the blanket, Aaron fluttered his eyes and closed them. His head listed to one side, and he slept.

# A New Approach

The next day in Artimé, Alex sat at his desk in his office, which was once known as Mr. Today's office. Some of the older Unwanteds still referred to it as such out of habit, and Alex didn't mind. It still looked almost exactly like Mr. Today's office since Alex had had little time to do anything to it after he'd been forced to step into the role of head mage.

The one noticeable difference was that the monitors behind the desk no longer showed any images of the activities in Quill. Instead they hung useless and dark. Alex had puzzled over the strange phenomenon for a while when he first noticed it upon

LISA McMANN

returning to Artimé, but it didn't take him long to realize that it probably had something to do with the wall around Quill coming down.

Now Alex wished for a bird's-eye view into Quill as a new plan began to form in his mind. What were the people of Quill doing? How had they handled the ice? Were they afraid of Gondoleery, or did they support her? Did they even understand what was happening?

He considered doing a flyover with Simber, but he didn't want to frighten anyone or make Gondoleery suspicious of anything, for such an act could be considered threatening. And while Alex fully intended to threaten the high priest of Quill with his new plan, he did not wish to give Gondoleery any warning at all.

He pondered his options for hours, forgetting all about dinner. Eventually he heard the Museum of Large's door creak open, accompanied by excited chattering in the hall. The first meeting attendees were arriving. Alex could hear Lani speaking expertly about where to find things to someone who must surely be Sky.

Alex's stomach twisted at the sound of Sky's voice, which

had never fully healed from when she wore the thorny neck-lace of Warbler. He was in love, it was true. But he wasn't quite sure how she felt about him. She'd taken a step back in their relationship due to his stupidity, but she was slowly coming back to being his friend. And they'd come awfully close to a kiss on the ship as they returned home from the Island of Shipwrecks, though the sight of the help sign on the gorilla island had ruined that moment. If he could just keep cool and stop himself from messing things up, there might be a kiss in his future. But then Alex sighed, because that would cause old problems to resurface, he was sure.

The two girls entered the room with Sean Ranger right behind them. Sean, whose leg was nearly healed, walked on his own with only a magical support fashioned by Ms. Octavia, the octogator art instructor, to aid him. She was accustomed to fixing limbs of all kinds. And while she couldn't just give a human a whole new leg like she could do for Captain Ahab or Florence or any other statue, she built this contraption, which allowed Sean to walk normally without putting full pressure on his leg. Now it could finish healing properly while also giving him the freedom to walk without assistance.

LISA McMANN

This was the first time all three of them were present at one of Alex's office leadership meetings, and they seemed eager and nervous to be there.

Alex welcomed them in. "Sit anywhere, except not that giant floral sofa—that's Florence's spot. And Ms. Octavia prefers one of the small chairs up front, because otherwise she can't see."

The three looked around. "Your office looks just like the miniature version," Sky said. She had been the one to find the mini mansion in the gray shack back when Artimé had disappeared.

"Why, yes," Alex exclaimed as if it were the most brilliant thing said in his lifetime. "It does. Exactly like it." He perched comfortably on the corner of his desk and glanced up at the artwork on the wall. "See there? All those crazy dots." He shook his head, remembering how hard it had been to figure out what they meant.

"Do you still remember the words?" Sky asked.

"All but the fourth one," Alex said. The two shared a laugh that Lani and Sean didn't get, but neither Alex nor Sky offered to explain.

LISA McMANN

Others soon arrived. Florence, Simber, Ms. Octavia, Claire, Samheed, and Carina could see the entrance to the not-very-secret hallway, so they walked in easily. Most found chairs to sit in, and Simber lounged on the floor.

Alex welcomed them all.

Once everyone was settled, Alex turned first to Sean, Meghan's older brother. "How are you?" he asked.

Sean gave a small smile. "I'm holding on. I went into Quill and told our parents yesterday. Just to let them know."

Carina glanced over at him and slipped her hand in his, then pulled a handkerchief from her pocket and dabbed her eyes with it. She'd lost her young husband in the first battle with Quill, and her mother, Eva Fathom, not long ago. Of anyone, she could definitely relate to Sean's great loss.

"How did your parents react?" Alex asked. The numb feeling inside him was still there when he thought of his own dead parents.

"They didn't really react at all. It's just the kind of behavior you'd expect from people in Quill," Sean said. "It's maddening, but I shouldn't have thought it would go any differently."

"I'm sorry." Alex swallowed hard. "I miss Meg, more than I

know how to say. It's a loss I don't understand no matter how hard I try."

Samheed stared at the floor, eyes full of pain, but he didn't speak. She'd died saving him. Lani reached out and rested her arm around his broad shoulders.

"We all miss her," Lani said. "She was terribly brave. Braver than anyone I know."

Others murmured or nodded, and a few wiped away tears. Simber remained still, head bowed.

"She died protecting Artimé," Alex said. After a moment, he sniffed hard and cleared his throat, and went on. "I invited you all here because I want to make sure we are doing everything we can to continue protecting Artimé."

He told them about his conversation with Liam and what little information he'd gathered about Gondoleery Rattrapp. "No one seems to know much about her," he said. "We need to change that." He looked at the team before him, all smart and competent. "And . . . I think we're doing something wrong."

Eyes around the room met Alex's. "What are we doing wrong?" Carina asked.

LISA McMANN

Alex looked at her. "We're waiting to be attacked again."

The group was silent, either puzzled or contemplating.

The head mage hopped off the corner of the desk and elaborated. "Mr. Today taught us not to fight unless it's to protect ourselves. And I still believe his method is the right one. However, each time after we've been attacked, we work on defense so that when the next attack comes, we can handle it."

"What's wrong with that?" Claire asked, sitting up in her chair. "We *should* keep working on that."

"I agree," said Alex, "but that's not the only thing we should be doing. High Priest Gondoleery has made her intentions known. She told us clearly that she intends to take over Artimé. And she *has* attacked us, with ice. Isn't that enough? Are we going to wait for her to get stronger and attack us again? I don't think this was what Mr. Today had in mind. So let's start with this, like we've always said: We will not be taken without a fight. True enough? Can we all agree on that?"

Everyone nodded or voiced their agreement except Claire, whose face was concerned, but she continued to listen quietly to see where Alex was headed with this.

"Good," Alex said. "And do we all agree that Gondoleery

has attacked us with ice, thus starting our next battle already?"

A few in the group frowned along with Claire, but eventually they agreed once more.

"So," Alex said, "by Mr. Today's method, do we have grounds to retaliate?"

Almost everyone eventually came to the same conclusion. "Yes we do, Alex," Florence said, speaking as the head warrior trainer.

"I'm not so sure about this," Claire said under her breath.

Alex didn't hear her. "I agree, Florence," he said. "I believe it's time to switch things up and go on the offensive, friends. And I think we must do it now, or we will soon find ourselves mourning dozens and dozens more deaths. It's frightening, and I can't stand the thought of it. Frankly, I'm quite scared of losing more of *you*, my friends and advisors."

Simber lifted his head. "What exactly do you prrropose we do, Alex?"

Alex looked around the room and took a deep breath. "I propose we take Gondoleery out and end the attacks for good."

Claire lifted her head, alarmed. "What?"

"Do you mean you wish to kill her?" Simber asked.

Alex hesitated. It sounded horrible to put it that way. They could try putting her in a permanent freeze spell. But all it would take was one person with magical abilities to release the spell, and that could be any number of people—surely Gondoleery had supporters in place by now who could do such simple magic as release spells. It was too risky. So Alex stood firm. Gondoleery Rattrapp was dangerous, unpredictable, and way more powerful than anyone they'd ever come up against. Potentially, she had the power to destroy Artimé if she chose to do so.

Finally, Alex nodded. "Yes, Simber. We need to kill her."

The room was silent.

Only Simber spoke. "Well, it's about time."

# The Plan

Y ou want to assassinate Gondoleery Rattrapp?" Claire said, shaking her head slightly. "That's not going to be an easy task. Do you realize what could happen if you fail?"

Alex had thought plenty about it. "Yes. It means we'd be in deep trouble."

"Alex," Claire said, leaning forward, "Artimé has seen enough trouble in the last few years. Gondoleery has power and magic we've never faced before. If you attempt this and fail, she's not going to give you a free pass. It could mean the end!"

"The end . . . of what?" asked Alex, confused.

LISA McMANN

"The end of Artimé," said Claire. "The end of us."

Alex, taken aback, was silent for a moment. Then he frowned. "I understand your concerns, Claire," he said. "Thank you for voicing them. But if we attempt this, we cannot allow ourselves to fail. And if we *don't* attempt it, we also risk losing Artimé. The stronger she gets, the more danger our people are in. It's only a matter of time." He paused for breath, then added, softer, "I think we need to take her out as swiftly as possible before it's too late to stop her."

Claire considered that for a long moment, frowned over it as she ran through it once more in her mind, and then reluctantly nodded. "All right," she said, giving up. "All right. I see your point. Do what you have to do. You have my support. And I'll continue to work on defense with the Artiméans as always."

Alex gave her a solemn look. He didn't need her permission, but he respected her greatly and wanted it. "Thank you."

Claire nodded. "Just . . . get it right. The first time."

Alex nodded. "We will."

"So you're really for it, Sim?" Alex asked later, after Claire and the others had gone and only Florence and Simber remained

LISA McMANN

to help Alex plan the attack. "You believe we should take down Gondoleery?"

"Yes," growled the cat. "We prrrobably should have done it weeks ago."

"Why didn't you say so before?"

"You didn't ask."

Alex blinked. For a moment, he was speechless. He looked at Florence, who seemed just as surprised. "What?" Alex asked finally. "You're saying now I have to ask you every time I want your opinion? Even if you have something vital to say, you won't say it unless I ask the right question? When did this start?"

Simber sighed. He'd been quiet during the meeting and seemed more grumbly than usual now. "It's how you learrrn best," he said. "If I speak up too much, you count on me morrre than you should."

"Oh, come on. That's ridiculous." Alex shook his head, more frustrated than ever. "I haven't done that since before Mr. Today was killed and you sank in the sea. You're full of yourself."

"And you'rrre too comforrrtable," roared Simber. He got to his feet. "I might not be herrre foreverrr, you know!" The windows shook.

LISA McMANN

Florence watched the two, fascinated. They rarely fought.

Alex stared at the cat. "What's *that* supposed to mean? Are you leaving Artimé?"

"What?" Simber said. "No! Of courrrse not. But I can't keep telling you what to do. If you want my opinion, ask me. Otherrrwise don't expect it."

Alex raised his hands, completely confused. "I don't even understand what's happening right now," he muttered. "I just transported an entire party of Artiméans off Shipwreck Island—safely, mind you—virtually without you. What's your problem? Did I do something to offend you? If this is about Sky and me being stuck there, and the Florence thing with not enough magic carpet components, we would have figured it out without you, I'll have you know."

"I should hope so." Simber's chiseled jaw creaked as his stone teeth snapped together. He stared at Alex, nostrils flaring.

Alex stood tall and stared back, growing more defensive and angry as the seconds passed. He had no idea what had set Simber on edge. And he wasn't going to back down without an explanation.

Florence leaned forward on her sofa, propped her elbows

on her knees, and rested her chin in her hands, fascinated by the sudden flare-up and standoff.

After a minute, Simber relaxed his stance and turned his head. "Sorrry," he said gruffly. "I'm worrried about Gondoleerrry." He turned and paced toward the door, restlessly shaking his head. "Herrr ability to crrreate firrre is morrre dangerrrous than anything we've everrr been up against. Ice is bad enough, but firrre . . ."

Alex rested his gaze on the beast, trying to figure out if Simber was speaking the truth about what was bothering him. He couldn't tell. "We'll be careful," he said softly. "How hard can it be to take down one person when we have all of Artimé on our side?"

Simber stopped in his tracks and turned his head back to look at Alex. "That's exactly the wrrrong way to look at herrr. If therrre's anyone you should be afrrraid of in this worrrld, it's Gondoleerrry Rrrattrrrap." He paused, giving Alex a hard look. "And you should feel it in yourrr bones, Alex. Like I do. I shouldn't have to tell you." He paused. "*That's* what my prrroblem is."

Alex watched, jaw slacked, as Simber walked out of his

LISA McMANN

office. "You don't even have bones!" Alex called out. Simber didn't answer. When he had disappeared, Alex turned to Florence with a questioning look. "Didn't I just say I wanted her dead? I don't get it."

She tilted her head and raised an eyebrow. "Don't ask me," she said. "I think there's something deeper bothering him, but I don't know what."

"I can still hearrr you," came a gravelly warning from the balcony.

Alex sighed and shook his head. "Good night, Simber," he called. "We'll plan the attack in the morning."

"Harrrumph," said Simber, and soon the mansion trembled as the giant cat loped down the stairs to his spot at the front door.

# The Evil Twin

T he next time Aaron awoke, he was drenched in sweat and shivering profusely. He lay on his side, facing a rocky wall with no window, his blanket flung off him and just beyond his reach.

Every muscle in his body ached, and every bit of his skin hurt. His head pounded endlessly, and when he reached up to touch it, he found that it was wrapped in a bandage of some sort.

When he became aware that he was in a very strange and unfamiliar place, his stomach clenched in fear. *The pirates*, he thought. Had they brought him here? What were they going to do to him?

This time his memories were more distinct. He recalled the way the pirates had burst into his office and captured him. The way they'd thrown him into the boat. The way they'd starved him and spit on him and dragged him through the stormy sea for days with no water. And now, here, the storm still raged all around. Where was he? He had to get away. He had to escape!

With all his strength, he pushed against the mattress and tried lifting himself up, only to fall back again. He breathed hard, the air slicing his lungs, and tried again. Once more his strength gave out and he landed, twisted, on the cot.

A wave of nausea interrupted his efforts, and he began sweating again. He tested his voice, crying out for help, but it came out grainy and weak, nothing like the commanding voice of a high priest. He gave up.

When a shadow fell over his face, Aaron was too tired to open his eyes. But when someone slipped his arm around Aaron's shoulders and hoisted him up, putting a cup to his mouth, the boy lashed out blindly, slapping it aside. The back of his hand connected with the jaw of the one helping him, sending the man sprawling.

A moment later, Aaron could hear a low chuckle nearby and the voice of an old man saying, "Ah, there you are, Alexsan. I think you are going to be just fine after all."

Pain ripped through Aaron's stomach. Again, someone confused him for his brother. How was it possible that everybody in the world seemed to know Alex? Why couldn't Aaron ever be recognized?

He'd pretended to be Alex in the past. But this time Aaron wasn't going to let it happen. He was tired of it. He was Aaron Stowe, high priest of Quill, and he had done a lot of impressive things on his own, thank you very much. He was really getting sick of his brother always being the one people knew—and liked. And Aaron was tired of hiding conveniently behind his brother's fame, when Aaron should be known as the famous one for becoming the youngest high priest of Quill ever. He'd vaulted to the top in an amazingly short amount of time. And people ought to know about it. If Aaron's name was going to be known in this world, he'd better start using it and standing behind it, because clearly nobody else was going to vouch for him.

With all the energy he could muster, Aaron opened his

eyes. He blinked a few times and looked at the blurry face of the ancient little man who had returned to his side.

"I'm not Alex," Aaron rasped, his voice like gravel. "I'm Aaron." He closed his eyes and breathed, and added, "I'm the twin everybody hates."

# Stealth and Trickery

A day later, Alex met up with Florence, Simber, Samheed, Lani, Carina, and Sky. This time they took advantage of the beautiful day by sitting on the lawn. Simber seemed back to his usual self, and nothing was said of the previous day's fight between him and Alex. But Alex was determined to make his new idea work without Simber's assistance.

"Florence, start us off," Alex said. "What's our best move? Storm the palace?" He'd secretly always wanted to say that.

"No," Florence said. "We want to draw her out of the palace. There are too many places for her to hide inside—right, Simber?"

"And too many innocent people inside who could get hurrrt," Simber said, and by the look on his face, Alex could tell he was remembering their visit to the palace with Mr. Today, when Aaron had nearly killed Alex after sneaking up on him.

"Yeah, you're right, of course," Alex muttered reluctantly.

"And," Florence continued, "we'll want to make this a definitive action—one move to take her down, and it's done. Like Claire said, if we mess this up and she gets away, she's going to know what we're willing to do to stop her, and we definitely don't want that."

Alex nodded. "Great. So we need a few of us to infiltrate Quill and keep an eye on the palace without being recognized. You four would do well at that," he said, pointing to his friends.

"But won't we look conspicuous with our orange eyes and scars?" Lani asked.

"Come on," Alex said. "You're all mages—well, Sky not so much, but we'll help her, and she's creative. Can't you each come up with a disguise? Think back to Will Blair's days."

"Hey," Samheed muttered. "Take it easy."

"Oh, I see," Lani teased. "You want us to disguise ourselves as Aaron and take over?"

"Um, no, please," Alex said. "That plan didn't really work out well for Will, did it? I want you to look like ordinary Quillens walking around, which shouldn't be hard to do. Most of you have done it before."

Sky looked bemused and a bit uncomfortable. She was beginning to wonder what use she could be. "You could paint me invisible," she said.

"Where's the sport in that?" Samheed said. "Besides, the invisibility paintbrush spell doesn't last long enough, and wears off without warning. I don't even carry it anymore. It's a fun spell for goofing around, but not really meant for serious stuff."

Alex gave Sky a reassuring smile. "Don't worry. I'm sure Mr. Appleblossom has some costumes and can help you all with whatever magic you might need to keep you from being recognized."

Florence glanced at Simber. "I still have my mask from the masquerade ball. Maybe I can be a part of this."

"That'll worrrk," Simber said dryly. "Nobody will suspect a thing."

Alex grimaced. "I'm afraid you two will have to stay here. You're way too hard to disguise."

Sky couldn't hold back her reservations any longer. "I don't do magic," she said. "Not well, at least, and I don't know my way around Quill at all. Are you sure I'm the right person for this?"

"Oh, Quill's easy," Samheed told her. "It's one big oval road around the perimeter of the island, with quadrants of houses inside." He scratched his head. "Anyway, the palace is at the far west end. Just go left out of Artimé and follow the road— you can't miss it. It's the uninviting gray structure on the hill, with the crooked turret that sticks up quite high. Maybe you can stay on this half of the island so it'll be easier to find home again in case you get lost."

"Will we be working all together or separated?" Lani asked.

"You'll likely be together some of the time," Alex said. "But it depends on our approach. Let's figure out our plan of attack, and then we can look at that."

He addressed Sky specifically. "Yes, Sky, to answer your question, you *are* right for this job. I want you as a lookout. You're stealthy, you can run fast, and you're extremely clever— you'll be able to get yourself out of any situation easily. That's why I chose you, okay? Don't worry about the magic. The rest of us will have it covered."

LISA McMANN

63 « Island of Graves

Sky frowned. "Okay," she said, still a bit dubious. "Keep going."

Alex moved to continue, but before he could, Simber cleared his throat.

Everyone looked at him. After a moment, Alex realized the cat was waiting to be asked his opinion. He resisted the urge to roll his eyes. "Simber, what concerns do you have?" he said, only a little patronizingly.

Simber ignored the tone. "We haven't seen evidence of it, but accorrrding to Liam, Gondoleerrry might have firrre powerrr of some kind. In a deserrrt land like Quill, that can be verrry dangerrrous."

Alex nodded and waited to be sure the cat was done. "Right," Alex said. "I've been meaning to ask you, Lani—is there anything in that *Element-ary* book about fire?"

"I don't think so. It's more weather related. I'll check and get the book back to you."

"Thanks," said Alex. "Anything else to add, Simber?"

"No, thank you."

"All right, then. Moving on. Brainstorming time. How can we get Gondoleery out of the palace alone?"

The group members thought.

"Is there a Purge coming up?" Carina asked. "That would get her to the Commons."

"Not for a while," Florence said.

"What if . . . ?" Samheed said. "No." He fell back into his thoughts.

"She must go out now and then," Sky said. "Does she still have a house in Quill? We might just have to keep watch for a few days and see if there's any pattern to her movements."

Carina narrowed her eyes. "But does she go anywhere without a driver? I doubt it."

"Liam told me where to find her house in Quill," Alex said. "But he also told me that while there is sometimes glowing coming from the windows, it disappears if she answers the door, so we might not find anything there. Worth a look, though."

"What if . . . ?" Samheed said again, eyes lighting up, but then he slumped. "No."

Everyone but Lani snickered at him.

Lani, who had been quiet all this time, closed her eyes. "Hang on," she murmured, then nodded sharply, as if she'd just figured out a very difficult equation. "I've got it," she said, eyelids flying open.

"Tell us," Alex prompted.

Lani gathered her thoughts a minute more, then began. "If Gondoleery doesn't go anywhere on her own, I'll simply disguise myself as one of her drivers. When she decides to go somewhere, I'll drive her in this direction to the desolate area of Quill instead. You guys can be waiting, and we'll . . . we'll put an end to her reign right then and there," she said. "Now," she added, sitting up triumphantly, "knock some holes in that plan, why don't you."

"Seriously?" Samheed asked.

"Yes," Lani said.

"Well, for starters, you don't know how to drive."

Lani's mouth fell open. "Minor detail. How hard can it be?"

"Second," Samheed continued, "how will we know when you're coming with her? Are we just supposed to lie in wait for days? How will we recognize you if you're disguised as a driver?"

Lani's chin shot up. "I don't . . . Wait. The gargoyles. That's where Matilda comes in. We'll have Charlie with us, and Matilda can let us know when Gondoleery's going to go somewhere. She can follow Gondoleery out the door, and I'll sneak her into the back of the vehicle when Gondoleery's not looking. Then Alex can take Charlie through the tube and get to you, and you'll know precisely when I'll be coming."

Alex rubbed his chin, listening and thinking.

Samheed's face turned skeptical. "Okay, but aren't most of her drivers men?" he asked.

"So?" Lani replied. "When I said disguise, I'm talking full-blown impersonation. I'll become not just a man, but a specific man she'd recognize."

Sky looked up. "Maybe Liam could help. I bet he knows some of the drivers."

"Yes," Lani said, growing even more excited. "Yes, that's a great idea. He could help me with the disguise." She looked from Alex to Florence for approval. "What do you think? I think we have something here. There are a few minor issues, but nothing we can't overcome."

"I like it," Carina said. "It's not too complicated, and nobody else gets hurt."

"It's a *little* complicated, though," Simber argued.

"Yeah, like when Lani crashes a vehicle she doesn't know how to drive," Samheed said.

Sky elbowed him. "Stop," she said. "We'll figure that one out. Lani, does your father know how to drive?"

Lani's eyes lit up, and she made a face at Samheed. "Why yes, Sky, my father *does* know how to drive. He can tell me what to do."

Alex tapped a finger to his lips, deep in thought, trying to come up with every possible thing that could go wrong. "What happens to the guard you're impersonating?"

Lani's lips parted as if to answer, but soon she closed them, then opened them once more. "I'm not sure," she admitted. "Do we give him the day off?"

Alex smiled. "A day off? You've forgotten what it's like to live there. Drivers are Necessaries. They don't get a day off unless it's Purge day, remember?"

"Yeah," Lani said, scowling. "I remember."

"So . . . maybe we have to kidnap him," Samheed said, and now that he could picture himself doing something dangerous, he was starting to like this plan. "I'll kidnap him and freeze him somewhere out of the way so nobody notices him. He won't get hurt."

Alex frowned, not sure it would work logistically to have Samheed freezing a guard by the palace at the same time he was lying in wait for Gondoleery, but they'd work those details out.

Florence glanced at Alex, and then addressed the group. "I think the plan has a lot of potential. There are definitely a few things we have to address before I'm willing to sign off on it, but they are all problems we can overcome. So, if Alex is on board with the plan . . ." She turned back to him. "Are you, Alex?"

"I think so. Yes."

"Good. Then you four," Florence said, pointing to Lani, Samheed, Sky, and Carina, "can get to work researching your disguises, while Alex and I pound out the details."

Alex nodded. "Everybody feel comfortable? Sky, Mr. Appleblossom will have everything you need to blend in with the people of Quill. Lani, I'm pretty sure the drivers have a specific uniform, so maybe you should come with Florence and me before you start working on yours. I'm going to bring Liam in to discuss."

"Sounds good," Lani said.

"Questions, anybody?" Alex asked.

Carina frowned. "Yes. I'm not sure I like you bringing Liam in on the plan. I mean, he's . . . you know. One of them. Like . . ." She shook her head. "Never mind. I know he can't go back to them after Gondoleery sent him to the Ancients Sector. It's just . . . it's a little scary, trusting people who have spent so much time living in that awful palace."

Alex pursed his lips. "We need him."

"I know," Carina said. "But it makes me feel very uncomfortable. Not that long ago he was working against us."

Simber lifted his head, and this time he didn't wait to be asked for his opinion. "I've been arrround a long time," he said simply. "I've seen many people enterrr ourrr worrrld frrrom Quill. And therrre's one thing I have witnessed about behaviorrr. Therrre arrre few people who arrre borrrn evil and will die evil. Some become evil because of the influence of otherrrs and, forrr a time, ignorrre orrr burrry what theirrr innerrr trrruth is telling them. But I do know that humans who have been influenced to do evil arrre capable of change once they grrround themselves and follow that innerrr guide." He looked around. "And sometimes people like that become the biggest herrroes because they have so much morrre to prrrove."

LISA McMANN

Simber paused, then continued. "And therrre's one perrr-son who stands out as a prrrime example of this, and I don't want any of you to forrrget him."

"Who is he?" Carina asked.

Simber spoke humbly. "His name was Marrrcus Today."

LISA McMANN

# Ishibashi's Horrible Secret

When Ishibashi heard Aaron say that he wasn't Alex, he nearly fainted. Instead, as the young man's eyes closed and he fell into a troubled sleep once more, Ishibashi could only stare at the face he'd assumed for days was his friend.

Could Alex be delirious? Or was this person in the scientists' shelter telling the truth? Ishibashi racked his memory, going back to the conversation he'd had with Alex. The mage had said he had a brother—a brother who was his enemy and had killed Mr. Marcus Today, no less—but he hadn't mentioned that his brother was an identical twin! How could

LISA McMANN

Ishibashi have known this was the evil one? There was nothing about the sleeping young man to indicate he wasn't Alex, other than the words he'd just uttered.

Ishibashi's heart pounded as he realized the full extent of what he and Ito and Sato had done.

"The seaweed," Ishibashi said, his hands rising to cover his face as the horror came to light. By putting that tiny bit of healing seaweed into Aaron's mouth, they'd given the power of extended life, maybe even *unending* life . . . to a murderer.

Ishibashi hobbled from the room, his legs weak. He stumbled into the greenhouse, where he found Ito and Sato, and he told them in their native language what he'd just discovered.

The three stood in shocked silence for a long moment before the questions peppered the air, but all Ishibashi could tell his comrades was that they had done something they'd agreed never to do, and now they had the full responsibility of it on their hands.

When the three realized the extent of their mistake, Ito addressed the other two in a voice most serious. "There is only one thing we can do," he said. "We have a responsibility to fix our mistake. And because we cannot kill him, we can only change him. We must hope he does not try to harm us."

"And," said Sato, "we must protect all of society from him by keeping him here, for if he tries to escape the hurricane, it is certain that he will make it out alive."

Ishibashi nodded. His friends were wise. And he, having been the one to slip the seaweed into Aaron's mouth, took the most responsibility. "I will take charge of this mission," he said. "It is my duty."

Ishibashi watched over Aaron, and when the former high priest awoke again, Ishibashi was there.

Aaron blinked. For the first time, his mind wasn't filled with fog.

Ishibashi stood up so Aaron could see him. "I will get you some tea," he said firmly. "You must drink it, not throw it. Not slap it away."

Aaron focused on the man, who was definitely not a pirate. "Who are you?"

"You will call me Ishibashi-san. Do you understand me?"

"Barely," said Aaron. He didn't know what to make of the man's gruff behavior and unusual accent. But he wanted some tea. Desperately. Why did the man think he would throw it? "It's about time somebody treats me the way I deserve to be treated," he muttered.

Ishibashi put his hands on his hips and frowned at the young man, who was now completely distinguishable from his twin just by the words that came out of his mouth. But the old man didn't answer. He went to the greenhouse.

"He's awake," Ishibashi reported to the others. "Please make the most bitter tea you can, Ito," Ishibashi said. "I have a feeling he is going to be trouble."

While Ito went to the kitchen to prepare the tea, Ishibashi considered the task at hand. What would they do? They were stuck with him.

By the time he was serving the tea to Aaron, who complained angrily about it, Ishibashi promised himself one thing: Aaron must never find out that he might live forever.

# Making Preparations

Inside the mansion's vast kitchen, Thisbe and Fifer played in a corner near the food-delivery tube. They climbed over Crow, who was taking care of them. A few Unwanted chefs moved about, filling room service orders and designing elaborate fruit carvings and intricate vegetable dioramas in preparation for the next meal service.

Whenever a room service order came in, the kitchen staff quickly whipped up the desired food item, plated it in grand and elegant fashion, and wrapped it in magical sparkling cellophane that was designed to disappear into thin air once the recipient was ready to eat. The chef then handed the package to one of the twins to place gently in the tube for delivery. And for their young age, they seemed to grasp the importance of the task, at least a little. They hardly ever dropped a dish.

It was Fifer's turn next to place a plate in the tube. She took great care to set it gently in the right spot.

"Good job, Fig," Crow said. He pulled both children away from the tube. "Now watch it disappear! But stay back here with me. We don't want you to disappear with it." He smiled to himself at the thought—what a surprise that would be for someone to get a small child delivered with her meal.

Across the room at the kitchen bar, Alex and Lani enjoyed lunch with Liam and filled him in on the plan to take down Gondoleery Rattrapp. At first they only gave him the information that was necessary for him to help them, and once they'd explained the plan, Alex made Liam promise he wouldn't speak a word of it to anyone.

"I—I promise," Liam said with the utmost sincerity. "You saved my life. I shall never betray Artimé." He looked at his plate of food, overwhelmed by the variety, the color, and the amazing freshness of it all.

"Thank you," Alex said. "That's a promise we'll hold you

to." He hesitated, and then said earnestly, "I'll tell you that not everyone was in agreement on whether you should be told this information. But I believe you'll prove me right in trusting you."

Flustered, Liam set down his fork and fussed with his sleeves, which still hung nearly to his fingertips. "Why *are* you telling me this? How am I supposed to help you?" He rolled the fabric nervously between his thumbs and forefingers.

Alex looked at Lani, who picked up some sketches from the counter next to her. Alex had drawn them. They were depictions of the palace drivers. He'd done it from memory, but it had been a while since he'd seen a driver, and back when he had—when Aaron paid a visit to give Alex Mr. Today's robe—he'd been too angry to take much notice of the man's appearance.

Lani showed the sketches to Liam. "We need to know exactly what the driver uniforms look like. Alex drew these. Are they even close? Can you remember any details?"

Liam studied the drawings. He shook his head a little bit, then looked up. "I don't even understand what this is, really. How'd you even . . . you know. Do this? It's like the things on the walls in the hallways . . . very puzzling indeed."

LISA McMANN

Alex looked confused for a moment, and then his face cleared. "Good grief," he said, beginning to chuckle. "It's called a picture. I'm starting to understand all too well why Mr. Today seemed so absentminded when we first arrived here." He fumbled around in his robe pockets, pulled out some colored pencils, handed one to Liam, and flipped over one of the pieces of paper on the counter.

"This is a pencil," Alex said. "You've certainly seen a pencil by now, haven't you?"

"Yes," said Liam, examining it. "Aaron had one. And they're everywhere around here."

"Right. So you just have to touch the pointed end to the paper," Alex said.

Liam obeyed.

"Now press firmly, but not too hard, and move it across the paper."

Liam gripped the pencil awkwardly. He drew a short line, and the tip snapped off. He gasped in horror. "Oh no—I'm sorry!"

Lani laughed. "That's exactly what happened to Alex the first time he used a pencil! Remember, Al?"

Alex grinned. "I do. Sean was teaching me in the lounge." Alex took the pencil from Liam and drew his fingers over the tip. A new point grew from it. He handed it back to Liam, who cut down on the pressure and drew a few weak, wobbly lines on the paper.

"It takes some practice," Lani confided. "I'm not very good at it, myself."

"Please," said Alex. "You're good at everything. You can act, sing, draw, tell stories, invent things, design new components, experiment with who knows what . . . and you read like you're on fire, so you know more than anybody."

"Oh, I know that's all true," Lani said. "I'm decently good at a lot of things. But I don't really have a specialty I'm extraordinarily good at, like most people do." She shrugged, not at all bothered by it. "Everybody's different, you see," she said to Liam. "In Quill you're all supposed to be the same. Not here." She gave him a critical glance, sizing him up. "You're pretty old to be finding the thing you're good at, but I suppose it could still happen for you."

Liam smiled. He set down the pencil. "I think that's enough for now," he said, looking proudly at his scribbles. He turned over the paper and returned his attention to Alex's drawings of the driver. "Okay, so you call this a—a picture of the driver," Liam mumbled, trying to understand the concept of art. Once his mind accepted it, he began to compare the drawing to the way he imagined the drivers. But it was hard. He hadn't been taught to think that way.

"The jacket is the right length," he offered finally, pointing at the front view, then at the back view. "Long, to around mid-thigh, with that slit in the back. But the buttons are wrong. There should be two columns of four silver buttons—it's double-breasted. And this looks so stiff. The material is more . . . " He searched for the words. "Flimsy, I guess. The uniforms are very old and worn. Patches on the elbows and such."

"Do you want to draw the buttons where they're supposed to go?" Alex asked.

"Oh, no." Liam looked afraid. "I—I'll mess it up."

"It's okay," said Alex. "This is just a rough sketch. I'll redraw it. But I'm not sure I'm going to get the buttons and patches and the lay of the fabric looking right without actually seeing it."

"Ooh," said Lani, her face lighting up. "I guess we'll have to go spy on the palace, then," she said. "That's all there is to it."

Alex's first instinct was to say no, it wasn't safe. But then his smile became devious. "I think you're right. We'll go along the shore and sneak up the hill. We can stay hidden in the rubble and just see what we can see."

"Perfect." But Lani's smile soon turned to a frown. "Oh drat."

"What is it?" Liam asked her. "What's wrong?"

"I only wish we could get close enough for me to really study a driver's face." She scrunched up her nose, thinking. "I'm afraid that'll be the downfall of this plan—me not getting the impersonation just right. The face has to be very close, or Gondoleery will notice."

At Liam's puzzled look, Lani explained. "I'm going to use magic to disguise myself to look like one of the drivers. Do you happen to know which driver would be most likely to take Gondoleery somewhere? I'll need a description of him. Maybe you should come with Alex and me so you could point him out." Then she shook her head, frustrated. "But it won't be close enough, I'm afraid. Isn't there any way to see them up close without them seeing me? I'm going to need a good long

LISA McMANN

look, and Alex will have to get all the features just right in his drawing so Mr. Appleblossom and I have something solid to work with."

"You could use the invisibility paintbrush for that," Alex suggested.

"Oh, right!" said Lani. "Of course!"

"Hmm." Liam sat up and leaned forward. He pressed his lips together, as if he were thinking very hard.

"What is it?" Alex asked him.

Liam hesitated, then put a finger in the air. "I think, actually . . . ," he began, his eyes darting from Lani to Alex to Lani again. He leaned even closer to them, as if he had a secret to tell. "That is," he said, and cleared his throat, "I believe there is a tiny ch-chance that I might actually be able to help you . . . perhaps even more than you anticipated."

# Spying on the Palace

While Florence and Claire held the first Magical Warrior Training for the newest members of Artimé—the Warbler children who had been catapulted to Artimé's shores a few months before—Alex, Lani, and Liam headed west along the shoreline, staying low and close to the water. They picked their way over the rubble from the destroyed wall, keeping watchful eyes on the land and the road that ran parallel to their path up the hill a few hundred yards to their right.

"Maybe we should have taken the boat," Alex said. "We'd get there faster."

"No way," Lani said, hopping deftly from one rock to the next. "Someone would be sure to see it buzzing on the water, and knowing the people of Quill, the sight of it would cause a panic. We're much less noticeable walking along the shore."

They continued to where the shoreline curved and the elevation increased slightly, indicating they were on the approach to the palace end of the island. Now and then they heard the echo of the portcullis clanging open or shut.

"Guards and palace workers coming and going," Liam explained. "The gate to the palace is useless now that the wall is down, but I'm not sure anyone has figured out quite yet that you can just walk around the south side of the portcullis now, if you really want to."

"No wonder Justine was afraid of the creative thinkers," Lani muttered.

Alex kept a wary eye on the rise of land, but no one seemed to be guarding the palace grounds along the place where the wall used to be. When at last they could see the turret directly up and to their right, they turned toward it and began climbing the rubble-covered hill, staying low to the ground. They could hear the rumble of a jalopy revving up and fading into the distance.

"Aaron figured out how to get the vehicles running more smoothly," Liam whispered to the others as they neared the top of the hill and peeked over, witnessing the plodding of workers around the palace and the vehicle disappearing down the hill. "H-he made a . . . a contraption to squeeze the oil out of nuts. I've never seen anything like it."

Alex shot Liam a quizzical glance. "He did?"

"I swear it," Liam said.

"Shh," Lani said, pointing to the door to the palace.

A guard stood on either side of it. A few yards closer to Alex, Lani, and Liam, three drivers congregated near a line of vehicles. They didn't speak; they merely stood together, waiting to be called upon.

"Sometimes they stand there all day with nothing to do," Liam whispered.

"It doesn't look like we can get any closer without being seen," Lani whispered. "Do they ever walk over here?"

"They might," Liam said, very seriously. "Then again, they might not."

Lani and Alex exchanged raised eyebrows and went back

LISA McMANN

Island of Graves » 86

to studying the drivers. Alex took a tiny sketch pad and pencil from his robe and began to draw.

Once Lani had fully scoped out the area, she pulled an invisibility paintbrush from her vest pocket and painted herself with it. "Back in a few," she said, and Alex could hear her climbing up the rocks. But when she started across the gravel driveway, her footsteps were painfully loud over the loose rubble, and rocks tilted and moved under her. The drivers didn't seem to notice or care, but one of the guards looked up. Lani stopped moving.

When the guard turned back to her thoughts, Lani tried to get closer, but the fresh rubble was like crunching across a layer of spun-sugar brittle. The guard heard her again and took a few steps toward her, beginning to peer about.

Lani froze and was forced to wait several minutes until she was certain the woman had forgotten about the noise. Finally, with every ounce of caution and care in her step, she retreated back to the hiding spot where Alex and Liam waited.

"That's not going to work," she said. Over the next few minutes the spell wore off and she reappeared, a bit at a time.

Liam frowned as he watched the drivers. "I'm going to try

to get the attention of the one on the end nearest us," he said. "Follow me."

Liam slid down the rocks so he could stay hidden and moved farther west, past the side of the palace. Alex and Lani followed close behind. When Liam climbed back up to look over the top of the hill, the other two remained crouched on the rocks.

Seeing that there was no one guarding this side of the building, Liam ran the short distance to the palace, pressed his body against it, and slowly peeked around the corner. After a minute he picked up a pebble and tossed it toward the drivers. He waited, and when nothing happened, repeated his actions, hitting the driver on the end. When the startled man turned to look, Liam frantically waved him to come over.

The driver's face slacked in fear. He looked all around to see if anyone else had noticed Liam.

Alex and Lani ducked. Slowly they lifted their heads again, finding the scene irresistible. Was the driver going to come closer? Alex readied his pencil and sketch pad, straining to get a good glimpse of the man's face and uniform, and hoping they wouldn't have to take off running.

After a moment, the driver mumbled something to the

others and walked slowly along the front of the palace toward the side where Liam was hiding. When the man reached the corner, he turned nonchalantly, and when he was safely out of sight, he looked at Liam, face awash with fear.

"I thought you was sent to the Ancients," the driver whispered harshly.

"I didn't go," said Liam.

"But you have to!"

"I won't. Keep my secret, I beg you."

"You're putting me in danger," the driver said, his eyes darting this way and that. "Her greatness ain't sending people to the Ancients anymore—she kills 'em outright if she don't like 'em now."

Alex and Lani looked at one another in alarm.

Liam paled. "Oh dear. I'm sorry. I'll make it up to you someday, I promise. But I need your help."

The driver silently considered the plea. "What 'appened to them babies?" he asked, eyes narrowed.

It took Liam a moment to realize that the driver was talking about Fifer and Thisbe. "They're safe too. But you must never tell anyone."

The driver's face softened. He looked at the ground. "What do you want?"

"Come with me. Just right over here. Only for a moment." Liam pointed down the embankment to where Alex and Lani were hiding. "Hurry." He started down the hill and motioned for the driver to follow him.

With a panicked look on his face, the driver hesitated, looked around, and then followed. A moment later, Alex and Lani were face-to-face with the man Lani would soon impersonate.

Alex began sketching at a frantic pace.

"Don't be afraid," Liam said. "This is *Alex* Stowe, not Aaron. Alex is the leader of Artimé, where Secretary . . . well, you know. And this is Lani Haluki." Liam hesitated as he realized that even after all this time, he didn't know the driver's name.

No one noticed, for the driver had started at Lani's familiar surname. "Haluki?" he asked. "Like the old high priest?"

"He's my father," Lani said, holding out her hand. "What is your name?"

The driver looked surprised to be asked such a question, for he was accustomed to answering to "Driver!" most often. He shook her hand. "I'm Sully," he said, his voice hushed. "Your father was a kind man."

"He still is," Lani said. She smiled and, after a moment, removed her hand from Sully's grasp, all the while studying the man carefully, noting his mannerisms and gestures so she could imitate them properly. The man gazed at her with respect.

Seeing an opportunity, Lani caught Alex's eye, wondering if he saw it too.

Alex nodded ever so slightly and held back, giving Lani the reins to present their predicament.

"We've got a big favor to ask you, Mr. Sully," Lani began.

"Just Sully," said Sully.

"Sully," Lani agreed.

"What is it?" Sully grew fearful again. "I ain't sure if I can . . . You see, since the ice disappeared, High Priest Gondoleery's been fuming, and striking people down . . . dead." He looked at Liam. "Now you—you been good to me too, Governor, but I can't risk no more trouble for my family. Not with her shooting fireballs this way an' that wherever her whimsies takes her."

LISA McMANN

Alex's face clouded over, and he stopped sketching. "It sounds even worse than I imagined. What else is Gondoleery doing to the people of Quill?"

"So far it's just the ones what get in her way," Sully said. "Palace workers and whatnot. But she's plotting to do a full sweep of Quill, pretending to ask the people what they are needing, then shooting them down with her magics if they say anything."

A burst of wind seemed to come from nowhere, sending up a cloud of dirt and nearly knocking Alex and Lani over. Silt rained down on them.

Sully looked fearfully over his shoulder at the upper floor of the palace. "That kind of thing ain't natural—that wind. It's her doing," he said.

Alex and Lani exchanged a serious glance as they righted themselves and shook the dirt from their clothes.

"Sully," Lani said, taking the man's hand.

Sully looked at her. "Yes, miss?" He seemed to gain confidence being so close to an offspring of the one good high priest Quill had ever seen.

"We need you," Lani said earnestly. "We want to overthrow

Gondoleery Rattrapp before she hurts anyone else. She's gone too far."

Fear sparked in his eyes. "Overthrow?"

"Destroy," Alex said.

Sully looked at Alex and cringed—the young man looked exactly like Aaron, who was awful. "And then what?" he asked. "You take over the island with your killer beasts and monsters?"

Alex reared back. "Wait. Killer beasts?"

"The one that killed Secretary. We heard all about 'em from Governor Strang. What else do you got in there? No, sir. Nobody here trusts your crazy world full of Unwanteds and monsters." He said it matter-of-factly.

Liam cringed, and Alex's pencil froze in his grip. He cast his glance away, looking over the gentle waves of the sea as he recovered from the verbal blow. He knew the man didn't know any better. But would it always be this way? It would, he decided, until somebody taught them, like Mr. Today had taught him and his friends.

Lani dropped her eyes, but her temper rose. Keeping her voice low, she said, "If the Wanteds are really so intelligent, why can't they see we're trying to help them? Aren't you afraid Gondoleery will take you down next?"

A weary look came over Sully's face, and he sighed. "I work long days for a little food and water for my family. Every day of our whole lives we live in fear: Will the high priest let me go home today? Or will she find a reason to send me to the Ancients? Now she's gone even further. But . . . ," he said, and lost himself in thought for a moment.

"But what?" Lani asked softly.

Sully looked at her. "Sometimes I think the high priest striking me down without warning might be the best thing that could 'appen to me."

# A Proper Disguise

Leaving Liam, Alex, and Lani with nothing to say, Sully wearily climbed up the hill behind the palace and returned to his post. The three stood for a long moment, then soberly picked their way down the hill and walked back to Artimé.

Upon their return, Lani and Alex met with Mr. Appleblossom to give him the drawings and to begin working on Lani's disguise. She'd use magic to transform her features, and Mr. Appleblossom would help with the costume.

Once the costume making was well under way, Alex returned to the mansion to brood about the state of things.

LISA McMANN

Tugging at his mind was the question Sully had asked following Alex's announcement about intending to take down Gondoleery. "And then what?" Sully had asked. And indeed, Alex hadn't thought about that. Would the island become one land or stay separate? Who would be in charge? Perhaps Alex should leave it as it is and put Haluki back in charge of Quill.

"It depends what the people of Quill want," Alex muttered, but immediately he knew that was more difficult than it sounded, because the people of Quill didn't know how to make decisions. They'd been trained to have no opinion. They didn't know what they wanted. They only knew what was familiar. And he doubted his own ability to motivate them in any way, especially after what Sully had said about nobody trusting the people of Artimé.

A few days later, as Alex studied the pile of books he'd selected from the Museum of Large's library, trying to find the most deadly spell possible, he heard a noise. He turned to look, and gasped.

"Sully," he said, alarmed, wondering how the man had found his way into the somewhat secret hallway. But then his surprise faded, and he grinned. "Lani, I sure hope that's you!"

"It is," she said in Sully's voice. "Hope you don't mind me leaving the 3-D doorway up so I can get up here. How do you like it?"

"It's good!" Alex said. "Even your voice. How did you do it?"

"Concentration, imagination, and a little help from Mr. Appleblossom's junk drawer," she said mysteriously. "Not sure how long I can hold it—I'm figuring that part out now. It seems easy enough as long as I concentrate and stay in character, though. No ten-minute limit on this spell."

"It's really weird seeing you like this," Alex admitted. "You've even got his little eye twitch down."

"You think it's close enough?"

"Definitely," Alex said. "How are the others coming along?"

"Their costumes are ready. Just waiting on the plan of attack."

Alex nodded. "I've been studying some of Mr. Today's books. Found a journal here that's fascinating, but he wasn't into deadly spells until our group of Unwanteds showed up, I guess." Alex frowned. "He didn't seem to be too worried about Artimé being discovered until I came along."

LISA McMANN

"We know you wrecked it for all of us," Lani teased.

Alex didn't smile. He would never quite get over the fact that it was his fault the fighting had happened in the first place. And while he tried to push past the guilt as Mr. Today had told him to do, it still hung there in the back of his mind. He sighed. "Anyway . . ."

Lani, still disguised as Sully, gave a crooked smile. "Anyway," she agreed. "Look forward, Al. Here's your chance to create a surefire spell just to destroy Gondoleery."

Alex nodded and closed the book he'd been reading. "You're right. And I think I have just the thing in mind that will do the job."

Lani rubbed her man hands together. "What is it?"

But Alex only smiled. "You'll see," he said. "But I want you to know I got the idea for it from you."

# One of a Kind

Later that day, Sky found Alex standing barefoot on the beach, staring at the sand and occasionally moving his feet through it. "What are you looking for?" Sky asked. "Did you lose something?"

Alex looked up, his heart quickening at her unmistakable voice. She had her long hair piled on top of her head, the natural highlights like thin rays of sunlight bursting from a knot there. Her light brown skin drank up the sun, and her orange eyes sparkled despite Sky's earnest intentions to help him find whatever he was looking for.

"I found it now, thanks," Alex said, looking at her, and then blushing because he sounded ridiculous. He hastened to say something less stupid. "Where've you been? I've hardly seen you in days."

"I've been learning my way around Quill and practicing being a person from there," Sky said. "What a horrid place. Mr. Appleblossom has been helping me. He even made a pair of disguise eyes to cover up my orange ones."

Alex smiled sadly. "I hate that you have to cover up your eyes, even for one day." He reached out and ran his thumb over her bare shoulder.

She smiled back at him. "Oh, don't be so dramatic about it." She put her arms out and pulled him into a friendly hug.

Alex laughed, surprised that she would hug him, as it had been a while since she'd acted so friendly. He relaxed into her, resting the side of his face against the side of hers, and closed his eyes, his heart longing for something he couldn't describe. He knew that whatever it was, he didn't have it. But this was close. He slid his hands around her waist and held her, and they stood together like that for a long moment.

Alex wished he had a clue about what might be on Sky's mind. He could smell her skin, tropical and sweet, like pineapples and coconut. Without thinking, he pressed his lips against the curve of her neck.

Sky stiffened. "Alex," she whispered.

It brought him around. Hastily he pulled away and stepped back. "I'm sorry."

She looked at him, brow furrowed, and her lips twitched. Alex thought he saw longing in her eyes, or maybe that was just what he hoped to see. As much as he wanted to kiss her, he knew she was not going to give in and let him, or kiss him back. Alex had caused their breakup, and if he ever wanted the chance to kiss her again, he'd have to first figure out how to lead a nation without messing it up, while having successfully deepening relationships at the same time. And then convince Sky that he'd succeeded in doing it.

Unfortunately, at this moment Alex had a crucial spell to create, and he couldn't afford to make a mistake. He dropped his gaze and focused on the sand once more. "I was actually looking for a small stone," he said gruffly, and cleared his throat. "Just the right kind of stone, the kind that you can see through as if it's glass. I've seen a few in the past, which made me think it would be perfect for . . . for something, but there aren't very many of these particular stones, and they're hard to find. Because they're clear, I mean."

Sky, grateful for the distraction, walked a few steps away and began sifting through the sand with her toes. "What's it for?" she asked.

"A spell component."

"A new one?"

"Yes."

Sky glanced at him. "Is it for Gondoleery?"

"Yes." Alex didn't say more. It was going to be the most formidable spell he'd ever created, and he was already deep in thought over how to do it just right.

After several minutes of searching in silence, Sky spied something sparkling in the sunlight. She picked it up and examined it, squinting at it. "I think I found one," she said.

Alex looked up eagerly and hurried to Sky's side to take a closer look. She dropped it into Alex's open hand. "Is this the kind you mean?" she asked.

"That's it!" Alex said, peering at it. "Thank you. It's the perfect component for the spell I have in mind."

"Do you need a few more?" Sky asked, raking her toes

through the sand once more. "Since you're putting all this work into creating a new spell, I mean. Seems a shame to make just one. What if you misplace it?"

Alex thought about how he'd feel if he lost such an important and deadly item and shook his head. "If I misplace this component, I'm not fit to run Artimé," he said in earnest. "It'll be extremely dangerous if it gets into the wrong hands." He pinched the stone between his thumb and forefinger and slid it carefully into his robe pocket for safekeeping.

Sky tilted her head. "Well, then. If you're sure."

"Yes," he said decisively. "I'm sure. I don't want any more of these things to exist. Ever." He gave a resolute nod. "I'll have this ready by tonight. Tomorrow we'll put our plan in action. I'll alert Charlie. Can you let the others know?"

Sky nodded. "We'll be ready." She reached out to give his arm a squeeze, then stopped and instead dropped her hand to her side. "Good luck," she said with a half smile.

"Thanks. And . . . I'm sorry about before." He held out his hand in friendship, and awkwardly Sky shook it.

The two walked to the mansion together. Inside at the foot of the staircase they parted ways: Sky continuing on to the tubes, and Alex ascending the steps to the upper level, where he would attempt to fill the tiny glass spell component with the darkest, deadliest magic he had ever tried to create.

In the morning, the team assembled. Alex left his colorful robe with Claire so he wouldn't stand out, and wore a component vest dyed gray to blend in with the clothing colors of Quill. He carried his typical arsenal of spell components in his vest in case he ran into trouble with the palace guards, along with the small bit of glass that sat alone in one pocket. He tied his hair back and wore a brimmed hat so he wouldn't be easily recognized or mistaken for Aaron as he lurked around the palace.

Lani still looked like herself but wore a driver's uniform that was way too big for her, having decided that if things moved quickly, she didn't want to have to take the time to change into it. She loosely pinned up the fabric so she could walk properly.

Alex tried not to worry too much about Lani, but he couldn't help it after what had happened to Meghan. "Are you sure you can do this?" he asked.

"Yep," said Lani. "I'm still sure. Just like the last time you asked."

Samheed, Carina, and Sky were dressed in the gray, thread-bare clothing of the Necessaries. In the colorful world of Artimé they looked eerily out of place, like refugees from Quill. Carina and Samheed hid components wherever they could find space in their clothing, while Sky declared she preferred fighting her way, with her wits and her fists, if the incident called for it. And Charlie, who was already communicating with Matilda, wore nothing, as usual, and awaited the signal that would tell the Artiméans that Gondoleery was planning to go out.

"Everybody ready?" Alex asked, offering approving glances at each member of his team. "I sent instructions to your black-boards this morning. Are we clear on the plan?"

They all nodded.

Samheed took a step forward. "I've been working on some-thing for you," he said, and held out a handful of strange-looking scatterclips to Alex. "I call them stickyclips," he said. "I just perfected them last night using some of that rubber cement stuff we got from Ishibashi's island. Thought they might come in handy at the palace, Al. You just throw them like scatter-clips, but instead of them sending your enemy flying backward and pinning him to the nearest solid object, these will actually

LISA McMANN

hit your target and pull him directly to you wherever you are. That way you can do whatever you need to do to him while remaining out of sight."

"Great thinking, Samheed," Alex said, taking the clips and looking them over. "These are excellent. Thanks." He secured them inside his bulging vest pocket and looked up. "Okay, it's time to go. Lani, you and I will head out along the shore with Charlie. Sam, Sky, and Carina, you'll go to the desolate area as discussed, and take your places. Have components ready, but remember—you're Necessaries in trouble, waving down the vehicle, and you don't know how to do magic. Don't fire any spells if you don't have to, or Gondoleery will know something's up."

"Got it," Carina said.

Samheed echoed her. "Got it."

Sky shoved her hands into her empty pockets and nodded.

Alex continued. "If all goes according to plan, I'll pull Sully out, Lani will replace him, and once Lani's safely on the move with Gondoleery, Charlie and I will sneak around to Haluki's, take the tube back here, and meet you guys in the desolate area well before Lani gets there with Gondoleery. I'll be ready with the special spell." He patted the nearly empty pocket of his vest. "She won't know what hit her."

"What's the spell called?" Samheed asked.

Alex frowned. "I don't even want to say its name aloud until I have to," he said.

And with that, the parties dispersed. Before Alex set off, he let Florence and Simber know they were heading out. The rest of Artimé remained for the most part oblivious to the plan that could leave Quill without a leader and change the island forever.

# Aaron's First Lesson

**W**hen is this incessant storm going to stop?" Aaron asked Ishibashi. "It's driving me mad." He rested on his cot, his head propped up by two pillows.

"Never, thanks to you," said the old man. Instead of helping Aaron drink his morning tea like he'd done before, he set the cup on a small table about five feet away from the boy.

Aaron frowned. "Thanks to me? You're saying I caused this storm?"

Ishibashi set up a chair next to the table and sat down. "Do not give yourself so much credit. Arrogance is ugly. What I am saying is that the reason the storm is still here is because of you. There is a difference."

Aaron eyed the cup of tea. "Please. What in Quill could I have done to cause a storm to rage incessantly?" He pointed at the table. "Bring the tea to me."

Ishibashi ignored the command. "You are responsible for the storm's continuance because you killed the man who was trying to end it."

Aaron struggled and sat up, indignant. "I did no such thing!" he said. And then the realization of truth came over him. He clamped his mouth shut and turned his face away from the man. "Bring me the tea."

"You did not kill Mr. Marcus Today?" challenged Ishibashi.

Aaron turned his entire body away to face the wall. He pulled the blanket up around his ears and didn't answer.

Ishibashi studied the boy. "I see. Where there is shame, there is hope."

"What is *that* supposed to mean?" Aaron asked. "I am not ashamed of anything! Now *bring* me my *tea*, Ancient!"

Ishibashi stood up. Silently he picked up the little table with the cup of tea on top of it and moved it another five feet away from Aaron, set it down, and then left the room.

After a minute, Aaron turned his head slightly, curious as to why Ishibashi wasn't answering. "My *tea*," he said once more, and then, when it still didn't come, he grew angry enough to roll over.

The former high priest stared, seeing the table with the tea even farther away than it had been before. He sat up shakily, furious at the old man. Who did he think he was, anyway? "Hey, Ishi Mushy, or whatever your name is, get over here! This is not funny."

But the man didn't return.

Aaron flounced back in his bed, making his injured shoulder stab with pain. He stared hard at the ceiling while his stomach twisted in hunger for the horrible tea that tasted so awful, yet it was the only thing Aaron had.

Well, today he didn't have it. It was far away, growing cold.

"This is ridiculous," Aaron muttered. "I can't believe this treatment." His ranting grew louder, and he hoped Ishibashi could hear him. "If we were in Quill," he shouted, "I would have sent you to the Ancients Sector fifty years ago! Your incompetence and insolence is absolutely *astounding*!"

LISA McMANN

Finally, when no one appeared, Aaron, clenching and unclenching his fists, rolled slowly off the cot to his hands and knees. "Are you happy now?" he screamed. "I'm practically fainting from the pain!"

He crawled, head and face pounding, his right arm useless and dragging across the floor as he went the agonizing distance to the table. When he got there, he rested a moment, exhausted. Then he rose slowly and unsteadily to his knees. He reached for the cup, and then, in a moment of panic, wondered if it was all a trick. If Ishibashi was as horribly mean as he seemed, maybe he had put nothing in the teacup.

But that fear soon disappeared, for the cup was full as before. Aaron rolled to a sitting position, trying not to spill the tea, and sipped the horrible drink, which was an unappetizing lukewarm temperature by now. "You're a horrible person!" he yelled between sips. "And your tea is disgusting!"

He drained the cup, shuddered, and tried to throw it at the wall to show the man how much he hated him, but he had so little strength left to put into the throw that the cup just bounced on the floor and didn't break. Aaron stared at it. "Even your cups are stupid!" he screamed. His voice echoed through the chamber.

Could they hear him? Aaron had no idea how big this place was. He didn't even really understand who these people were, or how he'd gotten here, or where he was. Ishibashi hadn't told him anything.

Aaron could smell something delicious wafting in from another part of the giant maze of caves. He nearly yelled, "Bring me some of that food!" but he stopped himself just in time, remembering what happened when he demanded Ishibashi bring him some tea. Maybe Aaron would just wait and see if they brought him something to eat. But now . . . he looked at the distance to his cot. His arms and legs were shaking from the effort he'd made. The trip back to the bed looked formidable.

Finally, he began to slide across the floor using his left forearm to pull himself along. He made it only a few feet before his arm collapsed and he face-planted on the floor. The pain was blinding, and a wild sob escaped his lips as he waited for the agony to abate. With his eyes closed and his body spread out on the floor halfway between the table and his cot, Aaron rested his cheek on the cool rock and lay there, unable to move.

"Help," he called a while later. But no one came to help

him. He was not surprised. After a miserable hour, Aaron was convinced that no one was coming to his aid in any possible way, so he picked himself up once more, and with a tremendous effort, made it back to the cot. He fell onto it, too weak to put the blanket back on himself.

It was going to be a long road to recovery.

For everyone.

# Aaron Grows Desperate

That evening, when Aaron's stomach cried out in pain from hunger, he could keep silent no longer. Had they forgotten he was there? He could smell various foods cooking throughout the day, but Ishibashi delivered none of them.

"I'm so hungry!" Aaron called, writhing in the bed. "I know you have food out there. Why won't you feed me?"

This was almost worse than being stuck in that fishing boat, tied to the pirate ship.

Aaron racked his brain, trying to figure out why the men weren't feeding him. He began to argue with them as if they'd offered reasons for not feeding him. "If it's because you're mad about Mr. Today," he called out, "you should just get over it! I didn't even mean to kill him. He just . . . he was there . . . so suddenly . . ." Aaron frowned. He still didn't like thinking about that. It was horrible. And that time seemed so long ago and far away.

He carried on, wailing harder as his hunger intensified. But still no one came. "Did you all fall over dead?" he called. "Are you too deaf to hear me? Or are you just mean and horrible people?"

After a while, Aaron, exhausted, turned to begging. "Look, Ishi-what's-your-name, I'm sorry, okay? Please, can you just bring me something to eat? Just a little something?" But still no one came, and Aaron finally gave up.

He turned away from the opening to the room as he had before and stared at the wall while the wind howled and thunder crashed around him. Soon it was dark, and finally, after shedding a few tears, he fell asleep and dreamed about starving to death.

Aaron awoke before dawn to find Sato picking up the empty teacup and walking away with it.

"Ishibashi!" Aaron called out. "Anyone! Some food please?"

But Ishibashi did not come back, not even with tea this time.

# Plan in Motion

Luckily, all the parties involved in the attack on Gondoleery had brought food and water with them, for Gondoleery didn't go out at all the first day. In the desolate area of Quill, Sky, Samheed, and Carina took turns keeping watch overnight. Just down the hill from the palace, Alex, Lani, and Charlie spent an uncomfortable night on the rocks, waiting for a sign from Matilda that Gondoleery was heading out somewhere.

"Are you sure you can drive one of those vehicles?" Alex asked Lani for perhaps the fourth time.

"I'm sure," Lani said. "My dad told me everything about

how to do it. He said they go really slow, so it's not like anything can happen. The hardest thing will be getting it started."

"You know how to do that, too?"

"Yes," Lani said, growing annoyed.

"Glad you're the one doing the disguise and driving parts, that's all I can say," Alex said.

"Me too," said Lani.


It was early the next morning—before dawn—when Charlie tugged Alex's sleeve, waking the mage from a restless sleep.

"Is it happening?" Alex asked, sitting up and peering through the darkness. "At this hour? She's going out now?" He wiped his eyes with his sleeve and hopped up.

Charlie nodded emphatically and shook Lani awake.

Lani scrambled to her feet as if she hadn't just been sound asleep, and unpinned the sleeves and legs of her costume. Quickly she smoothed out the wrinkles. Without a word she faced away from Alex and began to concentrate on becoming the character of Sully the driver, knowing no one else could carry out their tasks until she'd succeeded with hers.

Alex crept up the hill and peered at the drivers, Charlie

staying close behind. Alex could tell there were three drivers standing in the usual spot, but he couldn't tell which one was Sully. He looked over his shoulder. "It's too dark," he whispered to Lani. "I can't see. I think I'm going to have to take them all out."

"That's fine," Lani said calmly, her body still swimming in the driver's uniform as she worked on getting into character. Her eyes were closed. A moment later her body began to fill out the suit, and her face stretched and completely redesigned into Sully's. In minutes, her entire shape and size had transformed from a teenage girl into a middle-aged man.

When she was confident she had solidly transformed into the character of Sully, she opened her eyes and took a deep breath, let it out, and whispered, "Ready when you are, Alex."

Alex waved to let her know he heard her, then snuck to the side of the palace and pulled out Samheed's stickyclips. He only had one handful, so he sized up his targets, knowing he had to hit the farthest driver just right so that the other two would be caught in his path, thus dragging all three back to Alex at once. He waited until they shuffled a bit, lining up nicely, and then he wound up and sent the handful soaring toward the one farthest from him. With no time to watch the spell work, Alex sank his hands into his pockets once more, pulling out freeze components. He had them just in time, for an instant later the three drivers were standing in front of him, completely shocked.

Alex froze them before they could utter a sound, checked on the guards to make sure they hadn't noticed, and signaled to Lani that the coast was clear for her to take their place. She, as Sully, walked stiffly to her station just as a guard poked his head out of the door.

"Driver!" barked the guard, looking this way and that.

"Yes, sir," Lani said in Sully's voice.

The guard looked at Lani with a sneer. "What are you doing back here?"

Lani froze. "What?" she sputtered, scrambling to understand his meaning.

The guard came over to Lani and put his face in front of hers. "I said, what are you doing back here?" he barked.

"I—I'm back to drive the high priest, of course," she said, trying hard not to back away, though the guard's breath was hideous.

Alex watched in dismay. What was happening? Alex tore his eyes from the scene and took a hard look at the three drivers he'd frozen. Close up, with dawn finally on its way, he could see their shadowy faces.

None of them was Sully.

Alex stifled a gasp and gripped the side of the palace, turning his attention back to Lani. Where was the real Sully? And what if he showed up?

The guard frowned. "You left Governor Strang without transportation? What's wrong with you? I'll have one of the others drive the high priest."

Lani shrank back as she supposed Sully would do in a situation like this and risked a glance in Alex's direction, but he was too far away for her to make out the expression on his face. Try as she might, she couldn't quite put the pieces together. The only thing that was clear was that Sully was already out with Governor Strang and must not be among the three drivers Alex froze. She didn't know what to say to the smelly man.

And then she did.

Her fear turned to disdain, and she straightened up a little. "Ain't you heard? The other drivers was taken sick. I'm all you

LISA McMANN

got for now, so I came back." She paused, then added, "The governor said it was fine."

The guard looked to the area where the drivers normally stood, finding no one there. He appeared uncertain, but soon the silence was disturbed by a clatter coming from inside the palace, and the guard scurried to open the door for the high priest.

Lani stepped quickly to the nearest car and opened the door to the backseat. She kept her head down, but occasionally peeked inside the open door to the palace. Gondoleery Rattrapp, her aubergine caftan fluttering, exited the palace and strode to the vehicle. The guard scurried behind her, leaving the palace door standing open. Lani bowed as the high priest got into the vehicle, and while Lani's head was lowered, a movement at the door caught her eye.

*Matilda!* Sure enough, Matilda the gargoyle darted outside after the guard and ran to the back of the vehicle, hiding behind it. Once the guard helped Gondoleery into the car and returned to his post, Lani closed Gondoleery's door. She strode to the back of the jalopy, hoping she could figure out how to open the trunk.

LISA McMANN

She fumbled with the handle in search of a release button, and finally found the lever she needed. Sweating, she released the catch and swung the hatch open. While Matilda climbed inside, Lani pretended to rearrange something, fearing they were about to be caught at any moment. To Lani's amazement, no one at the palace noticed the oddity. The guards generally seemed as lifeless as any Quillen, and clearly weren't as alert at this early hour as they had been the day Lani was invisible.

"Driver!" barked Gondoleery. "What's taking you so long?"

"Safety check," Lani called out. She gave Matilda a warm smile, then hastily closed the back of the vehicle, went to the driver's door, and got in, her eyes searching frantically for a clue to where the ignition was. Her father had told her to look near the right side of the steering wheel, but because of her nerves, she found herself searching the left. Finally she realized her mistake and located the ignition. But there was no key inserted in it.

Lani's heart dropped. She fought back the panic. For a second she had no idea what to do, but then she quickly patted down her driver's uniform pockets. Of course there was nothing there.

LISA McMANN

"I apologize for the delay," she said. She burst from the vehicle and ran in the direction of Alex, past the guard.

"What's going on?" the guard shouted at her.

"I'm feeling sick like the others," Lani called back over her shoulder. "Have to vomit! You know? Back in a moment." She sped to the back of the palace and rounded the corner.

Alex, who had seen her coming, figured out what the problem was. He was hurriedly searching the drivers' pockets, pulling out all the keys he could find. He shoved them at Lani.

Her hands were shaking. She closed her hand over the keys. "They think I'm chunking up my breakfast," she said, and nearly began laughing hysterically.

"So I heard," Alex said. "Take a breath. It's going to be fine. Just take your time and find the right key."

"I think I should try to freeze her while I have her in the backseat, once we're away from the guards and the palace. Then you can finish her off. Doesn't that make more sense? I'm worried she's already suspicious."

"If you can manage it, that's fine, but concentrate on driving."

Lani nodded. "I'll only do it if I have a sure shot."

LISA McMANN

"Okay." Alex reached up and gripped Lani's man shoulders. "I'm going to watch from here until you make it outside the palace grounds, and then Charlie and I will see you at the designated spot. Take it slow. You okay?"

Lani nodded.

"Okay." Alex patted her on the back. "I think you're done puking now."

Lani sucked in a deep breath. "Okay. Yes. Thanks." She smiled and turned around, ready to hurry back to the vehicle. But as she rounded the corner of the palace, she ran smack into the guard, and with a loud *ooof!* the two bodies went tumbling to the ground.

# A Wild Ride

Alex gasped, then automatically reached for a freeze component and sent it soaring at the guard. He lunged for the guard's legs and dragged the man behind the palace before anybody else could notice, while Lani got to her feet, scrambled to pick up the keys she'd dropped, and dusted off Sully's suit.

"Go, Lani!" Alex whispered. "Before the other guard notices!"

Lani needed no further urging. She took long strides to the vehicle, got in the driver's seat, and shoved the first key in. It didn't fit.

LISA McMANN

"What in Quill is going on around here?" Gondoleery barked. "If I had another driver I'd zap you dead right now. Get me to the Commons immediately"

Lani, deep in character once more and feeling as if she were the true Sully, felt a chill spread through her. Her fingers trembled. "I'm sorry," she whispered. She dropped the first key on the floor of the vehicle and tried the second one.

The second key didn't fit either.

"Come *on*," muttered Gondoleery. She pointed her finger at Lani and shot a tiny fireball, hitting her in the back of her head.

"Oh!" Lani recoiled, her hand automatically going up to the wounded spot and tamping out the smoldering bits of hair. "Ouch! Please don't do that!" Blindly she shoved the third key into the ignition, praying for it to fit.

It did. Lani turned it hard and held it for a second or two, like her father had told her, waiting for it to sound like a real running vehicle. The engine roared, then screeched angrily. Lani let go of the key, and the engine quieted and stayed chugging. She'd done it!

She breathed heavily and looked around for the gearshift. Once she found it, she ducked her stinging head to look at the pedals on the floor. "The pedal on the right makes you go," she remembered her father saying. She found the gear stick next to her and gently pushed it, testing its resistance. It didn't budge. Cringing, knowing Gondoleery could shoot a fireball at her again anytime, she gripped the stick and shoved it, hoping to land it in the right place. When it moved into gear, she pushed her foot on the pedal on the right. The engine revved a little. She pushed the pedal harder, and they started moving.

Sweat poured off Lani's head now. She gripped the steering wheel until her knuckles were white, and pressed harder on the pedal. The vehicle picked up speed down the driveway. She tested the steering wheel, finding that slight movements of it didn't really do anything. Peering ahead in the weak morning light, she aimed for the portcullis.

Behind the palace, Alex watched, barely able to breathe. When the vehicle began to move, Alex left the frozen drivers and the guard where they were, scrambled back down the hill to Charlie, picked him up and carried him like a baby, and began running from rock to rock around the curve of the island. He had to get past the portcullis and cross the road to Haluki's house as quickly as possible, and hopefully catch a glimpse of Lani driving slowly, steadily, and successfully toward the desolate area. He moved as quickly as he could while carrying Charlie. The weight of the stone gargoyle was going to slow him down—he knew that much already. But Charlie wasn't a fast enough runner to keep up, so there was no other way.

The vehicle was rapidly picking up speed as Lani drove down the hill. With the palace gate in sight, she sat up higher in the seat and leaned forward over the steering wheel. Why wasn't the gate opening?

The vehicle's velocity continued to increase. Lani's father had said the Quillitary vehicles moved painfully slowly, but that didn't seem to be the case today. If somebody didn't open up the gate soon . . . Lani pulled her foot completely off the gas pedal and wildly began to feel around for the other pedal, which was the brake. She got her shoe stuck between the two pedals for a moment, still unused to her large Sully feet. She panicked and looked down, trying to free it. Giving it a hard yank, she pulled it loose and looked up at the road. The gate loomed in front of her, still closed.

Suddenly two guards jumped up from their sleeping positions on the ground and scrambled to open the gate, but it was too late. They could only leap out of the way as the jalopy crashed into the iron structure, sending rusty metal pieces flying through the air.

Lani gasped, knowing the high priest could kill her at any moment. But she also knew that Gondoleery probably wouldn't do that as long she was driving the vehicle, because then they'd crash. Banking on that tiny bit of comfort, Lani forced herself to breathe and kept going.

"Well!" exclaimed Gondoleery as the gates clattered to the sides of the road behind them. "That was unusual."

Lani cringed, waiting for punishment, but she was also intent on keeping the vehicle on the road, which was much harder to do than she had expected. It kept trying to turn to one side, so Lani was constantly tugging the steering wheel toward the other, causing them to bounce and sway.

"You know, driver, I always hated that gate," Gondoleery added dryly.

"Yes, your greatness," mumbled Lani. Her foot finally landed solidly on the brake pedal, but every time she pushed on it, they lunged forward uncomfortably, so after a while she just rode down the hill trying not to swerve too wildly.

LISA McMANN

"I say, driver," Gondoleery said, rising up and leaning forward. "Is something wrong with this vehicle?"

"Oh, most likely, I'm sure," Lani replied. "Dozens of things." She began improvising the way Mr. Appleblossom had taught them in theater class. "The treads are broken," she said, "the joist is, ah, completely melted through, the grids are nowhere to be found, and . . . we're out of chicken grease." She caught Gondoleery's frown in her rearview mirror.

"I thought Aaron came up with a new substance to replace the chicken grease," Gondoleery said suspiciously.

"Right," Lani said quickly. "This vehicle hasn't gotten any yet, though."

"It's going awfully fast for a vehicle that is out of oil," Gondoleery muttered. She flounced back in her seat.

As they reached the bottom of the hill and the road flattened out, the jalopy began to slow down. Lani, who'd barely gotten used to handling the steering wheel alone, without using her feet on the pedals at the same time, now began to panic. Worried that Gondoleery might attack her if she stopped, she pressed down hard on the gas pedal. The vehicle lurched forward, the tires spinning and spraying loose gravel behind

LISA McMANN

them. Lani and Gondoleery were flung back in their seats, and the car began swerving and sliding.

"Sorry!" Lani exclaimed in a voice too high pitched to be Sully's. *Stay in character!* she commanded herself. *You are Sully!* She lifted her foot off the pedal and gripped the wheel, trying to straighten the vehicle's path. This was so much more difficult than she had anticipated. And if she lost her concentration as Sully, she'd also lose her disguise, which would foil everything. She had to stay calm—had to!—and get this trip under control.

Once the ride smoothed out, Lani began to breathe normally, and she reinforced her role as Sully. By the time she had her wits about her again, Lani remembered that she was supposed to be going somewhat slowly to give Alex time to get to the meeting spot. But this vehicle wasn't moving anywhere nearly as slowly as her father had said it would—they were speeding along. She wondered if Aaron's new oil was responsible. They certainly hadn't factored that in.

Meanwhile, as Alex raced around the curve of the island on his way to Haluki's house, Charlie on his hip, he heard the shouts of the gate guards and the subsequent crash, and he saw one part of the portcullis come flying down the hill toward him.

But he also heard the vehicle chugging away, so he didn't stop to investigate what had happened. Instead he continued along the shore until the line of rooftops that covered the governors' houses came into view, then dashed up the hill to the main road.

When he saw that the road was clear and the dust was rising toward Artimé, he knew Lani was well on her way. He shifted Charlie to his other hip and dashed across the road to Haluki's house. "What's happening with Matilda?" he asked the gargoyle as he jiggled the door handle.

Charlie signed something, but Alex was so busy trying to get into the house that he didn't catch anything the gargoyle was saying—not that he understood much sign language, anyway. And there was no time to try to decipher it now. Lani must have been going a lot faster than Alex anticipated to have been raising dust that far down the road, and he was starting to worry that he wasn't going to make it to the desolate area in time.

Once inside Haluki's house, Alex ran straight to the office. Holding Charlie to his chest, he entered the tube in the closet and slammed his hand down on the button. Instantly he was transported to the mansion. Wasting no time, Alex sprinted out of the kitchenette, past his office and private quarters, past the Museum of Large and the two mysterious doors, and out onto the balcony. He raced down the stairs, crying, "Open the door, Sim!"

Simber obliged. "Need help?" he growled.

"No thanks!" Alex yelled, running through the open door. "She'd know something was up if she caught sight of you."

Simber shook his head, eyes worried, but Alex was long gone and didn't see it.

Once outside Artimé, Alex turned a sharp left on the road that led to the palace. It wasn't far to the desolate area.

From under Alex's arm, Charlie frantically began signing.

"She's almost there?" Alex guessed. He pushed his body even harder, his lungs and thighs burning, and his arms aching from carrying the heavy statue.

Charlie nodded.

"Buckets of crud," Alex muttered. "She's driving way too fast!" Still running, he adjusted Charlie and reached into the pocket where he kept the special dangerous component. He pinched it between his fingers and carefully extracted it.

In the distance Alex could see Sky, Carina, and Samheed standing by the road facing away from him, watching a dust cloud that rose up, growing steadily closer. They appeared ready to fake an emergency and flag the vehicle down. Thankfully, without any help from Alex, they'd seen the dust and figured out Lani was coming. Alex felt a moment of relief. But soon the outline of a vehicle pushed out in front of the dust and an occasional glint of the morning sun bounced off the rusting chrome.

Charlie signed frantically with his two-thumbed hand in front of Alex's face, but Alex only picked up on a few words like "fast" and "soon." "Got it," he panted, even though he hadn't. He hoped Gondoleery wouldn't look past Lani's head to see him running toward the vehicle, but it couldn't be helped. He had to get there!

The young mage pressed on as the vehicle grew alarmingly closer, but he was having trouble getting enough breath to propel him any faster, and his body threatened to collapse. He pushed himself to his limit, but it wasn't enough. The vehicle's arrival was imminent.

With Alex too far away to do anything, Samheed, Carina, and Sky jumped out into the road. The vehicle swerved and slowed. Alex stumbled, overcorrected, slipped on loose gravel, and fell to the road. Charlie jumped from his arms just in time as the spell component flew from Alex's grasp. The gargoyle reached out and nimbly caught the component between two thumbs as Alex skidded to a stop on the ground behind him.

Stunned and in pain, Alex lay still for a second, then came to his senses and scrambled to his feet, his breath too ragged to even allow him to say thanks to Charlie. He took the component, staggered forward, and left Charlie behind.

"Hide," Alex warned Charlie in a ragged voice. It was all he could manage.

Charlie hopped to the side of the road and lay down in the ditch, then crawled up to the edge of it to watch.

Alex focused on the scene before him and picked up his speed once more. The vehicle had stopped. The driver's window was down. Sky, Carina, and Samheed were gesturing and playing their parts perfectly. As Samheed took the lead role in acting out their predicament, Sky glanced over her shoulder anxiously, and saw Alex. Immediately she turned back toward the car and shifted her position to block Gondoleery from being able to see him approach.

Come on, Stowe! Alex urged himself. He was nearly within range now. With Sky blocking his view, he didn't see

Gondoleery open her door. He barely saw Lani leap out of the car. He could tell that *something* was happening, but he couldn't hear what anybody was saying.

Yet everything became instantly clear when Carina flew backward, a dagger of ice sticking through her shoulder. Samheed, blasted off his feet in a fiery burst, landed on the ground with flames taking hold of his clothing.

Alex's heart stopped. He saw Lani desperately searching Sully's pockets, but he realized at the same time she did that in this disguise, and in character, her component vest wasn't accessible. And Sky had little magical ability, if any. Instinctively, Sky moved back and put her hands in the air.

Alex had no trouble seeing Gondoleery now. The high priest raised her hand and pointed toward Sky.

Alex had no time to think. He slowed, raised his spell component with an aching arm, focused on Gondoleery, and let it fly, yelling at the top of his lungs, "Pulverize!"

At the shout, Gondoleery turned. She saw Alex and leaped toward Sky, trying to dodge whatever it was he'd cast. Sky grabbed the old woman by the face and pulled her to the ground, then tried to fight off the high priest's kicks and punches.

Lani's disguise began to melt, and all too slowly she began changing once more into the Lani everybody knew. She floundered inside the suit with her mishmash of Sully/Lani body parts, trying frantically to get the clothes off so she could help. Carina, still skewered, dove at Samheed, knocking him to the ground, and rolled him over, desperate to put out the flames.

Alex's clear component sailed slowly through the air, trying to reach its intended target. But Alex had been too far away and his body too spent to give it the proper launch. With Gondoleery rolling on the ground with Sky, the tiny component hit the side of the vehicle and bounced to the ground.

Then, with an excruciating cracking sound, the entire jalopy imploded, shattering into a billion tiny pieces. Alex watched in horror.

Lani dove for cover, still tangled in the suit. Gondoleery paused in her fight with Sky to see what the noise was, and Sky clocked her with all her might, three fast blows right in the face, knocking the old woman unconscious. And Charlie, behind Alex, came running soundlessly, except for his little footsteps, toward the huge pile of dust that had once been the vehicle. His arms were flailing, and his mouth was open in a silent scream.

# Disastrous Consequences

Alex gaped at the giant pile of dust that had once been a vehicle, and then he looked at his injured friends and began running once more, this time somehow finding new energy from his tremendous fear. He had to stop this! He couldn't lose another friend! He ripped through his pockets, desperate for heart attack spells, knowing full well he wouldn't find any because he refused to carry them. He'd vowed never to use them again after Mr. Today's death. And it had made sense for him then. But Gondoleery was a different matter, and it dawned on him that she was not just the most powerful ruler Quill had ever seen—she was more powerful than Alex and all his friends combined. And because she seemed to have no moral sense at all, she was a hundred times more dangerous than he'd ever imagined.

"Are you okay, Sky?" Alex shouted as he neared.

Sky lay on her back, chest heaving from the fight with Gondoleery, and then attempted to shove the limp woman off her. She stuck a hand in the air, indicating she was all right.

"What the heck just happened?" Samheed muttered, on his back at the side of the road. He stared glassy-eyed at the sky, and then at Carina, who was struggling to get off of him. She winced and fell, holding her ice-pierced arm close to her body.

As Alex reached them, fearing the worst, Samheed struggled to his feet, his clothing still smoldering. He beat what was left of his shirt with his fists, tamping out the last burning orange shreds. Not far away, Lani finally got the enormous suit off and ran to help Sky untangle herself from the unconscious high priest.

Carina rose to her feet. She grimaced, gripped the end of the ice blade, and yanked it out of her shoulder. She let out a ragged cry, nearly sinking to her knees from the pain, but then rallied. When she caught her breath, she held the ice out to Alex. "Break the clean part off," she said weakly. "Give it to Sam for his burns."

Alex nodded and cracked the ice over his knee. He tossed the bloody end to the ground and handed the other half to Samheed.

"The ice . . . will help the burns on your skin," Carina told Samheed.

Samheed held the ice, staring at it.

Alex sprang to help. "Put it against your chest," he said. "Like this."

"He's dazed," Carina said. "You all right, Sam?" she asked him.

Samheed shook his head a little as if just waking up. "Yeah. I'm okay."

"Good." With Alex helping Samheed, Carina turned to her wound, then gripped her shoulder tightly to try to stop the blood that flowed from it.

With Alex's help, Samheed gently pressed the ice to his chest, moving it over the burned skin and wincing as it went. "That was horrible," he said. He pulled the ice away. "It's cold."

"Yeah," said Alex, peering at Samheed's burns. He took the

ice and continued to do what Carina had instructed.

"We need to kill her," Samheed mumbled. He reached into the pockets of his Necessary disguise and pulled out melted and charred spell components, examining them and then dropping them to the ground. They were all ruined.

Sky and Lani limped over. "The high priest is out cold."

"Good work," Alex said.

"Are you going to finish her off, Al?" asked Samheed, who was beginning to sound more like his old self.

Alex looked over at Gondoleery. Her body was twisted, and a bruise had begun to swell around the old woman's eye. He frowned. "I don't have anything else lethal."

"What, you only made one component that did *that*?" Samheed asked, pointing to the giant pile of dust that Charlie was desperately digging through. Sky was the first to notice the gargoyle, and she watched him, puzzled.

"Yes," replied Alex. "And that evidence is precisely the reason why. We don't need spells like that in circulation."

"Maybe Carina has some good components—" Samheed began.

Sky interrupted. "What is Charlie doing over there?"

Alex and Lani looked over, and then they both gasped. "Oh no!" cried Alex. He dashed toward Charlie.

"It's Matilda," Lani said. "She was hidden in the trunk!" She followed Alex to Charlie's side.

Sky went to help too. "Do you think Matilda is pulverized because she was inside the vehicle?"

"I don't know," Alex said grimly. "She was the only one touching it when it happened." His chest tightened, and a grim realization came over him. Not just Matilda's life had been in danger when he cast that spell. He could have hit Lani, or Sky, or . . . The thought sickened him. "What was I thinking, making that thing?" he muttered, digging through the pile of remains. "What a stupid move. Please . . . she *has* to be okay."

Samheed, who was still reeling a bit and had stayed back, now turned to Carina. "How is your shoulder? Wait—Carina?" She stood slightly bent, her eyes glazed, her face expressionless. "Carina? Are you okay?"

"Hfff," she said, and dropped slowly to her knees. Her eyes rolled back into her head, and she fell face-first in the dirt and lay eerily still.

The back of her shirt was soaked in blood.

# A Missed
# Opportunity

Samheed dropped the ice and stumbled to Carina's side just as a shout rose up from Lani.

"I can feel something solid!" she said, covered in tiny dustlike particles. "Just here, straight down. An arm, I think."

Alex, Lani, Sky, and Charlie altered their search, and soon they found both of Matilda's arms. They gripped them tightly, and on the count of three they pulled with all their might. From under hundreds of pounds of pulverized-vehicle dust, Matilda emerged, eyes wide, scared, and unblinking. They rushed to get her away from the dust and gently sat her down on the

LISA McMANN

road. Charlie hopped to her side, knelt down, and peered at her face, cupping her chin and stroking the dust from her cheek with the utmost care.

Sky blinked hard, wringing her hands and feeling utterly helpless. "Is she okay?" she whispered.

Matilda sneezed daintily, dust spraying from her nostrils onto Charlie. He didn't seem to mind. Charlie signed, "She's okay," and Sky let out a breath of relief. So did Alex and Lani.

"Close one," Alex muttered. "Too close."

"Alex!" Samheed called.

Alex shouted over his shoulder. "We found Matilda! She's okay."

"Al, you need to come quickly." Samheed's voice was dead serious.

Alex looked up. His eyes widened when he saw Carina, limp in Samheed's arms, and Samheed swaying like he could fall over at any moment. "What happened?" He started toward them.

"The ice spear must have pierced all the way through her shoulder. She's lost a lot of blood. We have to get her back to Artimé right now." His arms trembled, and he took an unsteady step forward.

Alex reached him and quickly but carefully took Carina from Samheed's arms. Her face was gray and lifeless, like Meghan's had been, and he felt a wave of nausea come over him. But she was still breathing. There was still hope for her. "Come on, everybody!" he said, his voice edged in hysteria. "We have to go before it's too late!"

"But what about Gondoleery?" Lani asked.

Alex couldn't think. He could see Carina's pockets were still full, and he knew she always carried heart attack spells. But he couldn't stop thinking about how he'd nearly destroyed Matilda or pulverized Lani or Sky instead of the car. Balancing Carina on his knee, he reached into her pocket and pulled out a handful of heart attack spells and stared at them. They wavered before him. Slipping his arm under Carina's knees again, he stumbled toward the high priest. He stood looking over her limp, unconscious figure.

Alex squeezed his eyelids shut and closed his fist around the components. Mr. Today's face danced before him. The postscript of the old mage's last communication rang in Alex's ears. *Five heart attack components, what a waste! He could've done the deed with three.*

LISA McMANN

Aaron appeared in Alex's mind, a strange look on his twin's face as he'd handed Alex the robe. Fear, was it? Regret? It didn't matter. From that moment, Alex had vowed not to use heart attack spells.

"Just do it, Al!" Samheed yelled. "Hurry up, before Carina dies!"

Lani rushed to Alex's side. "I'll do it," she said. "Give me the components."

Sky stood silent at the side of the road, lips pressed tightly together. She had no say in this matter.

Claire's warning about getting it right the first time rang in Alex's ears. He opened his eyes and looked at the old woman—unconscious, feeble, and helpless on the ground. He couldn't do it.

"What kind of horrible person would I be if I killed her now?" Alex said, looking at Lani. "Or if I let you? She's helpless! I'm not a coward."

"Al!" Samheed shouted, staggering toward them. "You're being stupid! Let's do what we came here to do!"

"I said I'll do it, Alex," Lani said firmly. "Give me the components." She grabbed his arm.

He wrenched it away. "Look at her!" he screamed, staring at the woman. "Will you please look at her and think about what you are doing? No, Lani! I said no!" He turned away. "Let's go."

"Alex," Samheed pleaded. "Come on! At least take her with us as a prisoner."

Alex looked at him. "How?" he asked, incredulous. "My hands are full. You're not fit to carry anything, and we need Lani to help you walk. Gondoleery is way too heavy for Sky to carry alone. We don't have time for this!" Alex said. He balanced Carina once more, shoved the heart attack spells into his pocket and pulled out a freeze spell, awkwardly casting it at the old woman. "There! Happy now? I'll send Simber back to get her."

Samheed stared, anger boiling in his eyes.

Alex adjusted Carina's still body in his arms as he stumbled to the road. "I'm so tired of death," he muttered. With his vision blurred by emotion, he broke into a shuffling gait toward Artimé. "Come on!" he screamed over his shoulder, and didn't wait to see if anyone was following him. He began picking up speed as panic set in and he realized he really could

LISA McMANN

lose Carina, too. The thought of digging another grave for a friend filled his heart with dread.

Slowly Sky followed, with the gargoyles walking along beside her. Then Lani reluctantly turned away from the high priest and helped Samheed.

When they were long out of sight and the spell had worn off, Gondoleery Rattrapp opened her unbruised eye and stared at the sky. After a moment she sat up and began to decipher what had happened. She frowned in the direction of Artimé, completely puzzled by their leader's stupidity in not killing her when he had the chance.

Despite her pain, a deep chuckle rose from her throat, for she knew this battle was going to be far easier than she'd ever imagined.

By the time Simber came for her, she was gone.

# No Respect

Another stormy morning passed with no one doing a single thing for Aaron. His hunger was gnawing away at his stomach now, and he didn't know what to do. Why wouldn't they wait on him? Were they trying to starve him just because he accidentally killed Mr. Today?

Aaron gave up yelling and sat up in bed, holding his aching head in his hands. His shoulder was not as sore today, and his legs didn't feel like butter anymore. As the hours passed, all Aaron could do was think about how everybody had abandoned him.

LISA McMANN

"This wouldn't have happened if I'd said I was Alex," Aaron muttered. And even though he believed it to be true, the thought made him furious. He'd been mistaken for his twin a dozen times in his life, and when he'd gone along with it, he'd almost always gained in the end. Like when Alex took the blame for Aaron's infraction. Or when the rock in the jungle assumed he was Alex because of what Mr. Today had told him.

But those instances were becoming less and less satisfying. He didn't want to be Alex. He wanted to be himself. Why didn't anybody seem to respect him as Aaron like they respected Alex? He didn't have the faintest idea. He couldn't even get anyone to respond to him here, much less tell him how he'd arrived and what had happened.

By early evening, Aaron could take it no longer. He was desperate for water and food, and he could smell something irresistible. He rolled off the cot and crouched on the floor for a long minute, and then shakily he rose to his feet. His sight went black for a precarious moment, but it returned, and soon Aaron was taking a step at a time toward the doorway.

When he reached it, he grabbed hold and leaned heavily against it, breathing hard. And then slowly he followed

LISA McMANN

the wafting scent of food past a large open area, where a fire crackled and smoke disappeared through the ceiling.

Sitting around the fire on thin cushions were three old men eating out of bowls with strange wooden utensils. There was a fourth, empty cushion, and a bowl filled with colorful food sat in front of it, keeping warm near the fire. Next to the bowl was the teacup Aaron had tried to smash the day before.

Ishibashi looked up. "You will wait there until you have been recognized by the eldest in the room," he said evenly.

Aaron stopped walking and stared. He was not used to being spoken to like this. "What?" he asked.

"Do not speak!" Ishibashi said. "Wait." He took a bite of his food and then sipped his tea.

Aaron began to protest, but then thought better of it. With food so close, he didn't want to jeopardize his chances at getting some. His mouth watered. He waited.

Finally, Ito looked up. "*Suwarinasai*," he said forcefully. *Sit and eat.*

Aaron stared. He opened his mouth to speak, but Ishibashi stopped him.

"Do not speak," the man warned.

Aaron held up his hands in surrender to the strange rules, and finally Ishibashi nodded. "Okay, Aaron, you may join us for dinner."

Aaron, whose legs felt wobbly again from just standing there, was relieved to hobble forward once more. He could hardly handle the delicious smell of the food. He reached the fire at a record pace and awkwardly, painfully, lowered himself to the cushion on the floor.

He reached for the cup of tea and immediately drank it down. And then he picked up the wooden utensils from the bowl and examined them. "These are sticks," he said.

"Silence," said Ishibashi.

"But they're *sticks*. Don't you have a fork?"

Ishibashi stopped chewing and stared straight ahead, as if he were trying not to lose his temper. In his native language, the man apologized to his two comrades for the interruption of their very fine meal. He placed his bowl on the floor and stood up.

Aaron watched him nervously. "What are you doing?" he demanded.

When Ishibashi reached down to take Aaron's bowl, Aaron's eyes widened.

"No!" he said, pulling it away. "I'll eat it with the sticks!" He tried to shove some food onto the sticks but only made a mess. And Aaron, in his weakened state, was no match for the wiry man. Ishibashi snatched the bowl of food and the utensils away, disappearing out of the main gathering room, while Aaron began to whimper.

"You can't do that!" Aaron yelled after him. "That's my food! You said I could eat!" He turned to the other two and implored, "He said I could eat!"

Ito and Sato ignored Aaron and continued eating.

"What is *wrong* with you people?" Aaron said, beginning to get hysterical when he realized he wasn't going to get any food. "You're stupid! Don't you know who I am? I could send you to the Ancients Sector like *that* if we were back home. I hate you! I hate all of you! You are my enemies! I hope you die a thousand deaths!" His voice cracked. He choked back a sob. He struggled to get to his feet, falling down more than once in his attempt to get away from them, and staggered to the main entry, where he could feel the wind and rain of the raging storm, but he didn't care. He had to get out of this place. He had to find something to eat. As he maneuvered past the maze of rocks at the entry, the wind blasted him off his feet. He landed on his hands and knees in a puddle, the rain pelting his body. In an instant he was soaked through, and the raindrops blended with his angry tears.

He sank to the ground, turning his head toward the sky, and lay there, exhausted, unable to get up. Once again he drank the plentiful water from the sky, because there was nothing else.

A few minutes later, when no one came after him, Aaron slowly rolled himself over. Weak, he crawled back inside and sat in the entrance, his back pressed against the rock wall, eyes closed, jaw hardened. Water streamed down him onto the floor.

When Ishibashi walked past with a bundle of dry clothing and deposited it in Aaron's room of the shelter, Aaron didn't call out to him or demand anything. He didn't speak. He didn't even look at the man. Instead, he gathered his strength so he could make the journey back to his cot.

And once he finally made it there and managed to change out of his wet clothes and into the dry ones, Aaron eased onto the cot and fell asleep.

# A Rough Night

Alex had plenty of time to think as he sat by Carina's bedside in the hospital ward, waiting and hoping that she'd wake up. He spent most of the day with his head in his hands, his fingers threaded through his tangle of hair, thinking of all the things he could have done better.

Samheed slept in a bed nearby, Lani in a chair by his side. Neither one of them would speak to him.

And Alex knew that somewhere in Quill, the most dangerous person alive was probably cackling away, realizing that the head of Artimé was an idiot.

LISA McMANN

Once Simber had returned and delivered the news that Gondoleery was gone, he kept out of Alex's way. Florence stayed silent as well, knowing the incidents were still too raw and too recent for them to have a good discussion about tactics and to determine if Alex had done the right thing. That would have to wait a while. But not too long, for Gondoleery would certainly step up her game.

In the darkest hour of the night, Henry came up to check on Carina. "I brought you some water," he said, handing a cup to Alex.

"Thanks," Alex said. He took it and looked wearily at Carina as Henry checked her over. "How is she?"

Henry was quiet for a long moment as he assessed his patient. "She's doing better," he said after a while. "She'll be okay."

Alex let out a breath and pinched the bridge of his nose. "I'm so glad," he managed to choke out, relieved beyond measure.

Henry paused to watch the mage for a moment. He glanced across the room at his sister, who was watching too. Lani frowned and looked away, then leaned forward in her chair and rested her head on Samheed's bed.

Henry had heard the whole story by now from Lani. He'd never seen her and Samheed so angry with Alex before. Or with anyone, for that matter. It was disconcerting. Henry decided that as a healer, he had to stay neutral. And he was as loyal to Alex as he was to his sister after all they'd been through.

"How's Samheed?" Alex asked after a while.

"He's fine," Henry said. "We have good medicine to heal burns now. He can leave in the morning if he wants to."

"That's good."

"The high priest has some pretty powerful spells, though, doesn't she?"

Alex nodded. "Yeah, they're awful."

"I'll make sure we have lots of the burn medicine on hand for the future."

"That's a good plan," Alex said. "And something for the ice spears."

"We can handle those injuries too, if we get to them in time."

Alex nodded. "We didn't know . . . ," he began, trying to explain. "Carina didn't say anything about how bad it was."

Henry smiled. "I believe that."

LISA McMANN

Alex studied the boy. "You're really meant for this, Henry. You're an excellent healer."

Henry's smile faded, and he turned back to Carina, straightening her blankets. "Not quite good enough, though," he said.

Alex was taken aback. "What do you mean?"

Henry didn't look at him. "I should have saved Meghan."

Alex sat up. "Henry, don't do that to yourself. General Blair killed her. It was too late. Nobody could have saved her. Not even Mr. Today."

Henry paused in his work and said nothing. After a moment his fingers brushed against the tin box that had become a permanent fixture in his component vest. He glanced at Lani and Samheed, now asleep, and then at the mage. "Alex?" he said.

Alex looked up. "Yes?"

"Can I tell you something?"

Alex nodded solemnly. "Yes, Henry. Anything."

Henry looked away, his heart pounding as he remembered Ishibashi's words. He must tell no one about the powers of the magical seaweed. But surely he could tell Alex. Alex could help him decide when to use it, so that Henry didn't have to make that awful decision himself.

"Consent," Ishibashi had said. Giving the seaweed to save someone wasn't Henry's decision, or Alex's. It was the decision of the person who needed it, once they fully understood the consequences. If they didn't say yes, then Henry could not administer it.

Alex touched Henry's sleeve. "What is it?"

Henry looked at Alex for a long moment, then said, "If you were dying and someone had medicine that would heal you and keep you alive, perhaps forever, would you take it?"

Alex stared at Henry, and then, realizing Henry was completely serious, he thought about it for a long time.

Henry watched him think.

Many minutes went by. About the time Henry feared Alex had drifted off to sleep, Alex looked up and met Henry's gaze. The mage shook his head. "No, Henry," he said. "I wouldn't take that medicine."

Henry stared at Alex, a most intense look on his face. "Are you sure?"

Alex nodded. "I'm one hundred percent sure."

Henry sucked in a breath and let it out, and then he nodded. "Okay," he whispered. "Thanks. Good to know." He turned

LISA McMANN

to Carina, and then glanced back at Alex. "If you ever change your mind, will you let me know?"

Alex tried not to laugh. "Yes, I will."

Seemingly satisfied, Henry turned again to Carina and fussed over her for a moment, then excused himself.

Alex watched him go, completely puzzled. After a time, his eyelids drooped, and he rested back against his chair and slept.

# Aaron Does Something Right

**W**hen Aaron woke up the next morning to the most heavenly smells, he wasn't quite sure what to do. After a long night of dreams in which Ishibashi was constantly taking food away from him, Aaron was more exhausted than ever. He rolled over and glanced at the little table, noticing that someone had put a pitcher of water there. Did that mean water was all he would get today? Why wasn't Ishibashi explaining anything to him? Aaron had no idea what the man wanted of him, and he was tired of trying to figure it out.

After a while, with his stomach bucking in hunger, Aaron

LISA McMANN

got up and slowly made his way to the room that had the fire, where the old men were just sitting down to eat breakfast. Aaron's mouth watered at the sight of the food, and there was a steaming bowl and cup set up for him just like last night. He couldn't mess this up today.

He stood in the entry area to the large room and waited for the oldest one to notice him. After several minutes, with Aaron standing painfully still, Ito finally looked up and said something that sounded a little less gruff than the night before. "*Douzo tabete.*" *You may as well eat.*

Aaron glanced at Ishibashi, who didn't look at him, but seemed to nod just slightly, giving Aaron the courage to approach the fire and the cushion on the floor. He eased his way to the floor, noticing that he ached a bit less today than he had before. He looked at the bowl. It was filled with a little broth and some sort of grain, a variety of vegetables, and seafood. It seemed a very hearty meal, though totally foreign to Aaron. He glanced at the tea, which was familiar, and then watched what Ishibashi and the other two were doing.

He started with the tea, which was twice as bitter as it had been before, and he struggled not to choke on it. He drank it slowly, feeling the bitterness practically scraping the insides of his throat, all the way to his stomach. When he was finished, he set the cup down gently, and without daring to look anywhere but at the food in front of him, he picked up the bowl in one hand. Holding it close to his mouth, he wrapped his fist around the stick utensils and dug them into the food, trying to get a little bit of it to stay on. He lifted the sticks carefully to his mouth, ignoring the pain that stabbed through his shoulder. And with his hand shaking, he dumped the scant contents into his mouth.

The deep flavor of the food wrapped around his tongue and made his eyes roll back in pleasure. He dug the utensils into the food again, trying to get as much of the unfamiliar, delicious bits to stay on as possible, and then he poured the food into his mouth and almost swallowed it whole, wanting to taste it but not wanting to waste any time getting the food into his stomach.

Bite after awkward bite, Aaron ate as quickly as he could, always trying to remember not to speak or do anything to make Ishibashi mad. When he had devoured the last of the food and had poured the remaining broth down his throat, he was tempted to lick the bowl, but something told him that was taking things a bit too far. Instead, he set his bowl on the floor gently and clasped his hands in his lap.

His stomach bulged and finally stopped complaining. Aaron stared at the fire, not sure what he was supposed to do now, but even if Ishibashi yelled at him again, at least he'd eaten. The throbbing in his head began to subside a little bit, which was a welcome relief.

"Would you like more tea?" Ishibashi said, startling Aaron.

Aaron looked up, not sure what the right answer was. "Yes?" he said.

Ishibashi's eyebrows snapped together into a frown, causing Aaron to panic.

"Yes, please," the boy whispered, hoping that would help. When it seemed to calm the lines in Ishibashi's forehead, Aaron relaxed slightly and noted that maybe he should say please again in the future.

As Ishibashi lifted the teapot, Aaron realized he was to hold his teacup so Ishibashi could pour the liquid in. Silly, really, all the things Aaron didn't know about dining with people who weren't waiting on him.

When Ishibashi was finished pouring, he stared at Aaron.

Aaron froze, the teacup halfway to his mouth. *Now what?*

"Thank you?" Aaron whispered.

Ishibashi seemed satisfied. "You're welcome," he said. "How did you find your breakfast? Ito was our chef this morning."

Aaron looked at Ito, scared to death. "Delicious," he whispered.

No one yelled at him.

When it seemed there were no more questions, Aaron took a sip from the cup. This tea tasted surprisingly sweet, and he found when he drank it, some of the achiness in his muscles began to disappear.

Soon the three men were finished eating. They stood up, and Aaron got to his feet too, trying not to black out. He felt much stronger after the meal than he had before it, thankfully. The men exited the room with their bowls and cups, leaving Aaron standing there alone. Was he supposed to take his own dirty dishes away? *How disgusting.* A moment later, he sighed, picked up his bowl and cup, and followed them, finding himself in a kitchen.

He observed as first Ito, then Sato, then Ishibashi washed out their bowls and cups, dried them on a towel, and set them on a shelf. Aaron, who had only rarely washed dishes when he was living with his parents, watched very carefully to make sure he was doing it right.

Finally, when his dishes were dried and put away next to the others, and Ito and Sato had left the kitchen and gone outside, Ishibashi spoke. "It is the hour of calm. We have work to do. Tomorrow you will help. Today is your last day to rest."

Without waiting for a reply, Ishibashi left the room and disappeared outside.

Aaron, exhausted both in mind and body, found his way back to his room. And with a happy stomach, fell into a dreamless sleep.

# And Then He Messes Up Again

**A**aron learned quickly that the only way to get fed was by staying quiet and doing whatever Ishibashi, Ito, and Sato wanted him to do. He managed to eat a second meal that day without getting into trouble. And even though he had moments where all he wanted to do was yell at them to start treating him the way he deserved to be treated, he refrained, because for some reason with these particular people that tactic did not work at all, and it only served to hurt Aaron.

He wasn't a stupid boy. Clearly Wanteds were intelligent, or they wouldn't be sent to university or trusted with Quill's

167 « Island of Graves

LISA McMANN

secrets. And if Aaron had to cater to the strange rules of this island while he lived here, well, so be it. But once he got back home . . .

Home. He hadn't thought much about it, to be honest, which surprised him. He didn't miss anybody. Not really. The jungle animals, maybe. Panther. Oh, Panther—Aaron had made so much progress with her, and now she was probably forgetting everything. He hoped she was all right. Hoped her tail was intact. Hoped the spiders he'd created weren't nuisances to anybody. He was sure Panther would take care of them if they were. He chuckled softly as he pictured it.

Aaron didn't know how he was going to get home, but he shoved that worry way to the back of his mind. All he was concerned about for the imminent future was eating. Hopefully every day.

The next morning Aaron sat up and gingerly tested his injured body to see what parts were feeling better and what parts were still hurting. His general body aches from being tossed about and thrown onto the rocks were subsiding. His right shoulder still hurt, but he had limited use of it and his dominant hand now. His head was still shrouded in a dull throbbing pain, but the swelling around his nose and eyes had gone down. He could feel that the deep cut between his eyebrows was healing, as well as the long slice on his forehead at his hairline.

And now that he was eating, he felt his strength returning. Enough to get him from his bed to the fire room for breakfast, anyway. He wasn't sure what Ishibashi was expecting him to do during this "hour of calm," as he called it. But he hoped it wouldn't be much. He didn't see the point, really. If this place was in a perpetual state of storm, what good could possibly be done outdoors that wouldn't get ruined immediately? Maybe it was the only way these feeble old men could cope with the storm after all these years, he thought condescendingly.

He straightened his shirt collar and went to stand outside the fire room to wait for whatever it was the Ancient felt he had to say before Aaron could eat. "Controlling monster," he muttered.

Ishibashi looked hard at Aaron.

Aaron took a sharp breath. He hadn't meant to say that out loud. Had they heard him?

"You will wait by the entrance until the hour of calm," said Ishibashi. He picked up his tea and sipped it.

LISA McMANN

Aaron stared. "What?" he asked.

"Go," said Ishibashi.

Aaron's face got instantly hot. "What is the problem with you people?" he exclaimed. He clamped his mouth shut, his fists clenched at his sides. But he couldn't stop himself. "You're being so stupid!" He started toward his food, rage blinding him.

Ishibashi and Sato both rose immediately. Aaron kept coming.

"Stop," Ishibashi said in a horrible voice.

"I won't!" shouted Aaron. "I'm hungry and I've had it with your stupid rules!"

As Aaron advanced on the two little old men, Sato sprang at him with surprising force. Aaron crashed to the ground on his back. Sato flipped him over and sat on him, then cranked Aaron's injured arm behind him, making Aaron squeal in pain.

Sato lessened his grip. It was not his intention to hurt Aaron, only to subdue the larger, abler young man.

Aaron squirmed, to no avail.

Slowly Ishibashi walked over to stand by Aaron's face. "It is clear you cannot think beyond your own selfishness," he said quietly, "so I will ask you this. If you have no respect for us, why would we wish to feed you?"

Aaron, breathing hard, clenched his jaw and didn't answer.

Ishibashi wasn't finished. "I do not know how you came to be so different from your twin, but you seem determined to act like a spoiled baby. Perhaps your people tolerated it, but we will not. And until you figure out a way to leave this place, you are stuck here with us. So if you would like to eat the food we have worked hard to grow, catch, and prepare, I recommend you revise the way you think. Do you understand?"

Aaron squeezed his eyes shut and tried not to move, for every time he did, Sato's grip on his arm grew tighter and more uncomfortable.

Ishibashi's voice remained even. "On our island, the servant finds himself served first. For someone who is supposed to be intelligent, you are taking a very long time to learn that."

Pinned to the floor, Aaron wanted to shout. He wanted to fight back, to scream in their faces, to punch and kick at them. He wanted to teach these crazy old men a lesson of his own. But he was clearly outsmarted and outnumbered. He clenched his teeth to keep from saying what he wanted to say, and when he finally felt like he could control his temper and his tongue, he spat out, "Okay."

Ishibashi stood there a moment longer, and then he motioned for Sato to let the boy up. Sato did so skillfully, ready to take him down again in an instant if necessary. But Aaron lay there for a minute, gathering his wits, and then slowly he pushed himself up with his good arm. He got to his knees, and then stood and dusted himself off. Without looking at the three men, he walked to the door, stationed himself on the floor out of the blast of wind, and waited there as instructed. His face burned with embarrassment and rage.

He couldn't hear the sound of dishes clinking over the roar of the storm, but his stomach yelled at him just the same for messing up its chance to be fed once more. Aaron dug the heels of his hands into his eyes, furious and frustrated with himself. He had to pull it together and stop messing up. Because Ishibashi was right about one thing, at least. Until Aaron could figure out a way to get off this hurricane island, he was stuck here. With them. And, Aaron supposed, Ishibashi made a good point about the three of them doing all the work to create the meals. He hadn't really thought about that before. Didn't they enjoy making it, though? What else was there to do around here? It seemed like it would be a pleasure to have a

LISA McMANN

visitor to cook for. Not just an ordinary visitor—a high priest of another island.

"No one understands my brilliance," Aaron muttered. The wind carried the words away. He lifted his head and sighed deeply, then wiped his eyes and sat up straight, the strange words of Ishibashi still ringing in his head. "The servant finds himself served first." What was that junk supposed to mean?

There wasn't much time to ponder. As the storm's noise began to quiet, Ishibashi, Ito, and Sato filed to the kitchen with their dishes, and then came back out and headed toward Aaron. Aaron got to his feet and pressed back against the wall as they went past him, and followed them outside for his first calm view of what this island actually looked like.

When he saw it, his heart sank. It was quite possibly the ugliest place in the world.

# The Hour of Calm

**W**hen Aaron climbed into the scientists' ship, it was like he entered a different world. There were so many machines and contraptions, and Aaron had never seen anything like them before. His mood changed immediately, and he could barely stay quiet, but this time it wasn't because he was being an insolent jerk—it was because he was fascinated by all the tools and machinery. Compared to his oil-extraction machine, this stuff was so precise and perfect and mind-boggling that Aaron could hardly contain himself.

He soon adjusted his balance to the tilt of the boat, and

LISA McMANN

he didn't notice Ishibashi watching him as he marveled over a huge telescope for several minutes—though Aaron had no idea what the instrument was called. And he forgot all about the fact that he was somehow supposed to be working. Later, walking toward the bow, he found himself on the bridge peering at an enormous control panel. Absently he trailed his finger over all the switches and buttons, wondering what they could possibly be for.

Once Aaron had had a long look, Ishibashi called him over. The three men stood around the telescope. "We want to carry this telescope to the shelter," Ishibashi said. "Please help us lift it. We have not been successful lifting it on our own."

Aaron's interest was piqued, but he didn't dare ask any questions. He wondered if he'd get to learn more about it if it was inside the shelter. Obediently he took a spot between Ishibashi and Sato and wedged his good shoulder under the heaviest part of the telescope.

Ishibashi counted to three, and they all strained to lift the instrument. It came up off the ground, and Ishibashi grunted and pointed them forward. Aaron staggered under the weight until he got his footing as they walked uphill toward the ladder.

Aaron had no idea how the men planned to get the instrument down the ladder when they had to go single file, but he stayed quiet. He'd find out soon enough.

They made it to the area at the top of the ladder, where Ishibashi halted the crew. They set the telescope down and rested while Ishibashi reached for a rope. He made a harness and wrapped it around the telescope, then secured the other end of the rope to the ship. He pulled hard against the knots to make sure they were strong and reliable.

Ishibashi spoke to Ito in their language, and soon Ito was carefully making his way down the ladder to the ground below.

"Okay, Aaron," Ishibashi said. "We must hoist this telescope up and push it over the side, but do not let go of it until Sato and I have the rope taut in hand."

Aaron nodded and wiped the sweat from his forehead. He braced his feet, and when Ishibashi said go, he and the others pushed the instrument up with all their might. The three of them managed to lift the telescope just barely high enough to clear the ship's railing, and then they rested it there for a moment to catch their breath. Aaron looked below, where Ito stood waiting to guide the instrument to the ground.

The wind gusted, and thunder rumbled low in the distance. Ishibashi looked worried. "We have to hurry," he said. "But carefully. The glass inside must not break."

Aaron nodded, and when Ishibashi gave the word to continue, Aaron slid the base of the telescope over the edge. He held on, feeling his injured shoulder burn. But for some reason, he was intent on not letting this instrument break.

Behind him, Ishibashi and Sato grabbed the rope. "Okay, Aaron," said Ishibashi. "Let it go slowly. Try to keep it from hitting the side of the ship, please."

Aaron glanced over his shoulder to make sure the old men had a good grip on the rope, and that it was taut, and then he loosened his hold on the telescope. With one hand he guided it to rest gently against the side of the ship, and with the other he reached for the rope to help Sato and Ishibashi lower it. Soon, when it was out of reach, he put both hands on the rope and continued to help lower it. The wind gusted again, and the rain began pelting down. The telescope bumped against the side of the ship. Aaron moved faster.

Within a few minutes, they heard Ito yell, and the rope slacked. The telescope had reached the ground.

Ishibashi and Sato shouted back, sounding almost gleeful. They made their way down the ladder while Aaron watched from above. When they untied the harness, Aaron reeled in the rope and secured it before going down.

Aaron's arms and legs were shaky as he descended, more from exertion than anything else. Still, he hurried to the bottom and jumped down as thunder rolled in and the day darkened.

The four of them took their original spots and hoisted the telescope, then moved along as fast as they could without endangering it. Muscles burning, Aaron and the scientists made it to the opening of the shelter. They weaved their way between the rock slabs, careful not to knock the instrument against them, and when they finally reached the dry open area, they set it down once more. After a few moments' rest, they picked it up again and moved it into a well-lit room full of plants with a glass ceiling.

"Set it down here," called Ishibashi, and they all lowered the telescope to the ground in the corner of the greenhouse. Aaron stepped back and watched as Ito and Sato began examining the instrument, touching it gently as if it were very precious.

Ishibashi aimed the scope, pointing it at the glass ceiling

and looking into the small end. He made a dissatisfied noise and said something to the others in their language. They carried on a lengthy conversation.

Unable to understand what the men were saying, Aaron lost interest and looked around the room. It was a little bit like his Favored Farm, with a variety of plants and vegetables growing in strange, makeshift pots made out of tires and pieces of fishing boats. His eyes landed on a section where green pea pods grew, and he looked at them longingly, his mouth watering. After a moment, he realized the men's conversation had ended, and he turned his attention back to them.

They were taking apart the instrument and appeared to have completely forgotten about Aaron's existence.

Could he slip over to the pea plants and steal a few? What would they do to him if they found out?

Aaron swallowed hard. After a few minutes debating the pros and cons of stealing peas, he sighed and left the greenhouse and went to his room. Water would have to be good enough for now.

# A New Perspective

Aaron thought more about what Ishibashi had said—how the servant finds himself served first—and though he still didn't quite understand what it meant, some other thoughts seemed to swirl around that one.

Like the fact that these ancient scientists seemed so excited to get that telescope thing out of their ship so they could work on it. What was their motivation? Why didn't they just give up and sit around all day like the people of Quill—especially the Ancients, who were useless?

But these men weren't useless at all. They seemed to be

constantly tinkering with things and working on projects. The greenhouse was proof enough of that. It was so uncommon for Aaron to see anybody act so passionately about something, much less old people like Ishibashi and Ito and Sato. Granted, Aaron would have sent anyone like these men to the Ancients Sector years ago if he'd been in charge. It made Aaron think a bit. Did Eva Fathom have anything she was passionate about? What about the other people he'd sent to the Ancients Sector? He'd never thought about it.

The scientists' passion made Aaron a little jealous, he supposed. They had some pretty interesting things here on this horrible, desolate island. He wished he could get a closer look at the telescope.

After a rest, Aaron got up and made his way back through the shelter. He could hear the three talking excitedly in the greenhouse. And when he saw the broom that Sato often used to wipe away the water at the entrance to the shelter, and the puddles of water still standing on the rocky floor, Aaron remembered the servant line that Ishibashi had said. And then, almost as if his body were moving without direction from his mind, Aaron walked over to the broom, picked it up, and followed the trail of water all the way into the greenhouse. Then he began to sweep the water and silt back out of the shelter.

He wasn't going to lie—he wanted to make sure Ishibashi noticed him. Maybe it would get him something. Lunch, or at least dinner. But the three islanders were so intent on cleaning lenses and taking apart the telescope, and so giddy with their excitement when something went right, that Aaron didn't think they noticed him there.

As he swept, he thought more about how much they seemed to love that instrument, and he wondered if there was a way to bring more of the items from the ship into the shelter.

Not that he would touch them without being asked, of course. Aaron had learned a lot in the last several days. And it was actually sort of entertaining to watch the men in their enthusiasm. It reminded him of when he'd designed the Favored Farm, or when he'd made the oil press. Seeing them so intent on that telescope made Aaron wish for something like that—something that would wake him up inside like the oil press had done.

By the time all the water was swept out and the floor was

drying, Aaron realized something. He really liked sweeping floors. It gave his hands something to do so his mind could think, and it reminded him of doing similar chores with Alex when he was a little kid. He looked around and decided to sweep the rest of the open area.

The one thing that still surprised him was how rarely he thought about Quill and his home in the palace. And that was very strange, because when he'd been kidnapped, he was just about to take over everything . . . hopefully, anyway, once General Blair finished the attack on Artimé.

His eyes widened. That would have been weeks ago. Did Blair succeed? And who was running things now? Had Alex survived the attack?

He continued sweeping, finding home to feel so distant, almost like it wasn't even real. He wondered if that was normal, or if perhaps the trauma to his head had altered him somewhat. Maybe he cared less than he expected to because there was absolutely nothing he could do about getting back there. There was no way out of here. No way to escape. No way to build a boat, and Aaron had no idea how to sail one even if it fell into his lap. Especially with the hurricane surrounding the island.

"I might have to live here forever," Aaron said to himself in wonder. And then fear struck his heart. "What happens to me when they die? I'll be alone. Forever. I'll starve to death."

Perhaps he could try to find some materials to make magical animals to be his companions. The thought comforted him a bit, until he remembered he'd tried to make that strange statue come alive right before the attack. It hadn't worked. Maybe his breed of magic worked only in the jungle. At least the making animals part of it, anyway. Because the other magic he'd done in Quill worked just fine.

"Aaron," Ishibashi said, interrupting the boy's thoughts.

Aaron looked up. "Yes?"

Ishibashi was holding his bowl and cup. "It's time for lunch. Come. You can fill your bowl in the kitchen."

It seemed like hours since Aaron had thought about his hunger. He nodded, and then said, "Thank you," just in case it was required.

That phrase, along with "please," never seemed to hurt the situation, Aaron had noticed. The men were picky with their rules, but at least they were consistent. And Aaron had given up on being treated the way he was accustomed to. It wasn't going to happen here. If Aaron was going to be stuck with these people, he may as well try to tolerate their weird ways.

Aaron watched as Ishibashi filled his bowl with items from four different pots. The scent wafting from them was delicious. In the first pot was a brown grain. In the second pot, tiny pieces of raw fish. In the third, a colorful array of vegetables, including pea pods like the ones Aaron had thought about stealing earlier. And in the fourth pot was a boiling broth, which Ishibashi poured over his food, to make a soup. Aaron eyed the raw fish nervously, but he picked up his bowl and did the same. He followed Ishibashi out to the fire room.

Ishibashi sat down in his usual spot, but Aaron hesitated at the door, waiting for Ito to acknowledge him.

"*Douzo tabete,*" Ito said after only a minute or so.

*Progress,* thought Aaron. He pressed his lips together to remind himself not to say anything to jeopardize his chances of eating, and he moved to his spot and sat. Keeping his head down, he held his teacup out for Ito to pour tea into.

When the food had cooled enough for Aaron to eat, he took his utensils in his fist and dug in, trying to get food to float and land on top of the sticks. He chased the fish, which had cooked in the boiling broth, around the bowl, managing to get some now and then, and concentrating very hard on the task. He didn't notice the look Ito and Sato exchanged, nor did he see the smile that threatened Ishibashi's lips.

Aaron watched as Ishibashi, Ito, and Sato sipped the remaining liquid from their bowls, and he did the same. When they were finished eating, Ishibashi looked at Aaron.

"Tomorrow," he announced, "Aaron is chef."

# Harsh Words

Tensions ran high in the mansion between Alex, Lani, and Samheed. After a few days of completely ignoring Alex and stewing over what had happened with Gondoleery, Samheed finally stormed up the stairs and down the not secret hallway in search of Alex. He found the mage sitting at his desk, dozens of books spilling off piles, and him poring over two of them at once.

"Stowe," Samheed said, "I just can't get over how stupid you are."

Alex looked up. "Nice to see you too. Have a seat."

"I'll stand, thank you very much."

LISA McMANN

"How are your burns?" Alex asked.

"Fine, no thanks to you."

Alex blinked. "Okaaay."

"If you had gotten to us in time, I might not have any burns at all," Samheed said.

"I suppose that's true," Alex said. He could feel the first bits of heat prickling at his neck. "I made a mistake in timing, thinking that Lani wouldn't fly through Quill at breakneck speed when I told her to go slow."

"Leave her out of it," Samheed warned. "This was your idea."

"Was it?" Alex asked. "Was it really my idea to have Lani disguise herself as a driver and drive a vehicle when she's *never driven one before?*"

"You signed off on it," roared Samheed. "You're the head mage. It's your ultimate responsibility! Besides, that's not even the point." He clenched his fists at his sides.

Alex tried to breathe evenly, but it wasn't easy when all he wanted to do was punch Samheed in the stomach and throw him out the giant picture window onto the lawn. "What's your point, then?" he asked.

LISA McMANN

"My point is that you should have killed Gondoleery when you had the chance!"

Alex very deliberately closed the book he'd been looking through, pressed his palms on the desk, and rose to his feet. He folded his arms across his chest and looked at Samheed.

Samheed took a step toward him. "Well?"

"Thank you for your comments," Alex said stiffly.

"You wouldn't even have had to do it yourself!" Samheed said. "Lani would have done it. She was right there! She killed Justine, and she could have killed Gondoleery, and all of this would be over."

Alex's eyes flickered.

Samheed wasn't finished. "Do you even realize how huge a mistake that was? You said you weren't a coward, but you were. Just because Gondoleery can't defend herself doesn't mean you shouldn't take her out. She's *dangerous*, Alex. And she attacked us. A real leader would have killed her without blinking. You were a complete coward. And cowards don't make good leaders." Samheed ripped his fingers through his hair, growing more frustrated by Alex's refusal to yell back at him. "Alex, do you understand what I'm saying?"

LISA McMANN

Through clenched teeth, Alex said, "Why don't you spell it out for me."

Samheed stared at Alex, searching his friend's face, not finding whatever it was he was looking for. "I'm saying," he said, softer now, "that I don't know if I can trust you as a leader anymore."

Alex didn't flinch, though the words hurt more than he cared to admit. He didn't take his eyes off his friend's face. He just stared at him, a thousand defensive thoughts fighting to reach the forefront of his brain. Without fully realizing what he was doing, Alex reached up to his collar and unfastened his robe. Slowly, deliberately, he slid it off his shoulders.

"Do you want to do this job?" Alex asked, holding the robe out over the desk toward Samheed. He shook the robe slightly, indicating Samheed should take it.

Samheed glared. He didn't reach for it. "No, Alex," he said. "I don't want the job, and I never did. I just want you to do it right."

Alex gave him a patronizing smile, and his voice was eerily calm. "Oh, I see. Well, as I mentioned before, thank you for your comments. I'll consider doing something right next time. That really hadn't occurred to me until you SAID SOMETHING."

All of Samheed's muscles were tensed, and his mouth twitched with anger. But he held his tongue. After a moment he turned and stormed out of the office, his footsteps echoing down the hallway.

When all was silent once more, the robe slipped from Alex's grasp into a heap on the desk. He sat down heavily in his chair, closed his eyes, and let out a defeated sigh. A few minutes later, he opened his eyes and wearily went back to studying Mr. Today's spell books.

Not long after, Alex heard a new set of footsteps. He trained his eyes on the doorway, waiting to see who was coming this time.

It was Lani.

"Hey," Alex said. "Come in."

Lani marched in, eyes blazing. "So you're blaming this on me?"

Alex blinked. "What?"

"You told Samheed that I drove too fast and it's my fault the plan didn't come together, right?"

"Not exactly," Alex said. "I told him I made a mistake in thinking you would drive slowly as we planned, so I was off on my timing."

"Aaron fixed the oil problem, you know," Lani said accusingly. "The vehicles used to run very slowly but now they go faster. All Liam told us was that the vehicles run more smoothly. He didn't say anything about speed. And in fact, Alex, I did a great job delivering Gondoleery to the designated area. I'm sorry you weren't there yet. I had no way of knowing that since Matilda was hidden in the trunk, and I couldn't see her to find out if anything was going wrong." She crossed her arms and tapped her foot. "Besides, that's not the point."

"Here we go again," Alex groaned. "Tell me, then. What is the point?"

"The point is that you should have let me kill Gondoleery when we had the chance."

Alex nodded. "Okay. Anything else you need to say?"

"Don't talk down to me, Alex Stowe."

Alex's shoulders relaxed. "You're right. I'm sorry. I just heard this same complaint from Samheed, plus a few other choice insults, and I'm a little touchy at the moment."

Lani's chin jutted out. "Listening to people is part of your *job!* And when you're wrong, I'm going to tell you you're wrong."

"Yes." Alex closed his eyes briefly. "I am aware of that."

"It was a big mistake, Alex," Lani said. "It's going to cost us more lives."

"You don't know that," Alex said.

"It's really stinking likely, though, isn't it? Don't you think?" asked Lani. She frowned at the robe on his desk. "Why aren't you wearing your robe?"

Alex stared at her. He thought about offering it to her like he had offered it to Samheed, but he was afraid she might take it. And as much as he thought she'd be a great mage, and as much as he knew she'd do a good job, it wasn't what Mr. Today had wanted. So for now, at least, he had to keep it.

"I took it off," Alex said.

"Well, put it back on and get to work," said Lani, "because you've got a big mess to figure out."

Alex shoved his chair back and stood up. "Listen, Lani," he said. "It's easy for you to stand there and criticize me. And you have every right to do it. Maybe I deserve it this time. But what happened with Gondoleery is over now, and we have to look at what to do next. Neither Samheed nor you have offered any suggestions on how to fix things—you're just yelling at me."

"I'll yell all I want," Lani said, eyes blazing.

He frowned. "I understand why you're angry. But you don't know what was going through my head at that moment, and you didn't bother to ask. You don't understand what arguments I have with my own conscience about things. These are big decisions that I'm forced to make, and I have to live with them the rest of my life. There's no way I'm going to get them all right, but at least I have a method of deciding what to do, and it's based on stuff you know nothing about, so maybe you should try to understand why I didn't kill her before you condemn me for it."

Lani's eyes narrowed, but she didn't speak.

Alex went on. "I know you went through terrible things on Warbler—in many ways worse than what I went through here. But yours were a different kind of terrible from mine, and that makes me a different person from you. You haven't seen what I've seen, and you haven't lived through what I've lived through, and you can't possibly know how my past experiences influence how I make decisions today. Because you weren't here to see them." He let his hands fall to his sides. "And neither was Samheed."

Lani stared at him for a long time. Alex wished he could figure out what she was thinking so he could know if she was going to start yelling again.

Finally she spoke. "You make a good point, I have to admit. Maybe our experience on Warbler led us to think one thing was the right thing to do, and your experience here during the time Artimé was gone led you to see things differently."

Alex pressed his lips together and folded his hands in front of him.

"I'm still furious though," Lani said. "And I still think you made a mistake."

Alex nodded. "That's fair. I'm starting to think so too. Will you help me fix it?"

Lani rolled her eyes and sighed. "Well, of course. I always do. Let me think about it."

"Thanks." Alex looked down at his book.

"Okay." She stood for a minute, uncertain, then turned and walked out the door.

» » « «

An hour later, when Alex heard another noise in the hallway, he looked up, preparing for someone else to launch a tirade at him. This time it was Claire.

"Oh, hi," Alex said wearily. "Go ahead and tell me I made a huge mistake. I'm taking free punches today, so have at it."

Claire offered a small smile and pointed to the robe, still crumpled on the desk. "I'm not here to criticize. I turned down that robe once for a reason." She picked it up and began to smooth out the wrinkles.

"I appreciate it," Alex said. He gazed at her inquisitively. "So . . . what's up?"

Claire paused what she was doing. "I'm here with some bad news, I'm afraid."

"Oh," Alex said. "Is it Carina? Is she doing worse?"

"No, she's much better. It's something else, in fact, involving Gondoleery. We just received word that she's ended Aaron's tradition of rewarding Wanteds and Necessaries with food from the Favored Farm, and closed the farm doors to everyone."

"That's ridiculous. All the food will rot and go to waste!"

"Probably. But there's more news," Claire said. "Were you

aware that some Unwanteds moved back into Quill after my father was killed?"

Alex nodded. "Yes. They got tired of having no food or water."

"Well, last night Gondoleery sent them to the Ancients Sector. They were put to sleep this morning."

Alex stared. "You're kidding."

"I'm afraid not," Claire said.

"You mean, like Cole Wickett from my Purge year? He's—he's dead?"

"Yes, his name was on the list. And rumor has it Gondoleery believes that as she expands her magical abilities, the Necessaries will no longer be necessary. So she's going to practice her killing spells on them whenever they annoy her."

Alex's stomach roiled. If he'd killed Gondoleery, this wouldn't be happening. "I think I'm going to be sick," he whispered.

Claire moved around the desk and held up the robe. "No you're not," she said. "You're going to fix this."

Alex took the robe from her and nodded slowly, then slipped it on and fastened it around his neck. "Yes," he said solemnly. "I'm going to fix this." He turned to look at Claire. "Even if it kills me."

# Aaron Reflects

That evening after everyone had taken care of the dishes, Ishibashi invited Aaron into the greenhouse. Aaron was dying to know if the telescope had been put back together again, and if so, how it worked and what it was for. But he still didn't dare to ask many questions—they always seemed to get him in trouble. He glanced at it in the corner and saw a few pieces lying around on the floor surrounding it. That was as much answer as he needed.

"Tonight you plan your meals," Ishibashi said.

Aaron's stomach flipped, and before he could stop himself,

LISA McMANN

he blurted out, "I don't know how to cook anything." He closed his mouth quickly.

"You have eaten several meals here now. Did you notice them?"

"They tasted good," said Aaron.

"What did you observe about the food?"

Aaron's mind was blank. He shook his head. "I don't know."

"This is how you learn," Ishibashi said quietly. "You must be inquisitive about all things. Learn with eyes, imitate with hands."

"But I'm afraid," Aaron said, and looked down. He was ashamed. What if he made something awful, and Ito didn't like it? What would they do to him then?

Ishibashi sighed. "I am too old for this," he muttered. He pulled a stool over to the garden area. "Here. Sit."

Aaron sat down as Ishibashi got another stool and sat next to him. He took off his cat-eye glasses and looked at Aaron. "Who was our chef today?"

"I—I don't know."

"And who watered these plants today?"

"I don't know that either."

LISA McMANN

199 « Island of Graves

"Who caught the fish?"

Aaron folded his hands in his lap and studied them. "I don't know," he whispered.

Ishibashi was silent for a long time. And then he said, "Your eyes are focused on one person. Do you fail at everything?"

Aaron recoiled. How dare he! Who did this little old man think he was, speaking to him like that? He started to protest, but then he shut his mouth, realizing he had no words as powerful to fight back with. How did Ishibashi know about Aaron's failures? Had Alex told him?

Finally Aaron found his voice. "You don't know me," he said.

To which Ishibashi replied, "I am afraid I know you better than you know anyone in the world." He put his glasses back on. "Your glasses are invisible, and through them you see only yourself. You must turn your lenses around, Aaron. Windows, not mirrors."

Aaron frowned, not understanding anything Ishibashi was saying. "What does that have to do with me not being able to cook?"

Ishibashi smiled. "You'll figure it out. For now, you're welcome."

"For what?"

LISA McMANN

"For cooking your meals today."

"But I didn't know . . . ," Aaron began, still feeling defensive. "Oh." He looked around the greenhouse, overwhelmed with the choices. "Will you help me cook tomorrow?"

Ishibashi got off his stool. "I have other work to do tomorrow to keep our shelter running."

"But what if I make something terrible to eat?" Aaron pleaded.

"Then likely we will all be very irritable," said Ishibashi. Without another word, he hopped off his stool and left the boy alone to figure out how he was going to fix anything that would please the scientists . . . for all three meals.

Aaron muttered as he wandered around the greenhouse. But he knew now there was no use getting mad. He thought briefly about making the three of them go hungry tomorrow like they'd done to him, but he was pretty sure that wouldn't quite work the way he was imagining it. He picked up a frayed wicker basket from the corner and started to look all around the greenhouse. At least he knew a little bit about picking fruits and vegetables. He also knew something about nuts and saw an almond tree growing behind the pea pods. Maybe he could start with that.

He spent the rest of the evening choosing food items, changing his mind and choosing different ones, then sitting down at a small table in the kitchen to figure out how much to make and how long it would take him to prepare things. He knew that breakfast had to be served and eaten before the hour of calm began. Lunch was a few hours after they were back from working outside. And dinner usually happened when it was fully dark outside and the storm was nearing its worst.

When he went to bed, he saw that someone had put out the fire, which meant that someone also had to light it in the morning. He also noticed the broom had been put away. And he saw that the lights in the greenhouse had been dimmed.

In his room he noted that the first set of clothing he'd been given after he'd arrived in tatters was washed and folded neatly on his cot. "I wonder who did that for me," he said. He yawned and lay down on his cot, pulling his blanket up to his chin and telling himself to be sure to wake up on time so he could get the breakfast going.

The next morning, Aaron arose before dawn. He noticed the fire in the eating room was lit and going strong, and so was the one in the kitchen, where he began cutting fruit and chopping almonds. Having fire was a relief—he wasn't sure what he would have done if they had expected him to light that, too. "Gondoleery would come in handy for that," he said with a small chuckle. And then he laughed loudly as he pictured Gondoleery Rattrapp stuck here on this island with these three scientists. How would they get her to obey them? he wondered. It made him laugh so hard he had to set his knife down and wipe his eyes. He hadn't laughed like that since . . . since . . . ever.

Rummaging around the kitchen looking for serving utensils, Aaron flung open a drawer and stared at the contents. "Forks," he said, shaking his head in disbelief. "A whole drawer full of them. Unbelievable." But he didn't replace his sticks. He closed the drawer and found what he needed elsewhere.

When the time came for breakfast and Ito and Sato filed into the kitchen with Ishibashi at their heels, Aaron was sweating profusely, but he was ready for them. On the counter he presented a large bowl of smashed fruit pieces (he'd had a bit of trouble with the knife). In a pot on the stove he announced chopped almonds soaked in coconut milk with a prune on top, and in the teapot, orange tea, which was orange slices soaked in boiling water, since he didn't really know what tea from the containers on the shelves actually looked like.

Aaron wiped his forehead with his sleeve and stood at attention, trying not to appear anxious or look like he was waiting for someone to compliment him on a job well done. And then he remembered what Ishibashi said to him about turning the lenses around, and he remembered how the fires were already lit when he awoke.

He cleared his throat, nervous to speak, but deciding that if he got punished, he'd had enough tastings of the food that he wouldn't be too terribly hungry and could snack again while making lunch. As the three old men dished the food into their bowls, Aaron said, "Thank you to . . . to whoever it was that lit the fires this morning. I—we wouldn't have this fine almond cereal and orange tea without it."

Sato looked up at the boy, and then he looked at Ishibashi. Ishibashi translated for Ito and Sato, while Aaron's heart pounded.

"*Hai*," Sato said. He spoke a few more words in his native tongue.

Ishibashi nodded and turned to Aaron. "He says you're welcome, and he thanks you for your . . . interesting . . . breakfast."

Aaron's mouth twitched. He stood up a bit straighter and swallowed hard, and then he nodded slightly. "You're welcome," Aaron said, with an almost indiscernible bow of his head toward the man.

They finished filling their bowls with the curious-looking food, and when Aaron took his bowl last of all and followed the men to the dining area, he waited to be recognized as usual.

Ito said something to Ishibashi.

Ishibashi looked at Aaron. "Ito-san said you are the chef, and you no longer have to wait for permission to sit and eat."

Aaron felt a thrill chase up his spine. He was being rewarded. Finally. "Thank you, Ito-san," he said reverently, and sat down with his bowl. He held the teapot up for Ito and filled his cup, then Sato's, then Ishibashi's, and then he filled his own. The three looked at the tea very curiously and hid their strange reactions when they tasted it, but Aaron wouldn't have noticed, because he was too busy eating the first meal he had ever created. And to him, everything tasted absolutely delicious.

# Settling In

As the weeks passed, Aaron went from being
a whining, beastly little turd to a thoughtful,
useful young man. He still had his obnoxious
moments and his bad feelings, but he learned
to keep those inside and deal with them in private. Sometimes he punched a pillow in his bedroom when he thought
the scientists were being unreasonable. Other times he ran
outside for a quick dousing in the rainwater to cool off after
feeling like he wasn't being treated the way a high priest
should be treated. Whenever he did that, he could barely
stay on his feet, and he realized just how quickly he could

LISA McMANN

be swept away by the storm. That usually sobered him up a bit.

He learned how to be a better chef by doing it more often, just like Ishibashi said he would. And then he learned how to fish using the nets that Ito and Sato had set up on the leeward side of the island near some pretty fluorescent blue seaweed. But he was afraid to go into the water. He knew by now that he'd barely survived drowning. He wasn't eager to enter the sea ever again, especially one so rough as this.

The more Aaron worked, the more he forgot about his pain, and the stronger he became. His muscles filled out in a way they never had before, but he didn't seem to notice because he'd "turned his lenses around." The scars on his face grew less noticeable, but they didn't disappear, though his shaggy head of hair covered them much of the time.

One day, as Aaron ventured out farther than usual, chasing after a useful-looking scrub bush that had been uprooted by the wind, he found himself face-to-face with a strangely familiar thing.

The tumbleweed forgotten, Aaron stared at the glass tube before him, sheltered slightly by slabs of rock. "A tube," he

207 « Island of Graves

LISA McMANN

breathed, and as he realized the depth of its meaning, his hand rose to his mouth. He stepped inside it, out of the wind. Catching his breath, he looked at the control panel. It was broken, but most of the pieces were there. The panel was identical to the one in the tube in Haluki's house and the one in the jungle, both of which he knew quite well. "So that's how he knew Mr. Today," Aaron muttered.

Aaron scrambled to figure out what was missing and what needed fixing. There had to be a way to make it work! After all, Aaron was actually pretty good at mechanical stuff like this.

He dropped to the floor of the tube and stared up underneath the controls to see what things looked like from there. It seemed the main button that he guessed would take him straight to the mansion had no support base, which was why when he pressed it, it just fell through the panel to the floor. But could Aaron fix it?

Ishibashi had tools. Aaron had seen them in a little room that the scientists called their laboratory, where they'd been bringing various things from their ship to try to restore. Maybe Ishibashi had some tools he could use.

He looked all over the tube, making note of everything that

LISA McMANN

seemed wrong with it, so that he could try to repair it over the upcoming days—if Ishibashi let him, that is.

Just then another scrubby bush rolled by. Aaron chased it down and struggled to get back to the shelter with it before the storm was back up to full volume again.

Inside, Aaron had a small collection of tumbleweeds. He'd started collecting them for firewood but set a few aside in his room, thinking they'd be good to try his magic on once he got around to it. He tossed this one with the others and went in search of Ishibashi to ask him about the tube. He found him in the laboratory with yet another instrument from the ship that Aaron had helped the men carry inside.

Aaron made a noise at the door to let Ishibashi know he was standing there.

"Come in," Ishibashi said.

Aaron entered and looked at the new instrument, knowing now that it was more polite to ask questions than to blurt out his own needs. "What is it, Ishibashi-san?"

Ishibashi frowned, trying to think of the word for it in Aaron's language. "It is a seismometer," he said. "It measures the ground's movements, like with earthquakes and volcanoes.

LISA McMANN

When it works, that is." He tinkered with a few levers and knobs.

Aaron looked at the machine. "What are earthquakes and volcanoes?"

Ishibashi looked up, surprised. "The island where the pirates live is a volcano. I haven't seen it, of course, but Alex-san said as much. It blows fire and lava from the top of it now and then." He paused. "All the other islands here might be dormant volcanoes except for the crab island. Like this one, for instance, and possibly your island. I do not know. But perhaps I'll be able to tell more if I can get this instrument to work."

Aaron scowled, reverting back to his old ways for a moment. "Why do you call him Alex-san, but you don't call me Aaron-san?"

"Because you have not earned it yet," Ishibashi said. He fiddled with his glasses and went back to the seismometer. "Did you need something from me?"

Aaron pressed his lips together, not happy with Ishibashi's answer. "I was wondering about the tube," he said.

Ishibashi's hands froze. "Yes?" he asked. "What about it?"

"Why didn't you tell me it was there?"

LISA McMANN

"There wasn't any sense in telling you," said Ishibashi. "It's broken beyond repair."

Aaron, feeling sullen and defensive though he didn't quite know why, asked if he could have access to the tools and the supply room, which held a strange variety of salvaged items collected by the scientists and other visitors over hundreds of years.

"You may," Ishibashi said in measured voice.

"Thank you," Aaron said automatically. He turned to go. At the door he stopped and looked back over his shoulder. "Ishibashi-san?" he said.

Ishibashi looked up. "Yes, Aaron?"

Aaron fought to put into words the struggle he'd been feeling lately . . . though it was something that he thought had been inside him for a long time. It was hard to define. He shook his head. "Never mind."

Ishibashi studied the boy and watched him leave on slow-moving feet. "Aaron," he called out.

Aaron stopped and turned. "Yes?"

The old man didn't speak right away. And then he got up and said, "Come with me, please."

Ishibashi left the laboratory and walked to the greenhouse. He plucked two ears of sweet applecorn from different sections of the garden. "You see these?"

Aaron nodded.

"They are practically identical. The oblong pods, the red leafy tassel, the edible husk." He tossed one of them to Aaron and began to peel open the other one. "Open yours, too, please," he said. His sweet applecorn contained red apple pieces next to yellow and white kernels of corn.

Aaron complied. He peeled off the red skin, revealing light green apple pieces next to blue and red kernels of corn.

"What do you see?" Ishibashi asked.

"Deliciousness," Aaron said.

Ishibashi's eyes twinkled. "Both look delicious. Do they taste the same?"

"No," Aaron said, for he'd tasted and cooked with both many times by now. "The one you're holding has a lot of sweetness and goes best with something tangy like lime juice in a dessert. The one I'm holding is hearty and naturally tangy, and works better as a main dish with tomatoes and peppers."

Ishibashi looked at Aaron, pleased with what the boy had

learned in the time he'd been there. "That is correct," he said warmly. And then he tapped the boy's chest. "You are apple-corn."

"I—what?" asked Aaron. He was pretty sure Ishibashi was doing his weird metaphor thing again.

The old man held his ear of applecorn next to Aaron's. "You and Alex are identical on the outside and very different inside," he said. "But that does not mean you have to be bad because he is good." He shook the vegi-fruit. "Alex is strong in ways you are not." He grabbed Aaron's applecorn and shook it. "You are strong in ways Alex is not. This sweet applecorn has no bear-ing on how that sweet applecorn tastes. Both are delicious in their own ways. Do you understand what I am saying, Aaron? What matters is you." He hesitated, then softened his voice. "When you stop comparing yourself to him, you will find your true self. Be your own strong, Aaron."

Aaron looked at Ishibashi, feeling like the man had some intense ability to see inside his soul better than Aaron could see himself. And while part of it made sense, he was still confused.

"Which applecorn am I?" Aaron said, studying the two ears. Ishibashi slammed both vegi-fruits on the counter. "It doesn't matter," he exclaimed. "Aaron Stowe, you must be the applecorn that is inside of you. Peel back your husk, my boy, and be proud of your deliciousness."

Aaron stared at the two ears and began backing away slowly. "I think this just got a little too weird for me, Ishibashi-san. But thanks for the lesson. I'll . . . I'll see you later."

# Peeling Away the Skin

**D**uring the hour of calm, whenever Ishibashi didn't need him, Aaron went to the tube and tried time after time to get it to work. He found an old book and pencil that Ishibashi said he could have and used the margins to keep track of measurements, so that when he was stuck inside, he could work on building the missing pieces. But the job was painstaking since he had only a short time each day to test his progress, and he still wasn't very good at writing letters and numbers quickly—though he was improving with that on the Island of Shipwrecks as well.

After several days of watching Aaron work on the tube,

LISA McMANN

Ishibashi called Sato and Ito together to discuss it while Aaron was outside.

"The boy is very mechanically minded," Ishibashi said. "I am afraid he will succeed in fixing the tube. Which would be a wonderful thing in any other instance except the one we face with Aaron. I do not think he is ready to go back to Artimé. We must keep him here a little longer, at least, and do the best we can with him before we let him out into the world. One day he will discover the secret of his extended life, and if he has returned to his selfish, evil ways, it will mean a certain end to Alex and our friends."

"We may have to sabotage his efforts," Sato said, but he sounded reluctant to do so.

"Perhaps we can simply find other things for him to do during the hour of calm," Ito suggested.

"If he is mechanically inclined," said Sato, "I suppose we could have him take apart the rest of the large instruments in the ship and carry them inside piece by piece."

The three men looked at each other. Ishibashi nodded. "That is what we will do."

Ishibashi hurried out to redirect Aaron, and as soon as

Aaron was busily working in the ship, Ishibashi went back to the tube and studied Aaron's work. The young man had made great strides in repairing it. He'd gone much deeper in his attempt than Alex had. Aaron really did have a gift for understanding the way things worked.

"Maybe he can fix our telescope," Ishibashi muttered. He reached for a tiny spring, unhooked it from the tube controls, and slid it into his pocket, cringing all the while, but knowing he had to do it to stop Aaron from jeopardizing Artimé. He would keep it safe. And hopefully feel comfortable returning it someday.

After the hour of calm, Ishibashi went in search of Aaron. He found him at the entrance of the shelter, staring at the maze of rock slabs.

"Is something amiss, Aaron?" asked Ishibashi.

Aaron roused from his study. "No. I was just noticing how perfectly designed this entrance is. Every slab of rock is exactly where it needs to be to minimize the wind and rain that gets in through the doorway."

"Yes," Ishibashi said. "Whoever built it was very clever."

Aaron nodded. "I like it," he said. He shoved his hands

LISA McMANN

in his pockets and looked at Ishibashi. "Did you need me to sweep the floors today since Sato is chef?"

Ishibashi gave Aaron a rare toothless smile, for he had earned it. "Yes, please. When you are finished, would you like to try your hand at putting together the telescope? We have still not found the problem, and Sato is frustrated. It would please him very much if you could solve this."

Aaron didn't have to be asked twice. He'd wanted to have a look at that instrument since the day they'd brought it into the shelter. "Yes, of course!" he said. "I promise not to break it. I'm really . . ." He stopped.

"You're what?" asked Ishibashi.

Aaron blushed. "Never mind. I was about to brag, but that seems like something that would disappoint you."

Ishibashi put a hand on Aaron's arm. "You are making good choices. Perhaps your brag can be told in a different way, modestly. Think about it while you sweep."

Later, when Aaron had taken a long look at the telescope, he asked Ishibashi if he could take the entire telescope apart.

Ishibashi gave him a skeptical look. "We tried that already," said the old man. "What basis do you have for suggesting it?"

"Something has been put together wrong deep inside," Aaron said. "And I think I will be able to figure it out if all of the pieces are laid out. It's easier to build a machine than fix it. For me, at least. That's—that's part of my applecorn, I guess."

Ishibashi gave Aaron a discerning look. "Have you successfully built a machine before?"

Aaron looked down. "Yes, I have."

"Please tell me about it," said Ishibashi, "so I may determine your skill level and decide if you are capable of working with such a delicate instrument in the same way."

Aaron told Ishibashi about the oil press he'd made using bits and pieces of cast-off scrap metal. He explained how he could see the design in his mind, and that's what made him able to put it together.

Ishibashi seemed satisfied. "Was this your brag?" he asked.

Aaron nodded.

"You found a way to tell it, then, didn't you."

Aaron nodded seriously. "I guess I did."

Ishibashi stood up. "Very well, Aaron. You may take the telescope apart. All of the tools are at your disposal—there's no need to ask this time. I wish you well."

Aaron nodded. He was already trying to figure out where to start. As Ishibashi walked away, Aaron paused in his excitement to look at the man. And he realized that as harsh as Ishibashi had been with him at first, Aaron was really growing to like him, and more than that, to respect him. Respect was something Aaron rarely had for anyone. Even the feelings he'd had about Justine were based on fear.

What he felt for Ishibashi had perhaps started out with fear, because Aaron hadn't understood what was expected of him. But once Aaron had learned to change, the fear was taken away. Now Aaron found himself thinking of ways to make the scientists respect him. It was a quest that never got old, for there was always something new to work on.

Part of Aaron had no desire to ever leave them. And today, when Ishibashi had called him away from his work on the tube, Aaron secretly felt a little bit glad. Because if he succeeded in fixing the tube . . . he might actually have to go back to Quill.

The thought of that turned him cold.

Maybe that was important to his applecorn.

# Taking a Different Path

**W**ord had spread quickly through the leadership body of Artimé about Alex's failed attempt to take out Gondoleery, and when they'd heard that Alex hadn't taken the opportunity to kill her when he'd had a chance to, some of them couldn't understand why. Now, because of Alex's mistakes, some former Unwanteds were dead.

It was a serious story. Once the shock wore off, Alex expected people to become even angrier with him. He was angry with himself—why hadn't he at least used a permanent freeze spell? It was a terrible mistake made under duress, but

LISA McMANN

one a seasoned leader shouldn't have made. He didn't blame his friends for being mad. But to Alex's surprise, instead of people's anger toward him increasing, their negative feelings turned to deeply thoughtful concern for their world. They took responsibility too. Most of Alex's friends rallied around him, and they offered to help however they could in this time of need.

Samheed wasn't one of them, though. He remained upset and wouldn't speak to Alex. But Simber, who hadn't said much since the debacle, stood by the head mage. The cat let go of his previous strange behavior and once again began to offer a word of advice to Alex whenever a situation called for it, just as a faithful companion should do when times are tough. And Sky was there by Alex's side, like she'd been time and again.

Day in and day out for many weeks, Alex consulted with the people, creatures, and statues he trusted the most, trying to come up with a new plan—one that would actually work this time. And while Alex was anxious to stop Gondoleery as soon as possible, he didn't want to be sloppy about it or rush through anything again. Not this time. That could be a fatal mistake. But Alex's real problem was that there was no plan to

LISA McMANN

rush through. He didn't have anything in place. And he was certain that Gondoleery *did*.

The leaders reconsidered isolating the palace and attacking within its walls, but once more nixed that idea at Gunnar Haluki's urging. There were so many innocent workers inside whose lives would surely be in danger, he said. So while Alex didn't completely rule that idea out, he considered it a last resort.

As the days passed, a strange wind began blowing over the entire island, causing dust from Quill to fly up in squalls. At first the Artiméans didn't think anything of it. But after several days of it, they began to get suspicious.

"It's Gondoleery, no doubt," Liam informed Alex. "That's what Sully said, anyway."

Sean agreed. "Eva Fathom told me in one of our secret meetings that this could be next. Gondoleery is probably just beginning to figure it out. I bet it'll get worse. Is there anything you can do?"

"I've been reading a lot," Alex said. "I found Mr. Today's journal from when he created Artimé, and I think the sound barrier spell that he used to keep Artimé hidden can be reinforced to block the elements as well. I'm putting it in place this afternoon."

» » « «

Luckily, Alex's plan worked, and Artimé was cut off from the squalls, though the people of Artimé could see the occasional dust devil swirling just beyond the invisible barrier. And if they stepped through the barrier, of course, they'd be shading their eyes from the blowing sand like the Quillens were already doing.

Amid conversations about protecting Artimé and ending Gondoleery's reign, Alex continued tinkering with spells, trying to batten down the hatches of Artimé to protect it as much as possible from Gondoleery's wrath. But he didn't like having to do it. It reminded him of when he first came to Artimé and had to hide in the magical world, fearing the people in Quill. Would there ever be peace throughout their world? Or was Alex just too idealistic for thinking it was possible?

One afternoon Alex sat on the lawn not far from Henry's garden boxes—his greenhouse, Henry called it—which the young healer had constructed to hold the plants he'd received from Ishibashi. Alex wondered what all the plants were for. He'd have to ask Henry sometime. The sun shone and the sea sparkled, and the wash of waves on the shore was deceivingly

LISA McMANN

Island of Graves » 224

peaceful if Alex didn't look toward Quill, where an occasional burst of brown swirling dust was visible.

He kept waiting for Necessaries and Wanteds to grow concerned enough about the dust storm to seek shelter in Artimé, but they didn't come. Clearly, as Sully had told them, Governor Strang and Gondoleery had done an excellent job of scaring the Quillens into thinking Artimé was more dangerous than their own crumbling world. Alex shook his head, deep in thought. He had to come up with a plan—and soon. Gondoleery was growing stronger every day.

Simber, Lani, and Ms. Octavia approached the greenhouse garden area and joined Alex to brainstorm once more and see if anyone had come up with a good idea. They were in the midst of discussing Gondoleery's growing abilities in elemental magic, trying to predict what else she might be able to do, when Samheed walked up.

He shoved his hands in his pockets and said, somewhat gruffly, "Mind if I sit in?"

Simber, who knew that the two young men were in a long-standing argument, looked pointedly at Alex.

Alex's brow furrowed. "I don't know if that's a good idea,

Samheed," he said in earnest. "I mean, I get that you're still angry, and if you want to talk more about that, fine, but not right now. We're trying to solve problems here, not rehash old ones."

Samheed looked at the garden box on the ground, where a meandering iridescent vine had curled its way outside of its designated box and was beginning to wrap around Samheed's shoe. "I don't plan to bring that up," he said, shaking the vine off his foot and stepping away from its path. "I've got an idea, though, if you'll listen." He looked up at Alex. "You'll probably think I've lost my mind once you hear it."

Doubtful, Alex held his old friend's gaze. They'd been through a lot together since the Purge, both good and bad, and it had been really hard for Alex to hear Samheed say he didn't know if he could trust him as a leader anymore. But Samheed surely knew how to pique Alex's interest. "All right, sure," Alex said, relenting. "Have a seat. What's your idea?"

The group made room, and Samheed sat down. "Well, I got to thinking. Since Gondoleery is starting to kill off Necessaries, maybe we could get them to join us and revolt against her."

Alex shrugged, a bit disappointed that was the best Samheed had come up with. "Yeah, we thought of that already. But the

LISA McMANN

people of Quill are dead inside, and Gondoleery and Strang have been filling their heads with lies about how dangerous we are. We don't think we stand a chance of convincing them to join our side now."

Lani added, "You weren't there when Alex and I talked to Sully the driver. But he said that the people of Quill think the creatures of Artimé are all very dangerous. They believe our creatures and statues want to attack them, based on what Aaron and Gondoleery and Strang told them about Eva Fathom's death."

Simber snorted. "Well, maybe they'rrre rrright."

Ms. Octavia batted at the cat with her nearest tentacle. "Stop it. You're gentle as a lamb."

Simber growled but didn't respond. He nodded to continue the conversation.

"I know about the rumors," Samheed said to Lani. "I was talking with Liam about it."

"But you still think it could work, convincing them to join us?" asked Alex, incredulous.

"No," Samheed said. "Not that way, anyway."

"Then how?" asked Lani. "I don't get it."

"Well, this is where the crazy part comes in."

"I was wondering," Alex muttered.

"Quiet, Alex," said Lani. "Go ahead, Sam."

Samheed seemed uncertain about continuing. He made no eye contact, choosing instead to stare at a spot in the garden box. "See," he began, "Liam also told me that the people of Quill have really only been roused out of their complacency once before."

Ms. Octavia leaned in. "Have they? That's news to me."

"Yes," Lani said, tapping a finger to her lips. "That's right, they have."

"I'd forgotten that," Alex admitted. "It's true. According to Liam, anyway."

"Right," Samheed said, gaining a bit of confidence. "It was when Aaron was high priest and he began rewarding them with food. They responded to that in a way they never had before, and they were pretty loyal to Aaron after that even though he didn't pay much attention to them from that point on."

"So we should start offering them food?" asked Ms. Octavia. "Well, certainly, if it'll work. We have enough to spare."

"But the creatures and statues," Lani reminded the octagator. "The Wanteds and Necessaries are afraid of you. If we give them food, they'll think we're tricking them. So much of Quill is based on fear." She glanced at the instructor. "It's hard to understand if you've never lived there."

"Right," Samheed said. "I thought of that too." He slid his fingers over a particularly wide blade of grass, making it squeak. "But," he went on, "they responded to Aaron, right? And Alex looks exactly like Aaron. So I was thinking maybe Alex could, you know, pretend he's Aaron. He wouldn't even need a disguise, really."

"That's brilliant!" Lani exclaimed. She turned to Alex and grabbed his arm. "You could go into Quill and act it all out. You know—you're Aaron and you've returned to your people, and you start giving out food and doing what Aaron would do to get them to respond, and you show them you're friends with Artimé now. And you prove to them that we're safe, and convince them all to rise up against Gondoleery!"

Alex looked skeptical. "What happens when they discover I'm *not* Aaron? When they find out I lied to them and tricked them? Then what? Because you know they'll find out eventually."

"Oh, good grief, Alex," Lani said, frustrated. "Do you have to wreck every single good idea we have?"

LISA McMANN

Alex looked at Lani and sighed. "You know, the problem with you is that you jump on things too quickly and you don't think them through all the way. Which is also why you were caught flat-footed without any spell components to freeze Gondoleery in the car when you were in disguise, like you wanted to do."

"Yeah, like you would have let us kill her if she was frozen!" Lani said. "Apparently she has to be a split second away from killing you before you'll take her out. Isn't that about right, Al?"

Samheed ripped the tips of the grass from the lawn and threw them down. "I thought we weren't going back to this conversation," he said.

"I'm just giving an example," Alex replied evenly, "just like you gave me when you thought I did something wrong."

"Well, stick to the topic," Samheed said. "I think it's a good idea."

"I'll gladly stick to the topic," Alex said. "The answer is no, I'm not going to impersonate my brother. I think it'll backfire horribly in the end. And I don't want to spend one second of my time acting like him—not that I even know how! Besides,

LISA McMANN

how am I supposed to run Artimé if I'm busy being Aaron in Quill? How are the two leaders supposed to show trust for each other if they're never seen together? I can't be both people at once." He leaned toward Samheed. "This plan is fraught with problems. It's a disaster waiting to happen. Admit it."

Samheed frowned, thinking it over in silence.

Lani sat up. "I've got it—*I'll* be Aaron! I'll disguise myself and do all that stuff so you don't have to."

Samheed groaned. "This is sounding eerily familiar," he muttered. "And I think I can predict Alex's response."

Lani went on planning out loud as if she hadn't heard Samheed. "I'm sure I can figure out Aaron's mannerisms and stuff—he's got to be a lot like you, right?"

"He's *nothing* like me," said Alex.

"I mean on the outside," Lani said.

"He's nothing like me," Alex repeated, louder this time, "and Sam, you'd be right in your prediction, because the answer is, once again, no."

"Come on. Why not?" Lani asked.

Alex clenched his jaw, trying not to raise his voice. "Because you don't have a clue about how he'd act, or what he'd say, or how he'd say it. You've never spent time with him. You've barely even seen him. You don't know him *at all!*"

"Yes, but I know *you* really well—"

"WE ARE NOT THE SAME PERSON!" Alex shouted.

Artiméans on the lawn stopped mid-conversation to look at Alex.

"And frankly," Alex said, quieter now, "it's extremely offensive to me that you'd think so."

Lani stared at him, lips parted. "Sorry," she muttered. Hastily she closed her mouth and sat back, stone-faced. The silence was palpable.

"Excuse me," Simber said quietly.

Heated and breathless, Alex, Samheed, and Lani turned to look at Simber, who hadn't said a word in so long they'd almost forgotten he was there.

"What is it, Simber?" Alex asked after he'd gathered his wits again.

Simber's voice remained low, but the words he said were unmistakably clear: "Maybe the best solution is to find the rrreal Aarrron and brrring him back herrre."

# The Craziest Plan
## of All

The silence was eternal. And then Alex exploded. "Simber, have you lost your mind?"

Lani, Samheed, Ms. Octavia, and Alex all began talking at once.

"We just got rid of him, and now you want to bring him back?" Lani asked, incredulous.

"Great, then we'll have *two* dictators to deal with," muttered Samheed.

"I have to agree with Alex, Simber," Ms. Octavia chimed in. "I think you've lost your mind."

LISA McMANN

Simber waited patiently for the chatter to die down before he tried to explain.

"I rrreckon Samheed's idea is a good one," said the cat. "But, as you'rrre discoverrring, the simplest plan is often the best. The disguise idea is too rrrisky. Lani has no idea how Aarrron interrracted with his people in orrrder to make them trrrust him."

Lani scowled, but she didn't argue. Simber was probably right.

"And asking Alex to become Aarrron is prrroblematic. It will only weaken Arrrtimé and exhaust him to be going back and forrrth, trrrying to be stealthy. Plus it puts him at grrreaterrr perrrsonal rrrisk of an attack from Gondoleerrry."

"*And* I refuse to do it," Alex added.

"And therrre's that," Simber agreed.

"What's simple about bringing Aaron back here?" Lani asked, dubious. "Sounds pretty complex to me."

"It's not complex at all," Simber said. "We know he went east. And because the upwarrrd waterrrfall exists on that end of the worrrld, he can't go far. Therrre arrre only thrrree places Aarrron can be, corrrect?"

LISA McMANN

"Unless he's still floating around in a boat, yes," Alex said. He listed them: "The cylindrical island next to us, the gorilla island beyond that, and Ishibashi's shipwreck island."

"Rrright."

"*If* he's even alive," Samheed interjected. "How do we know that?"

"I just know," Alex said quietly.

"But why bring him back?" Ms. Octavia asked. "He'll team up with Gondoleery and cause us twice the trouble."

They thought about that for a moment.

"No," Samheed said slowly. "Gondoleery won't team up with him. She doesn't need him."

"Sam's right. She wants him out of the way," Alex said. "She'll want to kill him." He frowned.

Simber looked on as they figured it out.

"So why," Lani began, and then she stopped, scratched her head, and began anew. "What makes you think Aaron will do what we need him to do? Won't he just help us get rid of Gondoleery to try to put himself in the palace again? Then we'll be right back to the way it was before."

"Which would be an improvement from the current

situation, I must point out," Ms. Octavia said. "Aaron was dangerous, certainly. But he, at least, was somewhat manageable. Predictable, anyway. Gondoleery . . . is not."

Simber looked sternly at Lani. "If we make this move, Aarrron will do what we tell him to do, because if he doesn't, I'll kill him." He looked sidelong at Alex and added, "With orrr without yourrr perrrmission."

Alex studied his hands, clasped in front of him. After a pause, he nodded very slightly to acknowledge that he'd heard Simber and didn't disagree.

Satisfied, Simber continued. "Aarrron will be a lot easierrr to dispose of than Gondoleerrry, so if he trrries anything once she's gone, he'll be out too. He cerrrtainly won't rrrule Quill again. But it might be best forrr me to simply fly him back to wherrrever he was beforrre, once he's done the job we need him to do."

Alex was quiet. He'd worked so hard to forget about Aaron since he'd taken that irresponsible trip in the boat. And thanks to the Gondoleery situation taking all of his time, he'd succeeded. But here they were talking about bringing Aaron back. It was almost too much.

He racked his brain to come up with a reason to shoot down the plan. But as crazy as the idea sounded, it actually made sense. Aaron could rally the people of Quill better than anybody else. That wasn't saying much, but it was something. And it was the simplest, most solid plan they'd come up with after weeks of talking.

"It'll take too long to find him," Alex argued weakly. "The ship is so slow."

"Clairrre's boat is fast," Simber said. "And so am I, if it comes to that."

Ms. Octavia shook her alligator head firmly. "No. Simber, you must stay here. We need your protection. I don't like Alex going, either, but he's probably the only one who can convince Aaron to come with him and do what we want him to do."

"I'll go along," Lani offered.

"Me too," said Samheed.

Ms. Octavia shook her head again. "We need both of you here, alongside Simber, in case something happens." She looked at the cat. "Okay, Simber? We can spare Alex easier than we can spare you. No offense, Alex."

"It's okay. I get it," Alex mumbled. He couldn't believe they

LISA McMANN

were actually considering this. He hadn't had such mixed feelings since he tried to get Aaron to come to Artimé the first time.

"I'm not happy about that, Octavia, but I agrrree," Simber said.

Silence fell over the group as they tried to come up with other objections to the plan. When it appeared they had worked them all out, Simber looked at Alex. "You'rrre awfully quiet, Alex. What do you think? Can you convince yourrr brrrother to help us? Orrr will we need to take him forrrcefully?"

Alex took a long time to answer. He stared at his hands, but they were blurry in front of him as he imagined Aaron half-starved, injured, fleeing or hiding from the saber-toothed gorilla. He squeezed his eyes shut, trying to remove the image, but it wouldn't leave.

"Wherever he is," Alex said finally in measured tone, "he's in really rough shape. Or at least he was a few months ago when he was kidnapped." He opened his eyes, and his hands came back into focus. He looked up at the others. "I think he's got to be pretty scared. And yes, I believe he would come with me. Willingly. Gladly, even." Alex straightened, remembering it was his job to make official decisions. "Are we settled, then? Lani?"

Lani nodded. "Yep."

"Sam?"

"Yes. I'm in," said Samheed.

"And you trust me?" asked Alex.

Samheed hesitated a fraction of a second. "I trust you."

Alex looked next at Ms. Octavia. "And you, Ms. Octavia. Do you approve of this plan?"

"I do," Ms. Octavia said, "once I spend a little time preparing your boat."

Alex nodded. He turned to Simber. "I think we're all in agreement, then, Simber. I'll run it by Florence and Claire after Magical Warrior Training to make sure they agree."

Simber nodded. "Spike can follow along with you. She's verrry smarrrt. And we can send Charrrlie with you, too, now that Matilda has rrreturrrned to Arrrtimé. We'll be able stay in touch the whole way."

"Yes. That'll be good," Alex said, but he was feeling a bit numb and having trouble understanding his emotions about any of this.

LISA McMANN

239 « Island of Graves

"Good. We'll figurrre out the rrrest of the logistics this afterrrnoon. Go think about it forrr a while."

Alex and Simber exchanged a meaningful glance, and then Alex stood up. An angry dust squall pounded the barrier.

"There's no time to waste," Alex said. "Ms. Octavia, if you could prepare the boat in time, I'll leave tonight. If all goes well, I'll reach the nearest island by morning."

# Finding the Inner Applecorn

Except for the hour of calm, Aaron spent days hunched over the telescope parts, working from early in the morning to late at night, barely pausing to eat, and forgetting completely the next time it was his turn to be the chef. No one scolded him, though. Sato silently took care of it for Aaron. He'd grown fond of the boy, and as he was also fond of the telescope, he hoped for Aaron's success in fixing it.

Every day when the hour of calm was over and Aaron had returned to the shelter with whatever treasures he could carry from the ship, he made sure to sweep the rainwater back out of the entrance, and then he went to the corner of the greenhouse to work on the telescope.

Finally one afternoon Aaron connected the last piece. He called the scientists to help him place the telescope into its cradle stand. Once they lifted it and settled it in, Aaron stepped back and pointed to it modestly.

"I'm not sure if I have fixed it," he said. "Will one of you have a look?"

Ishibashi urged Ito to step in. Ito angled the telescope toward the glass ceiling as the rain slapped down hard on it, and he peered into the eyepiece in the smaller end. Aaron stared at the floor, silently begging the telescope to work.

Ito reached to adjust a knob at arm's length, never moving from the eyepiece. Then he turned a collar around the neck of the instrument. After a minute Ito said something in his language, which Aaron didn't understand. Ishibashi and Sato exchanged a hopeful glance. Aaron didn't dare ask for a translation. He lifted his gaze and watched Ito's every move.

Ito looked again and made a pleasant noise, and then he straightened up and spoke rapidly. Ishibashi and Sato began to converse excitedly, and they each took a turn looking through the eyepiece. Aaron stayed glued to the wall, hoping their excitement meant that he'd done it. And then, before he could see it coming, Sato, Ito, and Ishibashi turned and surrounded him. They shouted praises, and then Ito, whose eyes were shining, opened up his arms for an embrace while Ishibashi patted Aaron's back and said, "Good work, Aaron-san! You have done it!"

As Aaron hugged Ito, his eyes welled up at the words. Ishibashi had called him Aaron-san. He squeezed his lids shut, trying to stop the tears from leaking out, and found himself burying his face in the eldest man's bony shoulder. A lump of emotion blocked him from being able to speak.

Next Ishibashi was hugging him, and then Sato was hugging him, and that was more hugs than Aaron Stowe could remember having since he'd left home after the Purge. He couldn't control his feelings, couldn't stop the tears of relief and joy, so he hurriedly tried to wipe them away. Ishibashi noticed.

Aaron's mentor herded the other two men back to the telescope, giving Aaron a chance to pull himself together. "You'd better take a break now, Aaron-san," Ishibashi said with a toothless smile, "because Ito and Sato are already deciding which instrument they will make you fix next."

Aaron nodded and laughed. "Okay." He wiped his eyes on his sleeve and stepped out of the greenhouse, going to stand at the entrance of the shelter to get a breath of fresh air. He'd done it. And it felt amazing.

He stood near the entrance in a spot that would allow a bit of spray, but not the full force of rain, to refresh him, and marveled again at the perfect design of the rock slabs.

He thought about the strange, joyous feeling in his heart from accomplishing something these scientists couldn't do. He thought about the way the time sped by when he was working on a machine or putting together an instrument, or creating a spider creature. He thought about how Ishibashi had said that nothing else mattered but what was inside him. And he also thought about how, if Justine had discovered his ability to create things like this, she would have sent him to his death.

For the first time in his life, that thought didn't cut through him with burning, mind-numbing fear, and that rule didn't apply. In fact, stuck here on the Island of Shipwrecks, everything about Quill seemed entirely insignificant. With the spray soaking him through, Aaron smiled, and with growing satisfaction he looked out and said to the world, "I really think I could live here. Forever."

LISA McMANN

# A Journey Begins

Alex found Florence and Claire in the mansion. They listened to the plan and had much the same reaction to it initially as Alex did. Once they heard the reasons for going out to find Aaron, though, they came around just as the others had.

Claire gave Alex a refresher course regarding her boat, which was actually his first real lesson, as he'd only borrowed the boat unannounced in the past and figured out some of its workings on his own. "Remember it's magically intuitive," Claire said. "It'll automatically avoid rocks or areas that are too shallow. You can take it as close to an

LISA McMANN

island as you need to. It'll stop if it can't go any farther."

"Oh, that's right," Alex said. He remembered that from his first trip in the gleaming white boat with Mr. Today, when they'd skimmed around the island to enter the palace from the magically hidden back entrance. It was an excellent feature.

"Just set the location instructions and leave it," Claire continued. "And use the anchor spell if you need to go on shore anywhere."

"Right," Alex said. "Don't I have to steer it at all?" He'd always steered the boat before.

"Of course not," Claire said. "It's magic. If you want it to go automatically, you have to tell it where you want it to go—just like you do with origami fire-breathing dragons. But if you don't have a specific destination or direction in mind, you'll need to steer it manually."

"I didn't know it could do that," Alex said. "Sounds like I'll be able to get some reading done."

Florence spoke up. "We'll use the preserve spell on it in case the magic fails or something comes crashing into you. Then you won't end up in the same predicament as we were in before on the Island of Shipwrecks."

"I think Ms. Octavia is already working on preserving it," Alex said.

"Excellent," said Florence.

"The boat should be able to maneuver you through anything," Claire said. "Even the hurricane, if you end up that far. It's a very powerful machine."

"I'm glad to hear that," Alex said. "Wish we'd had that feature on the pirate ship."

"Me too," said Florence. "Spike is going to follow along, so she can assist you and get you back here in case anything goes wrong with the boat."

Alex nodded. "I'm sure we'll be fine."

"Who else is going with you?" asked Florence.

"Charlie. I'll bring my sign language book, don't worry. I've been learning a little every night before bed."

"Good. We'll keep Matilda here, then. There's no good way to get her back into the palace, though we need ears there more now than ever. Ah well." Florence trailed off, hand on her forehead, thinking. "Okay, so Spike, Charlie, and who else?"

Alex shrugged. "That's it. You need everybody else here in case something happens. I'll be careful."

LISA McMANN

The ebony warrior, towering over Alex, leaned forward. "Oh no," she said. "You are not going alone."

Alex took a step back. "Lani and Samheed offered to come, but I don't want to take any spell casters away from Artimé. You need them if Gondoleery makes a move while I'm gone."

Florence began to pace, making the mansion shiver the tiniest bit with each step. "You need another human to help watch for danger in the unfamiliar places. Charlie won't be able to do much to help you, and Spike certainly can't if you go ashore anywhere." She frowned and tapped her forefinger against her temple. "You can take Crow."

"But what about the babies?" Claire interjected. "We need him to take care of Thisbe and Fifer if we have to go into battle, so the rest of us are able to fight."

Florence frowned harder. "All right, then," she said reluctantly. "I'll ask Sky if she's willing to go with you. I'll miss her quickness, but with her lack of magical ability, she'll be better at helping you search."

Alex turned to hide the smile that kept trying to force its way onto his lips. If he were to choose anybody to spend a few

LISA McMANN

days with on a boat, it would definitely be Sky. He just hoped she'd agree to it. "That's fine," he said, his lips still twitching.

Florence wasn't oblivious. She knew he was pleased. "This isn't a pleasure trip," she warned. "Stay on your guard the whole time. You approach an island, you circle it, you call out for Aaron. If he's got any brains at all—and I'm not sure about that—then he'll be near the shore. If you must go ashore, find the best and safest way to land, and only land if there *is* a safe way. Find Aaron and get back to the boat. You saw what's waiting for you on that gorilla island. I didn't see it, but I know it was bad—Simber told me. I can't imagine Aaron could have survived if he made to that island."

"He's alive."

"So you say. Just be sure to always have a way out, and never forget why you're out there. And if you can't find him, move on."

"Okay, Florence, I get it," Alex said, beginning to get a little annoyed. "Are you seriously lecturing me on this right now?"

Florence stopped pacing. "Sorry. You used to be a little kid."

Alex grinned. "All right. Just stop worrying. I'll be fine, and I'll be back in a few days if I'm lucky."

"I hope you're lucky," Florence muttered, and went back to her pacing.

"Remember," Alex said, "I'll be in touch the whole time through Charlie."

"That's the only reason I'm letting you go." Florence stopped at the front entrance and opened the door. "I'm going to see how Octavia's doing with the boat. And to check with Sky." She left, closing the door behind her.

Claire put her hand on Alex's arm. "You've got plenty of components?"

"Yeah, thanks," Alex said. "Though . . ."

"What is it?"

"Maybe I ought to take some heart attack spells with me, just in case."

Claire nodded. She knew why he didn't use them. She didn't like them either, for the same reason. But this was different. "I would if I were you," she said.

That evening, with his vest loaded and an extra sack of spell components packed, Alex shoved a large handful of books into his rucksack. He included the sign language book, though with Sky along, he wouldn't need it quite as desperately as he'd thought. But he still needed to learn the language. Maybe Sky could help teach him on the boat. Alex packed a few more personal items and some clothes, and then sent an order to the kitchen for his favorite to-go meals for the trip.

He checked his pants pocket to make sure he had Simber's dewclaw in there in case he had to summon the cheetah with a seek spell. And then he loaded his rucksack on his back and headed out.

Sky met him on the lawn. She had her things packed too, and she didn't hide her grin when she saw him.

"Ready for some excitement?" he asked her.

"Ready," she said.

Simber, Florence, Copper, and Ms. Octavia were there to send them off, as well as Samheed and Lani and the others who wanted to wish the travelers well on their journey. Crow was nearby with the twins to say good-bye too.

The boat floated in the lagoon, ready to go.

Ms. Octavia was all business. "I've installed a magical water fountain on board so you'll have freshwater to drink at all times," Ms. Octavia said. "It'll never run out. And I've got boxes and boxes of food that the kitchen delivered. Most are in the cabin and a few are in the hold as backup in case you get lost or stranded somewhere and it takes us a few days to get to you. You'll find blankets, toiletries, music and art supplies, tools, a healer's kit—everything you could possibly need." She smiled proudly.

"Sounds like we'll have enough food for an army," Alex said. "At least we know what's important." He gave his instructor a hug and planted a kiss on the side of her snout. "Thank you, Ms. Octavia. We'll survive any disaster with this."

Florence spoke up. "I've put a sword and a dagger belt in there for you, Sky. Those weapons might also come in handy in case magic doesn't affect certain creatures you run into, like that eel."

"A sword! Good thinking, Florence," Sky said. "Thanks." She'd done some sword training with Mr. Appleblossom's stage combat class and knew how to use one—in a play, at least. She wasn't so sure about real life.

Simber frowned at the mention of the eel, but they'd seen no sign of any ominous sea creatures since they had left the Island of Legends, which led them to believe they really had killed it.

"That boat can outrrrun any eel," he said. "Be surrre it does."

"I will," Alex promised.

Fifer toddled over and grabbed on to Alex's pant leg. Alex picked her up and tickled her. She giggled.

"I'm going away for a week or so, little Fig, but I'll be back," he said to her, and sang in a silly voice, "I'm off to fetch my evil brother." Then he froze. "I mean, *our* brother," he said in his normal voice.

"That's weird," Sky remarked.

"Yes, very," Alex said. He walked with Fifer toward Thisbe and knelt on the ground by her.

"Good-bye for now," Alex said. "Do either of you have a hug for me?"

Fifer threw her arms around his neck. Alex laughed and kissed her cheek. Sisters weren't so bad, he decided.

He gave Thisbe a hug as well, and tried to kiss her cheek, but she was having none of it, preferring instead to pick a nearby reblooming flower—every time she picked it, another flower of a different color immediately bloomed in its place. It was an endless game for the little ones as the pile of picked flowers grew larger by the minute.

253 « Island of Graves

LISA McMANN

"The chefs can use those discarded petals for something, I'll bet," Alex said.

"I'll have the twins help me bring them into the kitchen," Crow said.

Alex grinned at the boy. "Thanks for taking care of them. They love you."

Crow shrugged. "I like taking care of them. They're all right when they're not both screaming at once."

"I agree," said Alex. He slapped Crow's shoulder and turned to the rest gathered there.

"Where's Charlie?" he asked.

"He's in the boat already," Sky said. She hugged her mother, and then hugged Crow. "And Spike is out there waiting." She looked at her little family. "Alex and I will be all right," she said. "See you soon. Find Matilda anytime if you want to check in and see how we're doing."

Copper gave Sky's arm a squeeze. "We will. Be smart like always."

"I will." Sky set down her rucksack, patiently waiting for Alex to finish saying his good-byes.

Florence picked up Alex's and Sky's personal items. "I'll

put these in the boat," she said, and waded out into the water.

When all the warnings and reminders had been given, and all the hugs had been warmly received, Alex and Sky struck out in the water for the shiny white boat, climbed in, and got settled.

Alex took the wheel, and soon, with the sunset at their backs and with Spike's faux-diamond spike glinting fifty yards off to starboard, they were on their way.

# Just Friends

Once Alex manually had the boat speeding over the waves at a brisk clip, he commanded it to aim for the nearest island to the east. He hoped that was enough information, and it seemed to be, for as soon as he said it, the boat adjusted its direction slightly, the wheel moving of its own accord.

Alex took his hands off it and watched. And to Alex's great surprise, part of the dashboard slid aside, revealing a miniature blackboard. There was no face or personality to this blackboard, unfortunately—or fortunately, as the case may be—but there was, in fact, a map that appeared. And on the map were seven islands. They were headed directly for the cylindrical one.

"Wow," Alex said, and motioned Sky to come over. "Check out what happens when you use the direction spell."

A gauge appeared in the corner of the blackboard. *Estimated time of arrival: 9 hours, 14 minutes*, it read.

"This is cool!" Sky said. "Does it give any information about the islands?"

"No. It just marks their location in the sea."

"Oh." Sky was less than impressed. She'd gotten used to the conveniences of magic and had high expectations.

"I'm sure Claire would have told us if it had that," Alex said. "It could have saved us some trouble."

"The waterfalls aren't on here, though, so that wouldn't have helped us."

"Yeah. The strange block of land isn't on here either. Nine hours, thirteen minutes now."

"Sure isn't." Sky yawned and dropped into the passenger seat. It was soft and cushiony. She leaned her head back and breathed in the salty air. "This is awesome," she said. "So we can sleep while it's driving us places?"

"Sure," Alex said. "Spike will let us know if danger's afoot."

"Or afin." Sky wrinkled up her nose and laughed. "Get it? Never mind. That was dumb." She picked up her rucksack and pulled out a book to read.

"It was kind of dumb," Alex admitted. He sat across from her and began to unpack. "Look, there's room to put your things away if you want. And each seat folds all the way flat like a bed for stretching out."

He lined up his books on a small shelf, and then stowed his extra clothing in the tiny cabin at the front of the boat. Charlie had claimed the cabin space immediately upon boarding, saying he didn't like looking at the water very much. But he was happy to share it with all the supplies they'd brought along.

Sky put her books on the shelf next to Alex's, except for the one she was reading. It felt a little awkward being trapped on a boat for days with the person she liked, so she immediately grabbed a book and curled up with it.

As darkness fell over them, the dashboard glowed with enough light to read by. The two lounged on opposite sides of the boat with an aisle between. They maneuvered their seats to fold down into beds, which felt almost as soft as any bed in the mansion. They both read their books intently, saying little to one another. Occasionally Alex glanced at Sky, and if she looked up, he pretended to check the dashboard map to see their progress and make sure they were still on course. They always were.

After a time, Sky drifted off to sleep, and her book tumbled to the deck. Alex reached over to pick it up, and then he stood at the ship's wheel for a long moment, gazing into the darkness, and laughed a little at his full trust in the boat's ability to keep them from crashing into something.

From the side of the boat, Spike called out, "Is everything all right, the Alex?"

"Yes, it's perfect. Is it all right with you and the sea?"

"It is," replied the whale.

Alex smiled and glanced at Sky, whose back moved gently with her breathing. He turned back to the water, but he couldn't see Spike. "Good night. Wake me if anything seems unusual."

"I will," said Spike.

Alex pulled two blankets from the tiny cabin. "Good night, Charlie," he said, signing it at the same time.

Charlie signed good night.

Alex closed the cabin door and draped one blanket over Sky. He pulled the other over himself as he lay down. The sea air filled his lungs, and soon he was asleep as well.

It seemed like only a minute had passed before he was opening his eyes to daylight. The boat had slowed considerably, and as Alex sat up, he saw the towering wall of the cylinder island only feet away—almost close enough to touch.

What he didn't see, on the opposite side of the island, was a floating creature unlike anything the Unwanteds had ever seen before.

# Island Number Seven

**A**lex balled up his blanket and threw it at Sky's head. "Wake up!" he called. "We're here!"

Sky groaned. She pushed the blanket aside and yawned.

Alex rubbed the sleep from his eyes and looked at the towering island. It was huge—much larger than he had remembered, but he'd never seen it close-up before. The smooth, sheer cylindrical island appeared to be entirely formed from light brown rock, with muted orange waves of color swirling through it, void of any particular pattern. It rose straight up into the air hundreds of feet.

LISA McMANN

The boat slowly moved around the perimeter of the island, and the map on the dashboard flashed the word "ARRIVED" in green letters, which disappeared when Alex took over the steering wheel. He increased the speed slightly, staring at the immense wall before him for any clues on how he and Sky might be able to land. Was there an opening in the wall somewhere?

Sky got up and stretched. She took in the new scenery for a moment, looking all the way to the top of the island at its spikey crown, where flowering ivy dangled down a short distance. She folded and put the blankets away. "See anything?" she asked.

"Not so far," Alex said.

"What did Spike say about it?"

Alex turned and scanned the water. "I haven't seen her yet this morning." He sped up the boat a bit more to see if the whale was visible around the curve. "Spike!" he called.

"There she is," Sky said, moving to Alex's side and pointing to a flash in the morning light. She opened the center of the windshield and hopped onto the bow, where there was even more cushioned seating. Straining forward over the railing at the point of the bow, she tried to see what was around the curve.

Spike saw them moving in and came toward them. "There is a something floating," she said, moving alongside the boat.

"What is it?" Alex asked. "A boat?"

"No. It is alive," Spike said.

"A floating, living creature?" asked Alex. "Like a duck of some sort?"

"Oh, no, the Alex. It is not a duck. It is hiding from me. I cannot see it, but I know it is there."

Alex's lips twitched. He glanced at Sky, who was trying not to smile at the whale's odd way of speaking. Turning back to Spike, he said, "Do you think it's afraid of you? Is that why it's hiding?"

"I do not think so." Spike ducked under the water for a moment, disappeared, and came up on the other side of the boat. "I think it does not want to be seen by anybody. When I follow it, it stays out of sight around the curve of the island, even when I go very fast."

Alex wasn't sure what to make of it. "Do you think it's dangerous? Like the eel?"

Spike blew water from her blowhole. "It is not like the eel. I cannot tell if it is dangerous, but it does not want to attack us."

"How do you know that?" asked Sky.

"I can feel it in the water."

"She's intuitive," Alex reminded Sky.

"Can you talk to it?" Sky asked Spike.

"I cannot get close enough to talk," Spike said, "but if I go one way around the island and you go the other way, one of us might."

Sky raised an eyebrow at Alex. "Is that a wise idea?"

Alex shrugged. "We need to go around the island anyway to see if there's anyplace where Aaron might have accessed it." To Spike, he said, "Okay, you go around to the right, and we'll go around to the left, and if at any time you think there is danger, just make a loud noise or something. Hopefully we'll hear you."

"I will do that," Spike said.

The two parties split up, with Alex and Sky spending more time looking at the rock face than worrying about whatever floating nonduck thing was out there.

As they scoured the rocky cylinder, Sky and Alex became

more and more sure that Aaron couldn't possibly be on this island. The only way to access it was to fly up to the top, it seemed, like the birds that circled overhead.

Sky absently combed her fingers through her hair before securing it in a ponytail. "Do you think there's any sort of door under the water, like with the Island of Fire?" she asked.

Alex peered into the water. He could see a short distance underneath the surface, but the smooth rock looked no different below the water than above it, except for some wispy green algae growing on it. "I can't see any openings," Alex said. "But I haven't been looking all the way around. I'm not sure we want to waste much time checking, either. Remember, as far as we know, Aaron can't swim. His chances of finding an underwater entrance to this island are about a million to one."

"That's true," Sky said. She leaned forward over the bow. "Can you go a little faster? I want to see this creature Spike's talking about."

Alex increased the boat's speed, and soon they were on the shady side of the island a quarter of the way around from their starting place. The sheer wall didn't vary much. There were few cracks or crannies, and the divots and irregularities that could be used as hand- or footholds were too far apart to be used for climbing. Eventually Charlie emerged from the cabin, and he helped study the island, looking for a way in.

As the boat continued, Alex became more and more certain this seventh island was determined to keep everyone out. "I wonder if we could scale the wall in some other way," Alex mused. He thought about spells that might help with this, but he had nothing prepared that would do the trick.

Sky looked up and blanched. "That's an awfully long way to fall," she said. "I hope you're not thinking about trying."

"I don't have any components that'll work," Alex said. "Unless you want to try scatterclips on me at just the right angle."

"Um, no, thank you," said Sky.

Alex grinned. "Besides, Aaron wouldn't be able to get up there either."

The two of them stared at the crown of the island, contemplating their options.

In their silence, a faint, faraway noise could be heard.

Alex looked at Sky. "Did you hear that?"

Sky tilted her head, trying to identify the noise. They heard it again. "It's just a bird, I think," Sky said after a while. "It didn't sound like Spike."

Alex nodded. He turned the wheel to follow the island's curve, and the sound came again, louder this time.

"Wait—it *is* Spike," Sky said, sitting up. "Isn't it?"

Charlie nodded emphatically.

"I wonder if she found the floating creature," Alex said. He increased the boat's speed, and Sky went up to the bow and leaned forward, straining once more to see around the curve.

A moment later she reared back with a shout and tripped over her feet trying to back up. "Stop!" she cried to Alex. "Go back! It's huge!"

Charlie ran into the cabin and shut the door.

Alex slammed the boat into reverse, but not before he caught a glimpse of what was most certainly the floating creature Spike had been talking about.

This was definitely not a duck, nor any other type of bird. Curled up like a snake with four short legs and floating completely on top of the water, the black, shiny creature had a

LISA McMANN

giant, gaping mouth filled with multiple rows of teeth, a regal plume of scales, like feathers, shooting up from the back of its head, and a thin tail that was so long it appeared to have no end.

It made a strange cry, and fire shot from its mouth. Its tail lifted into the air like a rope lasso, and the creature headed straight for the boat.

# The Mysterious Coiled Water Dragon

Aaah!" Alex shouted, and cursed under his breath as he fumbled with the boat's controls. "It's a dragon!"

"Like the origami fire-breathing kind?"

"Yeah, only a thousand times bigger and alive!"

"Why is it in the water?" Sky asked, frantic, scrambling over to grab the sword Florence had given her.

"Does that matter right now?" Alex asked. The magical boat skimmed backward over the water, and Alex and Sky remained frozen face-forward, unable to take their eyes off the dragon.

LISA McMANN

The dragon, seeing the boat retreating, closed its mouth and stopped pursuing them. Alex slowed the boat to a stop so they could look at it from a safe distance. "We come in peace!" Sky yelled out.

The dragon's ears twitched.

Sky glanced at Alex. "It heard me," she said. "Did you see that?"

Alex nodded, not taking his eyes off the creature. "Do you think it understands us?"

"I don't know," Sky murmured. She called out, "We don't want to hurt anyone. We are looking for someone. A human, like him." She jutted her thumb at Alex. "Have you seen him?"

The dragon coiled up its extremely long tail. Its short, stocky legs, which ended in wide, webbed feet with three large, hooked claws, paddled the dragon through the water away from them.

"Wait!" Alex studied the creature, and wondered why the thing seemed vaguely familiar when he hadn't ever seen a real dragon before. "It's all coiled up on the water," he murmured. "A coiled water dragon. Where have we heard of it?"

Sky frowned and shook her head. "I have no idea."

Alex thought harder. Had Ishibashi mentioned it? "Oh!" he exclaimed after a moment. "It was Talon from the Island of Legends." He stood up on the captain's seat and hung on to the windshield. "Please wait! We are friends of Talon and Lhasa and Karkinos the crab, many days' journey to the west!" he shouted. "I am Alex, and this is Sky. Our whale is called Spike, and she means no harm!"

At this, the dragon stopped paddling. Alex could see Spike rounding the island, making a wide turn out to sea to keep from threatening the dragon.

When the dragon looked at Spike, the whale swam closer and spoke up. "We are the ones who saved Issie and the squid from the underwater pirate cage," Spike said. "Our friend Simber the stone cheetah broke the glass."

The three Artiméans peered anxiously at the dragon, which eyed them one at a time. Finally the dragon lifted its regal head, shaking out a scaly, shimmering mane, and a female voice boomed out over the water. "Approach without fear."

Alex and Sky dared not look at each other.

Softly Sky said, "If she belongs to the Island of Legends, why is she way over here?"

LISA McMANN

"Talon said she rules the sea," Alex whispered, "so maybe she just floats around. He told me her name, but I don't remember it."

"I am called Pan," the dragon said. "I am the ruler of the sea."

Alex flushed, wondering if she'd heard their whispers.

The dragon went on. "I am grateful to your people for rescuing our creatures." Slowly she uncoiled, and uncoiled, and uncoiled. Alex, Sky, and Spike all watched in fascination as she spread out to her full, tremendous length, from her oversized head to her streamlined body, stout legs sticking out from the thickest part, all the way down to her spiked, ropelike tail, which began slowly snaking through the water, surrounding Spike and the boat and pulling them toward her fire-breathing, scale-shimmering head.

Alex swallowed hard. Was this a trick? Were they about to get eaten?

The dragon lifted her head to the sky and roared, flames shooting thirty feet into the air.

Sky hopped backward, sword handle gripped tightly in one hand. She stood side by side with Alex, who reached his arm around her. Both of them shook with fear, and neither one was certain they were going to live through this.

From the cabin, Charlie opened the door and peeked out, saw Alex's and Sky's faces, and closed it again.

Once Pan had drawn them close to her and the island, she pulled her tail in and coiled it up once more, then lifted the coil in the air and began to rotate it. With a roar, she swung her tail up high in the air, where it stretched to a ridiculous length, never stopping until it cleared the crown and hooked on to something up there. The dragon grabbed its tail with its clawed feet and climbed up the sheer rock several yards.

"Wow," Alex said under his breath.

"I suppose that's one way up," Sky said.

The dragon, apparently settled while dangling twenty feet above the water, stretched its head down toward its rapt audience. "Tell me," she said, "how I can help you."

# The Journey
# Continues

Alex explained their plight to the dragon. "We're looking for my brother," he said. "He looks just like me. His name is Aaron, and he is the former high priest of Quill. Have you seen him? Is he on your island?"

The dragon regarded Alex. "I have not seen him," she said slowly.

Sky pressed her lips together nervously, then asked, "He's not . . . up there, or anything, is he?"

"No human has ever been," the dragon boomed.

"Oh, okay," Alex said, and though his feet felt like they

were cemented in place, he leaned back slightly as if the powerful voice were pushing him.

The dragon regarded Alex for a long moment before speaking once more. "I have seen no one resembling you."

Alex gulped and nodded, knowing they should just leave, but not quite satisfied enough to do so. "If—if I may ask . . . ," he began.

"You may," boomed the dragon.

Alex lifted his chin bravely. "Is there any entrance to the island, or any sort of cave or nook nearby that a human might cling to?"

"There is not," said the dragon, sounding slightly impatient.

Alex dropped his gaze. "Okay, thank you." He glanced at Sky, who had carefully put the sword aside, and then he went on. "I . . . we . . . I guess we should go, then. We have to find him." He looked at the boat's controls, not daring to move. "Is it all right if we . . . go?"

"Yes," said the dragon. She didn't move.

Alex glanced up at her. "Thank you." He hesitated. "By the way . . ."

"What is it?"

"Have you seen our friends lately? Talon and Karkinos and Issie? Is Karkinos . . . doing all right?"

"Karkinos is ill," Pan said, her voice less booming now. "He's growing steadily worse."

Alex and Sky exchanged pained looks at the news. "I'm so terribly sorry to hear that," Alex said.

"Me too," said Sky.

"And me," said Spike.

"If—if you see them," Alex said, "will you give them our best? And . . ." He trailed off, knowing there was really nothing else to say. "Thank you," he added feebly. "Thank you for your help today. It was nice meeting you. We'll continue looking."

Alex put his hand on the ship's wheel and spun it slowly, turning the boat to the east to continue their journey. "If there's ever anything we can do for you, please come to me," Alex said over his shoulder. "We are from the island to the west." He thought for a moment, and clarified. "The southernmost bit of the island, that is. Artimé. Someone else rules the rest of the island. Someone . . . evil."

Pan nodded wisely, as if she already somehow knew this, but Alex didn't question her.

As they rounded the island, the dragon called out in a terrible voice, "Wait!"

Alex swung the boat around, and they looked back at the dragon. "Yes, Pan?" called Sky. "Can we help you?"

"The stone cheetah who broke through the glass . . . Is it true that he flies?"

Alex turned fully around. "Yes, he flies very well," he said.

Pan lifted her head. "And was it you who gave him wings?"

Alex shook his head. "No, it wasn't. The mage who came before me created him that way."

Pan seemed saddened. "I see. And that mage is dead now." After a moment, the dragon bowed her head, as if indicating they were free to leave.

Alex was surprised she knew so much about Artimé when he knew so little about her, but perhaps Talon had told her everything. And, he supposed, as the ruler of the sea, it was probably her job to know what was going on. Alex studied the dragon, and curiosity got the best of him. "Pan," he ventured, "are you in need of wings?"

LISA McMANN

Pan seemed to regret having asked the question. Absently she pulled her body up the wall by her tail, and finally she said, "I do not ask for myself, but for others."

Alex nodded. "I understand. If I ever figure out how to make something fly, shall I seek you out?"

"Karkinos is more important," stated the dragon. "You must help him first."

The request left a knot in Alex's stomach. He didn't have a clue how to fix Karkinos. They hadn't even had a chance to start working on a solution. "I will," he found himself promising, and he hoped he wouldn't regret it.

"Because of your kindness," Pan continued, "a word of caution as you journey eastward. Nothing good lies ahead of you. I advise you to turn back now."

Alex looked down. "Thank you," he said. "But I'm afraid we must continue."

Pan nodded. "May safety ride with you, then."

With that, the ruler of the sea dug her claws into the side of the island, dropped her tail deep into the water, and then curled it up, capturing three large fish quite expertly in its grasp. Then, tail hanging and fish struggling, she lunged her

LISA McMANN

body upward and scrabbled to the top of the wall, swung her tail up and over the edge, and dropped the fish into the cylinder. Then she perched on the ledge between two points of the crown and watched as Spike swam and Alex guided the boat in the direction of the next island.

Sometime later, when Alex looked back over his shoulder at the seventh mysterious island, the dragon was gone. But there were several thin trails of smoke rising from the top of it.

# The Orange-Eyed Children

Back in Artimé, Crow sat on the beach next to Carina, who had recovered nicely from her ice-spear wound by now. Sean sat on the other side of her. The three turned their backs on the dust squalls in Quill and tried to enjoy the weather as Thisbe, Fifer, and Carina's son, Seth, methodically scooped sand into tiny buckets and poured it over their legs.

On the lawn behind them, Florence and Claire were working with the newest batch of spell casters, teaching them to master the basics—scatterclips, invisibility paintbrushes, fire steps, stinging soliloquies, clay shackles, and the like. As usual, there were some older Artiméans who joined the training sessions to improve their defense and attack skills. But this time the vast majority of the students were young immigrants with orange eyes and neck scars, who had been catapulted onto Artimé's shore as human weapons from Warbler, one island to the west. The Artiméans had later learned that the parents of these children had deceived Queen Eagala by offering up their children as part of a secret plan to save them from the queen's oppression and give them a better life.

By now the Warbler children had settled in. Though they missed their parents terribly, compassionate Unwanteds had stepped up as they always did to offer comfort. The students had been taking classes for months with Ms. Octavia, Mr. Appleblossom, Claire Morning, and the other instructors, and some had already discovered what they were especially interested in—art, music, design, construction, theater, storytelling, inventions, and many other things. Now, in Magical Warrior Training, some of them found that they were decent spell casters, too.

Crow, who didn't care to do magic and didn't like fighting at all, watched over his shoulder, trying to identify the best future mages of the bunch. He'd known some of the children before, from when he and Sky lived on Warbler. One of them, the pale, blond girl he'd translated for on the day of the attack, seemed to be quite a serious force. Her name was Scarlet. A boy a year or two older than Crow was also learning magic quite easily.

Carina turned to see what Crow was looking at. "Who's that?" she asked him, watching too. "The boy next to Scarlet."

"That's Thatcher," Crow said. "He's almost as good as Scarlet. Not quite."

Sean turned to look. "Ah yes, those two. I've been watching both of them lately. They're good." He turned back to check on the toddlers and make sure they weren't straying too close to the water. "Claire said she's got a good-size group of Warbler kids who are really starting to do well with their magic."

Thisbe came up to Crow and patted his cheek with a sandy hand. Crow smiled at the girl, and she dumped her sand on his stomach. "Oh, thank you!" he said, as if he sincerely meant it.

"Ax?" said Thisbe, looking around.

Fifer paused what she was doing and looked up. "Ax?" she echoed.

"Alex went away in the boat," Crow said. "Bye-bye. He'll be back in a few days."

Thisbe frowned. "Boat."

"Uh-oh—I need more sand on my belly," Crow said, patting it. Seth ran over and provided it, and then the girls did too.

Carina looked on. Crow was so tolerant and good with the little ones. It warmed her heart to watch him. She glanced at Sean and gave him a sparkling smile. He leaned over and kissed her.

Crow peeked at them, only a little embarrassed. When the kiss went on a bit too long for his liking, he turned to watch Magical Warrior Training once more. His friend Scarlet was stealthily aiming a component at Thatcher while the boy joked around with Claire and Florence. The boy's dark brown skin was a few shades lighter than Florence's ebony hue, and his hair was black and curly. A moment later his hair exploded, turning bright pink.

"Flaming color spell," Crow remarked with a grin. Florence's rumbling laughter could be heard across the lawn as Thatcher tried to figure out what had just happened to him and who was responsible. Scarlet pretended to be very focused on her components and never cracked a smile to give herself away. Crow

LISA McMANN

admired her for a moment before turning his attention back to the children. He glanced sidelong at Carina and was relieved to see that she and Sean had stopped kissing.

"Do you think their parents will ever escape from Warbler?" Sean said. "It would be awful if they never got reunited."

"If they don't escape," Carina said, "I suppose we'll have to rescue them."

"Add them to the list," said Crow.

Sean laughed softly. "The never-ending rescue list."

"If the kids keep working hard on their spells," Crow said, "maybe they'll be able to help." He pressed his lips together. Maybe he ought to be over there too, learning magic so he could help rescue the Warbler parents. The thought made his stomach cramp.

"I hope so," said Carina. She stretched out her shoulder gingerly. "Because I'm about ready to retire."

Crow flashed her a worried look. "If I didn't have the twins to look after, I would probably be better at magic," Crow said, feeling guilty.

Carina looked sharply at him. "Crow, do you *want* to learn magic and fight?"

Crow looked down. "I mean, I feel like I should. . . ."

"Stop," Carina said, holding up her hand. "No. There's no guilt here. There are plenty of people in Artimé who choose not to fight. Every person decides for himself—that's the way it has always been. But you have a much more important job. Do you realize that? The head mage of Artimé has entrusted you with the care of his sisters. That's a pretty big responsibility. Do you enjoy your job?"

Crow nodded at the sand as Fifer clocked him in the head with her empty bucket. "I love it," he said. "It's the best job in the world."

Carina put her hand on Crow's knee. "And I love to fight. I was only making a joke before. Magic and fighting for Artimé make me feel alive inside. And working with children makes you feel alive, right?"

Crow nodded again. He lifted his head to look at her.

"We do what we love here," Carina said. "Right? Okay?"

"Okay," Crow said, relieved. With a big sigh, he flopped back in the sand, a tremendous weight lifted from him. And then Thisbe plopped down on his stomach, and Fifer poured a pail full of sand over his face.

LISA McMANN

# Regrets

With the boat operating on Alex's command and heading for the next island—the one with the gorilla—Alex and Sky delved into the stacks of books they'd brought. Sky's were mostly books about science, nature, and animals, which she'd gotten from Lani, hoping to find something that would help them in case they came face-to-face with the gorilla.

Alex's books were all from Mr. Today's library in the Museum of Large, and topics consisted of magic, ethics, and weather, and volumes upon volumes of the old mage's journals, which spanned over fifty years of his life.

LISA McMANN

Sky initially set out to find everything she could about goril-las, but now, in the back of her mind, she was also looking for information on crustaceans, in case there was anything useful about fixing the ailing health of the giant crab.

They studied in pleasant silence, trying to cram as much information into their brains in the time they had. Every now and then one of them broke the silence with a few interesting lines from what they were reading.

"Gorillas like fruit," Sky said, eyes glued to her page. "They're also supposed to be gentle." She snorted and looked up. "I'm not sure if this book is going to help us at all."

"Doesn't sound like it. The saber-toothed gorilla I saw was not gentle. And the only fruit it ate was probably whatever that pig had in its stomach."

"Ew," muttered Sky. "Thanks for that visual."

"You're welcome." Alex reached over to her seat with his foot and poked her.

She grabbed his toes and bent them backward.

"Ow!" he yelled, half laughing, and quickly pulled his foot back to his own side of the boat.

Sky grinned slyly and kept her eyes on her book.

They retreated back into silence.

While eating lunch later, Alex looked up from his book. "I just read a journal entry from Mr. Today where he mentions Ishibashi. He was talking about the tube."

"Does he say how to fix it in case it ever breaks?" Sky asked sarcastically.

"No, of course not." Alex was tempted to jab her with his foot again, but he valued his toes. "He also doesn't say here how he met the scientists. I wonder if he wrecked on their island too?"

Sky nodded. "I've wondered that as well. I wish we'd thought to ask Ishibashi when we were there."

"I really regret not asking Ishibashi to tell us everything he knew about Mr. Today," Alex admitted. "I was so preoccupied with trying to get off that island that I didn't take the time to really talk to him."

Sky closed her book and sat up. "It's understandable. Plus he didn't seem to want to talk about certain things, like where he came from." She stood up and wandered over to look at the map on the dashboard. "It'll be dark when we get there," she said.

"We're not going on shore unless we can see," Alex said. "We'll have to wait until morning to look for Aaron."

"Yeah." Sky lifted her head to the breeze, closed her eyes, and inhaled deeply. Then she reached her hands up and stretched.

Alex watched her. The sun and sea air filled her brown cheeks with the glow of life. Impulsively, he reached over to the steering wheel and cranked it to one side.

Sky, thrown off balance, shouted and landed hard in Alex's lap.

"Oof," he said, recoiling, and grabbed her around the waist.

"You did that on purpose," Sky said, squirming and laughing. She leaned down until her face was aligned with his.

"Maybe," Alex said. He looked into her eyes.

"We're probably going off course now," Sky murmured.

"Good thing we don't have to be there until morning, then."

Sky grinned. "Aren't you going to let go of me?" Her lips were dangerously close to his.

"Do you really want me to?" he asked.

"You're the one who needs to concentrate so badly," Sky said. She moved back an inch.

"You're so practical," Alex said, cringing. But he knew she was right. He loosened his grip so she could stand up if she wanted to, but kept his fingers lightly laced around her waist . . . in case she didn't.

"I don't know about that," Sky said. "If I were really practical, I'd point out that you don't have me to blame as a distraction for totally mucking up your Gondoleery plan."

"Oh, really?" Alex's lips parted at the insult. "Is that right?"

"Isn't it?" Sky said coyly. "Think about it, since you're thinking about regrets. And you should consider this: Maybe you're just looking for something to blame when things are naturally going to go wrong sometimes anyway." She paused, thinking. "Or you're just looking for a way to explain the fact that you're a human who is constantly faced with new dilemmas, and therefore you're going to fail sometimes."

Alex frowned. "Wow, that was direct. Anything else?"

"I'm not insulting you, Alex," Sky said. "I'm pointing out that you are probably the biggest perfectionist in the world, and you think that someday, when all the stars align and when all the conditions of your life and relationships are exactly perfect, you will never fail at anything." She chuckled under her breath and shook her head a little. "And when you've driven everybody away to accomplish that impossible feat, well, *that's* when you'll figure out that you've become the biggest failure of all."

Slowly Sky sat up straight and pulled out of Alex's grasp. Alex dropped his head back on the cushion, her words stinging hard.

Sky squeezed his shoulder and stood up, moving over to the control panel. "Looks like the boat put itself back on course automatically after your little stunt," she said, looking at the map.

Slowly Alex sat up, feeling bruised all over. "That's good," he said, his voice hollow. After a moment he picked up his book and pretended to read once more.

Sky gave him a pitying glance, which he didn't see. But she knew he needed to hear what she had to say. The problem was, maybe he needed to hear it from somebody other than her.

*But no one else knows about our private conversations, about the fears and dreams he reveals to me,* she argued with herself. And no one else could see it the way she could. Still, she hadn't meant to hurt his feelings. She just wanted to point out what was painfully obvious . . . to her, anyway.

LISA McMANN

The afternoon passed slowly, Alex barely grunting whenever Sky offered up a tidbit about gorillas or an interesting fact about crabs. And after a couple hours of it, Sky began to wonder if Alex was ever going to get over his bruised feelings, or if he'd stay mad at her forever.

As they sped along, the sun was high overhead. Sky snapped her book shut.

Alex, startled by the noise, looked up.

"It's because I love you, Alexander Stowe," Sky said abruptly, barely able to comprehend what she was doing. "That's why I said those things. Because I . . . because I love you."

# More Regrets

A lex stared.

And Sky choked. Before her mouth had finished forming the words, she regretted blurting out her confession of love. What was she thinking? And the more Alex sat there staring, the more she felt she had to do something fast.

"I mean, as a friend! A—a—a sister!" Sky nearly shouted, even though Alex was sitting across from her.

She slapped a hand over her eyes. *What?* she thought. *No! Not as a friend! A sister? Stop talking!*

Alex continued to stare, his face awash in conflicting emotions

LISA McMANN

and settling on complete confusion. "So, um, do you want to maybe try that again from the beginning?" he finally asked.

"No! Nothing!" Sky said. Which didn't even make sense. She turned abruptly and went to the bow, her face burning and her insides twisting. She crouched on the seat cushion and gripped the chrome railing, leaning out over the water. Why did she say it?

The first part was true. She loved him. She'd loved him for a long time, at first as a friend, but never, ever like a sister. Ugh! And while she wasn't romantically dramatic enough to declare she'd been in love with him since the moment she'd laid eyes on him, she was pretty sure she'd fallen in love with him the day he swam out to her raft when she'd foolishly set out to save her mother on her own.

But then she'd gone and ruined everything. *Like a sister?* Where did that even come from?

And now she was trapped. She'd have to stay on the bow of the *Claire* forever or try to melt into the cushions and disappear.

"Hey!" Alex called out. "That wasn't awkward or anything."

Sky cringed. "Shut up and toss me some books."

LISA McMANN

The day wore on, and soon the sun was beginning to set. Alex, still confused about what had happened, wasn't quite sure what to think. First Sky had told him all his faults, and then she said she loved him . . . like a sister. What was that all about? It felt like a punch to the gut.

If there was something Alex had never envisioned about his relationship with Sky, it was her acting like a sister to him. Had something changed? Had he been so self-absorbed that he'd missed it? Or maybe this was all part of how he was "pushing people away," as Sky had accused him of.

He grumbled to himself as he read Mr. Today's journal. Sky had certainly pulled out all the stops in that speech. She hadn't held back in telling Alex all the things that were wrong with how he was living his life as head mage. The words had stung. They *still* stung. And he was having a hard time understanding why she had decided to attack him like that.

Was there any truth to it? Had he been using her as the reason for his failures? And just why was it that Alex always expected to get everything right, every time? Nothing about his job as head mage was comfortable or easy. None of this was familiar at all. And Mr. Today had really left Alex completely unprepared.

Sky seemed to think it was okay to fail once in a while—that people expected that. But Alex hadn't felt that way. Not ever. Alex looked at every decision he made as all-important and absolutely crucial. If he failed, he was a bad leader. If he succeeded, well, then he was just doing his job. Every failure he'd made was mortifying. What would the people of Artimé think of him if he couldn't get something right the first time? They'd revolt. Or fire him, or something. Or worse, they'd call him a failure. It was much safer for Alex to analyze everything, determine the cause of his mistakes, and try to eliminate those things from his life.

"Like now, for instance," Alex muttered under his breath. He'd been staring at the same page for half an hour, analyzing everything that had just happened. If this most recent distraction caused him to fail at finding Aaron, he was going to be really mad.

Abruptly Alex closed his book and stood up. Feeling restless and trapped, he moved to the stern of the boat and looked back in the direction of the cylindrical island, which was gone from view by now. He shoved his hands into his pockets and filled his lungs with air, then let the breath out slowly as he watched the sun disappear. Sky had told him it was okay to fail and said she loved him, which had given him the most amazing rush of feelings. And then she had ruined it all.

Alex sighed, contemplating the situation. They were stuck together on this boat for the next few days, at least, in close quarters. It was beyond uncomfortable. He wasn't sure how to face her. The tension was horrible. Maybe if he didn't look at her until after dark, it would be easier. Maybe they could pretend that whole scene had never happened, because they couldn't very well go on like this indefinitely.

When night fell, and the lush, green island number six was in sight, lit up by the moon, Alex finally stopped trying to avoid Sky. From the captain's seat, he looked at her for the first time in a long time. And, to his relief, she was sound asleep.

He gazed at her for a moment, then pulled out the blankets. He dropped one on his seat and carried the other one to the bow and draped it over her, tucking it in so it wouldn't blow away. With the soft glow of the moon illuminating her face, she looked otherworldly—too good to be true. A sharp pain

LISA McMANN

297 « Island of Graves

stabbed through Alex's heart as he fought the urge to brush the hair from her face, hold her in his arms, and kiss her soft lips.

He turned away and went back to his position at the controls, verifying they were still a few hours from reaching the gorilla island. From his perch, he looked out over the water, scanning it for Spike, whom he'd forgotten about most of the day.

"Spike?" Alex called in a low voice, growing fearful at the realization that he hadn't noticed the whale in a long time. Was she still with them?

"I am here, the Alex," said Spike from the other side of the boat. With a splash, Alex caught sight of the whale's tail, and then a moment later, Spike surfaced at Alex's side.

"Good," Alex said. "I was worried we'd lost you."

"I was being quiet like the Alex and Sky."

Alex chuckled softly. He was proud of his creation. She was so smart, yet wonderfully naive in her early stages of life. "So you heard the conversation?" Alex asked.

"Yes, it was very interesting, thank you."

"Did you learn anything?" Alex asked. "Because I just got more confused about life."

"Oh yes," Spike said. "I learned that you are very hard on yourself."

Alex considered that. "I suppose I am," he said. "But I want everything to go right."

"It goes the way it goes," Spike said. "Sometimes your right isn't the same as the other people's right."

Alex blinked. He wasn't sure what Spike was trying to say. "But my right is the only right," he said, a smile playing at his lips.

Spike didn't answer at first. And then she said, "That makes me feel scared, the Alex. I don't like it."

"I'm sorry, Spike," Alex said quickly. "I was only teasing. Making a joke. I didn't mean it. There are many different rights, and many different wrongs, I think."

Spike blew a spout of water from her blowhole. "Thank you for teaching me what your joke voice sounds like. I will understand next time."

Alex rested his chin on his arm and watched the whale swim effortlessly through the water. While he watched, he wondered if he had really been joking at all.

LISA McMANN

# Circling

Alex endured a troubled night of sleep as the questions ran endlessly through his head. Did he really think his way was always the right way? Did he look for people and things to blame his failures on? And why was he so afraid to fail? Because that much was true—he admitted it. The thought of failure was frightening to Alex, and he never truly considered it an option in any part of his life.

Which was entirely ridiculous. He didn't expect anybody else to get through life without failing sometimes. So why did he expect them to think that of him?

LISA McMANN

It was because he was the leader of Artimé. A great weight had been thrust upon him against his will. He could have walked away. But he hadn't. He'd taken it on, and somehow that had landed him here—a teenage ruler with responsibilities so heavy even Mr. Today had been weary holding them. And that was before the chain of rescues and battles.

When Alex opened his eyes, he stared at the sky and knew that he needed to make some changes in his life. He had lost perspective. And he'd been too hard on himself. And that, he believed, made him a weaker ruler, not a stronger one. He'd lost his sense of instinct as he'd mired himself in people's high expectations. He'd lost creativity, no doubt, when he'd put all sorts of rules on himself. He'd stopped himself from feeling things for Sky . . . or at least he'd tried. It was almost like a piece of Quill still ruled inside his brain, telling him what he could and couldn't do. Telling him he wasn't good enough, and that failure was wrong. Telling him not to feel his feelings.

The thought was shocking. As hard as he'd tried to turn from Quill's rules, he was still fighting them every step of the way, and he hadn't even realized it. Until now. Until Sky punched him in the face with it.

LISA McMANN

A splash woke him from his reverie. He sat up and looked over the side of the boat, which floated several yards off the coast of the lush island. Sky was swimming, getting some exercise after a long day. Or maybe she was still trying to avoid him after yesterday.

"How's the water?" Alex called out.

She ignored him, or more likely she didn't hear him, and kept swimming in a straight line parallel to the shore. Alex took the wheel and commanded the boat to troll in the water a short distance behind Sky, and then he stripped off his shirt and jumped in next to her.

She yelled, startled, and then grinned and spit water in his face and kept swimming.

*Phew*, Alex thought, treading water and grinning back at her. Things were going to be okay.

After several hundred yards, the two climbed back into the boat, refreshed, and Alex turned it to circle the island. He took a good long look at it. They were coming up to the area where they'd seen the word "HELP" spelled out in bones, and as he toweled off, he began to watch for it. Common sense told him

LISA McMANN

that if someone had been able to make a sign there, chances were that it was at least a little safer than other parts of the island.

"Maybe we can spot the gorilla as we circle and then speed around to the other side of the island and start searching there before it gets to us," Sky suggested. She pulled out a container of breakfast items that the kitchen had prepared for them and took one out, attacking it ravenously. "How do they keep this so fresh and hot?" she asked, her mouth full. "I love magic."

"That's something I definitely don't know how to do," Alex said.

He turned back to look at the island. Two-thirds of the island was at or only slightly above sea level, and he could see an old ship that had run aground about a quarter of the way around the island from them. The other one-third of the island rose up sharply. "I'm hoping we don't have to go ashore at all," Alex said.

He scanned the beach area as they rounded a sharp point of the island. When they came upon the bone sign, Alex gasped. "Sky, look," he said, pointing.

Sky looked, and she gasped too, almost inhaling a rather

LISA McMANN

large bumbleberry from her breakfast pie. She licked her fingers quickly and stood up. "It says 'come back.'"

"I know," Alex said reverently.

"That means . . . that means . . ."

"It means somebody changed the sign since we passed by here last time," Alex said.

"Do you think they're talking to us? Did they see you and Simber fly over, I wonder?"

Alex shook his head. "I don't know. We know there have been other ships passing by besides us—Simber saw one, remember?"

"Maybe it's Aaron who changed the sign, asking the pirates to come back."

"Maybe." Alex's insides twisted. Could they be close to finding Aaron? Part of him hoped for it, and part of him never wanted to see his twin again. The conflict was eating him up.

"Let's not waste any time, then," Sky said. "Pull up as close to shore as you can and start circling. We'll call out his name and see if he answers."

Alex hastily shoveled down the rest of his breakfast and then guided the boat toward the shore, letting it determine when they could get no closer. It moved around shallow spots and kept them within spitting distance of land.

"Keep an eye out behind us, Spike," Alex called to the whale. "Let us know if you detect any signs of life."

"Yes, the Alex," said Spike. "I can feel something strange, but I don't know what it is."

"The gorilla, maybe," Alex said. They moved along slowly, calling out Aaron's name regularly and trying to see through the bushes and trees that grew all the way to the island's edge. Both Alex and Sky pretended like yesterday's blowup had never happened, and it was easy not to actually look at one another since they were both looking so hard to see through the brush.

It was the largest island of the seven, and other than some birds chirping occasionally and a rustle of a bush now and then as an unknown animal startled and ran, there didn't seem to be much happening—along the shore, at least. The only interesting thing they saw was the shipwreck, but it was abandoned and so old there couldn't possibly be anyone left alive from whenever it wrecked. They didn't dare go ashore to look at it.

By the time they'd made it around the low end of the island and the land began to rise up out of the water, it was midafternoon.

Faced with the rocky high side of the island, Alex stopped the boat in the shade, and they took a break to eat.

Sky poured water from Ms. Octavia's fountain and handed a cup to Alex, who was rummaging through a crate of lunches. He pulled out Sky's favorite meal no matter the time of day, and handed it to her: sweet applecorn on toasties with platyprot eggs, which cooked up multicolored and presented beautifully. The food was exactly the right temperature, and Sky dug in hungrily.

Alex pulled out his favorite, a thick seafood chowder with a slice of fig-jam toast, which he'd taken a strange liking to ever since Fifer shoved a piece of hers into his mouth. He smiled, thinking of her as he took a bite.

"What's funny?" Sky asked.

"Just thinking about my sisters." He laughed. "It's still weird to call them that."

"So you like them?"

"Yeah, I really think I do," Alex said. "I mean, all right, obviously I was a little unsure at first. But . . . they're okay. They're nice."

Sky wiped her mouth. "I saw one climbing up the staircase the other day calling out 'Ax! Ax!' It was so cute."

"Really?" Alex sat up. "Are you serious? Do you think she was calling for me?"

"Of course! I mean I certainly hope she wasn't calling for a real ax."

"Which twin was it?"

"I don't know. I can't tell them apart."

"It doesn't matter, anyway." Alex couldn't stop grinning. "Ax. That's cool. It makes me seem really tough, too."

Sky groaned. "Great." She folded up her empty plate until it made a bright popping sound and disappeared, then rinsed her hands in the water fountain.

Alex hesitated, wondering if now would be a good time to tell her that he'd been thinking about what she'd said. But he didn't want to start an argument when they needed to look for Aaron. Besides, he was still thinking about it. A lot.

So he commanded the boat to begin circling the island once more, this time from a bit more of a distance so they could keep an eye on the rising accessible part of the land.

"Aaron!" he shouted.

"Aaron!" echoed Sky.

A moment later Alex frowned. "Do you hear something?"

Sky nodded. "Something's rumbling. Reminds me of the hurricane after the hour of calm, when the thunder starts rolling back in."

They were silent for a moment, watching the highest point of the island but unable to really see anything except for the grass and trees on the downward slope before the land dropped off and became sheer rock.

"Spike?" Alex called softly. "I'm going to speed around to a spot where we can have a better look. Charlie, you might want to get in your safe place in the cabin. Sky, hang on. We're going to fly."

Charlie moved toward the cabin but stayed on deck to watch. Alex pressed down on the throttle until they were skimming over the water full speed ahead to the south side of the island, where they'd seen the come-back sign. Even with the noise from the boat, they could both tell that the rumbling sound was increasing.

As they rounded the highest point of the island and sailed to where the waterfall was visible and the land sloped quickly to just above sea level, Sky touched Alex's shoulder and pointed. Alex cut the motor so the boat drifted just offshore.

It looked as though the center of the island was moving or shifting toward them. The trees and long grasses waved in a single giant motion, and for a moment, Sky thought the island was about to split in two. After a few curious minutes of watching while the thundering increased, she caught a glimpse of black and silver, and then more black and more silver, and as the sound grew, a tremendous beastly cry rang out.

Charlie dove for the safety of the cabin as a stampede of what seemed like hundreds of silverback saber-toothed gorillas burst through the thick brush and flattened the grasses. They barreled straight toward the beach in front of the boat, growing larger by the second.

"Oh my—" Sky breathed. "Look at them all! They're not going to stop." She gripped Alex's arm. "Alex! They're not stopping!"

And she was right. The front line of gorillas reached the sand, continued toward the edge of the shore, and plunged into the water without even slowing down. They splashed in the direction of the boat, their fangs gleaming.

"They can swim!" Alex yelled in fright. He lunged for the controls, trying to turn the boat around, but he was so flustered that he fumbled everything. Finally, with the grunting carnivores nearly upon them, he managed to shout out a command to the boat to head straight out to sea. As the first gorillas reached out their clawed fingers and grabbed the side of the boat, the vessel kicked into gear, shaking most of the gorillas loose. But one held on. With saber teeth just feet away, Sky jumped to the other side of the boat and dove for the sword, while Alex tried desperately to shake the beast off by grabbing the wheel and steering as wildly as he could.

Off balance, Sky pulled the sword back and slammed it down on the gorilla's arm. The beast roared in pain, its open mouth wide enough to fit an entire human head. Alex grabbed spell components and began throwing scatterclips at the beast, but they seemed useless. The gorilla wouldn't let go of the side of the boat. It began to pull itself up as Sky cracked it over the head with the sword. She could smell its sickening rankness.

Alex pulled out a handful of heart attack components and looked at them. He cringed, took a breath, and closed his hand firmly around them, winding up for the throw. "Heart attack!"

LISA McMANN

he cried, sending them soaring at the beast. The gorilla seemed stunned for a moment, but it still didn't let go. Instead it gripped the side of the boat with its elbow and began hauling one leg up over the railing.

"Get off!" Sky screamed. She slammed the sword down again, then pulled back and sliced it sideways through the air, smashing it with all her might into the gorilla's head.

The creature wobbled, and its hand slipped. But with a mighty reach of its other hand, the gorilla grabbed the back of Sky's shirt and yanked her toward its face. Sky twisted around and slammed her elbow into the creature's eye. She tore herself from its grasp, sending her sword skittering across the deck. The back of her shirt was shredded from the beast's sharp claws.

After dodging and fighting off multiple gorillas, Spike finally caught up to the boat. She tried jabbing the stubborn gorilla with her spike, then grabbing its legs in her mouth to pull, but every time she got a grip, Alex yanked on the steering wheel, which sent Spike flying and trying to catch up again.

Alex, who was still trying to shake the creature off the boat, pelted the gorilla with half a dozen more heart attack spells, but the beast wouldn't die. Sky regained her footing and, with a mighty raging yell, grabbed on to the seatback and kangaroo kicked her feet at the gorilla's mouth. She landed on the railing, stomping on the gorilla's fingers. Then she jumped back to the deck, picked up her sword again, reared back, and shoved it into its leg.

The gorilla howled and snapped at Sky and Alex, its sabers dripping with saliva.

Alex shot one more round of heart attack spells. This time the gorilla's head finally flopped back. And with a last swerve of the boat from Alex, the creature's grip released. It fell backward with an enormous splash into the water and sank.

Stunned, Sky staggered to the side, chest heaving, hands shaking. The sword dropped from her hands to the deck, its blade covered in blood. Alex shouted a command to the boat to continue at full speed, and ran over to her. He flung his arms around her and held her.

Once Sky realized she was safe, her body began shaking uncontrollably. She hid her face in Alex's neck and started to sob, and he held her, stroking her hair and whispering in her ear, and they stood there in the speeding boat together until both of them stopped trembling.

# Back to the Island

**D**oes that sting?" Alex asked, dabbing the deep scratches on Sky's back with some salve Henry had put in their healing kit.

"Not bad," Sky said, cringing. She lay on her stomach on her fold-out seat as Alex tended to her wounds.

"It's a nice set of stripes."

"I'm just glad I still have a head attached to my body," Sky said. "A water attack was not something I expected."

"Me either," Alex said, mad at himself. "And I should have. I don't know why I didn't expect that the gorillas would leave the island and chase us. I just didn't think hard enough about

LISA McMANN

them being able to swim like that." He handed Sky a towel and then turned his back so she could change into a new shirt that wasn't shredded or covered in saber-toothed-gorilla blood.

"See, there you go again," Sky said. "We also had no way to know there were so many of them. Give yourself a break for once." She pressed her lips together, vowing to say no more, and slipped into a lightweight shirt.

"I get it, okay?" Alex said with a groan. "I've been meaning to talk to you about that."

"Oh." Sky wasn't sure what to say, so she changed the subject. "Okay, you're good to turn around again." Gingerly she tested out how the shirt felt against her scratches. "This is going to be really uncomfortable for a few days, I think."

Alex turned to face her again. "Henry said the salve should help quite a lot after about half a day. The healers are getting good at this stuff."

"And see, there's something you did that was really successful—you made healing a priority when Mr. Today didn't have much of anything in place before." Sky eased to her seat and perched on the edge of it. "Anyway, I can't force you to realize what you're doing to yourself—you're just going to have to see it on your own. Now, let's go back and finish this island. I'm ready."

"Are you sure?"

"We need to find Aaron. The sun's going to set soon," Sky said. She gazed at the island in the distance. "At least we know what we're up against now."

Alex swung the boat around and directed it to take them back to the island. He pulled out his supplies and reloaded his vest pockets, thinking about the horrible attack. He'd used heart attack spells during it, and he didn't regret that for a minute. The experience was probably the most frightening thing Alex had ever faced without Simber or Florence nearby. And he'd survived it.

Sky was a maniac—they'd both be dead without her and her quick thinking with the sword. Clearly Alex's spells intended for humans were not about to take down a nine-hundred-pound gorilla. He thought about the magic and wondered if there was anything he could do to his current stash to strengthen it.

"So, what's the plan?" Sky asked as the island drew near. "Stay back if we see any gorillas?"

Alex laughed uneasily. "Yep." He trained his eye halfway up the mountainous side where they'd first noticed the movement and pointed. "That extra-lush area there, next to the waterfall—I think that's where some of them came from. Others came from the clearing near the river on the low side of the island, several hundred yards from where the old ship ran aground."

Sky studied the area he pointed to. "If you look really closely all around the clearing, you can see the grasses moving in waves," she remarked. "Like they're just walking through it."

Alex nodded. "Okay. So they were there the whole time. We must have set them off somehow when we began yelling again after lunch."

Sky nibbled on the jagged edge of a fingernail that had been torn to the quick in the fight. "It was echoey on that side. Maybe that was it." She shrugged. "I can't imagine how your brother could have survived on this island for months, but I'll give him the benefit of the doubt. I think we should anchor on the cliff side, within sight of the bone sign, and wait for him to find us."

"I agree," Alex said. "We've made it all the way around,

LISA McMANN

though the last bit was pretty fast. Spike," he called, "did you see anything around the side before the gorillas started attacking?"

"Nothing," said Spike. "But I will not leave your side again."

"I know," Alex said. "Thanks. Intuitive or not, there's no way you could have predicted *that* was going to happen." He glanced sidelong at Sky, who was giving him a pointed "I told you so" look.

He smirked back at her and continued. "I think everybody in earshot probably knows by now that some sort of intruder was here. The gorillas were loud enough."

The sun was beginning to set, and the waves calmed. Alex set the anchor on the mountainous side of the island a hundred feet offshore for safety. Spike roamed around the boat, keeping a watchful eye on the island for anything that might move.

"I feel that there is a human somewhere," Spike said at one point, but she had nothing more than that information to offer.

While waiting to be noticed, Alex and Sky finished cleaning up the boat. There were several scratches in the gunwale from the gorilla's claws and teeth, but nothing worse than that, thanks to the preserve spell. They buffed the scratches the best

LISA McMANN

they could and washed down the entire deck, the dirty water draining through the floor vent. Soon everything was crisp and clean again.

Alex folded down a sofa cushion at the stern where he and Sky could both sit and eat dinner together while hoping for signs of human life.

And as darkness fell, so did any awkwardness that remained between them.

"You were right yesterday," Alex said after a while. "I don't know why I always set such high stakes for myself." He leaned back on the sofa and propped up his feet. "I think it has something to do with Quill and how I was raised. I knew I was going to be Unwanted for three years before my Purge. I think living with that knowledge and shame somehow makes me want to prove something now—that I'm not a failure in the eyes of the people of Artimé like I was to my parents and to Quill." He laughed softly. "I don't know."

"Just because you fail once in a while doesn't make you a failure," said Sky. "It makes you real."

"I know that. It makes sense when you say it. I just forget easily, I guess."

LISA McMANN

"Then I'll keep saying it until it gets pounded into your thick head."

Alex's mouth twitched. "Okay." He looked over at Sky, who was sitting gingerly on the edge of the sofa. His face filled with concern. "Still hurting, huh?"

Sky managed a smile. "Just being careful. It hurts to lean back."

"That'll make for a rough night," Alex said. "Want more salve on it?"

"Yeah. Thanks."

Alex got up and went into the cabin for the healer's kit, then applied salve to Sky's back once more. The scratches were red and angry-looking. "You want something for the pain?" he asked. "It'll help you sleep."

Sky considered it but shook her head. "I don't want to be groggy if something happens with Aaron. I'll be all right." She yawned.

"Here," Alex said, stretching out onto the sofa. "Rest with me."

Sky eyed him suspiciously.

"I'll be good," he said.

LISA McMANN

Gingerly Sky crawled next to him and curled up on her side, facing him.

"How does that feel?" Alex asked, letting his chin rest against the top of her head.

Between them, Sky's hands slipped into Alex's. "Pretty good," she whispered.

Alex closed his eyes and gave Sky's hands a soft squeeze. Before long, they were both breathing deeply, fast asleep.

They slept so soundly that at first they didn't hear the voice.

But Charlie did.

# The Song in the Night

A lex thought the song was part of his dream. He was back in Artimé, and Meghan was practicing in Ms. Morning's classroom, just like old times. But then Charlie yanked on his hair, and Sky stirred and sat up, and Alex woke from the dream and remembered Meghan was dead.

But the song was still there, sweet and lilting, like a lullaby.

"Do you hear it?" Alex whispered.

Sky nodded. "There's no way that's Aaron, though. It's a girl."

Alex eased himself off the sofa, careful of Sky's injuries, and went to the side of the boat. "What's happening, Spike?"

"It is a girl on the island. She is singing a story to us, I think."

LISA McMANN

"Where is she?"

"At the very top, near the mouth of the waterfall."

"We can hear her from that far away?"

"The night and the calm water carry her voice," Spike said. "Listen please. She is telling us something."

Sky joined Alex at the side of the boat, and they listened, trying to make out all the words. Alex quickly pulled his magical notebook and pencil from his pocket and began to scribble down everything he could understand.

> *I am singing from this tree—*
> *My voice soothes the gorillas in their sleep.*
> *Will you please stay and rescue me?*
> *They let me live but won't let me leave.*

The voice quieted, and then it began again, soft and lilting. The first line was muffled and sounded foreign, and only a few words came through before the voice strengthened.

> *I am Ka . . . rica*
> *I am . . . and stranded here.*

*I see you there in your white boat.*

*Please don't leave. . . .*


The voice quivered, and the rest of the line was muffled.

"Did you get that?" Sky whispered when the voice was quiet again.

Alex shook his head while scribbling out the last bit, and then they held the notebook to the soft boat lighting and read it over.

"This part I think was her name," Sky said, pointing to the first line of the second verse. "I didn't catch it either."

"I wish she'd tell us how to rescue her," Alex said. "It sounds like she's trapped."

The song began again.


*The creatures sleep at night.*

*I am lucky that they like my voice.*

*They keep me trapped in this tree to sing for them,*

*Overlooking all the graves.*


*There were many who were stranded here.*

*You saw the . . . ship on the other side.*

Now only bones and graves remain,

And books to tell the stories of their deaths.


I came from storm to storm and landed here,

My sailboat sinking, body torn apart.

I made it to the waterfall

Before they found me and took me to their lair.


Now I live here in this ancient tree.

I steal away for food when they stampede.

Sometimes I change the bone sign on the beach,

But only if they stampede to the north.


Can you please let me know if you can hear me?

Just sing back; don't speak or yell.

Try to imitate the lilt of my voice

And they will stay asleep . . . I hope.


Alex looked at Sky. "I can't sing," Alex said. "I'm terrible at it. Can you?"

Sky almost laughed. "You're the creative one," she said.

"And my voice is scratchy from the thorns. I don't . . . I mean . . ."

Spike spoke softly. "You are both silly to argue about this right now, I think."

Alex nodded. "You're right, Spike."

Sky scowled. "Okay, I'll do it. You'll probably just scare them all." She'd sung once before with Meghan, who had said she had a warm tone or something—Sky couldn't remember. Meghan was just being nice. Sky took a deep breath and let it out, trying to think of what to sing so that it wouldn't sound completely stupid.

> *We can hear you—there are two of us.*
> *We will help you escape.*
> *How . . .*

Sky panicked, trying to think of what to say, then kept going.

> *How can we rescue you?*
> *We don't want to die.*

"Good job," whispered Alex. "Beautiful. You should sing more."

"Thanks," Sky said. It didn't sound half bad.

They waited. There was a long silence. Sky pictured the girl in the tree and wondered what it was like for her to finally hear an answer. Tears sprang to her eyes as she thought about how she'd feel in the same situation.

Finally the song began again.

> *I am crying tears of joy and thanks.*
>
> *I've been stringing vines for months to make*
>
> > *a rope.*
>
> *I need two days or maybe three to finish.*
>
> *Then I'll run for the cliff and rappel down.*
>
> *That way you can stay safe in your boat.*
>
> *Is there any way you'll wait for me?*
>
> *I know it is a lot for me to ask—*
>
> *I am desperate on this Island of Graves.*

Alex and Sky looked at one another. "Two or three days?" whispered Alex. "We don't have that kind of time."

Sky's face was grim. "We need to save her, but we'll have to figure out some other way. We've got to find Aaron."

"Can you ask her if he's here?" Alex suggested.

"Yes, I was planning on it. What else?"

"Ask if there's another way for her to escape, like now, tonight."

"Got it."

Sky gathered her thoughts, and then began to sing:

> *Is there any other way to rescue you tonight?*
> *We're on a desperate search for someone else*
> *And have no time to lose.*
> *His name is Aaron. . . . Is he there with you?"*

They waited, and a few minutes later, the sorrowful reply came.

> *There is no other way to leave tonight.*
> *Gorillas sleep on the ground below my feet.*
> *I must finish my rope, then wait for daylight,*
> *And sneak away when they are on the hunt.*

LISA McMANN

*I have seen no humans anywhere;*

*No one has landed since I arrived.*

*I have the highest viewpoint of the island.*

*I assure you, sadly, Aaron is not here.*

Alex and Sky exchanged a glance. The girl paused, then continued in a sad couplet.

*I understand your urgency.*

*Perhaps one day you can come back for me.*

Sky put her hand to her forehead, squeezing her eyes shut, and sighed. "There's got to be something else we can do," she whispered.

"There is," Alex said. "Since Aaron isn't here, he's got to be on the Island of Shipwrecks. We'll collect him and come back for this girl on our return."

"Brilliant," Sky said. "They should make you head mage or something."

"Knock it off," Alex warned. "You sound like you've been cavorting with Clive, my wise-guy blackboard."

Sky elbowed Alex in the side and thought about what to sing. "Be quiet now. I'm thinking." Soon she began again.

> Our journey takes us one more island to the east.
> When we are finished there, we will return.
> A week or less, I guarantee.
> Do not lose hope. . . . Just finish your rope.

The girl responded shortly.

> My gratefulness to you is bigger than the sea.
> Beware the hurricane's dangerous grasp.
> Though often now I wish that I were there.
> Give my best to Ishibashi-san.

Alex's lips parted in surprise.

"Did you hear that?" Sky whispered excitedly. "She must be the girl that Ishibashi told us about. The one who escaped."

"And she ended up here." Alex shook his head. "Boy, has she had a string of bad luck."

"She's been working on that rope for months—did you

LISA McMANN

catch that?" Sky gazed up at the island with respect. "And I think Ishibashi talked about the girl leaving his island last year. We barely survived a day here, and we didn't even step foot on it."

"Impressive," Alex agreed. "She must be terribly lonely. It's amazing she hasn't given up or gone crazy by now." Then he scratched his head. "I wonder which island she's from."

"The Island of Fire, maybe," Sky said. "It's the only option, isn't it?"

Alex thought about it. "Not Warbler, since she's singing. Not Legends or Shipwrecks, since we met everyone there. And Pan said no human has ever been on that seventh island. Unless she's from Quill."

Sky shrugged, thinking about the other chunk of land on Lani's map and the dead passengers in the air vessel that had crashed in the sea near Artimé. "Or somewhere we haven't discovered yet."

"Maybe," said Alex. The idea seemed crazy. But it would certainly explain a few things.

When they were sure the girl was done communicating with them, they saw no reason to stay any longer. Alex commanded the boat to head to a spot a mile from the Island of Shipwrecks so they could figure out exactly how they were going to get to shore without dying in the process.

Meanwhile in Quill, Gondoleery was making some changes. She commanded Governor Strang to draft Wanteds into the Quillitary and begin training them. She visited the university to seek out eager students who were desperate to advance in Quill and appointed them to her newly formed high priest protection squad. And by now she'd figured out that Sully was the weak link in her driving staff who had given help to the enemy.

She killed him with an ice spear to the heart.

# Return to the Island of Shipwrecks

The boat was still speeding toward the easternmost island in the chain when Alex and Sky awoke early the next morning. Spike swam with the boat as usual, sometimes a little ahead of it, sometimes a little behind. And Charlie stayed in the cabin, preferring the safety of it whenever the boat was going fast.

True to Henry's word, the salve had helped Sky's wounds considerably overnight, and she was moving about much more comfortably by morning.

"Six hours to go before we get there," Sky said, looking through the shelf of books for a new title. "Unfortunately that means we're going to miss the hour of calm, which worries me a bit. I know Ms. Morning said the boat could make it through anything, but she hasn't seen this hurricane." She pulled out a book, looked at the cover, and put it back. "How do you suppose Aaron managed to survive the hurricane?"

Alex liked that Sky had never questioned him about Aaron being alive—she just believed him. "I have no idea. But if he's truly there and not still on some ship somewhere, I'm sure the scientists are helping him." He frowned. "Those poor guys. They probably had no idea what kind of horrible person they were getting stuck with."

"They've probably had a fair share of horrible visitors." Sky laughed, and then she grew thoughtful. "Hey, I just remembered something. Didn't Ishibashi tell us that sometimes the pirates dragged their enemies to the Island of Shipwrecks and set them adrift in the storm?"

"Now that you say that, it sounds familiar," Alex mused. "I'd forgotten about it. That must be what happened with Aaron."

"So he's got to be there!" Sky said.

Alex imagined Aaron in a little fishing boat caught in the hurricane. "I can't believe he made it through that alive. I'm glad it wasn't me against that storm alone. But I feel guilty, because it should have been."

"If Aaron is as bad as you say, you can cut the guilt. He got what he deserved." She knitted her brows, her finger hovering over the spine of one of Alex's books. "Hmm." She slid it out and sat down to read.

"Yeah. Poor Ishibashi." Alex pulled out a book too, but he had trouble getting into reading today. His mind was more preoccupied with the girl on the previous island. The Island of Graves, she'd called it. It was very mysterious. And the old abandoned ship, which could have carried hundreds of people. They were all likely devoured by saber-toothed gorillas, leaving nothing but their bones and some graves. What was their story?

Sky paged through her book with the utmost attention. She was so enraptured by it that when Alex pointed out the massive circle of clouds in the direction of the Island of Shipwrecks, she didn't hear him.

Alex studied her, a smile playing on his lips. "Sky," he said.

"What?" she replied, tearing her eyes away from the book.

"I was commenting on the clouds," he said.

Sky glanced eastward. "Yep," she said. "Those are clouds all right." She glanced at the map on the dashboard and went back to her book.

"What book is that?" Alex asked.

"*Element-ary*," she mumbled.

"The spell book? Since when did you care about spells?"

"Since we're heading into a hurricane by choice," Sky said, not looking up. "I saw you had the book with you, and I figured if Lani can rid an entire island of ice, what's stopping you from ending the hurricane?"

Alex blinked. The thought had never occurred to him. "What a brilliant idea. Is there a section on hurricanes?" He crossed the width of the boat and sat next to Sky. "Can I read over your shoulder?"

"If you're quiet," Sky said. "We'll be there in five hours, so cut the chatter, will you?"

"Sorry," Alex said. He leaned over Sky's shoulder as she paged through the book, skipping over the ice and snow sections, which Lani had used. Occasionally she went back to a page she'd bookmarked about rain and pondered it, then continued.

"This is really something," said Alex, "you know? I can't

335 « Island of Graves

believe you thought of it. I can't believe I *didn't* think of it."

"Quiet," Sky said, and tapped the book.

Alex obeyed.

They remained like that until their backs and necks cramped from intense studying. By the time they paged to the end of the book, Sky had marked four sections, but none of them were what she'd been looking for. She straightened up and turned to Alex.

"Well," she said, "there's no hurricane section. Not even a mention of a hurricane anywhere."

Alex deflated. "It figures. I guess that idea was too good to be true."

Sky tapped her chin, thinking for a long moment. "I'm not so sure about that. I mean, obviously I don't know much about magic or how spells work, but it seems to me that you can break a hurricane down into wind, rain, thunder, and lightning, right? It makes sense if you just think a little differently." She handed the spell book to Alex. "I've marked those four spells for you."

Alex took it and looked at the sections Sky had marked. "Put them all together, you're saying?"

"Yes, exactly," said Sky. "Make a new, huge spell from the four that already exist. Is that a stupid idea?"

Alex began reading over the sections carefully. "I don't know," he murmured. "It seems pretty smart, actually. . . ." He wondered if it was possible. Sure, Alex had successfully made new components and instilled them with magic many times in the past, but this was entirely different. He'd need to create an enormous removal spell, like the dissipate spell but on a majorly heightened level. And it was a task that would require a chant that didn't already exist. Alex hadn't had much practice writing that kind of magic. He'd always used Mr. Today's journals and notes in the past, like with the Triad spells. Now *he'd* be the mage doing the experimenting. *He'd* be the one scribbling the notes in the margins . . . all for the sake of one day helping the next mage of Artimé.

The responsibility felt daunting. "It would take a lot of work to get it right," said Alex.

"If anybody can do it, it's you," Sky said softly.

But doubt kept creeping in. "Don't you think Mr. Today would have tried this since he was friends with Ishibashi?" He paged through the book, and then checked inside the front and back covers for additional notes, which Mr. Today had often scribbled in books after attempting to alter a spell. But there were none. In fact, while old, the book was in pristine condition, unworn, and the binding was still very tight.

"Maybe he didn't write this book," Sky said. "I mean, he can't have written *all* of the books in the library. There wouldn't be time to do anything else. So it might be that he just didn't know about it. Or maybe he looked and discovered there wasn't a section on hurricanes, so that stopped him—I don't know."

Alex turned the book over. "I remember someone saying once that Mr. Today never really did much with weather other than the occasional rain to keep things fresh in Artimé. It wasn't really his style of magic."

"Well, there you go," said Sky. "He probably never thought about it."

"Maybe," said Alex. "I'll see what I can come up with."

Alex paced the narrow aisle for hours, book in hand, frowning and rereading and puzzling over the individual sections. Was there a way to stop a hurricane if all he had were spells to control bits and pieces of it? It didn't seem possible that he

LISA McMANN

could put this puzzle together and perform such a grand and complicated thing . . . especially if Mr. Today hadn't done it. Maybe Sky was right that the old mage simply hadn't thought of it.

It was worth a try, anyway. As the Island of Shipwrecks grew nearer, Alex sat down with his pencil and notepad and began dissecting each of the four spells Sky had bookmarked, looking to see if there was any repetition or overlap among them. He scribbled things down and crossed things out, hemmed and sighed, then wrote furiously again, pages and pages, not noticing Sky looking on from time to time to see what progress he was making.

By the time the boat pulled to within a mile of the island and slowed to drift outside the hurricane's grip, Alex had reconfigured the four different elemental spells to reverse their effects and combined them into one all-encompassing spell so he'd have to concentrate very hard only one time. At least he hoped that was what he'd done. Soon he'd know for sure.

As the boat drifted closer and closer to the island, Spike reported a tugging feeling in the waters below like she'd felt before when they approached this island. Alex went over each element of the spell a few more times, looking for mistakes. When he was certain he'd done everything he could, he tried to relax his body and brain for a few moments so he'd be fresh to perform the magic. "How long have we been drifting here?" he asked.

"A few hours," said Sky. "You must be starving." She held out a sandwich.

He waved her off, too absorbed by the task to eat.

Looking through the wall of the storm, he could barely make out the scientists' ship on the land, where he'd transported it for them. He was too far away to see any signs of life . . . or signs of Aaron.

Alex's stomach knotted. He'd been concentrating so hard on the spell that he'd almost forgotten the main reason they'd come. This was it. His brother was most likely here. And Alex wasn't sure what he was going to say to him. He was ready to fight if he had to. Ready to take Aaron by force or by magic if necessary.

Of course, they had to make it safely to the island first. And despite the boat's magic and strength, Alex thought putting an end to the hurricane was a safer idea, especially for Charlie, who would sink like a stone if he somehow got tossed overboard. He desperately hoped this melding of ideas would work.

Sky ventured a question. "Did you figure it out?"

Pulled from his thoughts, Alex smiled at her and stretched his tense muscles. "Mostly," he said. "And if this actually works, you get the prize for being clever and thinking beyond the parameters of magic. But before I try it, I have a question for you. How did Lani perform the spell to remove the ice? I was sort of preoccupied at the moment and didn't notice."

"She did this." Sky stood up and put her hands in the air, fingers outstretched. "It seemed like she was trying to encompass the whole area," she said. "And then she chanted the words under her breath three times."

"Got it. Thanks." Alex rechecked his spell for errors and began muttering. There was a lot he could get wrong in figuring out how to reverse rain, wind, thunder, and lightning. And even more he could mess up by combining all of those reversed spells into one.

Seeing that Alex had sunk back into his thoughts, Sky stayed out of his way and waited patiently. Soon he was nodding, and then he was rising to his feet, book in hand, pencil shoved behind his left ear. He looked out at the storm for a long moment, regarding it as an enemy and trying to find its weaknesses, and then he set his jaw firmly.

"Okay," he said, glancing at Sky and Charlie, "I'm warning you. This could be awesome, or it could get ugly. You both might want to hide in the cabin until it's over."

They didn't hesitate to take him up on the warning, though it was a tight fit.

Once Sky pulled the door closed, Alex lifted his hands in the air, still holding the book in case he needed it. He started chanting, "Water to clouds—no." He stopped abruptly and muttered something under his breath, then crossed off the word "water" and replaced it with "rain." "Disastrous," he grumbled, shaking his head. "Come on, Stowe." He paced up and down the aisle a few times, talking himself through the entire chant one last time.

When he felt like he was ready, he returned to his spot and concentrated hard on the weather that hung over the island. After several moments, he lifted his hands and started chanting again, softly, poetically, and with more confidence this time. "Rain to clouds," he said, "and clouds to sky. Gray to blue, and yellow to shine."

He paused, took a breath, and continued just as confidently as before. "Gale to breeze, and swirl to brush. Lightning fade, thunder hush. Calm the sea and dry the stone. And warm the air to feel . . . like home." He'd added that last bit in hopes of giving the scientists pleasant temperatures as well.

It sounded right. It *felt* right. Encouraged, Alex repeated the entire chant two more times, neither his hands nor his voice wavering.

But when he uttered the last word, part of his confidence left with it. Alex closed his eyes and cringed. Maybe it would've been a good idea to practice parts of his totally new weather spell first before trying to tackle such a big job. Had he messed up? Again?

When the sound of rain slamming against the water stopped, Alex opened his eyes. Before him was a most incredible sight. The wind was dying down. The rain reversed direction and went up into the clouds. And when the clouds had reabsorbed the moisture, they began to disperse.

"Sky!" Alex called. "Come look!"

Sky burst out of the cabin, joined Alex, and watched as the lightning shot up and faded inside the dispersing clouds. The angry, choppy waves calmed to gentle swells. The loud thunder grew faint and disappeared, and the brilliant sun shone over the island.

Alex stood gripping the railing, waiting with dread for something to go horribly wrong like it usually did. He imagined all sorts of disastrous results now that he'd said the spell aloud. What if the sea was totally made of rain and he'd just commanded it to go into the clouds? Would it leave Alex and Sky plunging hundreds of feet to the sea floor to their deaths? Would it leave Spike and all the other sea creatures struggling to survive? He paled and sweat pricked the back of his neck. This was the moment when everything would fall apart.

But for once that didn't happen. All of the elements of the hurricane had disappeared, just as Alex had wanted them to. Nothing more, nothing less. He couldn't believe it.

His heart thudded in his chest. "Did I do it?" he whispered.

Sky watched the performance in awe. "I think you did it, Alex." She watched for another minute, a smile slowly spreading across her face as the weather rapidly lost all signs of trouble. "Yes, you really did! It's perfect! I bet you wish you could see their faces when they notice it," she said.

Alex was having trouble believing it. He'd done it. *First try!* And all while having Sky present, and about as close as humanly possible for the past few days. He tore his eyes from the glorious scene and turned to her, thrilled beyond belief.

"I did it!" he shouted, throwing the book in the air. "And it's all thanks to your cleverness!" As the book clattered to the deck, Alex slid his fingers into Sky's hair and pressed his lips against hers.

She didn't push him away. He felt electric! When Alex drew back, she laughed softly. "It probably helped that I'm not magical. I don't know the rules." She reached for his shirt and pulled him close for a second kiss. "And I'm really glad we're taking care of *this* before Aaron gets here."

"I agree," he said. "I'd like to do more of it sometime if you don't mind."

"Okay. Me too," Sky said simply. She lifted a finger in warning. "But only if you stop blaming our relationship for your mage problems."

"I will. I promise," Alex said, reluctantly breaking away. His eyes lingered on hers and his hand caressed her shoulder. "So . . . that thing you said about loving me like a sister . . . ?"

Sky narrowed her eyes, and her face grew warm. "If you ever bring that up again, we're through. Not even joking a little bit."

"Okay, okay," Alex said, laughing. He moved to the boat controls. "On that note, let's go see if we can locate my whiny little monster brother so he can make our lives miserable for the next few days."

"Eh," Sky said, "we can always leave him with the gorillas if he gets too unbearable."

# The Reunion

Now that the hurricane was gone, Alex commanded the boat to head toward the island. Of its own accord, it weaved toward the destination, avoiding the rocks and wrecks that were scattered about. The boat moved gracefully, and just as graceful was Spike, beside it.

"The tugging is gone, the Alex," Spike reported. "The water is smooth and kind now."

"Excellent news," Alex said. "It's so strange to see the island in this kind of weather. I'm going to bring us right up to the shore. Feel free to explore if you want, and if you see anything useful in the wrecks, pull it up for Ishibashi."

LISA McMANN

"I will do that with pleasure," Spike replied, "for I have been very curious about the wrecks and sad that I was unable to see them last time because of the storm." Spike disappeared under the water, and Alex, Sky, and Charlie stood anxiously in the boat as they approached the island.

"Do you see anybody?" Alex asked Sky.

"No," said Sky.

"You'd think they'd be out looking at the sunshine."

"They might be," Sky said. "Just not where we can see them yet."

The weaving journey to shore took longer than anyone wanted it to, but at least they weren't in danger of crashing into anything.

"The island is so much more beautiful when there's no storm," said Sky.

Alex nodded. The silence was strange.

A few moments later, when they were nearing the spot where Ishibashi's ship had sunk, Charlie hopped on one foot and pointed. Three small, old men were emerging from behind a stand of rocks. They looked around and almost immediately spotted the white boat. But of course they didn't recognize it.

LISA McMANN

Alex stood on the captain's chair and began waving with all his might. "Hey! Hello! Ishibashi-san!"

The men came rushing to the edge of the beach, and when the boat couldn't get any closer, Alex cast the anchor spell. Charlie opted to stay in the boat rather than chance getting wet—or overwhelmed from meeting new people. So Alex and Sky climbed over the railing, dropped into the water, and waded to shore.

"Alex-san, is it you?" cried Ishibashi. "You have brought your weather with you this time!" He laughed hysterically as he and the other two scientists danced around, hands pointing at the clear sky and not feeling any rain. They couldn't wait to embrace their friends.

When the two teens reached the scientists, they greeted their old friends excitedly, everybody talking at once.

"What have you done with our hurricane?" Ishibashi asked. Tears were streaming down his face. "I have not seen the bright sun nor felt a gentle breeze like this in many, many years."

"Do you want me to bring the hurricane back?" Alex teased.

"No! Please! But tell me you have done this, and that I am truly standing here and this is not a dream."

"It's true!" said Alex. "I have done this, Ishibashi-san,

LISA McMANN

thanks to Mr. Today's book and Sky's creative thinking. She believed I could stop the hurricane even though there wasn't a spell for it. So I created something new, and now you are really standing here in the sunshine."

Ishibashi's eyes shone. "Then you are a true mage, worthy of taking the place of Mr. Marcus Today. Indeed, you have done something Marcus was unable to do. And your actions will save many ships and many lives."

The words sank in, and Alex's heart swelled as he fully realized the scope of what he'd done. It was true, then. Alex had accomplished something Mr. Today hadn't been able to do. The scientists got the best gift imaginable, and no more ships would wreck here because of the hurricane. And it was all thanks to him and Sky, working as a team.

Sky squeezed Alex's hand. "Good job," she whispered.

"You too," said Alex, squeezing back. Maybe the secret was to spend more time with Sky, not less. He went to Ishibashi and hugged him, and then he hugged Ito and Sato, who couldn't stop chattering.

Ishibashi turned to embrace Sky as well. "Thank you for coming back," he said to her. "I am not surprised to learn that you are partially responsible for the success of the magic. And now we have this great joy." The old man lifted his face up to the sun, letting the warm rays soak into his skin. Tears continued rolling down his cheeks.

Sky took a step back and touched Alex's sleeve, giving him a questioning look.

Alex, still high from Ishibashi's praise, was jolted back to reality when he remembered why they'd come. He glanced at Sky. "Aaron's not here," Alex mouthed, surprised by how disappointed he felt. They both began looking around the island, but they didn't see the former high priest anywhere.

Finally, in a quiet moment, Alex spoke. "Ishibashi, I—I was just wondering if . . ."

"Oh!" Ishibashi said. "Alex-san! I have nearly forgotten in the excitement of this moment. But I think you know already, or you would not have come back so soon. Your brother—"

"Yes?" Alex blurted out. "Is he here? We've been searching for him."

Ishibashi smiled gently. "Yes, he is here."

Alex looked around expectantly. "Is he coming out? Where is he?"

Ito spoke rapidly, and Ishibashi nodded. The eldest scientist left, heading to the shelter.

"What's happening?" Alex asked.

"Aaron . . . is inside," said Ishibashi. "He is . . . he is . . ."

"Is he all right?" demanded Alex. "Is he hurt?"

"In a way," Ishibashi said carefully. "But not in the way you mean."

"Then what?" asked Alex.

Ishibashi looked grim. "He suspected the sudden change in weather was caused by you," he said. "And he did not want to come out. He is . . . afraid. Afraid to see you. Afraid you wish to harm him."

Alex was silent, trying to contemplate the meaning of that. "He *told* you that? He said he was afraid of me? It sounds like a trick."

Sky stepped in and put a hand on Ishibashi's arm. "Will you take us to him?"

Ishibashi's face became worried as Ito returned alone. He spoke to the two in his original tongue. The elder one frowned and shook his head.

Ishibashi turned back to Sky. "I will try," he said.

LISA McMANN

Alex set his jaw. It was just like Aaron to be troublesome and ridiculous. "Ishibashi-san," Alex said, "I have to talk to him right away. It's very important." He stepped around Ishibashi to go in search of his brother.

Sky grabbed Alex's sleeve. "Maybe Aaron needs a few minutes," she said. "We have that much time, at least. I'm sure this is a shock."

"Yes, Alex-san," Ishibashi said nervously. "Perhaps if I talk to him . . ." He seemed about to make another excuse when a voice interrupted the conversation from behind the scientists' ship.

"It's okay, Ishibashi-san. I'm here." Aaron stepped into view. He walked toward the group, shoulders squared, a grim, determined look on his face. "Hello, Alex," he said evenly. He looked at Sky. "Hello."

Alex wasn't sure what sort of greeting he'd expected—a fistfight or some yelling, sure. But a polite, simple greeting? "Hello," he replied.

Sky looked from one brother to the other as they stood eye to eye. And then she turned to Ishibashi, Ito, and Sato. "Ishibashi-san," she said, "how about you three show me your ship so that Alex and Aaron can talk privately. Or maybe I can see what's new in the greenhouse . . . or something?" She smiled brightly and took a step toward the shelter, hoping the scientists would go along with her.

Once Ishibashi felt certain the two enemy brothers weren't going to kill one another, he and the other men took the cue and invited Sky to have a look inside the shelter at the newly restored instruments. They left the twins standing on the shore, both of them wondering what the other was about to say.

# The Talk

Aaron and Alex spoke almost at the same time.

"It's quite shocking to see the sun so bright," said Aaron, while Alex asked, "Were you badly hurt?"

They both laughed uncomfortably, and Aaron invited Alex to speak first.

Alex's twin seemed like a different person to the mage. He wasn't sure what to think, but he was quite suspicious of it. Aaron had never invited Alex to speak first on anything. That wasn't his way at all. Had he lost his memory? But of course he couldn't have, or he wouldn't have remembered Alex.

LISA McMANN

Alex pointed to the scar between Aaron's eyebrows. "Were you hurt quite badly?" he asked again.

"I suppose I was," Aaron said. "I don't remember the first few days, but Ishibashi told me they found me down there." He pointed and began walking slowly toward the spot, with Alex alongside. "Ishibashi said I was in bad shape. I've got this scar too." He lifted his mop of hair to show Alex the longer scar on his forehead.

Alex nodded. "I thought as much," he mumbled.

Aaron seemed puzzled by the statement, but he continued, his voice taking on a bit of his old sharpness for the first time. "They thought I was you."

"Oh, I see," Alex sniped back at him. "So I suppose you faked being me as usual."

Aaron dropped his gaze. "No, actually. I told them who I was. Right away."

"Oh. Well, that's a surprise." Alex frowned. "You seem . . . better now. Physically, I mean," he hastened to add. He hadn't come to a conclusion on the rest of Aaron quite yet.

"I'm fine," Aaron said. He was getting tired of talking about it.

LISA McMANN

"Good," said Alex. "Because I—that is, we—will be taking you back with us. But don't get your hopes up, because you're not going to get to go back to the palace. But in exchange for us rescuing you, we need you to help us."

Aaron stared at him. "I'm not going back," he said. "I don't want to be rescued. I'm staying here."

Alex blinked. "What?"

Aaron looked at the blue skies overhead. "You're going to make sure it rains sometimes, right? Because we're going to need water for the plants, and to drink of course. And I actually like the rain. . . ." He trailed off. "I never knew I'd like rain so much."

"Right," Alex said. "Of course I'll add some rain. But you don't understand. We came here searching for you."

Aaron looked at Alex. "You did?" He seemed genuinely surprised. "I thought you came to change the weather because Mr. Today intended to try again before he—" He cringed.

"How in the world would you know that?"

"Ishibashi told me."

Alex sighed and pressed his fingers to his temples. This was not the way he'd envisioned this conversation. Not in the

LISA McMANN

slightest. "Anyway," he said impatiently, "you're coming with us because we need your help overthrowing Gondoleery."

Aaron's eyes widened. "Did she take over the palace?"

"Yes, and now she's killing everyone. She even sent our sisters to the Ancients Sector."

"What?" Aaron stopped walking.

"They're okay, though." Alex wasn't sure how much he was supposed to tell Aaron. "Somebody saved them."

Aaron had forgotten about his sisters, but at the mention of them, he felt suddenly protective. "So they're back with our parents?"

Alex stared. There was so much Aaron didn't know. He realized now that they couldn't just pluck Aaron off this island and go back to Artimé. They'd need a couple of hours with him first to explain everything. "We should talk," Alex said quietly. "Inside, with Ishibashi, too."

"I'm not leaving the island with you," Aaron warned.

Alex sighed. "We'll discuss that later."


The twins joined Sky and the scientists in the gathering room. Aaron automatically went for the broom when they got inside, but realized nobody had tracked rain in, so he set it down.

Aaron and Sky took turns filling the others in on what had happened since they had seen them last. The deaths of Alex and Aaron's parents seemed to hit Aaron harder than Alex had expected. And the former high priest seemed shocked by the severity of the battle with General Blair and the Quillitary, and the deaths of so many. Aaron, who had known Meghan all his life, appeared genuinely sorry to hear about her death, though he had once seemed so in favor of it. And everyone in the circle was shocked by the ruthless actions of Gondoleery, not to mention her magical powers, including the ice spell she'd cast over the island.

Sky focused on hitting Aaron where she thought it might hurt the most. "Gondoleery has taken away your incentive rations for everyone in Quill," she said to him, "and she's started killing Necessaries randomly in order to practice her magic, so the work in Quill isn't getting done. The livestock isn't being cared for, and the Favored Farm is going downhill fast." She looked imploringly at him. "I know you don't know me. And I don't really know you at all, either. But I came here with Alex to get you because we think you are our only hope in stopping Gondoleery. Every single one of Alex's advisors is counting on us to bring you back so we can rally the people of Quill and get them to help us fight her." She laid her hand on Aaron's forearm. "Will you come with us?"

Alex chimed in. "We'll bring you back here when it's over if that's what you want." He glanced at Ishibashi. "If that's okay, I mean. It's your island, and I wouldn't . . . well. You know."

Ishibashi bowed his head. "Aaron is welcome here," he said evenly. And then he looked at Aaron. "What do you think, Aaron-san?"

Alex's expression flickered at the term of respect Ishibashi used for his brother. Did Ishibashi respect Aaron? How could that be possible? Ishibashi was a very smart man, and Aaron was rude and horrible. Though he hadn't been today . . . so far. Maybe Aaron had changed here somehow. Or maybe he was faking.

"I don't want to leave here," Aaron said quietly. "I don't want to go back to Quill. Things are very different there. You don't understand."

Ishibashi nodded. "You're right. I don't understand Quill, nor would I tolerate it. Nor would I tolerate a dictator like

LISA McMANN

Gondoleery . . . or like the former high priest Aaron Stowe, for that matter." He smiled as Aaron scowled at the floor. "You know that already."

"I'm not that person anymore," Aaron said, almost painfully, finding it dreadful to say such things in front of Alex.

And Alex was flabbergasted over and over again as the conversation wore on. He couldn't believe half of what he was hearing Aaron say. "You must have hit your head really hard," Alex muttered.

"Be quiet, Alex!" Aaron said, his ears burning. He had a dozen insults on the tip of his tongue. They'd come back so fast it was frightening. But he didn't say any of them.

Sky gave Alex a pointed look. "Do you think you're helping by saying that? Seriously."

"Sorry," Alex said. "Look, Aaron, I like the way you're acting now. It's just freaking me out a little."

Ishibashi studied Aaron as Ito and Sato exchanged concerned glances over Aaron's sudden outburst.

"Aaron," Ishibashi said. "This is a decision you must make."

Aaron looked at Ishibashi, his face anguished. Everything

was good now. Aaron felt peaceful for the first time in his life. He was figuring himself out, and finding his inner applecorn, and freeing himself from everyone he knew before. He could be normal here because nobody was around to expect the worst of him, like Alex clearly did. He didn't feel like he had total control over his actions when Alex was around.

Granted, Aaron thought, this must be quite shocking to Alex. And Alex had come to expect certain things of Aaron, so it was reasonable for his brother to react the way he did. But if Aaron went to Artimé, what would they think of him? What would they say to him? Would he be constantly fending off their judgments even while he was trying to help them? How long before that would break him? And going back into Quill to talk to the people . . . He'd be thrust into the same environment that had made him into the person he was before he came here. To be perfectly honest, now that he'd gotten so far removed from it, Aaron didn't like that person any more than the people of Artimé did. Yet that person was still inside him, sometimes clawing to get out.

Ishibashi had told him once that it wouldn't help anything to hate himself. He had to let go of the things he'd done in

LISA McMANN

the past that he wasn't proud of. But now, thinking of going back . . . to *help* the Unwanteds of all people . . . it seemed like it would be impossible.

"I don't know if I can convince the people of Quill to do anything at all," Aaron said quietly. "I wasn't very good at it in the first place."

Once again Alex gawked at his brother, this time admitting he wasn't good at something. Another first. He kept his comments to himself, though.

"You were the only one who got them to do anything," Sky said. "And honestly, you're our only hope. It was Simber's idea to get you, if that makes you feel any better. So you can be sure he will protect you until the job is done. And he's the one who said we'd deliver you back to where we found you. Of course, he said that because he didn't want you in power again, which I'm sure you can understand, but knowing you want to come back here . . . well, that's even better, isn't it?"

Aaron brought his hands to his face and sighed heavily. "So Simber's not going to tear my head off?"

"No," Alex said. "And . . . and I wouldn't let him. Unless you do something stupid, like join sides with Gondoleery."

LISA McMANN

"I'd want to tear my own head off if that happened," Aaron muttered.

Sky and Alex exchanged a glance. "Sooo," ventured Sky, "you'll help us, then?"

Aaron rolled backward on the floor with an exasperated groan. "All right," he said. "I'll do it. And maybe then you can forgive me for Mr. Today."

# And They're Off

Ishibashi, Ito, and Sato exchanged worried looks.

"You have decided to go?" Ishibashi asked Aaron.

Aaron sat up. "Unless you want me to stay," he said, hoping Ishibashi would talk him out of going.

Ishibashi looked deeply into Aaron's eyes. "I want you to go. But I also want you to come back the person you are today. I am too old and tired to start over with you."

Aaron pursed his lips, and then he sucked in a deep breath and let it out. "I don't know if I can do this," he said quietly.

Alex, watching all of this, was beyond confused, but he knew to stay silent.

LISA McMANN

Ishibashi stood up. "Alex and Sky, will you meet me in the greenhouse please? Aaron, why don't you pack up your things? Do you need any food for the journey?"

"Not this time, thank you," Alex said. "We brought plenty." He took Sky's hand and together they walked to the greenhouse.

Aaron watched them go, and then he looked at Ishibashi. "Sky seems really intelligent. And really good at convincing people to do things."

Ishibashi smiled. "She is. And I think she will be a good ally for you."

"She doesn't know the old me," Aaron mused. "I think you're right. That's a relief."

"If you feel like you are losing sight of yourself, seek her out." Ishibashi put his hand on Aaron's back and walked with him to his room. "I'll get you something to carry everything in. We had a small trunk wash up several years ago that we never found a use for."

Aaron nodded. "Now that the hurricane is gone, are you and Ito and Sato going to . . . leave?"

"We have not discussed it, but I don't think so. Our life is here. And we have no boat."

"Oh . . . because . . ."

"We would not leave without telling you, Aaron-san."

Aaron turned his head, struggling with showing the emotion he was feeling. But Ishibashi came up to him, the tears running freely down his cheeks. "I will miss you," he said. "You remind me of someone I knew in another lifetime."

The two embraced, and then Aaron turned to get his clothes and the few things he'd collected in the time he'd lived on the Island of Shipwrecks. The tumbleweeds stood in the corner, untouched. Aaron had never gotten around to needing magic here on the Island of Shipwrecks. He'd hardly even thought about it. He picked up the tumbleweeds and brought them to the pile of firewood, then broke them down into manageable pieces for Sato.

He could hear Ishibashi talking to Alex and Sky in the greenhouse, so he went back into his room to straighten his cot and wait for the trunk and think about how all of this was going to go. Above all, he knew he didn't want to disappoint Ishibashi.

In the greenhouse, Ishibashi was showing Alex and Sky the telescope. "We were never able to properly thank you for bringing our ship on shore, Alex-san," Ishibashi said. "It

LISA McMANN

meant everything to us and has given us great pleasure since we saw you last. Thank you."

"You're welcome," Alex said. "It was nothing. Is there anything else you need?"

"I would never ask for another thing," Ishibashi said. "But if it is not too much trouble . . . perhaps one of the vehicles would be interesting to experiment with."

Alex smiled. "Not too much trouble at all. Now that the storm is gone, you can work on it all day long if you want to."

"That concept is something that will surprise us every day for a long time, I suspect," Ishibashi said with a smile.

Sky tilted her head. "We found out that a ship carrying vehicles like the one that sank here made a stop in Quill many years ago. It had been battered from a storm, and it unloaded some of the vehicles onto Quill to lighten its load, because the ship was damaged."

"Yes," Alex said. "It seems strange that the captain would come back to this hurricane island if he'd escaped it once already. You'd think he would avoid it at all costs."

Ishibashi looked at them. "Perhaps it wasn't the same ship. Or a different storm."

"Maybe," Sky said. "But Ishibashi, where else would there have been a storm?"

Ishibashi's face flickered. "Maybe it went down the waterfall that you told me about."

Sky studied Ishibashi's face. And then she asked, "Ishibashi, we have been to all seven islands, and we have met people from most of them. You said you do not remember which island you came from, but it's not hard to narrow them down. And most of the islands do not have fleets of ships or the ability to create dozens of vehicles. So . . . this might sound crazy, but is there any place that these things could have come from, other than the seven islands in this chain?"

Ishibashi broke the gaze and looked at his hands, clasped before him. "I believe there could be," he said quietly. "Another place where people build ships and vehicles."

"Where things fly through the air with people inside?" prompted Sky.

"Yes," said Ishibashi. "Perhaps."

"Another world?" Sky asked.

Ishibashi closed his eyes, a pained expression on his face. He didn't answer.

Sky backed down. She didn't mean to cause Ishibashi any pain. But these things had to come from somewhere.

"You were saying," Alex said, trying to assuage the situation, "about the telescope . . . ?"

"Yes," Ishibashi said, looking up. "Aaron fixed it for us. He also fixed our microscope, seismometer, centrifuge, and Geiger counter."

"I have no idea what those things are," Alex said, "but that's . . . Actually, it's not all that shocking. I knew he was creative, but in Quill, that word is a bad one."

Ishibashi nodded. "I have learned more about Quill in bits and pieces from Aaron. And I am worried about him. He came here a horrible young man—the evil person you told me about. It took all this time for him to find his true self. I fear it will not be hard for him to go back to his old ways." He hesitated. "I would keep him here if it were not for you and your dire situation. But you must try to see him in a new light now, and . . . and try to nurture that, if you have it in you. This experience will test him greatly."

Alex was still trying to wrap his mind around this new Aaron. He'd expected to have to take Aaron by force or by magic, and then fight to keep him from trying to claim leadership of the palace again. Now he was presented with a stranger who might have changed so much that he wouldn't be able to inspire the Quillens after all. Alex liked the change. He just wasn't sure if it would stick. And right now he had a problem in Artimé that had to be solved. He needed Aaron to be himself—the way he used to be.

Alex shook his head, thinking how crazy it was to say that. He'd wanted Aaron to change for years. And now he had, and Alex needed the old Aaron back. At least for a while.

Ishibashi's gaze fell on the container of iridescent seaweed on the greenhouse floor, and his face took on a pained look. He tapped his forefinger to his lips. "Alex," he said, looking up at the mage.

Alex tore his thoughts away from Aaron. "What is it, Ishibashi-san?"

Ishibashi gazed into the young man's eyes. They were identical to Aaron's, though slightly less troubled. "There's something I think you should know."

The man looked back at the seaweed and swallowed hard. Should he tell Alex about Aaron's potential to live forever? He

LISA McMANN

371 « Island of Graves

felt like he should, yet . . . He imagined the look on Aaron's face if Alex ever revealed the secret to him. Aaron would never trust Ishibashi again.

The old man sighed and shook his head. It would serve no purpose now to tell Alex the secret and could only cause harm. "I'm sorry," he said weakly. "It's not important. I've . . . I've forgotten."

Alex frowned. Ishibashi was acting weird again. "Okay," he said, not sure what else he should say.

The old man smiled and patted Alex's arm. He called out for Ito and Sato to join him, and the two men came over. Ishibashi spoke to the men, and they nodded and smiled.

Alex looked away, thinking about all the strange things he'd seen and heard today. "This . . . well, it's all a bit overwhelming," Alex said apologetically. "I'm going to go outside and enjoy your weather, and then fetch you a vehicle from the bottom of the sea so one day you can drive around your island." He turned toward the door, glad to have something normal to do. "While I'm out there, what sort of rain pattern would you like?"

Ishibashi consulted with Ito and Sato. Ito worked out a formula and handed it to Ishibashi.

"A quarter inch of rain every seven days would be perfect for our needs," Ishibashi said.

"Thunder and lighting or just rain?" asked Alex.

Ishibashi smiled. "Surprise us."

Alex grinned back. "I will. Do you like the temperature? It'll vary a bit, and be cooler at night."

"It's perfect," Ishibashi said. "If only we had more dirt, we could plant things outside. Perhaps we can transplant a few flowers from the greenhouse. . . ." He trailed off, making grand plans for their new island, and then came back to the conversation. "Thank you, Alex."

"Anytime," Alex said. He went outside to deliver on his promises. Ito and Sato followed him, eager to see the vehicle arrive on shore.

Sky stayed inside and walked with Ishibashi to the supply room, where he dug out the little trunk.

"I'm sorry if I asked too many questions earlier," Sky said to him.

Ishibashi put his hand on her shoulder. "I am not angry. They are hard questions to answer. And . . . some things are better left secrets, I suppose."

Sky didn't know what he was getting at, but she respected the man immensely. She would have to find her answers another way. "Thank you for your honesty," she said.

Ishibashi turned toward Aaron's room, hiding the pained look on his face. "I am not a perfect man," he said, which left Sky with even more questions.

When Aaron was fully packed and Alex had finished adjusting the weather and transporting a vehicle to the shore for the scientists to play with, everyone on the island gathered to say their good-byes. Aaron hung back with the scientists, reluctant to go. "I'm worried that you will die while I am gone," he said.

Ishibashi translated, then said, "You must not worry about that. We are too stubborn to die. And . . . perhaps so are you. Come back to us soon. And be careful."

"I will." Aaron cautiously waded out to the boat, having never done that before, and climbed aboard, sitting stiffly and awkwardly at the stern, trunk on his lap, while Alex commanded the boat to head west.

# Heading for Home

C harlie," said Alex, "tell Claire we've got Aaron and we're heading home."

"Don't forget about our stop," Sky said.

"They don't need to know about that," Alex said. "They might try to talk us out of going because it's so dangerous—you know how smothery Florence can be with me. We'll have Charlie send an update once we're done there."

Aaron watched the two interact. "Who's Charlie?" he asked.

Charlie poked his head out of the cabin and waved his two-thumbed hand.

LISA McMANN

Aaron stared. "Where have I seen one of those before?" he asked, shrinking back.

"In your closet in the palace," Sky said. "My, the Island of Shipwrecks really does look so much better when it's not deluged by a storm," she exclaimed. "Look how pretty it is in the late-afternoon sunshine."

Alex and Aaron turned to look.

"But the one in my closet wasn't alive," Aaron said. "And it had an ugly bow on its horn."

"Hey, watch it," Sky warned. "You're talking about Matilda, and the bow is cute. Just like her. She and Charlie can communicate from any distance."

"That thing was from Artimé? I thought it was Haluki's leftover . . . Oh. I get it now. You planted it in the palace. So she wasn't just a dead statue?"

"Nope," Sky said. "She was alive in your closet the whole time, listening in on your conversations and telling Charlie in Artimé what was going on."

Alex cleared his throat. "Do you really have to tell him all of our secrets?"

"Great," Aaron said. "You spied on me all that time."

Sky frowned. "Calm down, Alex. What's the harm in him knowing it now?"

Alex shrugged. "Maybe his little change of personality is just an act."

Sky stood up in the boat and put her hands on her hips. "Alex Stowe, this is exactly what Ishibashi was worried about. And he would not be very proud of you for saying that."

Alex looked over at Sky, and then glanced at his brother. "Ishibashi doesn't know him like I do."

Aaron looked away, letting the breeze hit his face. Maybe Alex was right. He might as well not even try. No one would believe he had changed so drastically. "I think this is a mistake," Aaron said. "I'm afraid I can't help you after all. Can you please turn this thing around and bring me back?"

"See?" Sky said, whapping Alex with a towel. "Quit being stupid."

"It's too late to turn back," Alex said to Aaron. "We're not stopping until we reach the next island."

"I think you two need some more time to talk," Sky said. She went up to the bow and sat down, her hair flying back, and her shirtsleeves billowing in the wind. She turned her back on Alex.

But neither Alex nor Aaron said a word. They rode in silence for hours, no one moving from their spots, until dusk fell. The Island of Shipwrecks was just a dot behind them, and the Island of Graves appeared on the horizon dead ahead. Everybody was hungry, but nobody made a move. Finally Alex got up and walked to the back of the boat. He sat down across from Aaron and leaned forward, putting his face in his hands. And then he looked up.

"Were you seriously sad to hear about our parents?" Alex said.

"Weren't you?" Aaron shot back.

"No, not really," Alex retorted. "They sent me to my death. I didn't have a lot of fond feelings left after that."

Aaron felt himself struggling, already losing his focus on who he was. This was going to be disastrous. He fought to find his center once more, and to turn his lenses around, and said quietly, "I really can't imagine what that must have felt like. At the Purge, I mean."

"It was horrible!" Alex said, balling up his fists. "I wouldn't wish it on my worst enemy. I wouldn't wish it on you."

Aaron was quiet for a moment, and then he said, "You said

you knew somehow that I was hurt. How did you know?"

Alex lifted his head and looked at his brother. "Because my soul broke in half, Aaron."

Aaron stared. "What?" he whispered.

Alex clamped his hand to his ribs. "My soul broke in half and part of it went to you. I can't explain it—that's just how it felt. But it hurt like nothing I have ever felt before. Worse than broken ribs. Worse than a broken heart. I knew you were dying. I could feel it."

Aaron swallowed hard, unable to speak.

Alex gave a sardonic laugh. "And when the pain went away, and I knew you were alive, I even went out to find you on my own. But then I came to my senses and turned back home." He shook his head. "And finally," he said bitterly, "finally I was ready to give up on you forever. I even managed to forget about you for a while. But then this happened."

"Are you saying you didn't want to go along with Simber's plan?" asked Aaron.

"That's what I'm saying." Alex sat up and faced forward, watching the pink-and-orange sky grow dark.

"Oh," said Aaron.

LISA McMANN

"But I did it anyway, because I need to do what's right for my people." Alex had a sharp tone to his voice. "Because I love my people," he went on. "I love them, and I want to do anything I can to save them, and to keep one more friend from dying." He choked back a sob, thinking of Meghan, and knowing Aaron would make fun of him for crying.

But Aaron didn't. He faced forward now too, and looked out over the water. How much pain had he caused his brother over the years? He was ashamed. Having all these feelings, and letting them be free, finally—it was hard.

Sky peeked through the windshield, unable to hear the conversation, but it was clear to her a conversation was happening. The brothers were nearly identical now in posture, though they probably never thought about things like that.

Finally Aaron looked at Alex. And he thought about Ishibashi, and knew what he needed to do.

"Alex," he said.

Alex turned his head. "What?"

"I'm . . . I'm so sorry for killing Mr. Today. It happened very suddenly, and I was surprised, and I just . . . I just reacted to him appearing in that room out of nowhere, ten feet away

LISA McMANN

from me. But I take the blame for killing him, and I was proud about it then . . . but not now. And I'm sorry. I am. I hope you believe me."

Alex groaned heavily and after a moment got to his feet. "I'm having a lot of trouble dealing with all of this right now," he said, more gently than he felt like saying it. But Aaron's new soft-spoken ways were influencing him.

Aaron nodded. He couldn't force Alex to acknowledge the apology. He could only make it.

Alex moved to the captain's seat and dropped into it, somewhat numb. Eventually Sky got up and handed out meals since no one else was doing it.

They ate in strained silence, and before Sky went to bed, she moved to where Alex was sitting. She rested a cool hand on his neck and placed a gentle kiss on the top of his head. He looked up at her, eyes grateful.

Aaron watched them, breaking apart a little inside.

Sky went into the cabin and came out with another blanket. She brought it to Aaron and showed him how to fold down the seat so he could sleep on it.

"Thanks," he said, looking at her.

Sky recognized the pain in his eyes, and for the briefest moment it brought her back to the rooftop of the gray shack with Alex—the expression was almost identical. "You're welcome, Aaron," she said. "Good night." She went up to the bow with her blanket and curled up on the cushions.

Aaron slept restlessly, but Alex stayed awake long into the night, trying to figure out why everything in his life felt like it had been completely turned upside down.

# But First, a Pit Stop

**A**fter daylight, with the Island of Graves looming large, Alex told Aaron that they were stopping to rescue a stranded sailor. By midmorning they had reached their destination. Alex guided the boat to the high side of the island where the gorillas couldn't rush at them, and where the girl would attempt to rappel down the rock using her vine rope. Hopefully it was long enough, for in daylight Alex could see exactly why she couldn't just let go and land in the water—because there were rocks below.

While they floated, Sky explained in more detail to Aaron what was happening and what they were doing here. His eyes

LISA McMANN

grew wide in fear as she described the gorillas, and he looked aghast when she showed him the scratches on her back. Though they no longer hurt, they were still very visible.

"Basically," Alex told him, "just sit quietly and say something if you see any gorillas coming our way, because they can swim, too."

Aaron grew pale. "Okay," he managed to say.

"But," Sky added, "if all goes well, the girl will be able to make it to the ground and we'll get her in the boat and be off without any of them noticing."

"Let's hope for that," Aaron said. "How will she know we're here?"

"She can see us," Sky said. "She knew we'd be coming back this way. She'll sing when she thinks it's safe."

They didn't have to wait long. Soon a girl's voice came floating down, letting the boat's occupants know that she was about to attempt her escape. "Stay where you are," she sang, "but leave if you are attacked."

"Well, that's generous of her," Aaron said dryly.

Alex shook his head. "As if we'd actually leave. We're not going anywhere without her."

Aaron looked at Alex. That was what Ishibashi was talking about—that good trait that Alex had. Alex really cared about people in trouble. No wonder he'd risked so much and tried so hard to find Aaron so he could come to Artimé to help them. Aaron used to hate that about Alex. But now he found himself almost admiring it.

Ten minutes later, a vine came hurtling over the side near the tallest tree. The end of it fell nearly all the way to the rocks.

"Looks like she finished it," Sky said. Another minute later, she pointed. "There she is," she said.

A young woman in tattered clothing began to descend the vine, bare feet pushing against the wall, inching her way down.

"She doesn't have anything to catch her if she falls," Alex said, nervous for her.

"Don't you have any magic you can use to get her here safely?" asked Sky. She gripped the railing. "What about those stickyclips?"

"They're gone," Alex said. "Samheed only made a few. I used them all to try to get Sully."

"Sully?" Aaron asked. "My driver?"

"Yeah—it's a long story. Anyway, they're gone." He went

LISA McMANN

through a mental list of spell options, but nothing he could think of would help in this situation, other than using scatter-clips to stop her from falling in case she should let go of the rope too early.

Just then, Sky's spine tingled. She turned to Alex. "Do you hear that?"

There was a tiny rumbling noise that grew louder. "Oh no," Alex said. "Stampede?"

"I hope they're going down the hill, away from her," whispered Sky. "Aaron, glue your eyes to that spot over there," she instructed, pointing to the beach a quarter of the way around the island. "If you see anything hitting the water, make sure to tell us." She opened the cabin door and signed to Charlie.

His eyes opened wide with fear, and he nodded.

Sky closed the door, leaving the gargoyle inside.

"Look," Alex said softly. "She's going faster."

The girl moved down the vine rope, pushing off against the rock wall and sliding a little bit at a time, but the rumbling soon grew to a monstrous thundering. She began singing, but with the noise, no one could hear what she was saying.

And then, one by one, heads appeared at the top of the

island, looking down on the girl. The gorillas pounded their chests and roared. The biggest one picked up the rope and started pulling the girl back up to them.

"No!" said Sky. "We have to do something!"

The girl started singing at the top of her voice, but with the gorillas roaring, Alex and Sky still couldn't understand her.

Alex grabbed his scatterclips and stood ready to throw them if she started to fall, though once she was pinned to the wall he wasn't sure what they could do. It would only buy them fifteen minutes or so before the spell wore off and she'd continue falling anyway. He didn't want to use them if he didn't have to.

"Do you think the gorillas will hurt her?" he asked. "Didn't she say they let her live there?"

"I don't know," Sky said. "I think so. But she didn't say what they'd do if she tried to escape." She couldn't take her eyes off the scene. The gorillas pulled the vine rope up and up and up, and the girl hung on for dear life. Her singing turned to shouting. Finally Sky understood something the girl was screaming. "Go to the graveyard! By the end of the river!" she was saying over and over.

Finally the gorillas pulled the girl over the edge. A few of them carried her above their heads and out of sight, while most of the other beasts had noticed the boat, and the thundering began once more.

Sky grabbed Alex's arm. "What are we going to do? I heard her say go to the graveyard by the end of the river. We have to go!"

Alex nodded. "Let's draw some of them into the water first to distract them from her." He swung the boat around and headed for the beach, where the words "COME BACK" were still there, though they looked slightly wobbly, like they'd been trampled a time or two.

"Hey!" shouted Sky. "Hey, gorillas! We're over here!"

"What are you doing?" Aaron exclaimed.

"Getting their attention," said Sky.

Aaron stared at Sky like she'd lost her mind.

Some of the gorillas heard her, and they went down the near side of the waterfall, while others moved more slowly over the rocks down the far side toward the flat area, not far from the old ship.

"Um, Alex?" Aaron said. "They're coming now." He tapped on Sky's arm. "Sky? Anybody? They're coming *right now*."

"Got it, thanks," Sky said. "That's what we want."

"Spike," Alex called, "we're luring the gorillas into the water. Keep an eye out, and don't be afraid to spear a few or let them chase you farther out to sea!"

"Yes, the Alex!" said the whale.

"She calls you 'the Alex'?" Aaron muttered under his breath as the gorillas plunged into the water. He grabbed the railing.

"She does," Alex said. He headed out to sea, enraging dozens of gorillas, then swung around and aimed for them, trying to draw even more into the water.

"I'd say we've got close to half of them out here in the water," Sky said. "Whoa, they're fast. Look out!"

Aaron leaped backward as if he'd been zapped. Half a dozen gorillas were suddenly in striking distance, and their saber teeth were enormous.

"Aaron!" Sky called. "Catch." She grabbed the dagger belt and tossed it to Aaron, then took the sword for herself. Stationed at the side of the boat, she began to warm up her swing whenever any gorilla got a little too close.

"I'm going to draw them out a little farther, and then head around to the ship!" Alex shouted.

"We'll still have half of them to deal with on land!" Sky shouted back. "We can't fight them all!"

"But if she told us to go to the graveyard by the river, I think we should get over there!" Alex said, steering and training his eyes on the ones approaching in the water. "Besides, the gorillas on that side of the river are moving very slowly down the mountain. We'll have time to figure something out. I hope."

Aaron, seeing a gorilla's arm stretching toward the side of the boat, yelled and stabbed at it with his dagger. The gorilla roared and retreated.

"Nice one, Aaron!" Sky said.

Aaron was too petrified to respond. He'd never actually used a weapon before.

Alex gave the boat a little burst of speed to get them out of reach. "I'm turning around now," he said, pulling away from the gorillas. "Spike, distract them so it'll take them a while to swim back to shore. Aaron, can you swim?"

"No," said Aaron, his voice filled with terror. "I've barely touched the water—that I can remember anyway."

"I figured as much," Alex said. "Don't fall out." He guided

LISA McMANN

the boat at top speed around to the low side of the island. "Hey, Charlie! I need you!"

Charlie peeked from behind the cabin door, and then at Alex's urging, came out the rest of the way.

Alex lifted him up to stand on the captain's chair and showed him where to hang on so he'd be safe. "I'm going to pull in next to the shipwreck," Alex said, "right up close behind it so hopefully the gorillas can't see us. Sky, Aaron, and I are going to go on shore. If you see any gorillas coming anywhere near our boat and we're not running like heck in front of them, I need you to save our boat and get away from this island. Okay? Just use this lever to go fast, and use this wheel to steer. I'll have you facing the right way and everything. You got it?"

Charlie nodded. He didn't seem scared at all.

"Give it a try," Alex said. "Drive around for a minute."

Charlie did exactly what Alex told him to do, and the boat zoomed toward the shore.

"Good. You're about as speedy as Lani, which is a good thing today," said Alex. "If you have trouble, Spike will be here soon to help you." He guided the boat all the way up to the shore, turned it around for a fast getaway, and stopped it in the shadow of the old beached ship.

"Sky, Aaron, ready? Come on," Alex said, shoving a few more spells into his pockets, not that they had worked very well on these beasts in the past.

Aaron looked at his dagger. "Is this my only protection?" he asked.

"I'm not giving you any spell components, if that's what you're asking," Alex said.

"What—you think I'd use them on you or something?"

"I don't know if you would at this point," said Alex. "Stay in the boat if you don't want to help."

"Aw, come on," Aaron muttered.

Alex ignored him. He hopped out of the boat onto the rocks and ran around the old ship, heading for the flat graveyard area. Sky followed, carrying her sword. And a moment later Aaron hopped out with his dagger and went after the other two.

They ran straight to the flat area near the mouth of the river, watching right and left carefully, but no gorillas were on this part of the island. Though they were coming this way, based on the waving grass and brush on the mountain.

"Wow," Sky said, bending down and pushing some grass aside. "Look at all these graves."

Alex and Aaron looked around. Dozens of mounds of dirt peppered the area, overgrown with grass and weeds. Each mound had a large rock marker at one end. There were words on the rocks, identifying the person buried there. Alex knelt down next to one and pushed the overgrowth aside. "'Marietta Plum, beloved performer and friend, d nov one, one nine one three,'" he read. He looked at another. "'William Strange, animal trainer, d feb two five, one nine one four,'" he said. "And look—'Figar Osari, ringmaster, d jan one three, one nine one four.' I wonder what a ringmaster is."

"I don't know. Some sort of lord of the rings, I suppose." Sky moved on to read more, while Aaron stood watch, too scared to look anywhere but in the direction of the thundering gorillas. How he wished he had Panther here to protect him now!

"'Imelda Fanzini,'" read Sky, "'primate trainer, d apper one, one nine one four.'"

"Why are we waiting here, actually?" Aaron asked nervously.

Sky looked up. "We're not sure, but the sailor seemed to

know what she was talking about. I wonder why this is where she wants us to wait."

"She probably has a reason after managing to survive here so long," Alex said. He moved to read another gravestone. "'Madame Fiona,'" he said. "'Mother to us all.'" He looked up. "I wonder what the story is here. It's wild."

"What do the numbers mean?" asked Sky.

"I'm not exactly sure," Alex said, "but I've seen numbers like that in some of the books we have in the library."

The thundering grew louder. Aaron shifted anxiously, looking all around. "Do you see the girl anywhere?"

Sky and Alex strained to look as well. Then Sky pointed up. "Look. She's jumping into the waterfall," Sky said in awe. "She's hanging on to a hunk of . . . something! See?" Sky watched as the girl free-fell a sickening distance. She landed at the bottom and disappeared in a big splash.

"Oh dear." Sky stood on her tiptoes and watched. "I hope she survived that," she murmured. A moment later, she spotted the girl again. "There she is! She's coming this way down the river."

"Unbelievable," Alex said, eyes landing on the girl. She

floated on a white board, paddling with all her might. Not far behind her, the gorillas were making their way down the rocky mountainside in pursuit.

"How did she get away from them at the top of the mountain?" Aaron wondered, his anxiety temporarily replaced by amazement.

"No idea," murmured Sky.

The gorillas began to gain on the girl now that they were reaching the bottom of the hill.

Alex watched the progress carefully, and once it became clear that the girl was planning to come straight down the river to them, he directed the other two. "Aaron, figure out how many gorillas we're dealing with. Sky, set yourself up halfway between the river and the shipwreck, there, and once we get the girl out of the river, Aaron'll run her behind you, so you can fend off the gorillas. Shout if you see anything coming from the other side of the river, but I'm pretty sure Spike is keeping most of those beasts busy in the sea." He ran forward several yards. "I'm going to try to slow them down," he called, and pointed at the spot of land next to the bank, concentrating.

"Glass," he whispered. As a sheet of glass appeared,

perpendicular to the river, he moved to the spot next to it and uttered the spell again. As each new sheet of glass appeared, Alex calmly put up another one next to it, making a giant glass shield that stretched from the bank of the river to the edge of the island. When the entire line was finished, he started a second row to reinforce the first line, going a little slower this time because the intensity of the concentration was beginning to sap his strength.

"I count thirteen gorillas chasing the girl," Aaron called. He gripped his dagger, his face awash in sweat and fear. "Will that glass stop them, Alex?"

"Maybe for a minute," Alex said. "It'll be a shock, anyway, and might distract them long enough for us to get the girl to our boat." He looked at his brother. "Come with me. We're going to stand next to the river, here. She needs to paddle beyond the glass barrier and then we'll pull her out, climb the bank, and make a run for our boat. Okay?"

"Okay," Aaron said. He felt sick to his stomach.

Alex pointed. "Go to the river's edge now and wave at her. Make sure she sees you and knows to come all the way down the river to you."

Aaron nodded, unable to speak, but he ran to the edge of the river and began motioning to the girl.

"Sky, stand by to fight," Alex called. "You've got the most useful weapon of all of us." He shook out his hand, wiped the sweat from his forehead, and planted a few more glass spells for a third, scattered layer.

The ground began to shake as the gorillas charged toward them, and the girl was getting nearer. With no time left for more glass barriers, Alex ran to join his brother. He climbed down the bank and stood in front of Aaron, ready to lend a hand to the girl, who was still paddling mightily.

Alex and Aaron waved their arms when the girl grew close. She stared straight ahead, fully concentrating, nodding her head only to acknowledge that she saw them. "Ten seconds," Alex called softly to Sky, not wanting to further enrage the gorillas, who would be plenty angry in about fifteen seconds when they hit the first line of glass shields.

"Five," he called, and then, as the girl came at them, she flashed a wide grin.

"Catch my board!" she shouted. Aaron and Alex leaned out over the water as she flipped off the board and tossed it up.

Alex caught it, and Aaron grabbed the girl's hand and pulled her out of the water.

Breathing hard, she scrambled up the bank with Aaron. Alex was right behind, using the girl's board as a shield between her and the gorillas. And then they ran.

The first line of gorillas hit the glass shields at full speed with an earsplitting crash, sending shards exploding to the sky and raining down everywhere. The gorillas stumbled, surprised, but continued on. They hit the second line of glass, and it crumbled too. Some of the gorillas went down. But the first two furious gorillas that didn't have a third glass shield in front of them were completely through the barrier. And they weren't stopping. The glass had barely slowed them down.

# The Rescue

To the ship!" the girl yelled, her voice hoarse. "Get to the old ship! They won't touch us there!"

Aaron pulled the exhausted girl along, his dagger raised, while Alex began flinging as many more glass spells and heart attack spells as he could to try to slow the gorillas down. Sky fearlessly ran toward the first gorilla, which was trying to head off Aaron and the girl. Some smaller beasts that seemed more affected by the glass walls moved sideways along them to the sea and jumped in to swim around them. Three of them caught sight of the magic boat and roared, then headed toward it.

From the boat, Charlie jumped up and down on the seat,

LISA McMANN

trying to get a better view. The gorillas advanced. "Go, Charlie!" Alex yelled. "Get out of here!"

The statue hesitated, then pushed the lever and tore out to sea.

Aaron nearly screeched himself at the sight of their ride leaving. He was most certainly going to die at any moment. He was sure of it.

Sky gripped her sword and swung with all her might, slamming it into the first advancing gorilla. It staggered and tripped, knocking over the second. Sky looked over her shoulder. "Run!" she screamed. Aaron and the girl sprinted past, a gorilla right behind them. Alex slammed the floating board into it. The beast rose to its full height and roared as Alex jabbed the pointed end of the white board into its gut, then sprinted away. Furious, it dropped down and loped after him.

"Get in the ship!" the girl cried to Aaron. "See the ladder? Now!"

"I see it," Aaron panted. "Stop screaming in my ear." He pulled the exhausted girl after him, and then picked her up and ran when she couldn't seem to get her legs to move fast enough anymore.

The remaining gorillas had scattered around the area, circling their victims. Sky darted toward the ship as the beasts in the sea turned away from their chase and caught sight of her.

Aaron and the girl reached the ship with a big silverback on their tail, and as Aaron hoisted the girl up and she climbed aboard, Aaron struck out at the gorilla with his dagger, catching it in the chest.

"Get up here!" the girl screeched.

The beast grabbed at Aaron. Aaron yelled and struck again. He started his climb up the ladder. Another gorilla reached them, grabbed hold of Aaron's leg, and began pulling. Aaron flailed, swinging wildly from the rung, and managed to land a backward kick right in the gorilla's nose. The creature loosened its grip and Aaron pulled out of it, then scrambled the rest of the way up, certain the gorilla would follow right behind.

But it didn't. It skittered away from the ladder with a hooting sound. From somewhere on the ship, the girl began making a racket that sounded like metal crashing against metal. Immediately the other gorillas backed off and began hooting warnings to their companions.

Sky, who was trapped by three gorillas that surrounded her

LISA McMANN

and kept her from getting to the ship, swung her sword wildly, connecting at every chance she could get. Her shoulders ached and her hands were numb, but she kept swinging, inching toward the ship.

Alex used the board as a shield and threw every spell imaginable, and finally discovered that the blinding highlighter was the only spell that actually had a full effect on the creatures. He quickly blinded the gorillas surrounding him, making them roar and wave their arms. Alex slipped between two and blasted the ones who were attacking Sky. One after another they grabbed their eyes in pain and whirled around, knocking into Sky and sending her sprawling. Alex ran to help her up, and the two made a mad dash between blinded, howling gorillas, all the way to the ship.

Aaron, bleeding from his shredded leg, reached down from above to grab the girl's board and help them as they scrambled up the ladder, while the girl continued to make the clanging noise below.

Alex shoved the board aside, and he and Sky flopped on the deck of the old beast of a ship, sweating and breathless, muscles quivering. As soon as they could manage it, they crawled away from the ladder, making the floor creak and a few rotten ship boards crack and fall away. The three lay heaving and bleeding, but alive, as half the gorillas still wandered about temporarily blinded, and others cowered several yards from the ship, distressed about getting too close to it.

"Where's the girl?" Alex asked when he had his breath back.

"She's down there making that noise," Aaron said. He took off his shirt and wrapped it around his leg, trying to stop the bleeding.

A moment later the noise stopped, and soon the girl appeared on a ladder, coming up through an opening in the deck. "Welp," she said, wiping her hands on her pants and glancing out over the sea, "that ought to keep them quiet. They'll go away eventually, and then it'll be safe for your boat to return." She stood there, her clothes still dripping and her light brown hair a knotted mess with sticks and leaves stuck in it. She was a little shorter than Sky. Her soggy, tattered shirt drooped off one shoulder, revealing a patch of fair skin. The rest of her was deeply tanned. She was thin—a little too thin, like she hadn't been eating normally—but muscular.

Alex sat up. "How is it they won't come on the ship?" he asked. "You saved us with this trick."

LISA McMANN

The girl shrugged. "It's the cages down below," she said. She had a strange accent. "I discovered it by accident pretty early on. They don't like the sound of the clanging, and they won't try to get inside the ship. I don't know if any of them are the actual animals that were caged on this ship or if they just learned from their ancestors to fear it, but it's one of only a few safe places on the island."

"Wow, that's fascinating," Alex said. He stood up and held out his hand to her. "I'm Alex," he said. "This is my brother, Aaron. Twins, if you can't tell. And this is Sky. We're from Quill and Artimé, two islands to the west."

The girl smiled, and instead of shaking his hand, she hugged him. Her eyes shone. "I can't believe this nightmare is almost over," she said. "Thank you so much for coming back for me."

"Of course," Alex said, hugging her back.

She pulled away and looked up at him. "My name is Kaylee Jones. I'm from America. I'm not sure where that is from here, but I know it's pretty far."

"America?" Sky asked. "Is that an island?"

Kaylee laughed. "Funny! No. You know, the United States?"

Sky shook her head. "I've never heard of that." She looked

at Alex. "Maybe it's that big piece of land on Lani's map."

Alex took note of the fading smile on Kaylee's face. "Maybe," he said to Sky.

Kaylee searched the faces before her. "You're not joking," she murmured.

"No," Sky said. "We've traveled all around the world and haven't ever heard of it." She was tempted to ask the girl about other worlds, like she'd asked Ishibashi, but the girl was in rough shape, and Sky thought it would be better to wait in case it upset her like it did the scientist. Instead, she offered a sympathetic smile. "I'm sorry."

Kaylee pressed her lips together. "No, it's okay. I . . . I had a feeling about this. Ishibashi tried to tell me. And then there's the ship's log . . . and everything that happened with that." She turned to look out over the water again and let out a small despairing sigh. It almost sounded like she might be crying.

Sky glanced sidelong at Alex, who shrugged. He glanced at the gorillas, most of which had begun grazing in the long grass nearby.

Alex turned and walked carefully over the rotting boards to the sea side of the deck, wondering where the white boat was. It wasn't hard to spot. It sat safely a few hundred yards offshore. He waved to Charlie, though he couldn't actually see the statue from that distance, and then he saw Spike's faux diamond–covered spike coming up alongside the back end of the old ship, which was in the water.

"I'll take you whenever you're ready, the Alex," Spike said when she sensed his presence. "Is everyone okay? Did you find the singing girl?"

"Yes, we've got her," said Alex. "You did good work, Spike—you kept dozens of gorillas from coming after us. We're waiting for them to get bored and leave."

Alex turned to the others. "Okay, people," he called softly. "Our ride is here, so as soon as the gorillas wander off, we need to head for home." He looked at his brother, who was still nursing the deep scratches on his legs. "Hey, Aaron," he said. "Tonight you get to learn how to swim."

# Circus Tales

S o you found Aaron, then," Kaylee said, turning back
after her momentary grief. "That's good."

"Oh yes," Alex said. "We did. Thank you."

Kaylee nodded, subdued, and clearly struggling
internally. None of the others knew quite what to do for her,
so they waited respectfully for her to gather her wits.

After a moment Kaylee took a deep breath, let it out, and
said, "Okay. We need to stay out of sight from the gorillas for
a while. Stay quiet so they forget about us. By evening they'll
head to the top of the mountain, where they sleep. Once

they're far enough away, they won't come after us when we jump into the water."

Alex relayed the plan to Spike. "Go to the boat and tell Charlie what's happening," he said. "Then ask him to tell Matilda that we stopped here to rescue a castaway, and everybody's safe, and we'll be on our way again by nightfall."

Spike swam out to the boat, and Alex returned to the group.

"I want to grab a few things from the cabin below before it gets dark," Kaylee whispered. "This ship is super old, but there are three logbooks. I've only had a chance to read the first one. It was written by the cabin boy, like, a hundred years ago."

Sky looked up. "Wow. Can I come?"

"Sure," Kaylee said. "Stay quiet. One on the ladder at a time—this thing is falling apart."

The two girls descended the ladder, which was missing a few rungs, to the deck below. Toward the stern, several tiny, narrow cabins lined the hallway. But Kaylee turned forward and went down a few stairs into a larger square cabin. There was a small bar with broken bottles everywhere, and a rickety old desk that was bolted to the floor. Kaylee headed straight

LISA McMANN

for the desk. She tugged open a warped drawer and pulled out three yellowed volumes. On each book cover were the words "Ship's Log."

Kaylee held them out to Sky. "See? I'll bet the whole story of this shipwreck and the people and gorillas on board, and maybe even something about the graves, is in here." Her eyes shone with excitement. "So far, in reading the first book, I've discovered that this whole tribe of saber-toothed gorillas began with just four animals about a hundred years ago. There's at least seventy of them now on the island—I've counted them enough times."

"Incredible," Sky said, carefully opening one of the log-books and looking at the strange handwriting on the fragile pages.

While Sky looked through it, Kaylee moved around the cabin as if she were at least a little familiar with it, pulling out papers and unpinning a giant map from the wall, which she folded up. "Do you want to see the cages?" asked Kaylee.

Sky nodded and tucked the books under her arm. Kaylee led her out of the cabin and down another level, where cages lined both sides of the ship. A few portholes up high on the

LISA McMANN

409 « Island of Graves

walls let light in. Some of the glass was broken or completely missing. Standing on her tiptoes, Sky could see the gorillas not far away.

They heard a slight noise behind them and saw Alex and Aaron coming down the ladder. "We were curious," Alex whispered.

The two stood side by side, looking remarkably the same except for their clothes.

"Which one is which again?" Kaylee asked. "Oh wait— Alex has the robe."

"Yes, and Aaron has the scar," Sky said. She grinned at the boys. "I guess people will be able to tell you apart now, at least until the scar fades."

Aaron smirked. "Don't go trying to imitate my scar now," he said to Alex.

Alex grinned reluctantly. "I won't." He was actually impressed with Aaron's willingness to fight the gorillas even though he'd clearly been scared to death. With a little training, Aaron might become a decent fighter. Though there was still something about Aaron that worried him. What if his evil twin was so sneaky that he really was faking this new alignment with Alex and Sky? But then again, what kind of idiot would willingly risk fighting gorillas if he were faking it? Aaron could have stayed in the boat, but he chose to help. He was either insane or truly sincere with his new attitude. Alex was starting to believe that Aaron might have actually changed for real.

"Obviously these are the cages," Kaylee said, keeping her voice low. "According to the logbook, this was some sort of animal transporter bound for a circus in the US when it got lost in a storm. Saber-toothed gorillas," she said, shaking her head. "Can you imagine that scene at the circus? What an attraction that would have been."

The three looked puzzled, and no one dared admit they had no idea what a circus was, or the US for that matter. They understood storms, though.

"It's all documented, you see," Sky told the boys, holding up the logbooks. She shivered. "It's creepy down here. All these creaking cages in the dark underbelly. No wonder the gorillas won't come near it."

Kaylee nodded expertly. "The original animals must have passed down the fear of this ship and the cages to their offspring after having been locked up in them the whole voyage," she said bookishly. "It couldn't have been a good ride through the storm."

Their new companion sounded so much like Lani that Sky and Alex just looked at each other and laughed. "You sound like one of our best friends," Alex explained, not wanting Kaylee to think they were laughing at her. "You'll get along just fine."

"Yeah?" Kaylee smiled sadly. "So . . . what happens now? I guess I go to your island with you, right?"

"That's pretty much the only option," Aaron said. "For now, at least."

"Anywhere but here," Kaylee said. "What's your island like? And how on earth did you do that thing with the glass walls? That was really freaky." She began to perk up. "Also, I don't know if you know this, but you have a talking whale."

Alex laughed, forgetting to be quiet, then covered his mouth. "Sorry," he whispered.

Kaylee hopped to see out the porthole, then pointed to the ladder. "Let's go back up," she whispered.

One at a time they climbed the ladder up two levels, staying low on the top deck so they would remain hidden from the gorillas. They kept their voices quiet.

Alex explained to Kaylee that Artimé was a magical land. He told her that he placed the glass shields on the ground with magic, and showed her a couple of little spells, like tapping his notebook to produce a pencil. She didn't believe it at first, but then Alex used the preserve spell on the ship's logs, and she marveled as the spell seeped over each page. Once the spell was complete, the brittle pages were flexible and protected from further damage.

"They're waterproof now too," said Alex, "so when we jump into the water, they'll be fine."

"That's fantastic," Kaylee said, turning the books over and admiring them. She glanced over her shoulder to check the sun's location, but it was hidden behind the mountainous side of the island. "They should start moving upland fairly soon. I'll let you know when it's safe to jump."

Aaron wore a perplexed look. "Why did you live up there in the tree at the top of the mountain when you could've lived here on this ship?" Aaron asked. "I mean, it's falling apart, but you'd be safe if you repaired it. And we could have picked you up from here in the first place instead of messing with the vine and the cliff."

"Two very important reasons," Kaylee said. She stretched out on her back and grimaced as her spine popped. "Oof," she said. "That was from the ride down the waterfall. My body has taken a beating on this island, let me tell ya." She twisted her back until she was satisfied.

"Anyway," she continued, "why didn't I just live on this boat? One, this ship is too far away from the river. I needed to be able to get water safely. Plus the water is a lot cleaner up at the top because the gorillas, um, spend time in it down at this end, if you know what I mean. And two, food. There's nothing but grass and weeds down here, and a herd of wild pigs, but I haven't been able to catch them and I don't have any way of cooking them. I'm sort of a vegetarian now, I guess," she said thoughtfully.

The others didn't know what the term meant, but they could guess, and they didn't want to interrupt.

Kaylee looked at her deteriorating clothing and scars all over her arms and legs from various cuts, scratches, and bug bites. "It's been rough," she said softly. "Really rough. I . . . For a while there I started to feel myself slipping away. Losing my mind, I mean." She ran her hand over her arm, wiping away a bit of caked mud from the underside.

Aaron watched her. "How did you manage to hold on?" he asked in a quiet voice.

"I'm used to being alone," Kaylee said. "I've trained for it. And I told myself every morning that I just had to get through one day, and surely someone would come tomorrow. . . ." She swallowed hard. "Making the vine rope helped. It gave me something to work for."

Aaron felt a wave of emotion sweep through him, though he wasn't sure why. All he knew was that he understood being alone.

"Getting back to my story," Kaylee continued, "I lived in this ship for a couple of days when my sailboat first sank out there, and then when I got deliriously thirsty, I made a run for the river. While I was there, the gorillas caught sight of some weird creature floating off the north shore—"

"Ah yes, I bet that was Pan, the coiled water dragon," Sky said.

"She rules the sea," added Alex.

Aaron looked mystified.

"Okaaay," Kaylee went on. "And I ran up there to see if I could find food. I found a lot of it, actually. Bird eggs, wild raspberries, mushrooms, and cattails by the mouth of the waterfall.

LISA McMANN

When the gorillas came back, I got cornered, so I climbed to the top of the tallest tree. They tried to get me, and for whatever reason, I started singing, because I couldn't think of anything else to do to save myself. And they liked it. They made a pet out of me."

"A pet," Alex repeated. "And they let you live up in your little cage at the top of the tree."

"Exactly. They didn't hurt me. They got a little aggressive when they wanted me to sing, so I learned quickly to start doing that before any tree shaking began."

"And you said they sleep up there?" Sky asked.

"Most of them. All night, a few always right at the foot of the tree. After the first few days, whenever the coast was clear, I got down for a bit to get food and water. I also started to make a vine hammock so I could sleep in the tree without stressing about falling out. For the first few days I figured I was going to die at any moment."

"I've felt like that before on a raft in the sea," Sky murmured. "It's a terrible feeling."

"Yes," Kaylee said. "But I got the hang of it eventually. Pardon the pun, ha-ha."

Aaron didn't know what a pun was, but the other two laughed.

"I started making the rope several months ago once I realized I had to do something to keep my sanity, and the cliff offered me the best chance of escape. I can see all the way around the island from up there in case a ship came by. I was really hoping the rope thing would work, but the stinking gorillas are wicked smart and they foiled it. They basically just pulled me up and put me back in my tree cage, which I knew they would do. They heard you out by the beach—that was smart, by the way, to draw them out to sea. Can you believe it? Gorillas are not usually swimmers, but these guys are *not* normal. Anyway, once you came on land, they saw you and took off to eat you."

She took a breath. "Whew. So plan B was in place. I never wanted to do what we ended up doing today, let me tell you, but there was no other choice." She rubbed her backside. "My board is not made for waterfalls."

Alex nodded toward it on the deck nearby. "Is that part of your sailboat?"

"Nope," said Kaylee. "The sailboat sank, but I grabbed this

as we were taking on water. It's a surfboard. Haven't you ever seen one?"

Alex shook his head. "It just floats, like a raft?"

"Yes," said Kaylee. "You ride on it. I usually stand up when I'm on an ocean with big waves, but that method doesn't work very well on a river, so after I jumped I had to lie down and paddle it."

There were so many unfamiliar things Kaylee was telling them, and Alex and Sky had tons of questions about where the girl came from, but the gorillas were beginning to move. Kaylee held a finger to her lips and pointed.

They all watched in silence for about twenty minutes as the gorillas lumbered away and began climbing the mountain.

"Stay quiet now," Kaylee warned. "We can continue this conversation once we make it to the boat."

# Back to Artimé

Once most of the gorillas had retreated and were on their way up the mountain, Sky brought Kaylee to the sea-side end of the ship and introduced Spike. As soon as Kaylee got used to the fact that Spike was a talking magical creature, she had no qualms about jumping twenty feet into the ocean below and riding on Spike's back to the boat.

"Stay quiet," Kaylee warned the others before she jumped. "Any noise will bring the gorillas thundering back here."

Sky nodded. She counted down, and she and Kaylee jumped first so Aaron could see what was expected of him. He had

LISA McMANN

so little experience with the sea that his fears were enormous, especially after nearly drowning. He didn't complain or try to get out of it, though. He was just more quiet than usual.

Alex knew Aaron was scared to death, and he actually felt a little sorry for his brother. They stood at the railing and watched the girls jump, and looked on as Spike swam under them and popped them out of the water so they were sitting on her back. Spike immediately sped out to the boat, which the boys could barely make out in the moonlight, and they saw the girls climbing on board.

Aaron's hands were clammy by the time Spike returned, and his legs shook as the brothers climbed over the railing and hung on.

"I won't let you drown," Alex said quietly.

"I wouldn't blame you if you did," Aaron said. "But I appreciate it."

Alex took his brother's arm. "We'll jump together on three," he said. "Take a deep breath as I'm counting and hold your nose. It'll be over before you know it."

Aaron swallowed hard and nodded. He was panting from fear, which made it hard to take a deep breath, but as Alex counted to three, he did the best he could. He closed his eyes and plugged his nose, and soon his stomach was flipping and he was screaming and falling and then he was plunging underwater, not stopping. His nose came unplugged and he panicked, his arms and legs flailing, and then he felt Alex pulling him up. From below, he felt the huge back of the whale beneath him, lifting him above the water. He choked and coughed, flailing face-first on the whale's back and trying to hold on to her smooth skin for dear life.

"You did it," Alex said from behind him. He climbed up next to Aaron and put his hand on Aaron's back. "You're not going to fall off. It's a whale. It's huge. Open your eyes and look."

Aaron opened his eyes and saw the expanse of whale on which he was riding. He coughed a bit more and then cautiously pushed himself up to sitting. Soon the whale was moving, and before long they were coming up alongside the white boat.

"That wasn't so bad," Aaron admitted.

Sky and Kaylee reached out to help him climb into the boat.

"Glad we girls went first," Kaylee said. "That impressive scream of yours woke some gorillas, I'm sure. Listen."

They heard the now-familiar rumble.

"It wasn't intentional," Aaron said.

Kaylee looked askance at him. "You're awfully serious," she said.

"Oh, he's from Quill," Alex said, toweling himself off and preparing to direct them home. "You'll understand eventually."

"Is that how you Unwanteds talk about us?" Aaron asked.

"Wow, unwanteds?" Kaylee said. "That's not very nice."

Alex held up a hand. "It's okay. It's not what you think. Well, I mean, it is, but we Unwanteds wear our title like a badge of honor because we were sent to our deaths and survived."

"Whoa," Kaylee said. "So clearly I'm not the only one with a near-death experience. This is probably a ho-hum sort of day for you. That explains a lot, actually."

"Ho-hum?" Sky asked.

"Casual," Kaylee said. "Ordinary."

Sky nodded. "Sadly, risking our lives has become a little too ordinary lately."

Kaylee looked nervous. "Maybe I'm better off with the gorillas after all," she said.

"Don't worry," said Sky. "We'll keep you safe in the mansion."

"Is there soap?"

"Oh yes," Sky said. "You're in for a treat."

Alex commanded the boat to go to Artimé with no further stops, and they set off around the south side of the island. Kaylee grew silent and watched it go by as they moved past the come-back sign and the rise of land and the tree at the top where she had lived for so long. "I can't believe I'm finally out of there. I was really starting to think I'd never . . . make it. . . ." Kaylee pressed her hand over her eyes and choked back a sob. "Ugh. Sorry," she said. "I am just all over the place emotional about this—seeing the island from the water again. Knowing I'm safe."

Alex gave her a friendly one-arm side hug. "Nobody here is going to make fun of you for crying—we're all pretty good at it." He gave Aaron a warning glance, but Aaron's gaze was elsewhere.

With the boat running itself and Spike keeping watch at their side, Alex ducked into the little cabin to get some food. He came out with his hands full and with Charlie at his side.

"Charlie," he said, "you did a great job saving yourself and the boat from the gorillas. Did you meet Kaylee?"

The gargoyle nodded, and his gray stone cheeks blushed pink. He ducked behind Alex's leg.

Alex grinned. "Any news from home?"

The gargoyle signed for a moment while Alex and Sky looked on.

"Storm?" Alex guessed, looking at Sky.

"Yep. The dust squalls in Quill are getting stronger," Sky said.

"Okay," Alex said. He looked at Charlie. "Tell Matilda to let Claire know that we should be home by tomorrow night."

Charlie gave three thumbs up and disappeared.

"You all continue to surprise me," Kaylee said. "A living gargoyle. What else have you got?"

"Just wait," Aaron warned. "The scary ones are back on their island."

"They're not scary if you're on Artimé's side," Sky pointed out.

"Which I guess I am, now," Aaron said. He shook his head and took the food Alex offered him. "Thanks," he said.

"And that still surprises me," Alex muttered. He'd rarely heard the word "thanks" from his brother's lips their entire childhood, and now he'd said it multiple times in the past two days. Ishibashi really did *something* to him, that was for sure. He started to wonder why he'd even liked Aaron as a child, because Aaron certainly hadn't treated Alex very nicely. Though there had been times when they were close, especially at night in their bedroom, talking about things they could never talk about in front of anyone. . . .

"Have a seat, Alex," Sky said gently.

Alex startled back to reality and realized he was standing in the middle of the boat holding his dinner. He laughed and sat down.

"Forgive me for inhaling this delicious food," Kaylee said, "but I can't seem to get enough of it. I have no idea how you kept this hot on the boat, but I want whatever you've got for my next journey."

"It's magical," Alex said. "And there's more food if you'd like it."

"I would," said Kaylee. She fished a rectangular device from her pocket. Its face was glass and cracked quite badly. She held

425 « Island of Graves

LISA McMANN

it up. "This is a real long shot, but do you happen to have a cell phone charger?"

The three just looked at her.

Kaylee's face fell. She sighed and put the device back into her pocket. "It's waterlogged anyway." She picked up her food again.

When everyone had finished eating, Kaylee attempted to work through her hair with Sky's brush, but found that after so long without using one, there was no hope. "I'm going to have to chop it off," she said. She didn't seem upset about it.

"I can help with that," Alex said. He produced a magical scissors that he used for his own hair whenever it got too out of control and handed it to her. Kaylee studied it for a moment, then handed it back. "Will you do the honors?"

Alex shrugged. "Sure." He took a good look at where the knots in her hair began, then started cutting. Thirty minutes later, Kaylee was peering into a mirror in the cabin, running her fingers through her new short bob and exclaiming with delight. "You could open up a shop!" she said. "How are you so good at this?"

"It's art," Alex said. "That's what I do."

Finally, when the activity settled, Alex asked Kaylee one of the questions he'd been wondering since they'd first discovered she was the same girl Ishibashi had spoken of.

"So we know you crashed on the Island of Shipwrecks and spent a few days there, and then you actually made it out through the hurricane, right? Only you ended up sinking off the shore of the Island of Graves. What happened?"

Kaylee, now wearing one of Sky's extra sets of clothes and snuggling under a blanket, shook her head and laughed. "I don't know why I'm laughing," she said. "It wasn't funny then, and it really isn't now, either, but I guess I can either laugh or cry about it, and I've cried enough.

"I managed to make it off Ishibashi's island during the hour of calm by trying to go with the wind instead of against it, then head over the big waves straight on. Which worked, actually, but in the process I hit some rocks. They tore up the sailboat, and it sprang a slow leak that I couldn't fix. After sailing slowly for a couple of days without sleep so I could keep bailing, I knew my only chance was to try to make it to the nearest island, which just happened to be the Island of Graves. So I pushed myself as hard as I could to get there. In the end,

I couldn't keep up with the leak, so I gave up and untied my surfboard. When the sailboat began to sink, I glided off on the board and watched my boat go down. It was . . . it was really sad. I'd been through so much with that boat. I can't even . . ." She shook her head and laughed again.

Sky gave the girl a hug. "I'm so sorry. That must have been awful."

"It was," said Kaylee, "but I'm still alive. Pushing through this disaster one day at a time."

"You made it," said Sky. "I mean, I know our island won't be home, but I promise it's scads better than the one we just left." She hesitated. "I've been curious to know where you came from before you ended up at Ishibashi's island," Sky asked. "Did you come straight from your . . . your land? How did it happen?"

"Well, it's sort of complicated," Kaylee said. "And I guess I'm not exactly sure how to explain it all. But I *can* tell you that I was in a race, I hit a terrible storm, and suddenly I found myself sailing up a waterfall."

# Kaylee's Story

Y ou sailed *up* a waterfall?" Aaron asked, his face etched in doubt.

"Hey, we sailed up a waterfall too!" Sky exclaimed.

"You did what?" Aaron asked, looking incredulous. "I have no idea half the things my brother has done."

Alex leaned forward. "But did you sail down a waterfall first," he asked Kaylee, "and then go upside down for a while before going up it?"

Kaylee frowned. "No, just up. I went through a really bad storm first. I was sailing around the world. Youngest competitor ever." She shook her head.

LISA McMANN

"We sailed around the world too!" Sky said. "We went past all seven islands."

Aaron tilted his head. "It's not nice to brag," he chided.

Alex blinked. Who was this person?

Kaylee looked at Sky. "All . . . all seven, huh?"

"Yes," Sky said. "Ours is the middle one. We went west, then ended up scrolling around to the east. That's what Samheed thinks happened, anyway, and he'd probably know."

"Samheed," Aaron said with a scowl.

"Aha!" Alex said, pointing at his brother. "That's the real you."

"Will you leave him alone, please?" Sky said. "Stop doing that."

Kaylee watched. "I have no idea what is going on with you all, but it's a little odd," she said.

"Tell me about it," said Sky. "Ignore them. And please, go on with your story. Did you see our friends on the Island of Legends?"

"I . . . um, no, I didn't," Kaylee said.

"Oh right, of course you wouldn't have, because you said you didn't go down the waterfall." Sky knit her brows, trying to figure out what Kaylee was talking about. And then she

LISA McMANN

looked up. "I have a feeling you and I aren't actually talking about the same thing, are we?"

Alex and Aaron stopped glaring at each other and looked at the girls.

"No," Kaylee said softly. "I'm afraid we're not."

"What do you mean?" Alex asked.

Sky turned to look at him. "I'm pretty sure she's talking about coming from a different . . . place."

Kaylee watched the faces around her as they tried to comprehend.

"Like that land on Lani's map?" Alex asked.

"You have a map?" Kaylee asked.

Sky nodded. "The land next to the islands. It's a real place, I'll bet. Lani was right."

Alex stared. "But there's no way to get there," he said.

Kaylee looked at Alex. "You're . . . you're absolutely certain? There's really no way to get there?"

"There's no way that I know," Alex said. "And we've been around this entire world. This is it."

"Then how did Kaylee get *here*?" asked Aaron, the most confused of everyone.

431 « Island of Graves

LISA McMANN

"The same way that thing came out of the sky and landed in the water by Artimé," Alex said slowly. "The same way some of those boats and ships ended up shipwrecked on Ishibashi's island. The same way all the vessel pieces and books and propellers and junk ended up in the Museum of Large. They come up the waterfall, or they get caught in a storm in the sky." He stopped talking, trying to figure it all out, but the concept was so large. "Storms—that's the way in."

"Kaylee," Sky said, turning to her, "is Ishibashi . . . and Ito and Sato . . . are they from another place too?"

Kaylee didn't know what to say. She looked from one confused face to the next. "Yes," she said, for Ishibashi hadn't asked her to keep it a secret. "They got caught in a storm like me. Their ship wrecked off the Island of Shipwrecks way back in the nineteen fifties while they were searching for another scientist's ship that had been lost at sea."

Sky, Aaron, and Alex stared.

"Are they from . . . that same place you're from? Am . . . Ami . . ."

"America," Kaylee said. "No. They're Japanese. They're from my world, though—pretty far away from where I live."

She shook her head. "This is blowing my mind right now, seriously. You have no idea."

They were silent for a long time, each of them trying to grasp the strangeness of the information they'd learned and trying to understand the references to places they never knew existed.

Finally Aaron spoke. "Then . . . where are we inside this bigger world you're talking about?"

Kaylee looked at him and shook her head. "That's the problem, friend. I have absolutely no idea."

# Talking Strategy

**W**ith the mystery unsolved and the hour growing late, the four humans took to their makeshift beds, the girls up at the bow and the boys sprawled out on the fold-down seats.

By morning, the Island of Graves was long gone and the cylindrical island was behind them as well, the speeding boat having passed by it in the early hours. There was no coiled water dragon in sight, but Alex hadn't forgotten about his vow to help the ruler of the sea if he could find a way to make things fly.

But that was the least of his worries. Charlie had woken Alex before the others with a report from home: Gondoleery

LISA McMANN

had begun to organize the Wanteds, forcing them under Strang's leadership to join the Quillitary. Now they were learning how to use weapons and drive vehicles. And the high priest was training a protection unit made up of students from the university.

As Charlie finished signing to Alex, and Alex confirmed that he understood everything, the gargoyle indicated that there was additional information coming in on the spot from Lani.

"What is it?" asked Alex.

Charlie stood frozen for a moment as Matilda relayed the news to him. His face grew sad. He began signing to Alex, too quickly at first for the mage to understand, so he had to start over.

Alex watched intently, the sign language book open in his lap. "Lani and Samheed . . . snuck into Quill?" he guessed. "To spy?"

Charlie nodded. He signed more words.

Alex watched, then paged through the book, trying to figure out a sign he wasn't familiar with. "Dead?" he asked, looking up. "Somebody's dead?" His stomach dropped. "Who?"

Charlie nodded. He spelled out a name.

Alex stared, stringing the letters together. "Sully," he whispered. "Gondoleery killed Sully?" When Charlie confirmed it, Alex dropped his head into his hands. "Oh no," he moaned. He was sure it was their fault.

Alex kept the news to himself for a time while the others continued to sleep, but once he got over the shock of Sully's death, he began to focus on Gondoleery's other recent actions. Eventually he nudged Aaron awake. He needed the former high priest's help.

"What is it?" Aaron asked, sitting up.

Alex gave him a grim look. "Gondoleery put Strang in charge of the Quillitary now that General Blair is dead."

Aaron wiped the sleep from his eyes. "Strang? That's . . . an interesting choice."

"Is he a big threat? I don't know much about him."

"He taught me a lot about the government," Aaron said. "He's very rigid about rules, but I don't think he would want a job like that."

"Do we have any chance to turn him to our side? Would he follow you?"

Aaron didn't answer right away. He was reminded again how hard this job was going to be and how much he just wanted to go back to the Island of Shipwrecks.

"I doubt it," Aaron said finally. "I wasn't all that nice to him, but I did make him a governor again." He shook his head. "He might listen to me, but he's such a rule follower, he'll most likely go along with Gondoleery—not because he approves of what she's doing, but because it's his job to follow the current high priest and carry out her wishes."

Alex gave Aaron a long look. He could tell Aaron was being honest. "Thanks," he said. "Is there any other angle we should take? Any group of people that would be more likely to join us—whether it's you they want to please, or perhaps there are some secret Artimé supporters?"

"Nobody I can think of right away," Aaron said. "Secret Artimé supporters certainly wouldn't want me to know about them. I'll keep it in mind, though." This would've been a good question for Secretary—Eva, as he thought of her now. She deserved a name. "Maybe Liam would listen to me. Whatever happened to him? Still at the palace, I presume."

Alex hadn't mentioned Liam at all, not sure if he wanted

Aaron to know about the man's double allegiance, like Eva's. But Aaron was going to find out soon enough.

"Liam's . . . sort of . . . with us," Alex ventured.

Aaron looked up.

"It's not what you think," Alex hurried to say. "When Gondoleery found out you were kidnapped, she snatched the title of high priest and sent Liam to the Ancients Sector. He was supposed to take our sisters there. But he escaped and journeyed over the ice with the twins, and finally made it to Artimé. So we took him in."

"So it was Liam who saved the girls?"

"Yes."

Aaron's face betrayed his bruised feelings. "Why didn't you tell me?"

"I—I was protecting Liam. In case you'd have been mad at him."

Aaron looked out over the water. "I know it's hard to trust me, and to believe that I've changed, but I have. Getting out of Quill and having a person like Ishibashi to slap you into shape—it's like I see everything differently now. Quill . . . I don't want to go back there."

"And you're not mad about Liam?"

Aaron shook his head slowly. "I'm surprised that he had the fearlessness to escape and not go directly to the Ancients Sector as he'd been ordered. I've never heard of anybody doing that before. I thought he was kind of weak, actually, but clearly he's a lot stronger than me." He turned back to Alex and looked at him thoughtfully. "Wait a minute," he said. "That's it! The Ancients Sector."

"What about it?" Alex asked.

"That's where you should start. Right away." He thought for a moment more and said, "They won't listen to me because I sent some people there. But find somebody trustworthy right away to recruit them. It won't be hard to convince them, because going to Artimé is a better choice than being put to sleep." He tapped his chin. "Like Gunnar Haluki. They'll go with him." He raised an eyebrow. "Especially the ladies."

"Whoa," said Alex. "Was that you making a joke?"

"Get used to it," Aaron deadpanned.

Alex smiled distractedly, thinking it through. It actually sounded like a viable plan. "Charlie," he called.

The gargoyle poked his head out of the cabin.

LISA McMANN

"Tell Matilda to find Gunnar and Henry Haluki. We need to talk to them right away."

Charlie nodded, already transferring the message to Matilda.

"Okay, I like this plan," Alex said to Aaron. "But how will they get past the attendant?"

Aaron nearly smiled. "It just so happens that you know somebody who has a secret code that will let the Ancients out."

# More Plans

**W**hen Sky awoke, Alex filled her in on the grim news of Sully's death and the rest of the developments in Quill, then left her to contemplate over breakfast with Kaylee. He returned to Charlie's side to await the meeting with Gunner and Henry.

Later, while Sky and Kaylee paged through the first logbook and discussed the amazing story of the animal-transport ship, Alex gave the order for Gunnar and Henry to release the people from the Ancients Sector.

Aaron and Alex continued their conversation about strategy. Through it, the brothers grew a bit more comfortable with each other, and while Aaron's sharp tongue came into play every now and then, Alex slowly became convinced that the harrowing experiences of the kidnapping and near drowning, plus the time spent with Ishibashi, had truly changed Aaron.

And Aaron began to confide a bit more easily in Alex, too.

As the former high preist waited for the island of Quill and Artimé to appear on the horizon, he paced and occasionally stared out over the water. He shook his head slowly. "I can't explain how much I don't want to do this, Alex," he said. "Not because I don't want to help you. I see Quill for what it is now, and I'm ashamed of my part in that. And Gondoleery is a tyrant and needs to be done away with. Plus I owe this to Artimé. But if you decided you didn't need me after all, I wouldn't be sad."

"But we do need you, Aaron," Alex said. "I'm sorry for what you're going to go through. I'm sure there are a bunch of people who aren't going to be kind to you after what you did, even though you're here to help now. They won't be expecting you to be a different person. It's really hard to get used to, believe me. And while it's too bad they're not going to trust you, and they might even be hostile, well . . . you deserve it."

"I know," Aaron agreed. "And I'll do my best to take it. I'm scared, though."

Alex had never heard his brother say those words before. "What are you scared of?"

Aaron thought for while, trying to find the words to describe his fear. "I'm scared that I'll go into Quill and act like the person I used to be . . . and then I'll want that life back."

Alex shook his head. "I get what you're saying, but you won't. At first, when we Unwanteds were sent out of Quill, we all wanted to go back, even though we had the magical world that is so much better than Quill—believe me, it's a million times better. But it took us a while to grasp what we had because it was so strange." He sat up. "You won't see it the same way you used to."

"You say that, but the people in Artimé welcomed you. They won't be welcoming me."

Alex hadn't pictured it that way, but it made sense.

"I'm just really confused," Aaron went on. He scratched his head and turned to Alex. "Anyway—let's talk through this plan. I've got some new ideas."

"Great. Tell me what you're thinking."

"You've got Gunnar and his son on the way to the Ancients Sector to recruit them," Aaron began. "And if Gondoleery is on the move doing unspeakable things, we're not going to want to waste any time. So I've been thinking that since we'll be arriving in Artimé sometime during the night tonight, we should strike in the morning."

"Strike with what?" Alex asked.

"I'm getting to that," Aaron said. "But first, can you mobilize people this evening to stealthily enter Quill and go door-to-door in the Necessary quadrant? Wait until darkness falls and all the people are home from their jobs. And tell them to meet at the amphitheater an hour before dawn."

"So early?" Alex asked. "Why?"

"Because they can't come during their work shifts. That would be a serious infraction that Necessaries won't even consider doing. Remember?"

"Yeah," Alex said, "I guess I do, now that you say it. What'll our people say to them, though, that will convince them to show up?"

Aaron thought for a long moment. "Okay, hang on. I'm thinking this one through."

While Aaron thought, Alex brought out lunch for the girls and Aaron and himself. "Another eight hours or so," Alex said. "Home after dark. And then we'll have an early morning. Early for Sky, I mean—not you, Kaylee. We'll get you settled in a nice room so you can take a bath or get pampered and sleep for days if you want."

"Pfft," Kaylee scoffed. "Find me a slingshot and some stones and I can fight with the best of you. Just, ah, you know—point out the bad guys to me so I know who to aim for." She took a bite of lunch. "And keep feeding me this stuff."

Alex grinned. "If you insist. I'd rather fight with you than against you, that's for sure."

"I'll worry about pampering and baths and getting my nails done when it's all over," Kaylee said. "Do you have a salon?"

"A what?" Sky asked.

"A nail salon . . . oh heck. A place where you get your nails painted."

"Oh!" Sky said. "We don't need a salon. You can get them

painted just about anywhere, at any time of day, because half the people in Artimé are painting at any given moment."

"Now we're talking," Kaylee said. "Fist bump!" She held out her fist.

Sky stared at it.

"Never miiiind," Kaylee sang, and the girls dissolved in laughter.

Alex went back to Aaron, who was pacing in the short, narrow walkway between the seats. "Any progress?" asked Alex.

"Yes," Aaron said. "I've been repeating it to myself so I don't forget it."

"We can solve that," Alex said, pulling out his notebook and tapping it to produce a pencil.

Aaron shook his head. "You're going to have to teach me that one."

"Maybe someday," Alex said, and a whole new cast of worries entered his mind. What if Aaron got access to spells during this attack on Gondoleery? Would he turn on them? He couldn't think about that now. "Go ahead."

"Okay. The people of Artimé should knock five times. No more, no less."

LISA McMANN

"Aah, the Necessaries' knock," Alex said, "so they know it's not a Wanted at their door. Good idea."

"And they should say these words exactly: 'The High Priest Aaron Stowe sent me. He's alive, and he's coming to save you and your family from Gondoleery Rattrapp. Meet at the amphitheater an hour before dawn tomorrow. Each Necessary who comes will receive a day's supply of fruit and nuts. May Quill prevail with all I have in me.'"

Alex scribbled down the words exactly as Aaron said them, cringing at the last bit. "Do they really have to say that 'May Quill prevail' junk?"

"Oh, I don't know," said Aaron sarcastically. "Do you really want them to believe you and actually show up?"

"Point taken."

"Good." Aaron looked at Alex. "You'll have to have another team go to the Favored Farm and break in to get food, I suppose. We'll need a lot of fruit and nuts."

Alex laughed. "I think our kitchen can come up with something sufficient without actually having to do that," he said.

"Oh," said Aaron. "In that case, bring along a tub full of whatever that sweet thing was that I just ate. What's that called?"

"Oh, that dessert," Alex said knowingly. "That's something one of the chefs found in a recipe book that washed up a few months ago. Our chef added her own special touch to it back when Gondoleery iced us. It's called rhubapple sugarberry pie—with pecan fig-jam ice cream."

Aaron patted his stomach. "I learned how to cook on the Island of Shipwrecks, you know. I'd like to make that sometime," he said.

Alex stared at Aaron for a long moment. "Are you sure you're not Lani disguised as Aaron?"

"What?"

Alex shook his head. "Nothing," he said. "You just keep shocking me."

# A Trip to the Ancients Sector

Gunnar Haluki donned a black cape so he'd look familiar and high priestly to the Ancients, and Henry Haluki loaded his component vest with lethal and nonlethal spells so he'd be prepared for anything—even Gondoleery herself.

The father-and-son team hadn't spent much time together lately with all the chaos and with Henry so engrossed in his work, so this quest felt a bit like a special adventure. Henry had never been inside the Ancients Sector before, and he was intensely curious about the medicines that were used there—especially the ones that actually put the Ancients to sleep.

LISA McMANN

Not that Henry wanted to do that, of course. He'd just always wondered about it. What did they use, and more importantly, where did they get it on the desert island? It was something no one seemed to know.

Even Gunnar Haluki didn't know. He hadn't been in power long enough to discover that information.

Armed with Aaron's secrets, they took the tube to their old house. Gunnar cringed only a little upon reaching his office closet, where he'd spent so much time tied up. He quickly stepped out of the tube and searched the room, making sure no one else had turned it into some sort of evil headquarters. Henry arrived a moment later. They spent a moment in the house, reflecting and missing the late Mrs. Haluki, who had selflessly died in battle against Aaron's Restorers.

And then they pressed on, leaving the house and heading toward the Ancients Sector.

"Do you think Aaron gave us the right secret code to release everybody?" Henry asked his father.

"What do you mean?"

"I mean he could have easily made something up as a trap."

Gunnar Haluki thought for a moment. "I think that's entirely possible."

They walked in silence as both of them mused over it.

"I think," Henry said eventually, "that Alex wouldn't have given it to us without being completely certain it was the right code. And Alex would know if Aaron was lying."

"Let's hope so," Gunnar said grimly. "But Alex has been wrong about Aaron before. His heart gets in the way sometimes."

Henry glanced at his father. Gunnar had never before confided in Henry about what he knew about the inner workings of Quill and Artimé, nor had he ever spoken so candidly about Alex and Aaron. Henry was nearly as tall as his father now, he realized as they walked. Perhaps his father was beginning to treat him like a grown-up as he did with Lani. He straightened his back and lifted his chin and waited to see if his father would say anything else.

Eventually, Gunnar did. "It's a wonderful trait to have, certainly. But for a leader it can be fatal."

"What trait?" asked Henry.

"Having a kind heart, like Alex. It gets in his way. Like with the assassination attempt."

LISA McMANN

"Do you think Alex should have let Lani kill her?"

Gunnar closed his eyes briefly. "That's not an easy question to answer when the subject is your child. No father ever wants to see his child have to kill someone and then live through the emotional consequences of that."

"But Gondoleery is so evil," Henry said softly, not wanting to be overheard in the middle of Quill. "I can understand it if she had some good quality inside her, but . . ."

"I think it's more complicated than that," Gunnar said. "If Gondoleery were seriously wounded and someone brought her into our hospital ward, would you ignore her? Would you let her suffer and hope for her to die because she's irredeemably evil?"

Henry pondered that for a long time. He knew for sure he wouldn't give Gondoleery any seaweed. But beyond that, it was too hard to know what he'd do in that situation. Was he obligated to try to heal all people no matter what their allegiance was? He didn't have an answer.

Soon they reached the Ancients Sector, and Henry turned his thoughts to the current task. They stood outside the door to the reporting office, looked at one another, silently going over the plan. Henry nodded when he was ready. Gunnar opened the door and stepped inside.

The attendant looked up. For a moment she seemed afraid, but then she hid her fear as the people of Quill were supposed to do.

"Greetings, former High Priest Haluki," she said formally.

Gunnar nodded and smiled. "Hello, Zora. This is my son, Henry."

Zora didn't acknowledge the boy. "Have you both been sent here?" she asked.

"No," Gunnar said. "I've come with a message from the high priest." He didn't bother to mention *which* high priest.

Zora's eyes widened. "What is it?" she whispered.

"You must release the Ancients to my care at once," Haluki said with authority. "All of them. Immediately."

The worker blinked and didn't respond for a long moment, and while her face remained bland, Henry could see the fear in her eyes.

Finally Zora spoke in a shaky voice. "And of course you have proof that this command is legitimate?"

Gunnar smiled disarmingly. "Of course."

"Well?"

Gunnar leaned toward her and whispered, "In the name of Quill, and upon your life, mine, and the life of the high priest herself . . . it *shall* be done." He stood up straight.

Zora stepped back, no longer able to hide her horror. She put her hand out, pointing at Gunnar, her finger shaking. "That's not it," she whispered, her face going pale. She shook her head rapidly. "She changed it. That's not it anymore." She looked around rapidly. "Guards!" she shouted. "Guards!"

Gunnar turned swiftly to Henry. "Now," he said quietly.

Henry's face was awash with fear. He grabbed a freeze component and sent it soaring at Zora, freezing her in place before she could shout again.

"Of course Gondoleery changed it," Gunnar muttered. "We should have expected that."

Henry stood poised, watching behind the table for the guards to come. Instead two of them burst through the door behind him and grabbed Gunnar. Henry whirled around and threw scatterclips at the two guards, sending them flying back

LISA McMANN

against the wall. Henry cast a blinding highlighter at each, then clay shackles, expertly avoiding hitting his father with any of the spells.

"Behind you!" Gunnar cried as he struggled to untangle himself from the guards' shackled limbs.

Henry spun around as three more guards came through a door behind the attendant. He shot off a backward bobbly head, a pincushion, a handful of scatterclips, and a fleet of fire-breathing origami dragons, which turned the room into chaos.

"Come on!" Henry cried, reaching out to help his dad. The two weaved around the disoriented guards through the back door, Henry armed and ready to take out anybody else who wished to stop them.

"This way," Gunnar said, taking the lead. He headed toward a community room where old people stood or sat aimlessly, all tethered with rusty chains to spikes on the wall.

"They chain them down?" Henry cried. "What a horrible thing to do." As he froze the attendants in the room and looked around for a key that would unlock the chains around the Ancients' ankles, Henry thought about Ishibashi and Ito and Sato, and how all of them would be in here chained to the wall if they lived in Quill. It made him furious.

Gunnar stripped the key from a guard's belt and began to unlock the Ancients.

"Is this it? Is our time up?" one after another said fearfully.

Henry soon realized they thought they were being brought to the sleep chamber.

"No," he said. "Oh dear, no. Not at all! We're here to free you. Do you recognize former High Priest Haluki?"

A few of them stared at the man, and looks of recognition crossed their faces. They nodded.

"Everyone," Henry said, "please listen for a moment."

The bewildered Ancients settled down.

Henry turned toward his father. "We've only got a few minutes before the spells start wearing off," he said quietly.

"Go back and make them permanent," Gunnar said. "We'll release them once we've got everybody out."

Henry nodded and took off to the main entrance as Gunnar spoke to the Ancients.

"Friends," he said, "I've come from Artimé to release you and ask you to help us. We must be very stealthy, and Gondoleery must not hear of this, or we will all be doomed. Do you understand?"

The Ancients nodded. "Clear as day," one of them remarked. "Though we're already doomed, so nothing really changes."

"True," Haluki said. "But everyone here knows that you do not deserve to die just because you're old. You are all valuable. Before dawn we'll give you your freedom whether you choose to help us or not."

"Help you do what?" asked one Ancient, rubbing her ankle where the shackle had been. The Ancients were more vocal than ordinary Quillens, perhaps because they realized they had nothing to lose.

"We're going to overthrow Gondoleery Rattrapp."

The Ancients stared.

Gunnar stared back, trying to gauge their reaction.

The Ancients turned and looked at each other.

Gunnar watched them.

A few of the Ancients began to turn the wrinkled corners of

LISA McMANN

their mouths upward into a smile. Others did the same.

Gunnar felt encouraged to continue. "Will you help us?" he asked as Henry returned.

The Ancients erupted in a wild cheer. Some began dancing around the room, others whooping and laughing.

"I think that's a yes," Henry said, sidling up to his father.

Gunnar nodded and put his hand on his son's shoulder. "I think you're right. Now, let's get this army organized."

# The Plan Comes Together

**W**hen the white boat and its occupants arrived in Artimé's lagoon after dark, there was no fanfare to greet them. Alex wanted it that way—he'd get everyone inside and settled so they could have a little rest before their early morning. Alex, Aaron, Sky, Kaylee, and Charlie said good night to Spike and waded to shore. They slipped inside the front door, finding Simber and Florence awaiting their arrival.

Alex quickly introduced Kaylee, who was speechless at the sight of the two living statues, and then Sky and Kaylee left to get a room assignment for the new resident. They

LISA McMANN

agreed to meet everyone in a few hours, when it was time to head into Quill.

Charlie wandered off to find Matilda. Alex motioned for Aaron, Simber, and Florence to follow him to his office, where they could meet in private and catch up on things.

In Alex's office, Simber eyed Aaron warily, but didn't ask him any questions. Aaron ignored the stone cheetah as much as he could.

Florence began, reporting to Alex that six small groups of Unwanteds had gone out to Quill to spread the message to the Necessaries. The groups were led by Mr. Appleblossom, Sean, Claire, Carina, Samheed, and Lani, and all but Carina's group, which had to travel the farthest, had returned so far. The leaders reported that the Necessaries seemed scared, and none gave any indication of whether they would show up in the morning, which Florence found to be deeply troubling.

"That's normal for them," Aaron explained. "They won't commit. Remember, an infraction like that could mean being sent to the Ancients Sector. They're not going to say anything ahead of time. I don't think you have to worry about them showing up. Some of them, anyway. Enough."

Florence watched Aaron carefully. "We'll see," she said.

Aaron, who very much wanted to retort, "Yes, you will," instead held his tongue and took a deep breath in and out, remembering Ishibashi. He couldn't disappoint the man. He must show respect in order to earn it. He knew how this worked now.

"Do we have the Necessaries' food ready?" asked Alex.

"The chefs—and yourrr sisterrrs, I prrresume—packed everrrything up," said Simber. "It's on the lawn, rrready to go."

Alex turned to Aaron. "What do you think about Simber and Florence being there at the amphitheater? Too scary?"

"Way too scary," Aaron said. "Why do you think more Necessaries aren't already living in Artimé?" He glanced at Florence and Simber. "Sorry."

Florence blinked, clearly puzzled by the new Aaron even though Alex had tried to warn them through Charlie.

"I don't like this arrrangement," Simber growled. "If Aarrron is bluffing and plans to turrrn on us, he could take his chance then."

Aaron looked up at the ceiling and sighed, but he kept quiet and let Alex talk.

"We'll take Charlie with us," Alex said. "He's small enough not to look threatening. He can relay everything that's happening to you through Matilda. You can be close by, but stay out of sight. If anything happens, you'll be right there."

Simber regarded Alex and nodded. "All rrright," he said.

"I'm fine with that as well," said Florence, "as long as every Artiméan is ready with spells in hand."

"We will be," Alex assured her. "I'll have Clive relay the message to everyone."

"And," Florence said, "no components for you, Aaron. We'll give you an empty vest, which will help protect you a little in case Gondoleery shows up."

"That's fine," Aaron said. "There won't be any need for magic at that meeting anyway, as long as Gondoleery doesn't find out about it."

"Alex, when do you expect to attack Gondoleery?" asked Florence.

"The longer we wait after the meeting, the better chance she has to find out about it," he replied.

"And the more time you give the Necessaries to back down or forget," Aaron pointed out. "If we manage to motivate them—and that's a big if—we need to strike fast. Give them an hour to bring their food home and talk to their loved ones, and then we go."

Florence looked down at Aaron. "You seem to have very good ideas," she said. "Why didn't you organize something like this against us when you had the chance?"

Aaron frowned. "My mind was clouded by a lot of other things," he said. "Getting away was the only way for me to see clearly."

"And now that you see things morrre clearrrly," Simber said, "do you want to go back to rrrule Quill again?"

Aaron dared look at the big cat in the eye for the first time. "No, Simber. Not in the slightest. If you would send me back to Ishibashi right now, I would thank you profusely and go without another thought."

Simber regarded him. "And yet you came willingly."

Aaron nodded. "I did," he said quietly. "I owe you that."

After a long moment, Simber dropped his gaze, seemingly satisfied that his own observance had rung true once more—that once a person leaves Quill, their mind changes and they see the world differently. He began to gnaw at his remaining

LISA McMANN

dewclaw, which had somehow grown a small callous near the cuticle.

Just then there was a noise at the door to Alex's office. Alex and the others turned swiftly, finding Claire standing there with a battered-looking Carina Holiday.

"What happened?" Alex cried, standing up and rushing to the door. "Are you all right?"

"It's the sixth group that went into Quill," Claire said gravely. "Gondoleery discovered them. Everyone but Carina is dead."

# And Then It Falls Apart

E ven Aaron was ripped apart by the news. Everything became more real than ever before. And Aaron felt extremely vulnerable. He was about to go into a situation he'd never had to face in the past, with no weapon but a dagger and no protection except for a flimsy vest. Gondoleery was *killing* people. Actually killing them herself. He'd known she was doing this before, and he'd heard about Sully by now, but to hear it firsthand, to see Carina standing there, singed and hurt and without her team . . . It was startling. What remained of the calmness of Ishibashi's world now collapsed at Aaron's feet. And then everybody turned to look at him.

LISA McMANN

He scrambled to think of what he should say. Clearly they weren't looking for him to tell them how sorry he was that it had happened. They wanted his thoughts on what to do. What would the Necessaries do if they found out this had happened?

"Did Gondoleery stumble across them on her own, or was she tipped off?" Aaron asked Carina.

"She was in a car leaving a house that was glowing orange," Carina said. "I don't think a Necessary tipped her off. We never expected her to be there in the Necessary quadrant. When we saw the car, we ran, but she shot fireballs and everybody went down. I—I managed to get away."

"What do you think we should do?" Alex asked. "Sounds like it was an isolated incident. Do we still go to the amphitheater in"—he checked the time—"two hours?" If so, there would be no sleep for them tonight.

"We have to," Aaron said. "I do, anyway—the rest of you can decide for yourselves, I guess. Even if Gondoleery knows about the plan, and even if the Necessaries get wind of what happened to your scouting group—I need to be there. My name was on that promise."

LISA McMANN

Now it was Claire's and Carina's turn to stare. But there was no time to talk about it.

"I won't let you go alone," Alex said. "I'll be there too. But we have to prepare for a fight."

"We'll all go as planned," Florence said. "Things aren't going to get better by us canceling the meeting in the amphitheater. We'll lose the Necessary support for sure if we don't show up."

"Plus Gunnar and Henry and the Ancients are counting on us." Aaron looked around at the group as several of them nodded. It was a lot easier working with a team of reasonable people rather than plotting everything alone and trusting no one.

Alex turned to Florence. "Do you have any more weapons? We have a few nonmagical fighters now. Sky has the sword and Aaron has the dagger. Do we have something for Kaylee?"

"Who?" asked Carina.

"Kaylee," Claire said. "The girl Alex and the others rescued from the island with the gorilla."

"Gorillas," Alex corrected. "Seventy of them. But that's a story for a different day."

"So there really was someone there on that island," Carina said. "And she wants to fight? That's great."

"I'll check with Siggy and find something for her," Florence said.

"All right, then," Alex said. "Anything else? If not, I'll prepare instructions for Clive to send out, and we'll be on our way shortly."

The small group had nothing more to add. They dispersed to handle their duties. Aaron stayed with Alex, and they went into the mage's private quarters. "Have a quick nap if you like," said Alex, pointing to his bed. "I have a feeling tomorrow's going to be a long day." He sat at his desk and began jotting down notes.

"Is this what it was like when you were preparing to fight the Quillitary?" Aaron asked.

That battle, and Meghan's death, were still very fresh, and Alex had often wondered if he'd gotten home sooner, would he have been able to prevent its terrible toll on Artimé? "No. It's nothing like that," Alex said sharply. He didn't explain.

Aaron got the hint and didn't press it. He sat down on Alex's bed. He'd never really thought about how it would feel to be among those who were attacked. Closing his eyes, Aaron wondered if Alex missed Meghan like he missed Secretary. If so, it must have left a wound in Alex's heart that ached terribly whenever he thought about her. And in a strange way it fired him up when he thought about destroying Gondoleery. She was killing people without warning, for no good reason, and causing pain to all the people who knew the dead. She had to be stopped.

Aaron lay down, but he couldn't sleep, so he looked at all of Alex's artwork that adorned the walls and ceiling, while Alex composed his assignments. With an hour to go before the planned meeting time in Quill, Alex called Clive.

Clive pressed his face out of the blackboard. He didn't say anything, but his pout made Alex wince.

"What's wrong, Clive?" Alex asked, but he knew the answer.

"You didn't tell me you were leaving."

"I know—it was a terrible oversight. I'm sorry."

"I didn't get a chance to tell you not to die. What if you had died?"

Alex tried to be patient, but he was running out of time. "You're right. I'm sorry. Now, though, I have a very important job for you."

469 « Island of Graves

"You're just going to dismiss it?" Clive asked. "Don't you care about the eternal guilt I'd feel if you *had* died?"

"Ah, but I didn't. So here's your chance to say it again since we'll be going into the most difficult battle we've ever faced. Are you ready to take down the instructions?" He shook the paper he'd written on for emphasis.

"Maybe I don't want to say it anymore," Clive said.

Aaron watched from the bed, fascinated.

Alex felt the heat rising to his face. "Clive," he said in a dead serious voice, "you have one second to accept this job or you're fired and Stuart is taking your place."

"Okay!" Clive said. "I was just joking around, sheesh. Whatcha got for me?"

Alex gave him the orders through clenched teeth. Clive became much more subdued when he heard what the assignment was. When Alex finished, Clive repeated it back to him, and then Alex gave the final okay.

He turned away from Clive and loaded components from the supply in his dresser into his vest, then slipped a robe on over his clothes.

Soon Alex had his robe pockets packed full of spells too.

He pulled a fresh component vest from his closet for Aaron, completely empty, and Aaron put the dagger belt back on. The twins were easily distinguishable for the sake of any Artiméans who might not yet trust Aaron.

"Are you ready?" Alex asked his brother.

"I am," said Aaron, and the two exchanged a look of trust for the first time in many years. He held out his hand to Alex, and Alex shook it.

From behind them, Clive cleared his voice. "Don't die," he said meekly.

Alex looked at the blackboard. "I might, just to spite you," he said. "Now shove off." He turned away and motioned to Aaron. "Let's go. It's time to assemble on the lawn."

# To the Amphitheater

It was dark as pitch. Alex and Aaron stood outside the mansion waiting for everyone to assemble. Sky and Kaylee arrived first, followed by Lani and Samheed. The latter two eyed Aaron steadily, trying to read his face in the light of Alex's highlighter.

Aaron had attempted to prepare himself for this moment, but it came very quickly. He dropped his gaze to avoid the stares, but kept his chin up and his jaw set. They had asked him here. There was nothing about his presence that he needed to apologize for. That didn't stop him from sweating, though.

He recited Ishibashi's lessons in his head. *Be your own*

*strong. To gain respect, one must first offer it.* Time would prove to them what Aaron's inner applecorn tasted like. He didn't need to feel shame or fear among these people. His presence was his apology.

Simber and Florence joined the front ranks. They'd walk with Alex and the others until the larger group turned off to go to the Commons of Quill, and then they'd keep watch for Gondoleery on the road from the palace. If she showed her face, Simber and Florence wouldn't hesitate to take her down.

Florence pulled Kaylee aside and spoke to her in a low voice about weapons, listing the options for the girl. Kaylee listened and chose, and Florence pulled a fencing sword from her quiver and handed it to the girl. "This is from Mr. Appleblossom's prop closet. It's real, and it's deadly. Choose wisely when you wish to use it. Did Sky explain what we're up against?"

"Yes," Kaylee said. "I understand, and I'm ready. I took two years of fencing at the club."

Florence looked puzzled, but there was no time to ask questions. Kaylee expertly tossed the sword by the hilt from one hand to the other, then slid the blade into her belt.

Simber seemed more anxious and showed more concern

than usual. He paced on the lawn as the people of Artimé who chose to fight assembled.

Alex watched the cat, troubled. "What is it?" he whispered when he passed.

Simber stopped by Alex's side and looked at the mage. "Whateverrr happens, you must keep going," he said. "I believe in you. You arrre an excellent rrruler. You have what it takes to lead Arrrtimé to victorrry and peace. And you have brrrought this worrrld back frrrom nothing on yourrr own beforrre. If you have to do it again, have no fearrr. You will succeed."

Alex's eyes grew wide, and his heart nearly stopped. "What are you saying?" he asked. "Artimé won't disappear. If it does, it's because I've been killed, and Claire and Lani and Sky all know the spell to bring it back. There's even an extra robe in the gray shack—I put it there some time ago. . . . It's important for the spell, you see. . . ." He faltered. It dawned on him that Simber wasn't talking about Artimé disappearing. He was talking about Alex having to inspire his people without his leaders there to advise him. He was talking about just in case. *Just in case every one of us is destroyed or killed.*

"It won't happen," Alex declared. "She can't destroy you."

LISA McMANN

Simber only looked at him. "Neverrr forrrget. No one is invincible." He sampled the air. "Send the seek spell the second you sense trrrouble."

"I will," said Alex. Simber was making him really nervous.

"And you, Aaron," Simber said, loud enough for many of the Artiméans to hear, "will be prrrotected as long as yourrr allegiance to Arrrtimé rrremains clearrr. We thank you forrr helping us."

Aaron looked up at the beast and nodded. "Thank you," he whispered.

Alex held up his highlighter, and Florence raised hers as well to get the attention of everyone on the lawn.

"Friends!" Alex shouted. "Thank you for your sacrifice for Artimé. Do you all have your water flasks and dust guards?"

The people nodded, some of them lifting stretchy tubular cloths in the air, which they'd wear over their faces to protect them from the dust squalls.

"Good," said Alex. "We'll arrive at the amphitheater and provide light and support for the Necessaries, so they will see they are not alone. Aaron will speak to them, asking them to join us, and if he is successful, we'll march to the palace and surround it. We'll give the guards and drivers a choice to join us or be frozen, and we'll swarm the entrances. You've all seen the diagram of the palace that Gunnar Haluki sketched for us, so you won't be entering blindly.

"Most important of all," Alex continued, "we'll provide the Necessaries with weapons, but they cannot compete against Gondoleery's magic. So we must protect them at all costs."

As his solemn words rang out over the silent crowd, one by one the Artiméans lifted their fists to their chests and tapped them to declare their solidarity with their leader. "We are with you, Alex!" they called out, until the air was filled.

Aaron swallowed hard as he watched his brother command this dedicated group of people. He felt a deep longing for what Alex had—so much respect and so much support. Aaron had almost felt that once, with the Restorers, but it hadn't lasted. Now he could see why Artimé remained strong and won battle after battle. It was their hearts that kept them in it. Their passion.

Aaron felt his anxiety increasing. How was he supposed to convince the Necessaries to embody that same passion when they were lifeless inside? He was starting from a much more difficult place. And if he failed to convince them, would Simber

LISA McMANN

think he hadn't tried hard enough, and that his allegiance wasn't clear? Would he have to worry about Simber killing him too?

Before he could ponder further, everyone began moving, and Aaron was pushed along with the crowd, following Alex. As they passed through the magical barrier into the ugly, dust-stormy world of Quill, and the Artiméans raised their dust masks to cover their noses and mouths, Aaron glanced back toward the jungle and felt a sudden desire to be there with a growling rock and a screaming panther, where he felt comfortable. If he stole away, would the Artiméans kill him? The temptation was real, but fleeting. He marched onward.

The giant crowd moved quietly down the road with their boxes of fruit and nuts and weapons in tow. Carina and a few others toted healers' kits as well. Everyone's clothing gathered dust from the storm as they moved. No one spoke. No one tried to override Alex's plan. And Alex was confident, walking between Florence and Simber with his head high.

Aaron took it all in. He found Sky and Kaylee and fell in step with them. He felt most comfortable with them—the two who hadn't known him before.

Sky gave him an encouraging smile. "Just think," she said, "if nobody shows up, you won't have to do a speech at all."

Aaron didn't smile. For a moment he selfishly hoped that it would happen. But then he thought about Gondoleery, and he knew that it would be the worst possible result.

As planned, when they reached the path to the amphitheater, Florence and Simber stepped aside. Alex turned down the path and continued leading the group. He glanced over his shoulder, squinting at the two statues, trying to get one last glimpse of their faces before they were swallowed by darkness and dust. Alex paused to salute them as he led the people. Florence saluted back, and Simber lifted his head like a king.

Soon Alex and his people arrived in the very center of Quill. Sean and Claire led the Artiméans to spread themselves around the giant half circle in an organized manner, while Aaron and Alex stepped up on the platform.

Aaron was lost, forced into this spotlight again. He walked slowly to the old, familiar podium and stood behind it. He placed his hands on the rotting wood and closed his eyes, remembering the times he'd stood here before. It was painful to stand here now. Tears sprang to his eyes for no apparent reason . . . and then because there was one. He was here to play a role—the role of the old Aaron Stowe. To be a phony. A fake. To lie to the people who had trusted him enough to risk their lives and come here.

There had been a time when he wouldn't have thought twice about it. But now . . .

"I don't know if I can do this," he muttered.

At his side, Alex either didn't hear or chose not to react. Aaron wasn't sure. The former high priest dug his elbows into the podium and held his head in his hands as the world began to spin. Jumbled thoughts and confusing phrases twisted together in his mind as the mantras of Quill collided with the proverbial phrases of Ishibashi.

"I think I'm going to be sick," Aaron whispered.

Alex put a hand on his brother's back. "No, you're not," he said. "Because look over there. Your people are coming."

# The Hour Before Dawn

From the direction of the Ancients Sector, Gunnar and Henry Haluki were the first to arrive in the Commons with upwards of twenty elderly Quillens. The Ancients stood proud as they accepted the weapons offered, and their eyes widened at the sight of the sacks of food they were given. Some began eating right away, and others held their goods close while studying the strange lights and the Artiméans who held them. They didn't seem particularly fearful, having been swept away from certain death. They were almost animated. Almost.

From the other direction a small group approached slowly.

The Artiméans gave them plenty of room to get by and make their way to the huge pile of crates in the center. Wordlessly they accepted the food first, and then, more tentatively, the weapons. They seemed confused about the weapons, but they took them without question.

"I count thirty-one so far," Alex said to Aaron, who was still leaning over the podium, face hidden by his hands.

Aaron didn't respond. He could feel his stomach churning. The pressure was intense.

"Three more people just stepped into the lighted area," Alex reported. He strained to see in the darkness beyond the amphitheater. "Good night!" he said. "They're coming. Hordes of them. Aaron, look! The place is filling up!"

There was no way to turn back. Aaron tried to breathe through his cold sweat and nausea, and finally convinced himself he was going to be fine. He looked up and saw the faces of more than a hundred Necessaries peering up at him, with more Necessaries streaming into the amphitheater from all directions.

When the people saw Aaron lift his head, a murmur arose. "It's true," they said. "He's here!"

Finally, even though there were still Necessaries arriving

and collecting their promised food, Alex put his hand on Aaron's shoulder. "We need to get started," he whispered.

Aaron nodded. *Be your own strong.* He wiped his hands on his pants, located Kaylee and Sky in the audience, and put on the face of the old Aaron. Then he took a deep breath and began.

"People of Quill," he said, his voice shaking slightly. The murmuring in the amphitheater quieted. "People of Quill," Aaron said again, "thank you for coming here. You've risked your lives for me. I cannot thank you enough." He frowned as Necessaries looked around uneasily, and realized he didn't sound anything like the old Aaron. He needed to stop thanking them.

"People of Quill," he said again, harsher this time, "I have heard about your troubles with the new High Priest Gondoleery, and I've returned because you need my help to survive. She may have told you I was dead, but I am alive and well, as you can see. I was kidnapped by pirates because they were threatened by Quill's strength and dominance in the world. And my brother, Alex, the mage of Artimé, and some of his people risked their lives to save me. We owe them a debt. And we owe ourselves one too."

The Necessaries looked lost and shifted uncomfortably.

Claire Morning and Gunnar Haluki frowned and exchanged glances.

Aaron's mind raced. He'd done better that time, but then strayed too far from the old Aaron again at the end. He had to pull the Necessaries back in. He continued. "In your hands is the food I promised. There will be much more food available to all the Necessaries once we destroy the High Priest Gondoleery."

A new murmur arose, and Aaron allowed it, giving himself time to gather his wits. He had to keep things simple. A dirty gust of wind rattled the podium, and Aaron coughed to clear the dust from his throat.

"You have been given weapons," he said. "These are to be used to defend yourselves against Gondoleery and anyone who tries to help her. Once we have done away with her, you will have access to the Favored Farm whenever you want. Do you understand?"

This, apparently, was something all the Necessaries understood. The murmur grew, and Aaron didn't stop it. He had them, just barely. It had to be enough. When the crowd quieted, he said, "Good. You have one hour to bring your goods home and return with your weapons. Do not go to work. Come straight here, and we will travel together to seize the palace. Go quickly now!"

The Necessaries looked at one another, waiting to see if anyone was going to do what Aaron said to do. Finally a few began to walk uncertainly toward home, and then others started to follow.

"Hurry!" Aaron called out, silently begging them to obey.

As Necessaries began to scurry toward their homes with their goods, Aaron relaxed a little, relieved to be finished. He'd done the best he could.

But in the audience, Samheed turned sharply toward a cluster of people who hadn't moved. He leaned toward Lani and whispered a question. She looked where he pointed. Her eyes widened and she nodded.

"Stop! Everyone stop!" Samheed cried. "Alex, she's here! Gondoleery's here! Attack or take cover!"

Alex spotted the cluster. As he ran to the front of the stage, it dawned on him that the people surrounding the evil woman must be her new protection unit made up of university

LISA McMANN

students. And there were more swarming toward her, surrounding her, and brandishing the weapons the Artiméans had given them.

*Oh no!* Alex thought. He waved his arms wildly to gain control of the crowd and repeated Samheed's words, shouting over the uproar.

Lani pulled components from her vest and split away from Samheed, trying to get to a spot where she could take the high priest down. Carina, Sean, and others followed her lead.

All around, people dove to the ground as a woman in the middle of the pack threw her dust veil back, revealing the evil Gondoleery. A fireball burst from her fingers and hit Samheed in the chest, throwing him to the dirt. And then she turned toward Aaron.

"How dare you," she sneered, and sent a bevy of fireballs toward him. Aaron ducked behind the podium as the fireballs thwapped against it.

Alex shot off a round of scatterclips, catching a few of Gondoleery's guards and sending them flying backward into the night, but he couldn't get a good shot at Gondoleery behind her layers of protection. She turned her focus on him and shot several spears of ice from her fingertips.

The head mage dodged and dove toward the back of the stage and leaped off, hitting the dirt behind it as the ice sailed over his head. Once protected from Gondoleery's attack, he dug frantically in his pocket for Simber's dewclaw. When he found it, he held it tightly, closed his eyes, and whispered, "Seek."

A glowing orb shot out from Alex's hand and disappeared in the storm, heading to the road where Simber and Florence were stationed. As soon as he saw the seek spell was success- fully launched, Alex grabbed a handful of heart attack spells and crept around the side of the stage, clearing the dust from his eyes and trying to assess the situation.

In the amphitheater, more fake Necessaries in the audience revealed themselves as Gondoleery's palace guards. They sur- rounded her as well, forming several additional rings of protec- tion around her while still allowing her to shoot ice spears and fireballs over their heads and between their bodies.

Gondoleery uttered a chant, and the blowing dust grew stronger. As Artiméans everywhere began flinging spells, Gondoleery and her people dodged them. The Unwanteds' accuracy was off because of the dust, which only made the high priest cackle. Just a few of her guards had been taken down so far.

Gondoleery scanned the stage, trying to find the one person she knew she had to kill in order to stop the Artiméans' magic from working, but she no longer saw him. And then her eyes alighted on the podium again, behind which she knew Aaron was still hiding. She slammed a dozen fireballs at it, and finally the old dried-up piece of wood caught fire. The strong wind fanned the flames.

"Get down here!" Alex shouted to Aaron. He jumped onstage and nearly tackled his brother, pulling him off the back to give him the protection of the structure. "What is this, your first battle?"

"Pretty much," Aaron said, feeling completely out of his element. He scrambled to his feet.

Alex stayed low and grabbed his brother's arm. "Come on. Stay protected. Follow me!"

The Necessaries and Ancients who'd remained in the Commons were running everywhere, disoriented and useless, and often getting caught in the crossfire. In the midst of the confusion, Simber swooped in overhead with a tremendous roar, causing the Necessaries and Ancients to run away in fright. Aaron watched helplessly as his entire recruiting plan back-fired, leaving him the sole Quillen to fight with the Artiméans.

Lani, Sean, and Carina had managed to put out the fire on Samheed's chest, and he was back on his feet, a bit singed but saved by the extra protection from the vest. They took cover behind the rows of seats that made up the curve of the amphi-theater, as did the other Artiméans who were still standing and able to fight. Alex and Aaron stumbled across Henry, grip-ping his side where an ice dagger had glanced off him, and they dragged the boy to safety so he could get bandaged up.

Not long after Simber's appearance, Florence came thun-dering in. Gondoleery turned all her attention on the war-rior, and Florence took the brunt of Gondoleery's fireballs for several seconds as she tried to weave through the throngs of hysterical, retreating Necessaries. Gondoleery soon discovered that her magic had no effect on Florence, but during the time she'd spent firing spells at the warrior, Sean, Carina, Samheed, and Lani had managed to take down several of her guards.

As Florence took on a handful of university students while trying to get to Gondoleery, Simber dove down from overhead in an attempt to grab the old woman. But she turned her weapons on the cat, sending a stream of ice spears at his underbelly. They clinked off him and dropped back to the ground, several pieces striking one of her guards and impaling him.

Gondoleery switched to fireballs. Simber dipped his wings and curved sharply, the fireballs missing him and being carried by the squalls into the Necessary quadrant nearby. Smoke added to the dust in the air, which made the visibility even poorer.

With her ranks thinning, Gondoleery paused in her firing and shouted something to her remaining protection crew. They lifted their rusty weapons and began to slice through the crowd of advancing Artiméans, traveling as a unit and heading toward the road in the direction of the palace.

Sean and Carina, anticipating Gondoleery's move, had slipped ahead to find barriers to hide behind. They reloaded their components, and once Gondoleery's pack came into striking distance, they began pelting her guards with heart attack spells, trying to cut deep enough into the layers of protection around the high priest to enable them to get to the woman herself.

With guards falling all around her, Gondoleery didn't seem to be bothered. She sent a dozen ice spears at a group of hidden Unwanteds, aiming for their arms so they wouldn't be able to throw their components, and she hit her mark.

The crowd scattered as Gondoleery began attacking anyone in the way, and soon she and her protectors were moving swiftly through the quadrant. Florence, who kept having to dodge guards swinging sharp objects, grabbed her bow and nocked an arrow so she could take a single deadly shot if presented with the opportunity. But Gondoleery was clever and kept moving constantly, avoiding spells cast her way and keeping a tall guard between her and the towering ebony warrior at all times. To her great frustration, Florence never had a clear shot.

By the time Gondoleery and her thinning ranks reached the road, Alex understood why she had decided to move in that direction. Stationed there, with a fleet of Quillitary vehicles, was Governor Strang and the new Wanted Quillitary recruits. With horns honking, engines revving, and a whole new battalion of guards running toward Gondoleery to fill in the holes in her human shield left by the fallen, Gondoleery's company took on renewed strength. Things began looking bleak for Artimé.

"Everybody take cover!" Alex cried, Aaron at his side. "Regroup! Reload!"

Simber flew over their path carrying wounded Artiméans and depositing them in a safe spot for Claire and Henry to attend to, seeking but not finding any opportunity to pluck the high priest from the ground.

Seeing Gondoleery's reinforcements arriving, Florence thundered out to the road to try to weave her way into the inner circle of human armor before it closed up again. As she ran, Governor Strang shouted a command, and suddenly a swarm of vehicles peeled out on the loose gravel road and charged toward the ebony statue.

"Florence, look out!" Lani cried. But it was too late.

The vehicles rammed at the statue's legs, trying to stop her. Florence nimbly jumped up and landed on the hood of one, smashing it and cracking her foot. She leaped to the next hood, crushing it, and then tried running across the tops of all of the vehicles that stood in her way. But the drivers began to anticipate her moves, and at the last second, a vehicle she was aiming for quickly slammed into reverse. Instead of stepping on the hood, Florence landed off balance with a jolt on the ground. Her already cracked foot shattered. Her knee buckled, and all her weight slammed down on that one point. It cracked and her lower leg broke off, leaving her helpless to walk and surrounded by vehicles.

Simber flew to Florence's side, roaring at the drivers, but they all rolled up their windows and were safe inside their vehicles for the moment.

"I'm fine!" Florence yelled to Simber. "I'm just stuck here. Follow them! I'll do what I can to help!"

Upon overhearing this, the drivers in undamaged vehicles raced around Florence to catch up to Gondoleery and her remaining posse of guards, while Alex shouted for all spell casters to huddle up if they were able.

Unwanteds, covered in a layer of dust and shielding their eyes from the wind, darted from their hiding places and found Alex. It was a decidedly smaller team than what he'd started out with this morning, but it was a strong one.

"We're not giving up!" Alex cried. "I let Gondoleery get away once, and I'm not going to let that happen again. I won't stop until she's dead. Are you with me?"

"We're with you, Alex!" the people of Artimé shouted.

"Take a moment to drink some water, wipe the sand from your eyes, and gear up for more," Alex said. "We need to overtake Gondoleery's party and reach the palace before her. We must keep her from getting inside. If we can stop her . . . we have a chance. A good one."

"Alex," Aaron said in a low voice, "there's a shortcut through the Wanted quadrant that will take us to the portcullis."

"He's right," Samheed said. "I used to take it all the time. We'll be able to head Gondoleery off at the gate if we hurry. And we can use invisible steed spells."

"Let's do it, then," Alex said, fumbling for the proper components and casting two invisible steeds, one for him and one for Aaron. "Climb on," he said. "Like this." Alex mounted the creature.

Aaron looked alarmed. But he tentatively reached out, feeling for the animal, and climbed on its back.

"Hold the reins and don't fall off. Samheed, lead the way."

Samheed led at a gallop. Alex set off after him and Aaron followed. Sean quickly cast two more steed spells for Sky and Kaylee, and the rest of the Artiméans came along behind.

Their steeds ran as fast as their feet could carry them. Alex kept a watchful eye on Simber, who was swooping in and out over Gondoleery's head so that Alex and the others would be able to tell where she was.

"Why doesn't Simber just grab her and destroy her?" Aaron asked, once he got used to being on the steed. "Can't he pluck her out of the crowd and take her away?"

Alex shook his head. "I don't know. Some really strange things are happening with him. She's obviously doing something to fend him off."

Following Samheed, they darted between rows of houses and across paths through the Wanted quadrant, and then veered sharply down the row of governors' housing. Occasionally Simber appeared above the roofs of houses, following Gondoleery and transporting wounded Artiméans out of danger.

As abruptly as the steeds appeared, the spells wore off, and one by one the Artiméans were deposited to the ground. They picked themselves up and began running the rest of the way.

"We're going to beat her there," Alex shouted over his shoulder. At Haluki's house, they turned and ran up the hill to where the portcullis used to stand. Now there was a gaping hole.

"Forgot . . . to mention . . . that," Lani said, breathing hard and pointing to the broken gate. "I drove through it when I couldn't find the brake."

"Nice," Samheed said, admiring it. "We can use the gates as shields. What do you say, Al?"

"Excellent," Alex replied. Breathless, everyone searched the sides of the road, grabbing whatever bits and pieces of the port-cullis they could find. They stacked the pieces up in the road, creating a barricade in front of them. And then they lined up, stretching all the way across the road behind the barricade, and looked down the hill at Gondoleery's approaching party.

Simber, seeing the Artiméans in the road, realized they could be run down by the Quillitary. He paused in his care of the wounded and began diving down and smashing one vehicle after another, rendering them useless. When the driv-ers got out of their smashed cars and tried to run to surround Gondoleery, Simber picked them up in his claws and flew them out over the sea, dropping them in.

"Her ranks are thinning," Alex shouted to his comrades,

LISA McMANN

who were all singed and filthy from mingled dust and sweat. "Arm yourselves, friends. Whether we live or die, this is the moment that defines us all."

The Artiméans pulled out their best spells. Samheed put up glass walls in front of the barricade, leaving room between for spells to be cast. Sky drew her sword, and Kaylee drew hers.

"We'll fire all at once," Alex said as more straggling Artiméans arrived to make a second line behind them. "We fight to end the fight. Give it your all. Wait for my signal."

Aaron unsheathed his dagger and looked at it. He'd have to throw it to do any good, and that would leave him weaponless. He would have to choose the right moment to use it.

Alex glanced at him. The Artiméans wouldn't have had these extra moments to prepare if it hadn't been for Aaron. And they had a better chance to take Gondoleery out with every Unwanted that arrived before she reached them. Alex pressed his lips together in a firm line, then reached inside his robe to his component vest. He pulled out a handful of heart attack spells and shoved them at Aaron. "Here," he said.

Surprised, Aaron fumbled the components, dropping some on the ground. He hurried to pick them up. "Are you sure?"

Alex pointed at the dagger. "What's that bitty thing going to do against Gondoleery's fireballs and ice spears? It's not fair for you to be standing here, risking your life, practically unarmed against her. I'll take responsibility for your actions," Alex said. "So don't mess up. You know the verbal component?"

"I—I—yeah, of course." Aaron held the heart attack spells in his hand and stared at them, remembering the last time he'd used them—to subdue Panther after she killed Eva. And he remembered the time before that, when he'd killed Mr. Today. Red and heart shaped, and so beautiful in flight with their feathered wings . . . yet they were deadly, and they'd caused Aaron so much pain and shame. He hated the sight of them. He couldn't stand holding them.

"No, thanks," Aaron said forcefully, shoving the components back at Alex. "I'd rather take my chances with the dagger."

Surprised, Alex let him pour the components back into his hand. There was no time to argue. Gondoleery was approaching. And she could see them.

"Everyone ready?" Alex whispered.

"Ready," they said softly.

"All together now, aim," Alex said, voice calm and steady,

as the high priest came within range, "and . . . fire!"

With shouts of various spells, more than thirty components flew through the air at once, striking their targets, and the outside layer of Gondoleery's protection went down. Aaron hung on to his dagger.

Gondoleery fired back, a round of ice spears shattering the glass shields and sending shards flying everywhere. Immediately she followed with a round of fireballs, which smacked the barricade, but none penetrated. She shouted a command, and a handful of guards rushed forward brandishing weapons.

"We've got them!" Sky yelled to Alex. "Focus on the old hag!" She and Kaylee rushed around the barricade with their swords and attacked the approaching guards, backing them off to one side so the Unwanteds could cast more spells.

The Artiméans quickly reloaded and sent off another round at Gondoleery, and then a third.

The guards around Gondoleery toppled to the ground as fireballs and ice spears peppered the rusty metal-gate barricade and zipped over the Artiméans' heads.

"Again!" shouted Alex. "That's the way!"

The spell casters shouted their spells and sent their next

round of components flying. When at last Gondoleery's inner guards had fallen and she was exposed, the Unwanteds sent a bevy of spells at her. She ducked and dodged, blasting a few Artiméans with ice spears.

When the next round of spells went out, Gondoleery fell too.

Everyone stared for a split second, holding their breath and watching the woman, before the Artiméans sprang into action, charging around the barricade. Simber swooped down. Aaron ran forward, dagger drawn, and Alex came right behind him, scatterclips in hand. They approached the pile of bodies cautiously, but Alex was nearly certain he'd struck the woman with his last heart attack spell.

Carina stayed back, not trusting any of it, trying desperately to see through the dust storm. Reluctantly she crept forward with the others, and then she saw something move. "Watch out!" she yelled. "It's a trick!"

With Alex and Aaron at close range, Gondoleery lifted her arm and pointed at Alex. Electric blue flames sparked from her hand in anticipation. With a primal cry, Gondoleery sat up and sent giant blue fireballs flying from her fingertips.

"No!" Aaron cried, shoving Alex out of the way. The first flaming blue ball flew between them, but the second slammed into Alex's stomach and sent him soaring backward, on fire.

Gondoleery followed Alex with her fingertips, fireballs bursting forth. Aaron jumped in the way and took the next two shots, fire exploding on his chest and the heat singeing his eyebrows and hair. The impact sent him reeling. With a surge of anger, he reared back and launched his dagger at the woman. It spun through the air, straight and true, striking her square in the chest. She staggered back and fell, and the dust storm immediately stopped. But Gondoleery managed to climb to one knee. Simber flew at her. She sent fireballs streaming at him. He weaved and dodged them, flying out of range to avoid them.

Aaron rolled on the ground, trying to put out the fire. Keeping his eye on Gondoleery, he shouted, "Alex! Are you okay?"

But Alex didn't answer.

With Simber out of her way, Gondoleery aimed and fired again. Alex took the hit, and his robe shot up in flames.

Aaron ran to help his brother, but Gondoleery bowled him down with another fireball.

The Artiméans exploded into action.

Simber bolted from the sky and flew toward Gondoleery. "You . . . will . . . not . . . win!" the giant cat roared in the high priest's face. He dove in front of the boys and spread his wings wide to protect them. With a grimace, Gondoleery dug deep inside her soul and poured out a round of blue flames, pelting Simber's chest and enveloping him in fire until she could cast no more.

Engulfed in flames, the giant cat roared a final command to the Artiméans: "Save . . . yourrr . . . mage!" And then he exploded, lighting up the morning sky. Simber's body returned to its original form, the sand from which the giant cheetah had been created. As the blue flames turned white, then red, and disappeared, the sand fell into a shapeless heap on the road.

In the instant stillness, the world stopped for a moment and shuddered, absorbing the shock of the explosion. Simber was gone. He was nothing. All that was left of him was a giant pile of sand, eerily settling in the suddenly windless land.

And then, as Alex lay hurt and unaware, the uninjured of Artimé ran to aid their mage, whose robe was covered in flames. Aaron came to his senses, found himself smoldering once more, and quickly rolled over to put out the fire. He lay there, exhausted and breathing hard, unsure if he could ever get up again.

But then a tiny bit of light caught his eye. On the ground in front of him, something silvery glinted in the morning sunshine. Aaron lifted his head and struggled to move toward it. With effort he reached out and plucked up one of the scatterclips Alex had dropped when he'd been struck. And just as everyone else was exclaiming over Simber or Alex, Gondoleery staggered to her feet once more, the dagger still stuck in her chest. She raised a shaking hand in triumph as tiny sparks spat from her fingers.

Fury fueled Aaron. With a tremendous cry, he pushed himself to his knees. He aimed the scatterclip and threw it at Gondoleery's face, shouting with all the passion he had inside him, "Die a thousand deaths!"

# The Pile of Sand

The scatterclip struck its mark, and Gondoleery fell once more. Forever, this time. She landed unceremoniously atop her dead guards. And as suddenly as the battle began, it was over.

Aaron sank to the ground with a whimper, trying to rip the still-smoldering vest off his body, and finally succeeding. It had saved his life—he was certain of that.

By now Lani and Samheed had smothered Alex's burning robe to extinguish the flames. They tore it off him and doused him with water from the flasks they carried, which woke him up quickly. Carina came running with her healer's kit to assist.

LISA McMANN

Aaron flung his burned component vest as far as he could, then coughed the smoke from his lungs and stood up, dazed. He stared at the giant pile of sand that had once been a living statue made by Mr. Today. A statue that had saved his life. Simber had said Aaron would be protected, and the beast had kept the promise and done it himself—and died doing it.

"Simber," he whispered. Aaron didn't know what to do. Did Alex know? Had he seen it happen?

With Alex sitting up and talking, people left his side to stare at the destruction or assess others' injuries. Soon Alex heard what had happened. He rose to his feet, and with a strangled cry, he staggered over to Simber's remains. The mage knelt on the road next to it, almost unable to believe the horrible sight. He fell forward, choking and sobbing. "No!" he screamed. "This can't happen! Not you! Not you!"

Everyone around them was in a state of shock and disbelief. Simber, their beloved protector, was gone.

Artimé would never be the same without him.

The Artiméans mourned together, and then alone, leaving Alex by himself next to the pile of sand, not wanting to intrude on the mage's intense grief. The young man had lost so many loved ones in his short life. It didn't seem fair that Simber had to die too. No one quite knew what to do to offer comfort to the brokenhearted leader.

After a while, Lani and Samheed came and knelt by Alex's side.

"Al," said Samheed gently, "I'm sorry." He stared at the sand, numb.

Lani was crying. She hugged Alex for a long moment, but he could barely feel anything at all. They sat together, the three of them, while Aaron looked on in silence.

Finally, Samheed got up and sighed wearily. "Stay here if you like, Alex. Lani and I will go with Sean and Carina to help Florence get back to Artimé. We'll take Sky and Kaylee, too, and as many others as we can find. Maybe all together we can lift her. And . . . we'll have to tell her the news about Simber."

Alex closed his eyes. He nodded numbly. "Thank you."

They stayed a minute more, but Alex didn't say anything. Finally they embraced Alex, and then Lani took Samheed's arm and they limped off together down the hill, with the rest of Artimé following. Aaron stayed with Alex.

The brothers remained next to the sand in the shadow of

LISA McMANN

the vacant palace, the smell of smoke and death lingering in the air and choking them.

"I get it now," Alex said dully, when all his tears had been cried. "No wonder he was so weird about Gondoleery and the fireballs. He knew. He knew that fire would destroy him. All this time he knew, and he didn't tell me. Why, Simber?" He became insistent. "Why didn't you tell me?"

But the pile of sand didn't answer. There would be no more answers from the wisest cat in the land.


As Alex lamented hour after hour, Aaron stared at the sand until his sight wavered. He closed his eyes and went to the jungle in his mind, all the way back to the day he first fixed Panther's tail. When he opened his eyes, he stared at the sand some more for a very long time.

Eventually, Alex got to his knees and pushed his aching body to a standing position. "Come on, Aaron," he said. "I can hardly stand to leave him, but I have to help back at home. My people . . ." He faltered.

Aaron didn't get up. He didn't even hear Alex. Instead, he crawled forward, reached out, and picked up a handful of sand.

He held it, feeling its heartbeat in his hand, then let it slide through his fingers.

"What are you doing?" Alex said, alarmed. "Don't! Don't touch him. It's . . . it's too soon."

The sand was warm. Aaron breathed deeply, picked up another handful and closed his eyes. Careful not to disturb the pile, he stood and held the sand high, as high as he could reach. He thought about Simber, picturing the creature's face and body in his mind. "Be alive," he whispered. "Live." He let go of the sand, and it hung magically in the air, taking the shape of a small triangle. Aaron didn't notice. He simply reached down for another handful and stood up again.

"Aaron, please," Alex said angrily. "What are you—" He stopped short when the second handful of sand hung in the air in the shape of another triangle. His mouth fell open. "Ears?" he whispered.

In the air, the ears twitched.

Alex held his breath, not wanting to make a sound to disturb his brother.

Aaron paid no attention. Eyes closed, he worked tirelessly, pulling up sand by the handfuls and letting it fall and cling to

LISA McMANN

an invisible outline that only Aaron could see. Within an hour Simber had a streamlined neck and back. The front legs came next, then the rear and the tail, and then the expansive wings, spreading wide across the road.

Aaron worked through the long, hot day, with Alex watching it all, completely in awe, until finally Aaron poured the front of Simber's face, filling in the cat's great teeth, nose, and jaw.

When there was only a tiny bit of sand left, Aaron drizzled it over Simber's face. It spread out into eyelids and whiskers. And then Aaron stood still for a long moment, his hand against the cheetah's side, feeling the sand harden and turn to stone, and the pulse of the beast inside it.

Aaron opened his eyes and stepped back.

The cheetah's eyelids fluttered. He rose to his full height and shook himself from ears to tail, as if he had just been given a bath he wasn't keen on taking.

"Simber?" breathed Alex. He choked on a sob and ran to the giant cat and flung his arms around his neck. "I thought I'd lost you again!"

The cat looked at Alex with love in his eyes. "And I, you,"

LISA McMANN

he said. And then he lifted his head toward Aaron and bowed. "Thank you, Aarrron," he said.

Aaron's lip quivered as he watched them, a tremendous ache swelling inside him. He nodded quickly, not trusting himself to speak.

Alex hung on to Simber, not wanting to let go, while the enormous cat began licking his paws, trying to smooth out some of the rougher patches of his body that hadn't landed exactly right.

And then Alex turned to Aaron. He opened his arms wide to his exhausted brother and embraced him, whispering the same words over and over and over. "Thank you."

Aaron froze for the briefest moment, and then he relaxed and hugged his brother back. "I didn't know I could do that," he admitted.

"I'm extremely glad to know you can," Alex said, wiping his tears away.

With the brothers having a moment together, Simber went back to what Simber did best. He snorted some stray dirt from his nostrils and sampled the air, and then stood on his hind legs, peering out over Quill as the sun began to set. "Alex," Simber growled.

Alex turned. "What is it?"

"Both of you get on my back. We need to have a look at something."

"Before we go . . . ," Alex began. He scrambled to pull out all of his preserve spells that hadn't melted. Quickly he pelted the cat with a layer of them, like Mr. Today had done when the cat was first created. When Alex was finished, the brothers climbed onto Simber's back, Aaron trying not to be sick with fear.

As soon as the boys were settled, Simber took a running leap over Gondoleery's dead body and rose high into the air. And as the sunlight weakened, Alex and Aaron could see it.

"Therrre," said Simber, pointing. "Smoke, rrrising frrrom the Commons and all arrround it." The enormous cat looked over his shoulder at the two exhausted mages. "Quill is on firrre."

# Epilogue: One Island Away

A pirate ship stood in the silent lagoon of Warbler Island, and the pirates aboard it didn't have to worry about being shot with sleep darts as they rowed in to shore in their fishing boat. Queen Eagala was expecting them.

The captain with hook hands and his first mate made their way down a hole in the ground to a tunnel and weaved through the orange-eyed, thorn-necked slaves of the queen. They headed toward her throne room, finding her just where they expected to—just where they had found her many times in the past when they needed slaves.

But this time the pirates weren't there with bags full of gold pieces to trade for workers. Queen Eagala didn't need any more gold—her people had made enough thornaments to last them a lifetime.

No, Queen Eagala had called the pirates there for a different reason entirely. This time she needed their help.

"Greetings, Captain Baldhead. First Mate Twitch," she said. She waved at the chairs near her throne, inviting the pirates to have a seat.

They sat.

"It seems my people have tricked me," said the queen, pressing her long, curling fingernails up to her lips. "And now all of Warbler's children are in Artimé." She uttered the island's name with a sneer.

"What's Artimé?" Captain Baldhead asked.

"It's the fringe group on the south end of Quill," Eagala said. "My brother's people."

"How did you manage to lose an entire generation?" Twitch asked.

Queen Eagala leaned forward and snapped at him. "That doesn't matter. I want them back."

LISA McMANN

Captain Baldhead narrowed his eyes at the queen of Warbler. "Why can't you go get them?"

"Because the Artiméans are magical people," Eagala said. "Much more magical than I am. And I need your help."

"Magical?" the captain asked. "We already got rid of their leader after he destroyed our reverse aquarium. He was weak."

Twitch looked at the captain. "But, Captain, the bloke we got was on the west side of the island, not the south," he said.

"Silence!" Baldhead said, striking at the other man with his hook hand and leaving a small gash in his cheek. "The whole island is nothing but trouble!"

The first mate sank back and pulled a handkerchief from his pocket to press against his wound.

Queen Eagala looked at the captain. "If you've gotten rid of their leader, I won't have to pay you as much as I expected to get my children back."

Baldhead frowned. "What are you offering?"

The queen smiled. "I thought you'd never ask." She got up off the throne. "Follow me," she said. She led the pirates down the hallway toward an exit and climbed the steps that led outside to the shipyard.

LISA McMANN

The pirates followed, and when they emerged from underground, they could see the silent Warbler workers putting the finishing touches on an enormous new pirate ship. "Designed with you in mind," Eagala said.

Baldhead and Twitch stared at the beautiful ship. The captain swallowed hard. "That's quite a beauty," he said.

Eagala smiled. "Yes, it is. Go have a look inside if you like."

The pirates nearly stumbled over their feet trying to get to it.

The queen waited patiently as they looked around, a smile playing on her lips. She knew it was an offer they couldn't refuse.

When at last the pirates returned, starry-eyed over the ship's elaborate design, Queen Eagala folded her hands in front of her.

"Well, gentlemen," she said, "are you ready to discuss a plan for the complete obliteration of the Island of Quill?"

# Acknowledgments

Greatest thanks to you, the faithful readers who have picked up this book. Some of you started reading at the very beginning in 2011, and others came along a bit later, but you are all ridiculously important to me. I have met or heard from many of you. You come from all age groups—from beginning readers all the way to teens, parents, grandparents, and great-grandparents. I am absolutely thrilled that this series is reaching across so many generations. Thank you for telling your friends and parents and grandparents and teachers and librarians and coworkers and children and grandchildren about Alex and Aaron and their stories. You are awesome!

These books wouldn't exist without the hard work of many people. Thank you, Michael Bourret, for nine years of wisdom, guidance, and friendship. Thank you, Liesa Abrams, for your kindness, expertise, passion, and brilliance, and for caring about these books. Thank you, Mara Anastas and Mary Marotta, for publishing me and for being so smart and thoughtful and diligent for the sake of kids' books.

Thank you, Jodie Hockensmith, Carolyn Swerdloff, Matt Pantoliano, Teresa Ronquillo, Lucille Rettino, Michelle Leo, Candace McManus, Anthony Parisi, and Betsy Bloom, for the long hours you put into publicizing, marketing, and introducing my books to the retail, education, and library worlds— your work is infinitely valuable, and I appreciate each one of you so much. You have done and continue to do tremendous work in a multitude of ways. Thank you once again to Lauren Forte—I miss you! And thanks to Julie Doebler.

Thank you to the amazing S&S sales team for placing the Unwanteds series into good bookseller hands all around North America, and thank you to all the good booksellers for welcoming me into your stores and for finding homes for these books with your customers. I am so grateful.

Thank you to Owen Richardson and Karin Paprocki for the amazing Unwanteds artwork and design. I am in love with every cover in this series and you keep surprising me with more and more incredible work.

Readers, I hope you love the Island of Graves as much as I do.

Alex's and Aaron's stories continue in

# THE UNWANTEDS

## BOOK SEVEN
## Island of Dragons

Turn the page for a sneak peek. . . .

# Fire

The desert land of Quill was no more.

Even though Aaron Stowe had implanted the fatal scatterclip into Gondoleery Rattrapp's forehead and cried out the words "Die a thousand deaths!" that ended her terroristic reign, the old woman's weapons had hit many unintended targets. The fireballs continued doing damage long after her demise.

The Artiméans limped home after the battle past dozens of small fires that burned throughout Quill. Fanned by the sea breeze and fed by the dry, brittle wood houses, the fires grew out of control. Soon every quadrant in Quill was engulfed in flames. Frantic Wanteds and Necessaries were forced to abandon their homes and flee for the only part of the island that wasn't burning: Artimé.

"Let's keep the Quillens moving!" shouted Alex Stowe, the head mage of the magical land of Artimé, as the people passed through the invisible weather barrier to safety. "All the way to the shore and the edge of the jungle, so there's room for everyone!" In the confusion, he turned to two of his closest friends, Lani Haluki and Samheed Burkesh. "Try to convince them that it's safe to go inside the mansion, will you? I'm afraid we'll run out of space out here."

"We'll try," said Lani, "but it's not going to be easy." The lawn was tightly packed with Wanteds and Necessaries. Lani and Samheed did their best to spread the word, while Alex hurried inside the mansion to expand the upstairs living quarters so they could house the refugees who agreed to come inside.

But it was a lot of work trying to convince the stubbornminded, fearful people of Quill that they wouldn't accidentally get any magic on them if they decided to take a room in the mansion until things could be sorted out.

Alex overheard an exasperated Samheed talking to an old

Quillen man. "Trust me," he said. "There's absolutely no way you are going to become magical just by sleeping in a nice bed for once in your life. Just come inside and I'll show you to your room."

When the stubborn man refused and instead sat down behind a bush outside the mansion, Samheed threw his hands in the air. "Fine," he said. "Sleep there forever, then. I'm sure I don't care." He went grumbling back through the crowd toward the weather barrier to try to direct some injured Quillens to the hospital ward.

Simber flew overhead, occasionally sweeping over the burning part of the island from a safe height, looking to rescue anyone who might be trapped. The orange flames weren't hot enough to harm him—not much, anyway. It had been the white- and blue-hot flames of Gondoleery's fireballs that had done him in. Nevertheless, the giant stone cheetah was especially wary after what he'd gone through. Simber knew that if Alex's twin brother Aaron hadn't acted so quickly to restore him, his sandy remains would still be on the road near the palace right now, burning with the rest of Quill.

Artimé owed Aaron a debt of gratitude, though a few were

having a hard time accepting that fact after all Aaron had done in the past to hurt the magical world. Alex was among the most grateful, though, for Aaron had done something that Alex couldn't do—he'd brought Simber back to life. While Alex sometimes struggled with the complexities of magic, Aaron's newfound abilities appeared almost effortless. Was there any limit to what Aaron could do? Alex was starting to wonder.

Needless to say, Aaron Stowe—former Everything, current Nothing—had earned a lot of respect from those who'd witnessed his unselfish actions. But he channeled his inner Ishibashi, kept his head down, and worked alongside the Artiméans to help with the injured and displaced people. And, being the closest thing to a leader of Quill, he found himself having to solve a whole new series of problems that came along with a community devastated by fire.

Once the fleeing Wanteds and Necessaries arrived in Artimé, they had no choice but to stay. Covered in soot and carrying what little they could salvage, they sought safety in the magical world they hated and feared. Some arrived defeated, some defiant, some overwhelmed, and some finally digging deep inside themselves and discovering their anger a little too late. And a few—mostly children—arrived with a tiny hint of excitement stirring in their hearts, for they had heard whispers about the happenings in Artimé, and they were not quite dead inside.

The heavy black smoke traveled westward with the wind, and it didn't take long for Queen Eagala and the hook-handed pirate, Captain Baldhead, to hear reports that something was amiss. After their meeting on Warbler, they sent out spies to see if the entire island of Quill was destroyed.

But Alex's magical weather barrier around Artimé proved to be one of the best spells the head mage had ever put in place. Soon the leaders of Warbler and Pirate Islands received word that the southern part of the island of Quill remained completely unharmed by fire and was filled with people. So they redoubled their efforts and continued planning the ultimate attack to destroy the magical land.

Alex and his people had other things on their minds.

The fires raged and settled and raged and settled again for weeks until there was nothing left to burn. During that time, Alex and his friends did whatever they could to assure their new visitors that they were safe now. Some of them, comforted by seeing Aaron safe and sound in Artimé, eased into their new lives a little at a time, trying to get used to the strange surroundings. Others chose to stay far away from the Unwanteds' mansion, sleeping on the lawn at the border between the two worlds, waiting until they could go back home. With no trained ability to imagine things, they couldn't fathom that Quill would look very different than it had before. But they'd soon discover there would be no home to go to.

When at last the fires burned out and it was safe to venture into Quill, all could see for themselves that nothing of worth remained. With no resources to rebuild, it seemed the Wanteds and Necessaries would be forced to stay in Artimé.

The annual day of the Purge came and went, unnoticed and obsolete.

# The Island of Artimé

But the people of Quill didn't want to stay in the magical land. Wanteds and Necessaries went into Quill multiple times over the following weeks to consider ways to rebuild. Sometimes they brought creative-minded Artiméans with them in hopes of someone coming up with a plan. But with no resources, there were no solutions, and the groups returned day after day covered in soot and feeling desperate for their old familiar land. Frustrations ran high. Soon even the most stubborn of the Quillens had to admit there was nothing they could do to rebuild their awful world.

With the long-term outlook seeming quite grim, Alex

called a formal meeting on the lawn for all the Wanteds and Necessaries to attend so they could talk about what to do next. He even borrowed a podium from Mr. Appleblossom to stand behind so that it would feel familiar to the people of Quill. It was a subtle gesture that was unfortunately lost on the dull-witted Quillens.

After greeting the crowd, Alex laid out the situation. "I've talked with my advisors, including my brother Aaron," he said. He pointed to Aaron next to him, since his brother's presence seemed to give the Quillens some sort of comfort. "Because there's nothing salvageable left in Quill, and because it would take years to remove all of the soot and embers and burned-out structures from the island, you are stuck in Artimé whether you like it or not. But I have an idea. With your permission, we'd like to expand our magical world to cover the ugliness."

The crowd, more vocal than it had ever been, began to murmur and complain.

Alex waited, then went on. "Once the magic of Artimé covers the entire island, I can make individual homes for you like you had before. And . . . ," he said, cringing, "I can make the land as bland as you want it to be."

Claire Morning and Florence, the giant ebony warrior statue, were standing at the back of the crowd, and they exchanged wry grins. It was hard for anyone in Artimé to believe that there were people who would purposely choose to have a bland world. But Aaron had suggested the option be offered, and it seemed to quiet the complaints a little.

"In fact," Alex said, bolstered by the reaction, "I can give you a similar layout to what you had before. I can even number the houses exactly the same, and just add some trees—and grass, if you want it—and schedule some occasional rain, which will help your living situations a lot. That way you won't have to limit yourselves to two buckets of water a week. Your gardens and farms will flourish, and you and your livestock and chickens will have plenty to eat and drink."

Mr. Appleblossom, who had been in charge of rescuing the livestock and chickens that had run from the fire into Artimé, nodded and smiled as the Quillens talked among themselves about this new development. Once Mr. Appleblossom had put all the farm animals in one place, he'd set up a nice corral behind the mansion where they wouldn't be bothered or frightened by the owlbats, platyprots, and other strange creatures that roamed freely in Artimé. The Quillen animals were flourishing on the food, water, and care that Mr. Appleblossom and his helpers had been giving them.

Kaylee Jones, the American sailor whom Alex, Aaron, and Sky had rescued from the saber-toothed-gorilla-infested Island of Graves, had found a bit of comfort in the sight of animals that actually seemed normal to her, so she had joined Mr. Appleblossom's team. She'd set up a petting zoo for the children from both worlds to enjoy, which was something she remembered loving from her own childhood. Carina's son Seth and the younger set of Stowe twins, Thisbe and Fifer, were frequent visitors.

Now Kaylee stood off to one side with Sky, Samheed, and Lani, looking decidedly healthier than she'd been at the time of her rescue. Upon her arrival, she'd been shocked by the gray, desert land of Quill—perhaps more shocked by it than by Artimé—and wondered how anyone could turn down the opportunity to have enough fresh water to drink. Yet before her eyes, a small group of Wanteds stubbornly argued and shook their heads, complaining about ridiculous things. She marveled at the stark difference between the two kinds of people on this island, and was infinitely glad that her rescuers had come from Artimé.

As the crowd grew louder in their discussion over whether grass should be allowed, and whether they wanted it to rain more, Alex leaned toward his brother. "Now what do I do?" he whispered.

Aaron put a hand on the podium. "You want me to step in?" he asked quietly.

Alex frowned. "No, I can do it. Just tell me what to say to them, because I have no idea right now."

One corner of Aaron's mouth turned up slightly. "Tell them that if they try having grass in their yards and they don't like it, we can always remove it so they can have dirt yards like before."

Alex sighed. "But I don't want to create dirt yards."

"Think of all the drawing they can do in the dirt when it rains," Aaron said, almost mischievously.

The look on Aaron's face caught Alex by surprise, as so many things had in the past few months. His brother was a different person now, thanks to his time on the Island of Shipwrecks with the three old scientists: Ishibashi, Ito, and

Sato. Alex still wasn't sure if Aaron had gotten whacked on the head a little too hard when the pirates had kidnapped him—that's how big his transformation was. But Aaron insisted he had still been an awful person when he'd first regained consciousness in the stone shelter, and Ishibashi had been quick to agree.

Alex smiled. "All right," he said. His insides felt complete now that he had his brother beside him. The two of them standing together with the same goals in mind was a dream Alex never thought could come true. Not like this. Not as friends, anyway.

Alex stepped back to the podium and lifted his hand in the air for silence, which came quickly. The Quillens were nothing if not militant about letting the person at the podium speak—even if he was someone they didn't trust. "We can always give it a try with the grass yards," Alex said amicably, "and if it turns out you don't like this luscious stuff massaging your bare feet every day, I will give you a dirt yard as before. Aaron will see to it."

Aaron nodded his promise to the people, and that calmed them immediately.

"Leave it at that," Aaron said under his breath. "Finish up—you're about to lose them."

Alex nodded. "Thank you, people of Quill. All in favor of having your own magical homes right where the old ones used to be, raise your hand."

The Wanteds and Necessaries had never been asked to vote on anything before. They looked at one another, confused.

"Just go ahead and put your hand in the air like I'm doing," Alex said, "if you want me to extend the magical world in order to give you your homes back. And if most of you agree, I'll do it."

Samheed stared from the audience and made a face at Alex.

Alex ignored him.

Aaron raised his hand as well to show the people. But no one wanted to be the first in the audience to do it.

"Okay, then," Alex said, hesitating a bit, trying to figure out what to do next. "How about this: Everyone who would like to have their own home back as I proposed, just keep standing there with no hands in the air."

No one moved.

"Good!" said Alex. "Excellent. That's all of you. I'll begin working on it right away. If everything goes well, we should have the first new homes ready in a matter of days. Thank you for coming!"

The people didn't move.

"And now you may go," said Alex, with a grand flourish that made Lani crack up and have to hide her face.

Alex stepped back from the podium and turned to Aaron as the Wanteds and Necessaries began to disperse. Only a few small groups stayed around to voice complaints. "Whew," he said. "Tough crowd."

"Yes," Aaron said. "That was pretty clever how you did that, though."

A group of five or six Wanteds approached Aaron.

"We don't want to live in the magical world," one said grumpily. "We want nothing to do with that Unwanteds magic."

Aaron and Alex exchanged a worried glance. "But . . . ," said Aaron, "there's nowhere else for you to live."

"We don't care," said the spokesperson.

Alex scratched his head, perplexed. How was he going to satisfy everybody?

But Aaron took hold of the situation. "No problem," he said. He turned to Alex. "Can you leave a small portion of Quill untouched by magic for these fine Wanteds?"

"I—" Alex began, then hesitated. "Well, sure, I *can*, but . . ."

"Very good," Aaron said smoothly. "Our problem is solved. Give them a bit of barren, burned-out land to live on." He thought about what Ishibashi might say, and added, "And make it as far away from here as possible."

# Aaron Longs for Home

I t had been a crazy few years for Aaron Stowe. He went from Wanted, to university student, to assistant to the secretary of the high priest, to leader of the Restorers, to high priest of Quill. He'd killed a kind magician; nearly killed his brother; sent his father to the Ancients Sector and made his only friend, Secretary, get him back; and sent Secretary to the Ancients Sector only to watch her die because he stupidly set loose a wild creature upon a group of innocent children.

That was a lot of horrible deeds to deal with, and Aaron would be lying if he said he didn't think about them often. He spent hours roaming the smoldering ruins of Quill alone, contemplating. He stood where the portcullis had been, and looked at the charred remains of the palace—his former home. Yet there was nothing he could think of that he missed about the place. Nothing had made that cold, gray palace feel as cozy as his cot on a rock floor in the middle of a hurricane.

Thinking back upon his life in Quill made Aaron feel numb inside. Everything he had once lived for was gone. He smiled ruefully, wondering what sort of metaphor Ishibashi would make from it. He missed the old man, sometimes desperately.

Every now and then Aaron thought about what it would be like if the pirates hadn't mistaken him for his brother—if they'd captured Alex instead, and Aaron had remained in power. Would he still be high priest, or would Gondoleery have ousted or even killed him by now? Would he still sneak to the jungle to be in the one place he felt at ease; among the misfits . . . the misunderstoods? Would he have eventually confided in Liam that he was so terribly uncertain about what he was doing? Or would he have kept it all in, as always? As one is expected to do in Quill?

And would he be raising his sisters to be bad like him? Thisbe and Fifer were almost two years old. When he looked at them, he couldn't imagine them growing up in that horrible, stark palace.

One quiet morning he sat on the lawn with his sisters, watching them play in the sand, making sure they didn't venture too far into the water. They were learning to swim, but it was the current that worried Aaron the most, knowing they could be swept off their little feet and pulled out to the sea.

Aaron could swim a little now. Not like Alex and Sky and the others, but at least he wasn't terrified anymore. Not really, anyway, though he still had nightmares about the little pirate boat and the hurricane. But he also had good dreams about returning to the Island of Shipwrecks.

Carina Holiday and her son, Seth, walked up to the beach. Seth ran over to the girls, and Carina sat down next to Aaron.

Some of Alex's friends had begun to trust Aaron by now. Simber, for sure, and Sky, of course. But Carina had kept her distance, watching him—he saw her and others, too, like Claire Morning and Samheed Burkesh, always, always watching him. And while Aaron knew their skepticism was deserved, it was hard to take, and it didn't feel very good. He wondered why Carina chose the spot next to him to sit.

"Good morning," Aaron said.

"Good morning," she replied, crossing her ankles and pulling her knees up. She sipped from a steaming mug.

Aaron watched his sisters shriek with joy when they saw Seth, who was a year or so older than them. They had become fast friends—most of the time anyway. As good friends as two- and three-year-olds could be, he supposed. "The girls really love Seth," he said to break the silence.

"He adores them, too," Carina said. "And I am rather enjoying this quiet morning."

"It'll be even quieter when the Quillens are gone," said Aaron. "Alex is going to start expanding the magical world soon."

"I was at the meeting," Carina said.

"Of course," said Aaron, feeling awkward. "Sorry I didn't see you."

If Carina noticed Aaron's awkwardness, she didn't indicate it. "I would imagine the Wanteds and Necessaries can't wait to go home," she mused.

Aaron nodded. He understood the feeling.

Seth started to pile and pack sand into a large mound. Thisbe waited until he was almost done and pushed it over. But Seth didn't get mad; he just started building it up again. Fifer played quietly by herself, singing a nonsensical made-up song.

"I guess she's like me," Aaron said, more to himself than to Carina. He looked up. "Thisbe, I mean. The one in red." Suddenly he felt strange for saying it, as if he were admitting something that made him very vulnerable. He still had a hard time with that, especially with people he didn't know well. Perhaps he always would.

Carina smiled. "Can you see their personalities emerging?"

"Yes. It's interesting. They're quite different from each other once you get to know them," Aaron said. "Thisbe plays hard and sleeps hard. She puts all her energy into everything she does—see?" He pointed as she knocked Seth's sand tower down again with her whole body, landing on the boy. Seth fell back, surprised, and laughed with Thisbe when she laughed. They got to their feet.

"Again?" Seth said to her.

"Again," Thisbe agreed. Seth started piling sand.

"And Fifer," Aaron said, shaking his head. "She's very gentle and . . . I don't know. Intensely musical, and thoughtful, I guess. Can a two-year-old be thoughtful?"

"I think so," Carina said. "Seth is that way too."

"Yet he puts up with Thisbe's games so well."

Carina nodded. "And the girls love each other, don't they? They seem inseparable."

"They are," Aaron said, thinking about so much more than just his sisters. "They're best friends. They couldn't live without each other."

Carina sipped her drink and watched the kids quietly. "You know," she said after a while, "I used to think that twins were trouble. Marcus and Justine. You and Alex." She swung her head to give Aaron a look of raw honesty. "Because it was really difficult with you for a long time, you know?"

"Of course." Aaron dropped his gaze. "I know."

"But you're proving that it doesn't have to be that way," said Carina. "You're showing your sisters something important, I think."

Aaron pursed his lips. He hadn't thought about that before. "Somebody wise told me that just because Alex was good, that didn't mean I had to be bad in order to be distinct from him. I could be a different kind of good."

"The man from the Island of Shipwrecks?" asked Carina.

"Yes." A spear of longing passed through Aaron. He looked

left, to the east, as if that would bring Ishibashi's island closer. But then he turned his gaze back to the girls, his face clouding over. He'd miss them. A lot. "Once we have the Wanteds and Necessaries settled, I guess I'll be free to go back there."

"Is that what you want to do?"

"It doesn't really matter what I want," Aaron said. "It was part of the deal. Alex found me, brought me here, and I did my job. I was never meant to stay."

Carina reached out, putting her hand over Aaron's, and gave it a gentle squeeze. "Thank you for helping us," she said. "You're an incredible mage—I have no idea how you were able to do so much without training. And I can't believe I'm saying this, but I'm very glad you came back. At least for a little while. If you decide to stay, well, I certainly wouldn't mind. You're all right, Aaron."

Aaron stared at her hand on his. He wondered if he'd ever get used to people being kind to him.

Later, when Aaron was alone and thinking about the responsibilities he had to attend to here on this island before he could leave, he found his mind turning to Panther. He went inside the mansion, past Simber and Florence, whose broken leg was restored. He climbed the stairs to the balcony and slipped down the not-even-a-faint-secret of a hallway. He went past all the doors, not knowing where some of them led, and into the kitchenette.

He stood for a moment in front of the tube, feeling guilty. One thing he hadn't told anyone about was his past visits to the jungle. He'd tell his brother eventually. He had to, so Alex could take care of the creatures once Aaron was gone. But he knew that when that happened, he'd have to confess to the rock and to Panther that he'd been lying to them. He'd have to tell them that he wasn't Alex.

The thought pained him, and the longer it lingered, the more painful it became. Maybe he would ask Alex to confess for him . . . but that made Aaron feel like a coward. A feeling he knew all too well.

*For now,* Aaron decided as he stepped inside the tube, *the jungle is my secret.* It was the only thing left that truly belonged to him. And he wasn't ready to give it up. He desperately needed one place to go where nobody stared at him or wondered if he was still evil inside.

# House After House

Alex had never spent so much time working on his concentration and spells as he was spending now. Once he'd found Mr. Today's journal that detailed how he created the world in the first place, Alex designed his own spell that would expand the existing boundaries of Artimé to cover almost the entire island.

It didn't all happen at once, unfortunately. He had to go bit by bit, section by section. Each section fell into place a little like how the hospital ward did whenever Alex had to expand that. As he pressed the invisible boundary outward, grass dropped down to mark his progress.

Once Alex had extended Artimé to cover up all but one small section of the charred remains of Quill, which he left for the cranky group of Wanteds as promised, he began working on the infrastructure, putting in a paved road where the dirt one used to be and laying down walking paths throughout the community. He widened the stream and had Ms. Octavia create a bubbling freshwater fountain in the Commons like the one she'd made for the *Claire*, so that the community could come and draw water from it whenever they needed it. Things were taking shape. Alex was careful to hold back so he wouldn't accidentally make Quill too beautiful. The restraint was almost painful.

Then Alex took to his office to work on a house component. He asked Aaron to help design the layout, and Alex created a prototype for the first house and tried it out in the vast open space in the Museum of Large. After a few tweaks, Aaron approved, and Alex had the design exactly the way the Quillens would want it.

The head mage called Samheed, Lani, Carina, and Sean Ranger to help make replicas of the component. The group spread out their supplies and tools in the Museum of Large, below the outstretched trunk and huge sharp tusks of Ol' Tater, the mastodon statue.

The new magical houses looked more like Wanted houses than Necessary ones, not just because the design was simple enough to replicate, but because Alex thought the Necessaries—who had been on the cusp of helping Artimé take out Gondoleery—deserved nicer houses than the ones they'd had. And it was easier to design and replicate one spell component than two, so Alex chose to do it as such. He decided that if any Necessary came to him demanding a smaller, less equipped home, he would gladly oblige.

When Alex finally had enough components for all the Quillen households, he began installing the houses one at a time in nearly the same layout as Quill had previously had, doing his best to work from memory and getting guidance from some of the older Necessaries who had known every inch of Quill.

By this time, the Wanteds and Necessaries were more than anxious to go back to their familiar-looking, yet slightly more colorful and less ugly world. Dozens of Wanteds and Necessaries moved into their new homes every day as Alex worked long and hard to re-create their world. Most of the recipients knew very little about how to express their thanks for a gift so huge, but some of them managed, which felt like progress to Alex. And a thank you now and then for the hardworking head mage of Artimé was very much appreciated.

The small group of cranky Wanteds who wanted nothing to do with magic settled in the charcoaled remains just beyond the Ancients Sector, across the island from Artimé. They were so blinded by their opposition to magic that they were willing to sleep in soot and scrounge for food and water just to make a point. Alex wasn't quite sure what that point was, but he didn't really care, either, as long as they didn't bother him.

And Aaron worked with some of the more reasonable Wanteds and Necessaries to try to make the Ancients Sector into something much more humane than it once was. He pointed out the willingness of the Ancients to help fight Gondoleery, thus proving their usefulness, and suggested the Ancients Sector be a place of respite for the elderly to go to on their own accord, where they could enjoy their last days without fear or chains, and be among friends.

Needless to say, Alex "forgot" to build the sleep chamber, and no one seemed upset about that.

As for the palace, Alex decided not to build one at all, and instead put a lighthouse with a lookout tower in its place on the top of the hill. For the time being, he appointed Gunnar Haluki to watch over the new annex, reassign jobs to all the people instead of just the Necessaries, and make sure the farms and animals were being nurtured properly. Gunnar asked Claire Morning to teach the Quillens how to make the most of their new situation, and she began by showing them how to funnel rainwater off their roofs into barrels so they wouldn't have to travel to the fountain to get it. They'd always have more than enough water to go around for people, plants, and animals.

With only a little grumbling, the people of Quill settled in to their new Artiméan-made homes, and life returned to almost normal.

A whole new adventure begins!

THE UNWANTEDS QUESTS

Dragon Captives

LISA McMANN

NEW YORK TIMES BESTSELLING SERIES